THE PARISIAN SPY

A RESISTANCE GIRL NOVEL #3

HANNAH BYRON

1

VERITAS

Boston, June 1938

Oftentimes a matter of life or death lies in the hands of doctors. It is considered a noble calling that comes with a high price tag of responsibility.

That sense of responsibility was certainly felt by the female graduates scattered over the trimmed lawn of Radcliffe College, prepping for their pre-med exams. The buzzing of the bees in the lilac bushes was drowned by the high-pitched voices of the students. As laborious as bees they cited the different bones in the thoracic cage and the chemical elements of the periodic table.

Behind this frantic labor towered the red brick building of Radcliffe College, nicknamed the Harvard Annex, with its distinctive white tower in the middle of the four-storied college. The all-female institute stood like a beacon erected to protect the future of America's brightest women, as started in 1882 with the illustrious first president and co-founder, Elizabeth Cabot Cary Agassiz.

Inside the building, in the College library, Océane Bell, dark-haired, cupid-mouthed, and slender, sat staring at page 100 of *The Principles of Mathematical Analysis* with eyes that saw nothing. Next to her was her best friend, Eliza Hutchinson, muttering calculations to herself while jotting down the answers to the intricate math formulas in her notebook. Now and then, she would flip back a page in the textbook and, nodding affirmatively, go on to the next sum. This had been happening for two solid hours and Eliza still showed no interest in a break or even a short, whispered chat. Neither seemed she aware of Océane's ostentatious sighs.

Océane knew she should concentrate on her final exam so she would be free for the summer. Ready to go to Boston University School of Medicine in the fall, as Harvard Medical School still did not accept women. But, for Océane, it seemed all too far in the future. Her motivation had been wavering during the entire exam period and she did not have a clue how to get back on track. Her brain was tired, her heart lusterless, her body ready to jump up and go.

Glancing sideways at Eliza, she found her pencil automatically drawing the lines of her friend's profile, a dark-blond curl slipping down the straight forehead, the perfect brow above a focused dove-gray eye with black lashes around it, the nose with the slight snub at the end, and the full lips always in a half-smile, even as she whispered formulas to herself as if they were prayers. Eliza's glass was always half full, trusting her every breath to the God she worshipped, and radiating a compassionate love for all mortal sinners around her. Of which, she, Océane, certainly was one.

Eliza studied with the same devotion she had for her God, adamant to become the first female doctor in her Congregationalist family. Océane sighed again, wishing she could be more like her and less like herself with her absurd longing to paint for hours and her doubts about her medical career.

"What are you doing?" It sounded surprised rather than irritated.

Océane shook from her daydream with a jolt and her pencil scratched over the page, turning Eliza's chin into a pointed beard.

"What? Nothing!" She snapped closed her notebook under the pretense of staring at the sums in the textbook.

"Do you want to go outside, OC? We can talk for a bit or study out loud together?" Eliza lowered her voice even further, as the librarian was looking in their direction.

The old lady with the tight gray bun as if it was screwed onto her head cleared her throat. Her first warning before expulsion.

Océane nodded. She was all too glad to be liberated from the stuffy library, longing to inhale some fresh air and have Eliza's attention for a while.

As they sat on the lawn five minutes later, their pleated skirts fanned out around them and their shoes kicked off, Océane pondered telling Eliza about her growing doubts regarding medical school but bit her lip and remained silent. Ever since they started as freshmen in 1934, the more mature Eliza had taken the sixteen-year-old from Chicago - the youngest student ever to enroll at Radcliffe - under her wing. Not that Océane needed the academic support. She had always been top of her class, skipping both a year in elementary school and in high school, but brainy as she might be, she had been just a young, inexperienced girl, living away from home for the first time in a strange, new city all by herself.

"Do you want us to go over the Polynominal roots together?" Eliza had already retrieved her math book from her bag and held it open in her lap.

Océane, showing no inclination to get out her books, shook her head. "I think I've had it for the afternoon, Elz. Maybe I'll study some more tonight. But I think I've got it covered anyway. I feel like going for a walk to Charles River. I want to sit at the waterside for a bit. Guess I'm missing the Lake at home."

"But I can't come with you." Eliza looked concerned. "I've got to leave soon to pick up my brothers from school. My mother's having the Church ladies to tea this afternoon." Eliza came from a strict Christian family on Savin Hill, where her father led the Pilgrim Congregationalist Church.

"It's okay, Elz. I probably need to be alone anyway for a bit. We'll see each other tomorrow. Last exam." Another sigh.

"Are you okay, OC? You've been mighty quiet, and I noticed you weren't really studying."

"Yes, I'm fine. Just a slight headache. That's why I want to go for a walk and sit near the water. It always helps."

"You're sure?"

"Sure as shooting."

They kissed each other goodbye and Océane waved one slender arm as she picked up her bag from the grass and slowly walked away from Eliza towards Mason Street. She had not gone very far when she heard someone shout her name.

"OC, wait!"

Recognizing Martin Miller's voice, she turned on her heels to see him standing next to his Harley Davidson, beckoning her. Thinking he wanted to take her for a spin on the old bike, as he sometimes did after lectures, she shook her head and kept walking. Martin called again. When she looked back, slightly irritated by his insistence, he had jumped on his ride and was coming towards her, his tie flapping over his shoulder and his bulk of a body making the bike sag under his weight. Though good friends, Océane was not too pleased, as the sociable Martin was for sure going to distract her from her wish to go to the waterside by herself and think things through.

Martin, a third-year student at Harvard Medical School, had befriended the girls two years earlier when he became Professor Lock's assistant, the anatomy lecturer at Radcliffe. It started with a chat during lunch and soon bloomed into friendship. Sometimes they went out for a coffee or to a mixed student party, both Océane and Martin being on-campus students. She knew, though, he secretly had a crush on Eliza, who hardly ever accompanied them given that her puritan father demanded of her to come straight home after lectures. Océane could not blame him for preferring the perfect Eliza as she took up the position as his companion. Martin was good company, there was no doubt about it. Just not now.

He brought the roaring machine to a halt next to her. She saw concern not annoyance at her uncompanionable behavior in pale blue eyes behind thick spectacles.

"Got a minute?"

She shrugged, not answering.

Martin, heavy-set and broad-shouldered, looked older than his twenty-three years, always formally dressed in the same dark-blue suit with white cotton shirt and striped tie. He had intelligent eyes under a ferocious mop of black hair, and a clumsy but endearing way of moving his burly posture. The only thing Océane found difficult to accept about him was his almost religious thankfulness for his medical schooling. Being the son of grocers from Milwaukee, Martin seemed to like stressing his humble background, making other people seem far superior to him. To her this was an absolute vilification of his superior brain. Martin's learnedness was impressive, and nine out of ten times put the privileged education of the rich kids to shame. And yes, she was one of those kids.

Staring at her friend without giving him an answer, Océane realized he must think her behaving oddly, not like her usual self. She couldn't help it. There was a strange knot in her stomach that made her slightly sick. So she stood, a statue nailed to the sidewalk, her school bag clamped to her chest, waiting for what he had to say. Martin was protective of 'his girls' as he called them, and it dawned on her there was a reason he insisted on seeing her now. From the way he looked at her, she sensed something was amiss.

"Care to go for a spin to Fenway Park? We need to talk."

"I don't know, Martin, I was going in the other direction, to Charles River. And I have to study for my math exam tomorrow."

"I know. It won't take long but it's kind of important." He looked at her, his broad face a mixture of begging and burden.

"Okay. But why Fenway Park?"

"You always say you like the park. A reminder of your Lincoln Park at home."

That was true. Fenway Park was one of her favorite spots. So she consented. It would be as nice to go down to the river there. After hopping on the back of the bike, Martin took off, zigzagging through the busy traffic heading for Anderson Memorial Bridge. After they had crossed the river, he zipped along the water down Soldier's Field Road. As always, on the back of the bike with the wind in her hair, Océane felt happy and carefree, momentarily forgetting her troubled state.

Martin brought the bike to a standstill and switched off the engine. It made a funny tuck-tuck-tuck sound. Océane jumped off while rearranging her wind-blown, dark curls, her full mouth still laughing.

"That was good!"

They entered the park at the Emerald Necklace. Océane inhaled deeply. The trees, all fresh and green after the night's rain, basked in the sunshine and offered pleasant shade for those who had come for a stroll along the river or to walk a dog.

Longing to break the awkward silence between, she cleared her throat. "You're mighty silent today, Mart, for the big talker you usually are. Things going on with you?"

When they sat down on one of the iron benches facing the shimmering Riverway, Martin opened his bag. "Not with me, OC. It's *you* I'm concerned about."

"Me? Why me?" She raised one eyebrow in an attempt to make it sound light and comical.

"This." He handed over what was her anatomy exam from the week before.

"Why do *you* have this? Did Professor Lock give it to you?" She stared down at the paper that was half corrected. It was full of red remarks and sentences crossed out. Her heart sank. This did not look good.

Next to her, Martin shifted uneasily on the hard surface, clearly uncomfortable. He spoke in that slow, professorial tone he adopted for teaching the undergraduates. "You know that Professor Lock is retiring after this semester and ... uh ... he's asked me if I'd be willing to correct these exam papers for him as he's quite bogged down with work. Of course, I said yes, knowing it would mean having to grade Eliza's and your work. But I thought you'd both pass with flying colors and saw no reason not to. But … OC … this is substandard. I wouldn't be able to grade this with more than an F."

He stopped talking while she stared down at the red-laced paper in her hands, a deep frown creasing her smooth brow. Instinct made her want to crumble it into a ball and throw it in the river, but she knew that was a ridiculous idea. She had failed and Martin knew.

A jumble of questions raced through her mind while her sickness increased. She had no clue how to react. Again, her body wanted to get up and run, run, run. Away from this, from Boston, from life. But her body remained slumped on the bench while her heart and mind raced like a span of uncontrolled horses with her bumping along in the carriage.

Martin was obviously giving her time to come to terms with her failure. She had to come up with an answer, but she didn't understand any of this. How was it possible? What had she done wrong? Had she forgotten to hand in one of the sheets? There must be an explanation for this mess, but the truth was that this was the result of her failing motivation, bitter as wormwood tea. A shiver went through her entire body. This could well mean no medical school after the summer.

In her agony, she wasn't even aware she was talking out loud. "Four wasted years of studying like crazy and for whom? For me or for my parents? Well, I don't care one fig about Boston University School of Medicine. I'd rather throw in the towel now and become an artist. Catch the last glorious sun rays over the inky-blue water of Lake Winnipesaukee with my brush. Live a life in freedom."

"But how are you going to tell your parents?" Martin's concerned voice cut through her desperate daydream.

Océane's cheeks suddenly reddened at the thought of her parents' disappointment. Passing down the physician genes had been their most ardent wish for their daughter. She had never dared tell them of her wavering motivation and her longing for a completely different life. Now the decision seemed to have been made *for* her. Until now all the exams had been a cakewalk for her quick, analytical mind, even without full concentration. Not in a million years had she anticipated this utter disillusionment in herself.

"I'll have to find a way to patch this up. This is not going to stop me." She handed her disgraceful exam back to Martin, who stuffed it into his brown leather bag. "Thanks for warning me, though."

He shot her a quick glance. There was increased worry in his Midwest voice. "What will you do, OC? I wish I could help."

She did not answer immediately, but the deep frown remained between her dark eyebrows. Then she perked up. In a flash she saw the answer, though it was a tricky one and she would have to figure out a way to make Martin consent to it. It meant sacrificing Eliza to some extent, dangling her before his nose, but they were the best of friends, after all, and Eliza would do the same for her should she find herself in such a knife-edge situation. Had they not promised to stick up for each other?

"Have you corrected Eliza's exam already?"

He nodded. "Straight A as always. So sorry, OC."

It really seemed to hit him hard but to Océane this was excellent news. Eliza would want to help her now, for sure. Not only because they were friends, but because she would want to be in the same class with her next year. It had been their dream for four long years.

Martin sounded disillusioned. "I guess this means you'll not be returning to Boston after the summer. What on earth happened to you, OC? How could you of all students mess up this relatively easy test? You knew you needed to pass it and it was merely a question of learning by heart. No brain power needed for this one."

"I don't know." Océane stared down hard at her hands, so like her father's, the long slender fingers – surgeon's hands or artist's hands? She sighed deeply. "That's why we can't let this happen, Mart. It would kill my parents."

Martin shot her another quick glance, two china-blue eyes in fleshy sockets scanning her face. Although he was generosity itself, there was this trait around his mouth that made him look like a sourpuss when diagnosing the patient, as he was now.

"What on earth are you talking about, OC?" But then she saw the bright eyes flash in understanding, and he shook his squabby cheeks forcefully. In his slow, doctorial voice he stressed, "If this is anywhere near where I think you want to go, the answer is 'no'. A straight out 'no'. I may come from a simple family, but we've got our morals, believe it or not. Can't do it, OC. Period."

The surprise was not that he'd seen through her plan - she would not have expected anything else from the bright brain next to her - but she was taken aback by the strength of her hurt feelings. To gain time, it seemed best to play the part of the innocent.

"I've no idea what you're talking about, Mart."

Martin searched in his coat pocket and fished out a package of Camel cigarettes. Knowing Océane didn't smoke, although they were considered the doctor's choice of cigarettes in the States, he lit one for himself and inhaled deeply.

"Let's take this from the beginning," he said, letting two blue plumes escape from his nostrils and evaporate in the late afternoon breeze.

OC thought he was becoming more like the psychiatrist he wanted to be, by the day. Martin Miller M.D. would undoubtedly be a good shrink.

"What is it that you want? Really want?"

A pair of white swans glided by, majestic and slow, their long necks held high as graceful ballerinas while the black-ringed eyes watched the students with suspicious curiosity, before the orange beaks went down to dip under the water's surface. Océane followed their movements with sudden clarity, as if wanting to draw the pair with minute precision in her sketchbook. Love and loyalty, bonded together for life. Life. It was so much more than ... this. What *did* she really want?

"The point is, I don't really know. Unlike you, medicine was thrown in my lap from birth, but I never considered a career in it. As a child I had so many dreams – writing, painting, photography, always more the artsy things than the scientific path. And I was good at art; I loved it. Love it."

Her voice trailed off as she played with the sash of her belted jacket, watching the swans now disappearing around the river bend. Another unvoluntary sigh escaped her.

"Go on," Martin nudged her gently.

"But then, when Arthur had … you know … the accident eight years ago, it was clear he would never be the one able to fulfill my parents' wish. I started to reconsider, not so much for me but to lessen their pain."

The words themselves, heavy and laden, hung in the air. The scene was in front of her eyes as vividly as if it was yesterday: Arthur, her lively, perfectly healthy, two-year-younger brother, performing antics on his bicycle in front of the house. Hit by a car. A stray accident. The end of everything. Everything normal and fun and light. Mom and Dad, Océane, Arthur.

She sat straighter as she remembered how she had been the first one on the scene. Not hesitating one moment. At the age of ten she'd performed the first-aid tasks she'd seen her parents carry out so often in their medical practice. Check the injuries, put him in stable condition, check his pulse, call out. Heeeeelp! But the dye had been cast then. Her future decided. Especially after the praise she had received for saving Arthur's life with her level-headed, swift action.

She felt Martin's warm touch on her coat sleeve. "I know that tragedy was formative for you, but I also know you've had doubts about a medical career; certainly in the past months."

Océane breathed in. "I know, but I have no choice, Mart. I have to stay in, and you have to help me."

He shook his head. "If I do that I risk being suspended, and then we're both out."

"What's your price?"

It was out before she could check herself. Fighting the nausea, she looked him straight in the eye, focusing on the one weakness she knew he had: a deep carnal longing for a woman's touch, his inability to set about making that happen. Martin was as shy and insecure as a stray dog, especially among the fast, rich university boys who scooped up girls as if they were spoons of ice cream. Everything about Martin was clumsy and clumpy. He was convinced his brilliant mind was his only asset. But it didn't stop him from his irrepressible desire for a soft girl in his arms; she could see it in his eyes and hear it in his breathing.

He hated himself for his carnality because, above all, Martin wanted to be a gentleman, worthy of Eliza, whom he desired above all women and worshipped like the Virgin Mary Herself. Though a doctor in training, Martin despised his own body and what it did to him.

Seeing how he now looked at her as she half flirted with him, with different eyes, the professorial air evaporated, Océane's fast-thinking mind decided against sacrificing Eliza. She would have to do it herself so his Eliza worship could remain intact.

"I'll let you kiss me. You know, really kiss me."

At these words, the hunger in his eyes increased. It was hard for her to watch. She really liked Martin but there was nothing romantic between them. She felt awful, a bad creature, like the women all dolled up in skimpy dresses and red lipstick she'd seen off Scollay Square. How on earth was she going to pull this off? Then she reminded herself that crushing her parents' dream was worse than kissing Martin. It made her straighten her back. She could see he was considering her proposal, despite also being astonished at this sudden angle his friend had taken.

"And how on earth do you think I can turn this around?" he grunted, obviously forcing himself to disguise the lust that already set him aflame.

Océane perked up. "That's the least complicated part, Mart. You leave the door to Professor Lock's office open. I sneak in and change some of my answers with the same pen I used for writing the exam. You only wrote with red on the first page. Let that stay as it is. When I've added more correct answers, you could opt for giving me a C. Fat chance Professor Lock will even look at our answers, he'll be satisfied with registering your grade."

"Mrs. Simmons, his secretary, always locks up."

"Yes, but you've got a key as well. You can go back after she's gone home and open it again. I'll go in when it's dark. Then you can be there first thing in the morning. Mrs. Simmons will never know the door was unlocked during the night."

"It's illegal. There's no way Professor Lock won't notice your first page being full of red remarks and inspect the next page and see there's nothing there. He might get suspicious."

"Well, he can't argue when the rest is good. If he asks you about it, you can say you checked with me, and I mentioned a black-out during the first part. He's retiring, Mart. He doesn't care two fiddle-sticks about former students. Nobody but you and I will know of our plan."

"*Our* plan? Your plan, you mean!"

There was a prolonged silence. Océane knew they both felt flustered and awkward about this shift in their friendship, adding a sexual tension to it that neither had foreseen nor sought. And then there was the seriousness of the consequences of her plan. Martin had been granted the responsibility to correct exams because he was as trustworthy as a farm ox. He would be breaking that trust and she was the one pushing him to it. Only because this small change in her exam results would mean a world of change in her life. She could see how much Martin was struggling. Yet, she had no idea on which side of the fence his decision would fall—his physical cravings or his impeccable reputation.

He lit another cigarette, shifting his heavy-set body uneasily on the corroded bench, which creaked in protest. Océane thought he resembled the hippopotamus she'd once seen maneuvering out of its sty in Lincoln Park Zoo, as if unaware of its own bulk as it clumsily banged against the door frame. She knew instinctively she should not go ahead with this foolish idea, but at the same time it seemed so marginal; so insignificant. Change a few sentences. She knew the answers, so in fact it wasn't even forgery. Only a belated reply. And it wasn't that she was a hopeless case. She had never gotten anything but A's and B's so far.

Waiting with bated breath for Martin's answer, she tried to imagine her parents' elated faces on her admittance to medical school. It was her sole motivation; she was doing it for them, not for herself. Sweat trickled down the back of her silk blouse as the sun began to vanish behind the treetops. A chill went through her slender frame. It was not the sun that warmed her, it was her heated fear.

How far would she have to go with Martin, and what would it be like? The only boy she'd ever kissed was Donald in sixth grade, and it had felt as if a wet flannel was slapping against her mouth. At least it had been over soon, and there had been no groping for her breasts. This time it would be different, but she would say *Stop* if it became too embarrassing for either of them. Another shiver went through her. Although she had seen human bodies in various state of undress countless times in her parents' clinic and during her own medical training, the idea of Martin's soft rolls, like unbaked bread dough, against her own body made her almost cry out 'no'. Sex and love were inseparable in Océane's view, and yet they were tradable. Apparently. Or at least she'd made it that way.

Just when she thought he'd never answer, the confusion in her mind stirring like a pot of hot soup, she heard Martin say, "I'll do it, but I don't want your kiss."

She did not even dare to look in his direction, her cheeks red as peony blossoms as she swallowed hard. She could not bring out one word, try as she might. Her throat was blocked.

Martin somehow managed to find his pedagogical tone again. "I'll do it for you, OC. Because I know what's at stake."

Almost choking on her tears, Océane managed to say, "Should things go wrong, I will take all the blame. Don't worry. I'll tell them I broke in or found the door open. I'll make something up ..."

"No need for that," Martin replied calmly. "We will both be guilty as hell. You're the only one I would do it for, OC. Well, and, of course, Eliza."

The look on his face made Océane cringe. There was so much unattainable love in it. It made her cheeks color crimson all over. How haughty of her to think he would even want to kiss her. She felt both humbled and tongue-tied, and another long silence fell between them.

The wooded park was quickly cooling off, with the setting sun creating a warm palette of Crayola and scarlet over the river, which turned the water into a glassy surface of diluted blood. *Where are my thoughts running to these days?* Océane thought as people began leaving the park to go home.

On stiff limbs Martin got up from the bench and stretched clumsily. He now looked even older than before, worried and weighed down. A wave of compassion filled Océane's heart for this good man, who risked everything that was important to him just to help her. She could not help herself and burst into tears after all, clasping her hands over her face while her shoulders shook. She was sure she would be punished for what she was doing to him.

A heavy paw landed on her quivering shoulder. "Don't fret, OC, certainly not at my expense. We have a plan now, don't we? I can't see a reason why it won't work. Come on, let me take you to your dorm."

"It's not that I'm afraid we'll be caught," she sobbed. "I'm crying about everything – for putting you in danger, for Arthur who's like a withering plant in a wheelchair, for my parents, and for myself because I don't know what I want."

Martin shifted from one foot to the other, clearly longing for this burst of emotions to be over so he could recompose himself.

Océane wiped her tears, picked up her bag, and rose as well, dragging herself to the park's exit. She'd only felt this miserable in the first weeks after Arthur's accident. Again, everything seemed so painful and difficult in her life, but she had to cling to the hope of Martin's generous offer.

2

THE FORGERY

T hat night in her narrow bed in the dorm, Océane could not catch sleep, as she tossed and turned. The fingers on the alarm clock crawled to 3 a.m. and still she had not slept a wink.

Martin would be working in the administration office the next day. He had instructed her to wait outside the door at the end of the afternoon so he could hand her the file with her class's exams without anyone seeing it.

Most students and staff would have left the college grounds by then. Océane would take the file to a silent place at the end of the corridor, find her own exam and fill in the missing answers. Martin would pass her by on his way back from the bathroom, grabbing the file from her desk in one swift movement. He'd mark her exam with a C and put it back in Professor Lock's cabinet for him to approve.

"Make sure you bring the exact same pen you used for the first exam," was all he had said.

Martin had not made a great deal out of it anymore after he had decided to help her. She knew his sole purpose was to solve this dilemma for her and give her space to think things through. Only for a brief instant he'd pondered accepting the physical reward she had offered as bribe but being the gentleman he really was, had overruled lust for friendship. This simple, generous deed increased Océane's guilty conscience. She had nothing to offer in return for the danger he put himself in on her accord.

In the dark of the night, as the shrill siren of an ambulance on its way to Peter Bent Brigham Hospital rose and died away, she stared hard and wide-eyed into the black space above her. Her mind fought vehemently with her heart. She knew she should stop this act of forgery now while it was still possible; lying and cheating was not how she was brought up; failing that test had been a sign that she *was* on the wrong track; it was a call to stand up for herself, to carve out a path that she felt was hers. Hers alone. At the same time, she felt paralyzed and scared. There was no way around it but to pass this test. A doctor she was going to be, one way or another.

In all her short life Océane had known she was groomed to take over her parents' clinic. She just could not see herself going home for the summer, tossing her medical bag on the ground, stamping her foot and saying, "I don't want to be a doctor. I might want to be an artist, I don't know, but I've failed my surgery exam so let me please figure out what it *is* I really want." She knew as certain as a squirrel would climb a tree that she didn't have the courage to utter these words and she hated herself for it.

After she'd moved from Chicago three years earlier to live on the university campus in Boston, the relief of not constantly being viewed as her parents' only hope hadn't been long-lived. The responsibility had soon become clear again. Dad and Mom were the kindest, most loving parents any child could wish for and yet she had shut up. Océane knew she could and should have told them then of her wavering motivation for a medical career. They'd eventually have understood, even if just for their daughter's sake, but it would never make them feel as proud of her as they were now. And she wanted them to be proud of her, above all else. Even if it held her in limbo. It lessened her guilt over Arthur, for spurring him on to do his bike stunts.

The gray morning light, slow and slurry, lifted its veil from the Boston rooftops. When it announced the new day had begun, Océane still had not slept a wink. She listened to the world coming alive both outside her student flat and inside. The shutters of nearby shops on Longwood Avenue opened noisily, a sharp metal rattling with a clang at the end. The drum of the morning traffic increasing below her window, cars, omnibuses and motorcycles racing passed, mingling the song of their engines with the buzz of human voices. Inside the Vanderbilt Hall, doors opened creakingly and closed softly as diligent students sped on their way to obtain an early spot in the Boston Medical Library.

It was as if Océane heard all the familiar sounds for the first time, her senses sharpened by her highly active mind and increased heart rate. The heavy traffic in noisy central Boston made her feel like the young girl in Edvard Hopper's Automat, sitting all alone, contemplating life as the busyness of the world raced by. She was alone in the scenery.

Growing up on the leafy Astor Street on Chicago's Gold Coast, the sound of traffic had been muffled by the trees and walled front gardens, but Océane had always longed to be in the middle of an exciting, bustling city where not only the rich and suburban families quietly went their way. She craved color, noise, variety, exotic and extravagant people. It was probably what made her feel she'd not found her true destination yet; it was not in the stately neighborhood on the shores of Lake Michigan and not in ancient, intellectual Boston where the level of your IQ was your most valued asset.

What Boston *did* have was this build-up to a rush hour, which reminded her of her grandfather's house on the Seine Boulevard in Paris. Everything about his house, the City of Light and her artistic, silver-haired grandfather Max - whom she'd nicknamed Maxipa - was enticing and dear to her. Visiting him every summer with her parents and little Arthur had been among the happiest events of her life but after Arthur's accident they'd stopped going overseas. With an acute, almost physical pain, Océane yearned for Paris. So much, that she threw off the covers and resolutely got up to wash and get dressed.

An hour later Océane stood staring at the pile of clothes and books strewn over her bed next to her suitcase, wondering how she'd ever fit it all in. Her parents were to arrive at the weekend to take her home to Chicago for the summer. The same panic that had held her in its clutches all night now manifested itself in the chaos on her bed. Despair about her upcoming act made her pulse quicken as beads of sweat formed under her heavy ponytail. She jumped when there was a soft knock on her door.

"Door's open!"

Eliza, soft and solemn, but with a smile on her kind, round face, stood on the threshold gazing at her, lucid gray eyes full of wonder.

"Are you busy or ...?" It sounded uncertain.

"Sure, come on in." Océane gestured with her arm.

Eliza slipped inside and closed the door. "How're you doing?"

Trying to act the host, Océane busied herself putting a stack of books and art magazines on the floor to clear a chair for her friend. She also kept busy so she didn't have to meet the scrutinizing eyes. Eliza sat down and she returned to her packing.

Still without making eye-contact, she muttered, "Known better times."

"I couldn't stop thinking about you, OC. I wish we'd studied together more often but you know ... having to look after my younger brothers when my parents are always so busy in the parish ... I just didn't have the time ..."

Why on earth had she given Eliza that phone call last night? Right, she had panicked after the meeting with Martin, but it would have been much better to keep her out of it. At least she had not told her the whole truth.

"It's *not* your fault, Eliza!" It came out sharper than she intended. "I mucked it up myself. Nobody else is responsible. I just didn't study enough." From below her eyelashes she could see Eliza glancing at the ink portraits stacked in the corner of her room.

"Do you know how you're going to tell your parents?"

"Nope!"

There was no way she was going to inform Eliza what she and Martin had planned. But her cheeks reddened. On her return to the lecture hall in September, Eliza would wonder how that was possible. She would invent a story about Professor Bell's influence to let her take a resit.

An agonized sigh escaped her. Though they were opposites in many ways, she loved Eliza dearly. Eliza was always kind, always loyal, to the extent that Océane sometimes had to repress her annoyance at so much goodness. Yes, Martin and Eliza would be a perfect match. Two do-gooders together, whereas she, Océane was as dark and difficult as her name. At least that was how she saw herself.

"It's hard being a good person." She wasn't even aware she said it aloud, a habit she had when her thoughts were obvious to her, and she needed to give them substance through words.

"What do you mean?" Eliza had picked up an art magazine featuring one of Océane's favorite contemporary artists, Jean-Jacques Riveau, the enfant terrible of Urban Realism Art in Paris. She turned the pages without really noticing both the precision of the painted buildings and people, nor the photographs of the dashing dark-haired artist who was responsible for their creation.

Océane's eyes followed Eliza turning the pages. Once again, her whole heart ached for Paris and for that life, Jean-Jacques Riveau's life. She sat down on her bed and folded her slim hands with the long fingers, so very much like her father's, between her thighs, her slender shoulders bent forwards as if under a huge weight.

"I mean," she began, "for some people like you, and also for Martin, being an honest and decent person comes naturally. You wouldn't even know how to act immorally or do something unlawfully."

Eliza's light gaze darted up from the page to fix on her friend.

"Neither would you, OC! You sound terribly morose and out of sorts today. Well, I guess, it's only logical just having found out you'll have to retake an entire college year because of one failed exam. You know what? Let's go to the Museum of Fine Arts today. That always cheers you up."

"You're a doll, Elz, but don't you have to look after the twins?"

"Not today. I told Mom I wanted to spend time with you before we part for the summer."

Océane's face lit up at the thought of strolling through her favorite museum with Eliza by her side, if only to kill the time until 4 o' clock. She also felt a surge of love for this introverted, sweet creature. The very last thing Eliza was interested in was art. Eliza was all about studying and working hard; there was not a thread of artistry or even free thinking in her personality. It probably had to do with her strictly Congregationalist background but whatever it was, it fitted Eliza like a glove. Océane sighed again. At that moment she would have given everything to be more like her.

AS THE WEATHER was a fine May morning and the museum lay only a few blocks away on Huntingdon Avenue, the girls decided to walk. The fresh air perked Océane up, as did the stop on the way for coffee and a bagel. With her arm through Eliza's, she felt quite revived, ready to face the dark cloud later that day.

She simply loved the entrance to the neoclassical exposition center of the Museum of Fine Arts. Built in stages from 1907 by the famous architect Guy Lowell, the 500-foot façade of granite and a grand rotunda was already considered a world-famous landmark. In 1915 a new wing had been added along The Fens to house the painting galleries. Océane had a particular fondness for the frescoes that the artist John Singer Sargent had painted to adorn the rotunda and the associated colonnades, but she did not want to linger there too long, knowing how it would bore Eliza to death.

"Why don't we visit the Period rooms in the Decorative Arts

Wing," she proposed, hoping Eliza would find that more interesting than the modern paintings, for which her own heart yearned. She had visited the newer Period section of the museum only once and rather briefly.

"Whatever you want, dear. If you prefer to go and look at these modern abstracts, don't let me stop you. I'll hobble behind you and pretend I understand."

"I don't want you to be bored on our last day together!" As she uttered these words, she had the distinct feeling that this *was* the very last time she would be with her best friend from college. *Nonsense,* she reprimanded herself. *Of course, I'll see Elz after the holidays.* Determined to shake off the feeling of dread, Océane quickened her step and gave Eliza's arm a thankful squeeze.

They had more fun than they'd thought to have, sauntering through medieval huts and 17th Century salons, pretending they were the inhabitants, catching fish in the river, or drinking tea from ancient porcelain cups. For a brief, delicious moment in time all heaviness about Boston University School of Medicine was forgotten. They were just two giggling schoolgirls on a playful outing.

At the end of their tour, they entered the ground floor galleries where Native American art was coupled with the Mesoamerican objects from Mayan, Aztec, Andean, and Native North American cultures. Suddenly Océane held her breath and stood stock-still. Eliza, who was still laughing about the statue of a half-naked man pointing a spear at her, looked at her friend in alarm.

"What is it?"

Océane did not reply. Her body went rigid while hazel eyes transfixed on a dark head bowed over the large, gleaming glass case, the side note of which stated it contained a 1000-year-old Mayan burial urn from Guatemala.

Eliza followed her friend's gaze but not understanding Océane's fascination with either the urn or the visitor, tapped her arm. "Are you okay?"

When she still did not react, standing as if in a trance, Eliza went over to the glass case to look at the urn, to see what held her friend's special interest. The man who had been studying the urn from close up, raised his head sideways and briefly nodded at the slim, modestly dressed woman next to him.

"Jean-Jacques Riveau!" Océane's voice broke hoarsely through the cave-like exposition hall, echoing dimly against the stuccoed walls.

The young man now rose to his full height and turned from Eliza to the woman who had spoken his name, a puzzled look in his moss green eyes. Océane kept staring at him, her lips pressed together, while her heart boomed in her chest like a wild horse. She was only vaguely aware that her intense staring might be considered rude, but she couldn't help herself.

"Do I know you, ma'am?"

He had a strong French accent, rolling his words in his mouth, which sounded exquisite to her ears. Riveau was a robust, muscular man, with the built of a stone mason or a wrestler rather than a painter. His thick, dark blond hair with a distinctive widow's peak was combed backwards and from under unruly eyebrows clear eyes looked straight at her as if gauging her worth as a model for his next painting. He had lean, bronzed features with a nose slightly out of joint, and firm lips that had a somewhat snarky expression, which she also saw reflected in his eyes. A man who weighed up the world in one gaze. He was still waiting for her reply, and so was Eliza, who had left the glass case to stand next to her.

Océane swallowed hard. "I'm sorry, forgive my impertinence, I'm ... I just like your work." She abruptly turned around and marched out of the exposition hall, Eliza following closely on her heels.

"What was that all about?" Walking fast to keep up with her, Eliza obviously tried to gauge her friend's uncommon behavior. Océane was normally outspoken, never shy or lost for words.

"Nothing!" she snapped. "Let's go home. I need to finish packing."

"But if you liked his work, why not talk with him? He's the guy in your magazine, isn't he?"

"Please just drop it, Elz. It's nothing. Just temporary stupidity." Gazing at her watch, she saw it was close to three. She would now have to find an excuse to part ways with Eliza to be in time for her meeting with Martin. "I'm not feeling well. So sorry. I want to lie down for a bit. I think it's the bad exam result. A nasty headache."

"Do you want me to stay with you? I've got another hour before I've got to collect the twins from school."

"No. I'm really not well. Sorry. Can we say goodbye now?"

They stood facing each other. Océane did indeed look miserable. Both the upcoming tampering and her inability to tell Eliza what was really going on, made her feel like a bad friend on top of everything else. Almost bending double with sudden stomach cramps, she realized it was also because all she'd eaten was that bagel. Her stomach was protesting.

"I'm so sorry, Eliza," she said softly as she took her friend in a farewell embrace, "I'll be alright after the summer. I'll miss you. See you in the Fall."

"We will, and I'll miss you, too," Eliza's said, kissing her and hugging her tightly.

"Thank you for everything," Océane sniffed, trying hard not to burst out in tears. "I'll be okay. Really."

"Will you write or phone me after you tell your parents? I want to know how you're doing."

"Sure."

AFTER KISSING Eliza goodbye for the last time, Océane tore herself free and with teary eyes made her way back to Vanderbilt Hall. Inside her dorm room she felt so ill, she threw all her stuff off her bed and lay down, checking her watch every couple of minutes. The agony of seeing her idol on the same day that her world came crashing down only aggravated her further.

"Oh, why did I need to make such a fool of myself in front of him?"

Rising from her bed, she angrily grabbed her school bag and made for the Office of Faculty Affairs on Shattuck Street. As she bridged the short distance to Martin's office, all her senses were heightened. The scent of grilled meat and mustard from the hotdog stall on the corner of Avenue Louis Pasteur, the sounds of a garbage truck claxon behind her making her jump, while the squealing wheels of a passing pram hurt her eardrums.

It felt as if she was walking outside her body, which had developed a mind of its own, moving closer and closer to the dreaded place of verdict, while her inner self seemed to be moving in the opposite direction. As an automaton, she swerved around passersby and crossed the street, entering the administrative department. Her feet directed her to the simple brown teak door stating 'Registrar's Office. No admittance for students.' She'd waited here for the end of Martin's shift several times, but this situation was altogether different.

Afraid her body would let her down and she would faint, she spied around for a place to sit but the corridor was a long, empty and ill-lit passageway with carpeted floor tiles in muck beige and a row of teak doors on each side. Only at the very end near the bathrooms stood a table, the table where she would eventually sit down and cheat. With her heart pounding in her chest like a hammer gone insane, she kept checking her watch. Five more minutes. Five times sixty seconds of terrible survival. Her ears were ringing, her knees almost giving in. She needed the toilet but there was no time.

It all took place as if in a blue haze. Martin, looking ashen-gray and even more unhealthy than usual, handed her the file without a word and closed the brown door again. As quickly as she could, Océane scrambled towards the loathed table, sure somebody would pop out of one of the teak doors any minute and cry out, "Here she is! Busted!" but nothing of the sort happened. Not yet.

She opened the beige paper file. Her eyes scanned the list of on the top, all straight A's until she came to the last column. With shaking hands, she shuffled through her exams until she found the culprit. Unscrewing her Parker pen, she no longer thought but added answer after answer on the lines she'd had to fill in a week before but hadn't. A niggling little voice in her head told her she wasn't cheating. She knew the answers. It had just been the wrong time.

The wrong time. Being in a place at the wrong time. It seemed the mantra of her life.

Goodbye, Martin, and thank you!

3

CHICAGO

A week later

Océane sat on the wooden swing in the back yard of the family mansion on Astor Street, idly dangling her feet. Since she returned to Chicago, she had not had a moment to herself. And she needed it. Leaving Boston had felt like a welcome flight, but her ordeal was far from over. Every moment she expected the dreaded phone call that she was found out and she would have to face her shame. The thought of how deceived her parents would feel after their exhilaration at her diploma, made her want to hide in the back of the family garden and never come out anymore.

Inside the house everyone claimed her. Her mother wanted to fuss over her, and her father wanted to know all the details of her Radcliffe education. Arthur was in constant anxiety, sensitive to the changes in the household now she had come back into his little orbit. He gesticulated wildly in his wheelchair, talking and shouting in his own language. Especially so when being put to bed at night. Océane had to stay in his room until he slept. It was endearing and heart wrenching at the same time.

She looked around the familiar garden. Here she had grown up, held her birthday parties, here she had taught Arthur to fish in the pond and to play ball. All signs of a children's garden had now been eliminated except for the dilapidated swing at the very back of the grounds near the tool shed. As neither of her parents had green fingers, the large plot with a fenced fishpond in the middle consisted mainly of a well-kept lawn, maintained by two gardeners on a weekly basis. The grass went right up to the ornate veranda that ran along the entire back of the white-washed wooden house. On the right was a walled tennis court and along the left side, where the garden bordered Lincoln Park stood tall oaks and pines. In one of the high oaks hung askew Arthur's old tree house, sagging dangerously with the floorboards come loose.

Océane breathed in the invigorating scent of the bristlecone pine, filling her lungs with a sense of nostalgia. As the tangy sweetness tickled her nostrils, it managed to lift her spirits. This was home, this was safe.

Bally, their six-year-old Irish setter who was actually Arthur's therapy dog, lay on his side in the shadow of the shed but kept a watchful eye on the young mistress's movements. He stretched his copper-haired hind legs and yawned audibly. He would not have minded a stroll through the park to hunt for rabbits or squirrels, but Océane didn't show any inclination to leave her sanctuary. It was Bally's afternoon off, as Arthur was at his physical therapy group and dogs were not allowed inside.

Though a work dog and devoted to the entire family, Océane knew she was his favorite as she was the one who would take him for long walks, telling him everything that was going on in her life, a squabble with a friend, a painting that had not come out right, her doubts about becoming a doctor. Today she was silent, not even sharing her inner thoughts, and the dog, sensitive to the needs of others, was on high alert.

"Come on, Bally, indoors we go." She jumped off the swing and smoothed her blue silk dress. "Official tea with Grandpa Bell, so we'd better be on our best behavior."

Bally reluctantly got on four legs and stretched his front ones. Like her, he yearned for the mysterious footpath in Lincoln Park, not sipping Darjeeling with an undercurrent of collywobbles.

"Not now, Bally." They dragged their feet up the veranda. "But tonight, when Arthur is in bed, it will be just you and me and my secret."

Bally wagged his tail while banging open the screen door with his long nose in a chirpier mood. Another secret they shared was their dislike of Grandpa Bell.

At that moment, the copper bell sounded at the back of the house to announce afternoon tea was served. Océane cast a quick look at herself in the gold-framed mirror in the hallway, making a grimace. Dark-brown locks, her father's hair, held together with a light-blue ribbon to make her look a presentable young woman; the hazel eyes and always-slightly tanned skin were untraceable family features. It was what she shared with her beloved French grandfather, though he was no blood relation, having adopted her mother as a baby.

"The gypsies have given you my skin, my little princess," Maxipa had once told her. "It makes us two of a kind. But never tell Mama. It's our secret." Her tone made her proud, so unlike her mother's almost porcelain white skin. She had inherited her mother's straight nose and high cheekbones. The mouth with the distinctly curved upper lip was also an unknown trait. Gypsies again?

"I'm just myself. And maybe part gypsy, part Océane," she told herself, as her black suede pumps clicked on the marble tiles on her way to the sitting room with Bally following on her heels.

"Stay there!" she ordered the dog, who heaved his brown body into the rattan basket outside the door. A dissatisfied groan sounded before he closed his eyes. When her father's family visited, Bally was not allowed inside the room. Just one of the rules Alan Bell Sr. issued in his son's house.

Océane hoped to slide into the afternoon room unnoticed. She was lucky. The attention was not on her. Yasmine, her grandfather's fifty years' younger third spouse, was having one of her fits because she had found a dog's hair on the settee which had miraculously worked itself into her new merino skirt.

"You know I'm allergic to dogs. Can't you have one of your maids do the hoovering before we come to tea? Bell Senior, say something about it. It's gross and it makes me sneeze. And it's not the first time!" She raised her painted face to her husband, whom she invariably addressed by his last name.

He, in an attempt to prevent a full out scene, patted her arm soothingly, which made her many bracelets tingle with a metallic, soulless sound. "That cursed dog," he muttered under his formidable mustache, "someone should shoot it."

Where Alan Bell Sr. was every inch the despotic patriarch of Bell's Construction Company, he always went soft where Yasmine was concerned. A trait she seemed to expect with the same aplomb as the fact she could spend her husband's fortune as she liked. It was difficult, however, for the rest of the world not to have a certain disdain for the third Mrs. Bell, whose only accomplishment seemed her youth and good looks.

Océane managed to sit down next to her mother on the couch unnoticed, thus saving herself from having to go over for the customary peck on the cheek from her grandfather. She didn't even have to look at her parents' faces, sitting stiffly upright in their own sitting room, to feel how the air was stifled with her grandfather's presence in it. Alan Bell Sr. and Yasmine managed to take over the lush family room and turn it into an exhibition space, where the visitors all moved and acted as if not in their own bodies, afraid to knock over something of value, or collide with each other.

The Bells' junior never managed to learn walking on eggshells. Each visit from the family's patriarch was an unplannable ordeal. Océane felt for her parents. Mother had told her that Dad had moved to France in 1910 just to escape his father's condescending bark and his endless string of misbehaving mistresses. But he had returned after the First World War, bringing his young bride with him.

It is a good thing Arthur isn't here, she thought. *He'd go berserk.*

Feeling her mother's rigidly upright backbone next to her, Océane glanced sideways at the fair profile. Her beautiful, blonde mother, so sophisticated and sweet at the same time, was sipping her tea in a studious manner, not seeming to taste the musky-sweetness at all. And that when tea and Agnès Bell were inseparable. Though raised in coffee-drinking France, her mother had in many ways adopted English habits.

She inched closer to her statue-like mother, inhaling the mixture of Chanel perfume and citrus disinfectant that seemed to be her permanent aroma. To feel her mother's safe proximity as a way of shunning away from an overbearing grandfather and a guilty conscience, Océane slipped her fingers into her mother's free hand. There was comfort in the soft, firm touch. Her mother put down her Wedgewood teacup to turn to her daughter. At forty-four Agnès was as sweet-looking and radiant as in her wedding portrait that stood on the sideboard, the white skin as fresh as dawn, a fine mass of blond curls around her oval face and the clearest robin's egg blue eyes.

The eyes that held her daughter's gaze were friendly but also showed her mother knew something was off. Océane cringed, squeezing the fingers in a reflex. How she hated secrets between them. Though every inch a rational scientist and ready to give her opinion if needed, Doctor Agnès Bell would never probe in personal matters. She was waiting patiently until Océane was ready to talk.

"You're okay?" she mouthed, giving her hand another squeeze.

Océane nodded. Her mother released her hand and pulled her closer, wrapping a slender arm around her daughter's shoulders. This was the sign Océane had been waiting for. Huddling her slight frame against her mother's and ignoring the stern look from her grandfather, she drew her legs sideways under her and felt safe and protected. Now she could listen to the conversation that went on like a Ping-Pong set across the light sunroom of the Bells' sitting room.

"That damn new Illinois congressman for Chicago, Matt Lutz, wants to prevent me from building a pier into the Lake to attract tourists. Thwarts me on every single plan I have. That cotton-picking fool. He's got no idea what he's talking about when it comes to business expansion. Well, he's got another thing coming, now he's dealing with me. Mark my words. There's no way Dr Matt Lutz with his fancy Harvard Degree is going to push me around, Thomas H. Bell. Not in a thousand years. I'm an honest and hard-working builder. I tell you, that Lutz is just one of those meddle-some Jews who's been elected to office by his sycophantic cronies from the academic world. That lot's bringing the whole country to a standstill. But I guess you voted for the damn bastard yourself, Alan Junior?"

There was no missing the sneer in the final remark. As it was more a statement than a question, her father refrained from react-ing. But Océane saw the line between her father's brow deepen. He looked like a cornered fox, ready to attack or to flee.

Océane felt her mother's body tighten again, though her face remained unreadable, almost sphinxlike, an expression she always adopted when Dad's family visited. Despite her mother's effort to look deadpan no matter what loud and boorish remark came out of Bell senior's mouth, her sweet face could never completely lose its soft loveliness. She could not hide her unease at the attack on her husband's political opinions.

Her father continued to ignore the remark and kept stirring his tea, his long legs in the navy-blue flannel pants crossed over each other, his body erect and poised. The beautiful gray eyes went from his teacup to his wife and daughter. He winked at them and raised his eyebrows as if to ease the tension, but she could see the muscles in his clean-shaven cheeks twitching. Océane smiled back at him with all the warmth she could muster. He grimaced back before returning to the study of his tea, as if looking for an answer to this ordeal amidst the tea leaves.

"Why don't *you* run for office, Bell Senior? You'd make mincemeat of the whole lot, now wouldn't you?" Yasmine Bell piped up, oblivious to the discomfort that hung in the room.

Only her own presence and that of her rich husband counted in the world. It struck Océane that this odd couple - he in his early eighties and she in her twenties - was actually like a weather clock. There was always drama lurking when these two were around but in some crazy way they seemed to keep each other in check. At least most of the time. There was the occasional explosion in which no one was spared, not even the crystal vases or the lacquered snuff boxes.

Both Alan Bell Sr. and his trophy new wife had little veneer and even less self-restraint. If it had not been so pathetic and her own family, it could have been funny, Océane thought. Her artist mind was already drawing a life-size Grandpa Bell with his B-actress-slash-society-girl as cartoonlike puppets standing life-size on his fancied amusement park pier. She seriously pondered getting up to grab her sketchbook but her mother's grip around her tightened, sensing what she was up to. How well Mom knew her.

"I might do indeed," Alan Sr. bellowed, "if that Jewish vermin continues to crawl through our District Office. I might indeed." He patted his Yasmine on the arm again, rattling the expensive bracelets.

Océane now lost interest in the conversation and felt herself relaxing against her mother, just seeing lines and light, forms that wanted to escape from her pencil onto an invisible page. Grandfather Bell continued to bark in his crude, overbearing voice while the others said little. There was only the occasional high-pitched interjection by his new bride. In her mind, Océane was drawing her father as he sat there with the garden light at his back, physically a younger version of his authoritative father, the same tall, slender built, dark-haired, gray eyed. Alan Sr. might be gray now but there was that same high forehead and penetrating eyes under dark brows, straight nose, decisive mouth. Dad was always clean shaven while Grandpa had this enormous mustache that made his face look wider. They were great models to draw, with regular features and a distinct air of confidence, but she knew she would never be able to draw her grandfather in a favorable way.

Where Alan Sr. was rough, unpolished and loud spoken, which showed in haughtiness and a certain debauchery, her father was restrained, sober and analytical but with a warm, loving heart. She drew Grandpa with bold, hard, thick lines and her dad's were more flowing, gentler strokes, more depth, simply with more love. Grandpa took, Dad gave. She was so engrossed in her mental drawing that she was unaware of being addressed. Only when her mother nudged her ribs, did she realize her grandfather was awaiting a reply.

"Sorry," she muttered, sitting upright and swinging her legs to the floor, "what was it you asked, Grandfather?"

"Manners in conversation most of all," he barked.

Océane had to bite her tongue not to reply that he should look in the mirror first. But her own fragile position made her behave as expected from her. "Could you please reply, Grandfather?"

She heard Yasmine sniff with contempt but ignored her.

"I was asking, young lady, what it is that you expect to do after the holidays. Your parents may still think it is a good idea to send you off to university, but I've told them that there's plenty of work in one of my offices. No need to squander more money on your education. A job as a typist would suit you fine. Well, that's my opinion but your father never thinks of asking for my advice. And be grateful I offer you a job." Again, that sneer.

Océane sat up straighter, her hazel eyes furious. "I'm going to be a doctor like my parents so, yes, I'll need to go to university for that. No question about it."

She was surprised at the conviction in her own voice, that she even was saying these words in front of her family when she was still doubting what to do with her life. But somehow this pompous grandfather provoked the words from her and now they were out. She felt relieved, standing by her parents. Not that she would ever consider working for her grandfather. Just like Dad, the less she was involved with them, the better.

But Alan Bell Senior was not done with her. "And what makes you so sure, young lady, that medical school will accept the likes of you?"

Her cheeks reddened. No way he could have known what she'd done at Radcliffe. Her mind raced. Her grandfather might be a bloated individual who steered clear from all things academic, but he was also an important man with a huge network of businessmen and magnates all over the States. She scanned his face but was instantly reassured. He was just giving one of his unwanted opinions. He knew nothing.

"Well, I graduated from Radcliffe. That's as good a ticket as it can be."

"Radcliffe is so passé," Yasmine declared, waving her red-nailed right hand as if brushing off some imaginary dust. "Ca-li-for-nia is where you should go, pet! Boys are spunkier there and also got plenty of ..." She rubbed the pointed-nailed thumb and index finger together to indicate the insides of their wallets.

Océane saw her father raise his eyebrows again, this time in despair, and she had difficulty not to burst out in laughter.

"Yassy, it's time to leave. Can't talk any sense in these academic brickheads. Let's leave them to it." Rising to his full length and straightening his fashionable pin-striped jacket, Alan Sr. suddenly pointed a finger at Agnès, who shot up as if being put on trial. "Don't forget the 4th of July garden party at our place, Mrs. Bell. Swanky jazz quartet and even Potter's children will be there. I expect you to take care of the salads."

Agnès gazed up at the formidable tycoon, nodding her deadpan face, visibly uncomfortable in her own sitting room.

BALLY WAGGED his tail in pure joy when the front door clicked shut behind the Bell's Senior.

"Good riddance." It was the first thing her father snapped as they returned to the sitting room and sat in their regular places.

"For the love of God, Agnès, I don't know why we put up with them every time. They insult us in our own home whenever they can."

Océane was well aware there was a trace of accusation towards her mother, which made her eyes go from one parent to the other. Her mother had sunk back on the sofa, looking withdrawn and unhappy.

"They *are* your family, Al." Her voice sounded tired, defeated.

"Your father isn't even your real father, and he feels more like a dad to me than this specimen." In his anger Alan, who could not sit still for long, started to collect the teacups and stacked them so roughly on the tray that the ear came off one of her mother's much-cherished Wedgewood crockery. Gazing at the broken cup, the pent-up anger left him like a deflated balloon. "Damn!" he cursed, "Sorry, darling, I'll get you a new one tomorrow."

"They are no longer for sale." Her mother's voice was small, and she was close to tears.

Seeing how distraught his wife was, he went over to her. Sinking down on his knees, he took both her hands in his before kissing them reverently. "Sometimes I think we should never have come back to the States. We were much happier in Paris, weren't we, my darling?" His voice was bitter and had an edge of begging.

Agnès shrugged. "We've built a nice life here, Al. And the children were born here. We have much to be thankful for."

Despite her dapper words to show that she had adapted to the New World and had come to terms with her heart always being pulled back across the Atlantic Ocean, a shadow slid over her pale, beautiful face. Océane was once again reminded of how homesick her mother could be for the country where she was born and for the father who had raised and loved her like his own flesh and blood. Biological bonds certainly did not guarantee love, so much was clear from the relationship between her father and grandfather.

"I'm not so sure anymore," Alan said morosely. Letting go of his wife's hands, he sat on the floor with his back against the settee and lit a cigarette. Blue plumes rose to the ceiling while they sat together in silence.

There and then Océane knew she would go to Boston University of Medical School. She saw her future before her as clear as if she were looking at Picasso's *La Vie*. Her life would be in the service of the other people's health. Just as she had been taught. If you loved your parents, the die was cast.

4

A FAILED ATTEMPT

That evening as Océane went up to her bedroom, she heard her father call from the sitting room, "Could you come in for a moment, OC? Your mother and I want to talk with you."

For a moment she considered feigning a headache or needing to catch up on some much-needed sleep, but there was something in her father's voice that made her retrace her footsteps. With feet that weighed ten thousand pounds she went into the same room where earlier that day the climate had been so stifling and sour. On high alert, she saw her parents looking relaxed, sitting each in their own chair. Her mother was reading a French novel while her father paged through his Academic Medicine Journal. They both looked up with a smile as she sat down on her own spot on the sofa.

"Tea, darling?" Her mother had her hand already on the bell cord to order fresh tea. Her parents were both having a port wine.

"No thanks, Mom, I'm fine. I was on my way to bed."

"Aha." Her father's falcon gray eyes scanned her face.

Océane couldn't help blushing. She wished her face wouldn't color every time she felt under scrutiny. He waited a moment, seemingly weighing his words, which made her feel more uneasy by the second. Her mother was also looking at her but with a softer expression. There was a tinge of sadness there, which made Océane swallow hard. In her lap her hands clasped together until the knuckles showed white. She hardly dared to breathe.

"I just had a phone call from Professor Lock." The words were spoken evenly but the emotions behind them were unmistaken.

"What have you done, OC?" her mother's clear voice, with its distinct European accent, broke through the air as the cry of a wounded animal.

For a moment she considered bolting out of the room, out the front door to never come back, go and hide at a faraway place where no one knew her or her shame.

"Well?" her father asked. "Please tell us what happened in Boston, dear girl. Your mother and I are really at our wits' end coming up with reasons why you thought it necessary to cheat in a final exam. Why, OC?"

No matter how hard she tried, she could not utter a single word. They stuck in her throat like sawdust. Tears welled up in her eyes, spilling over her lashes and dropping onto the front of her blue dress. "I don't know," she finally managed to squeeze out. It was no more than a contorted whisper.

Her mother came over and sat next to her. Just like that afternoon, she wanted to take her hand, but Océane pulled away from her.

"Whatever it is, darling, tell us! We can deal with the truth. We thought you were enjoying Radcliffe. If you didn't or thought it too difficult, why didn't you tell us?"

Her father cleared his throat, but there was no anger in it. "After I spoke with Professor Lock, who could give me no explanation for your behavior, I phoned Dean Jeremy Foster. He, too, said, there was no sign whatsoever of incompetence on your part, except on these last two exams. Your math exam was below standard as well."

Océane remained silent, biting her lip, sobbing softly.

Beside her, her mother said with a defeated tone in her voice,

"We really thought you wanted to go to Radcliffe as a prep for medical school. But now I get the idea we've pushed you to it. Is that it? Talk to us, child."

At this, Océane could hold back no longer and crying with unrestrained sobs threw herself in her mother's arms. "I wanted you so much to be proud of me, so much. That's why I did it. Don't you understand? You weren't supposed to find out. What went wrong? And what will happen to M–" She suddenly stopped wailing, the immensity of being found out and the repercussions it would have for Martin making her want to die on the spot. She hadn't spoken his name out aloud. This was her secret, their secret.

"Nothing will happen to you, my pet," her father assured her, mistaking the M for 'me'. "I have some strings to pull at Radcliffe through my position at Harvard. So all that will come later. All your mother and I want to know from you right now is why. Tell us the truth and we'll find out how to solve this afterwards."

"Let's have some tea after all," her mother interrupted, handing Océane her scented handkerchief, with which she dabbed her eyes. "A difficult discussion always gets easier with a strong cup of tea."

Her hand reached for the bell cord when they were shaken up by loud, almost inhuman cries coming from Arthur's ground floor quarters opposite from the sitting room. Without a moment of doubt, they sped out the room and into his chambers.

He was lying on the floor, having managed to fall out of his wheelchair. His whole body was convulsing, his eyes rolling backwards, showing the whites. He was about to lose consciousness. The night nurse had her hand in his mouth, preventing him from choking on his own tongue.

Both parents kneeled on either side of the tall, blond teenager who seemed engaged in a battle of life and death. Océane, nailed to the floor and wringing her hands, watched her invalid brother having one of the worst epileptic attacks he'd had so far and knowing there was nothing she could do for him at that moment, started praying, not even realizing she was doing it aloud. Meanwhile her parents were addressing Arthur in calming voices, caressing his limbs until the spasms finally died away. Océane was still reciting "Our Father, thou are in Heaven" when silence returned to the room. She'd seen his attacks many times, and knew it wasn't those that would kill him, but it broke her heart every time. His blond curls, so very like his mother's, lay damp against his temples as his eyelids lowered and his pallor slowly returned to normal. He was a big boy now, almost thirteen, his body growing normally, but his brain that of an infant. And the horrible attacks that sometimes came weekly, sometimes stayed away for a month, they took their toll on his deteriorating health.

"Why was he not in bed? And how could he fall?" She heard her father ask the nurse, who was busy taking the quilt from his bed so he could be laid in it immediately.

"He wouldn't sleep. He was so restless that I put him back in his wheelchair and pushed him around the room. He was happy, reaching for his helium balloon," the poor woman said, distraught, "and I just wasn't fast enough to catch him. I'm so sorry, Doctor Bell. The attack was so sudden. And he was so happy with Miss Océane's present. I really didn't see it coming or I would have put on his safety belt."

"It's alright, Nurse Janie," her mother said as she caressed the damp curls from her son's face. "Give me a flannel to wash his face."

During the scene that hadn't lasted longer than a couple of minutes, Océane had not moved, her mind in turmoil as her heart went out to her little brother ... and then to Martin. Arthur's attack had temporarily saved her from having to reveal her embarrassing failure to her parents.

Arthur, limp and exhausted after his attack, with the whites of his eyes still showing as his eyelids would not close, was helped into his diapers and pajamas in a combined effort by her mother and the nurse, while her father noted down all Arthur's vital functions on the clipboard that was always attached to his hospital-like bed.

While all attention went into getting Arthur to bed and comfortable, Océane's prominent thought was getting hold of

Martin on the phone. His fate was the worst of her nightmares. She could live with her own humiliation and a future that did no longer include medicine, but he couldn't. It was up to her to make sure his dream of becoming a psychiatrist was not blocked. But how?

"This is the moment," Océane murmured to herself, seeing her parents would be busy for the next ten minutes.

She tiptoed out, heading for the telephone in the living room. Unfolding the slip of paper with Martin's parents' phone number that was always in her pocket, she dialed the operator and gave the Milwaukee number.

Soon she heard a raspy voice saying, "I've put you through, you can talk now."

A deep voice, quite similar to Martin's answered, "Miller's Grocery, how can I help you?"

"Are you ... am I speaking with Martin's father?" Océane, suddenly aware she hadn't prepared for this, stammered as a result.

"Yes. Who's speaking?"

"It's ... I'm Océane Bell, I was one of your son's students at Radcliffe. Is he home? Could I ..."

"Sure, hold the line."

While she waited for Martin to come to the phone, she skipped nervously from one foot to the other. What now? She didn't even know how it had leaked out. Whether Martin knew or whether it had been just a talk between her father and Professor Lock as two Harvard professors.

"Hi," she said timidly when he said his name.

"Ah, OC, how are you?"

"Not very well, Mart. Have you heard?"

"Heard what?"

Océane sighed a breath of relief. There might still be a sliver of hope that Lock didn't know Martin was involved in the forgery. "So, you haven't? My Dad and Professor Lock talked. My parents know. You know, about what we ... um ... I did."

It became silent on the other side of the line. Playing with the coiled telephone cord she waited with bated breath what would come next.

"No, Lock didn't contact me. I've been home for a couple of days now, so perhaps he didn't want to phone my private number. What happened?"

"Well, that's the thing. I don't know yet. I was just summoned in by my parents when Arthur had one of his attacks. The only thing I know is that Lock knows I cheated. So I guess I'll have to hand in my diploma and get expelled. I'm sorry I'm bothering you with it when you're probably off the hook anyway. As soon as I know the details, I'll give you another call, okay?"

She heard a deep sigh on the other side. He didn't reply.

"I'm so, so sorry, Mart. I should never have asked you."

"It is what it is, OC. My dad has asked me again if I won't consider stepping into the business with him. He's getting old, you know, and he's got a heart condition. I'm working full-time in the shop now, so there's always a place for me to earn my keep."

"Noooo, Mart!" Océane wailed, no longer able to suppress her pent-up distress. "I have to take all the blame. I can't have you sacrifice your future. I'll find a way, I promise, I'll find a way."

"Whatever you come up with, OC, it's not going to make sense and you know it. How could you have known I was the one correcting your exam and stopped halfway and then miraculously you remember that you forgot some answers and decided to go and fill them in after all? We're both trapped as mice in a noose."

"I'm not going to rest until I'm sure you're staying at Harvard, Mart. I swear it. Got to go now because I hear my parents coming. Will give you a ring soon."

Océane dearly wanted to rush up to her bedroom and hide her face in the covers but her promise to Martin forced her to confront the situation head on. She would have to be careful, though. Arthur's last attack had been the heaviest she'd seen so far. Her parents' thoughts would be with their son, not on their cheating daughter. She peeped around the door and saw they were conversing quietly in French, the language they returned to when they were discussing intimate and personal things. She knocked softly, hesitantly. Her mother looked up, wiping a tear from her eye.

"Come in, darling," she said with as much enthusiasm as she could muster. Turning to her husband, she said softly in French, "*Cela peut attendre.*" 'It can wait.' This time her mother pulled the bell cord with force. "We need tea, strong tea."

Océane saw her father put the clipboard with Arthur's medical notes in his bag and wondered what was going on but did not dare to ask.

"So, sit, sweetheart," Agnès continued, patting the sofa seat next to her. "There's this other situation we have to solve."

Océane approached slowly, feeling pressed down by the deterioration of her brother's condition and her own failure to live up to her parents' expectations, but taking heart from her resolution to at least save Martin's skin, she said, "Dad, what exactly did Professor Lock tell you?"

Her father seemed to come from far away, his thoughts clearly more on his son's precarious health than his daughter's tomfoolery at Radcliffe. He cleared his throat but at that moment Bettina, their maid, brought in the tea and he waited until they were all served and she had closed the door behind her.

"Jack Lock phoned me this afternoon to tell me that his secretary had found your exam sticking out of a drawer in a rather odd way."

At this Océane colored, not knowing what had happened to her file after she'd returned it to Martin. Maybe he'd been caught red-handed when putting it back.

"Mrs. Simmons had put your exam on Jack's desk with a note saying she didn't trust it as it seemed things had been written on the last three pages with a slightly different pen while the first page was full of corrections in red."

While he talked, Océane tried to remember whether Professor Lock could know of her friendship with Martin. She hoped not.

"Jack contacted Martin Miller, who is his assistant and ..." Her father's falcon eyes rested heavily upon his daughter. "... I believe a friend of yours ..."

Océane cringed. Of course, Mom and Dad knew, she'd told them everything about the bright, poverty-stricken medical student from Wisconsin. She was trapped indeed.

"We've put two and two together," her mother now interrupted. "Although Professor Lock is still confused about what exactly happened with your exam, your father and I know this was forgery, Océane. And that is a very serious situation. We really want to know why you decided to go for such a severe measure. This is not like you and not how we raised you."

Océane glanced at her mother through her eyelashes with her head bowed. Her mother was deeply disappointed in her. So much was clear. "I will tell you everything, I promise," she started timidly, "but you must promise me one thing."

"I don't know if we can promise you anything, daughter." This was her father, stretching his long legs and searching for his cigarettes. He lit a Lucky Strike and blew out the smoke with force. "If this is what we think it is, we're all in a pickle. I happen to teach at Harvard, remember, and it's a small world."

"I know, Dad, Mom, and I'm sorry but I did it for you."

"Us? What do you mean?" both her parents exclaimed in surprise and at the same time.

"Yes, and that's why you have to help me save Martin's career."

She blurted out everything, in an urgent need to confess. Of her wavering motivation, her longing to be an artist, her guilt over Arthur's accident, her wish to be a good daughter. How some part of her wanted to be a doctor and some part of her wanted to explore the world and find out more about herself. While her parents listened in silence, Océane felt they slowly began to understand where she was coming from, how she'd come to take such an extreme measure. How they had to save Martin Miller's career.

Two cups of tea later, they sat in silence for a long time, until her mother said, "I agree with OC on this, Al. Although it goes against our morals, we need to save that boy's future. Stick with the version that OC realized she'd not elaborated enough on her answers, sneaked into the Registrar's office and hid in a cupboard until the secretary left. Did her thing, was caught almost red-handed and stuffed it back clumsily, then opened the door from the inside and left. That way Martin stays out of the story completely."

Her father was listening intently, then nodded. "On one condition. That you take a year off to find out what it is you really want to do. If after one year you still want to go to Art School, you've got my blessing, daughter. What do you say to that, my girls?"

"The fact remains that she won't be admitted to medical school should she want to," Agnès said pensively. "Forgery will make her suspended forever."

"Leave that with me, I'll discuss it with Jack and see what we can do. It's the only exam you didn't pass, so maybe he'll agree to a retake, not mention the forgery and let her off the hook."

"Thank you, Mom and Dad." Greatly relieved, Océane hopped off the couch and kissed both her parents. "And I'm sorry. Very, very sorry."

"Now we know why you did it, there's no reason to be sorry, sweetheart. There's just the matter what you will do with your gap year?" Suddenly her mother perked up. "I've got an idea! Why not go to Switzerland? They've got these one year-courses on etiquette and style. Not that you care much for these things, but they seem to be very good at teaching languages as well. You always said you wanted to learn Italian. And apparently, they offer lots of painting and sports. My father insisted I should go there before the war, but I just wanted to study at the Sorbonne, so I never went. Most of my Paris friends did, though, went to Lake Geneva and had a great time."

"Do you think that would be enjoyable for our bright little daughter?" Her father sounded doubtful. "Isn't that more a place to know how to catch a rich husband?"

"Well, we don't have to decide it tonight," Agnès said. "There are some other, more pressing matters we have to take care of first."

That night in her bed, staring at the ceiling and unable to sleep,

Océane pondered the idea of going to Europe, away from it all, a non-demanding course, mostly having fun, skiing and swimming and drawing as much as she liked, and the more she thought about it, the more attractive the idea became. Leave Boston and Eliza and Martin. But for a good reason. They would still be here when she came back.

Wouldn't they?

5

ON THE TRAIN

August 1938

As *Le Train Blue* weaved its way from France into Switzerland, slow and lazy as a blue caterpillar in the sunny morning, Océane sighed a breath of relief and momentarily closed her eyes. All she had to do now was leave the known behind, dive into this new world of European finesse and enjoy herself. For sure a ladies' only world where no career demand would be giving her stress. A time to explore the Alps, fill her always searching mind with silly spiel and fun.

It had been a nerve wracking and exhausting journey, first boarding the *SS Normandie* in New York. A teary goodbye from Mom and Dad. Arthur had not come down to New York with them but saying goodbye to him had been heart wrenching for them both. Seeing her brother's face behind her closed eyelids killed Océane all over. During her Boston years, goodbyes had never been longer than a couple of months. Home for Christmas, home for Easter, home for the summer. But now? She may not see him for another year and what if, what if?

It was impossible to shake off the past yet, no matter how hard she tried. Her life had been a train wreck ever since the last days at Radcliffe in June. Despite the many miles that now separated her from the States, the memories were under her skin and would stay there until they faded in the distant snow-capped tops of the Swiss mountains.

"Mademoiselle, is this seat taken?"

She peered through her eyelashes, irritated by the disturbance. Then she snapped up, her eyes wide open. "Yes!" She had blurted it out before she could think.

Why was he standing here? For a moment she thought he'd followed her, but that was an absurd thought. The moss-green eyes smirked but also held a shadow of perplexity. No doubt her rudeness. It made her recline even further into the plush seat. Jean-Jacques Riveau. What was *he* doing on a train to Switzerland?

"Sorry," she muttered, "go ahead. My mind was occupied. Forgive my rudeness."

"I was on my way to the diner carriage when I seemed to recognize you. Were you at the..."

"... the Museum of Fine Arts in Boston. Yes, that was me. Sorry for calling your name out there and then just disappearing. I'm ... I'm sort of clumsy at times." She spoke too fast, tripping over her words.

Jean-Jacques sat down opposite from her, perching on the edge of his seat, clearly not sure what this volatile girl would blurt out next. "I'm sorry I interrupted your train of thought."

His eyes were too intense, too mesmerizing. The sheer force of his gaze made her turn her head and look out of the window, seeing the landscape in a blur, her body hotly aware of his presence.

Jean-Jacques continued in his peculiar French-lilted accent, "Being an artist I know how valuable time for introspection is, so I'll take my leave now and let you be. I was ... uh ... just curious why you addressed me in the museum and then disappeared. I'm more used to it being the other way around. Devotees following me around, wanting to talk to me, have my autograph, you know, that sort of thing. Sorry, this makes me sound like a vain famous person who complains about the people who like my work. I didn't mean it that way. I try not to be vain."

In the glass reflection she followed his every move but still didn't dare to look at him.

"What's your name? Just tell me that. You know mine." His voice was very low, as if not wanting the other passengers to hear it.

His gaze forced her to look him in the face again. He was smiling, not that snarky smile, but friendly, almost shy. Océane held out her hand and felt his big, strong hand envelope her slender fingers. It felt warm, but she could feel the callouses on his palms.

"Océane Bell."

"O-ce-a-ne?" He repeated, letting the syllables roll of his tongue as good old wine. "What an exceptional name, so much depth and fluidity." He winked and she thought he was mocking her, as there was that trait around his lips again, but he added, "Your name is a timely reminder I have to finish my sea portraits. Been so focused on my city work lately. I couldn't stop painting the ocean during the sea voyage back from New York to Le Havre. The sea, the ocean, those waves, ah yes ..." He stopped talking, looking apprehensive now.

Océane thought his facial expressions were as fickle as the shadows of the clouds in front of the sun. His face was a painting in itself. He made an attempt to rise, clearly uncomfortable with her silence.

"Wait!" Regaining her confidence, she said, "What brings you to Switzerland."

There was the broad smile again and he sank back in his seat. "Oh that. A friend of mine has a chalet on Lake Geneva. He's holding a painter's retreat for a week, so I thought I'd join. I've been not as productive as I should be lately." A new nuance was added to his expressions, something wistful, almost melancholic. But he corrected himself. "Enough about me. What about you?" The intense green eyes focused fully on her.

Océane laughed. "I don't think I can tell you."

"Oh gosh, is it a secret? Are you a spy?" He brought his voice down to a conspiratorial level.

She shook her head, laughing. "No, I'm going to do the silliest thing I've ever done in my life. I'm going to a finishing school in Lausanne."

He looked pensive, scratching the two-day stubble on his chin. "You're doing what? You really surprise me, O-ce-a-ne. Somehow, I'd rather imagined you doing heroic stuff like rescuing people rather than folding napkins. The picture won't click."

Her face fell. There it was again. Her uncertainty about her future. Not knowing what to say, she simply fell into silence again.

Jean-Jacques waved his muscular arms in an apologetic way. "Sorry, I shouldn't have said that. Many young, accomplished Parisiennes I know have gone to finishing schools in Switzerland and had a great time there. You'll enjoy it, for sure."

"No need to apologize. If you'd asked me a year ago if I saw myself folding napkins, I would have said no. It is what it is."

"I guess you wanted to leave the States for a bit?"

"Yes. A clear break. Yes."

Though the words were on her lips to tell him her story, Océane held back, pressing her lips together. This man, this painter whose work and rise to fame she'd followed for the past two years, remained a stranger. And he wasn't interested in her. He'd have women hanging on to every one of his fingers, for sure. She should keep her distance. She wasn't a fool, not one of his *devotees* as he'd called them.

His expression was unreadable when he rose to his feet. "Well, no matter how dearly I'd like to get to know you better, Océane. I really should get to the diner now. My friend must think I've fallen off the train. I hope we'll meet again. Do come to my atelier, should you be in Paris. Here's my card. *Au revoir.*"

"*Au revoir.*"

And with that he was gone. The last press of his warm, rough palm still in hers, his card between her fingers.

Jean-Jacques Riveau
Peintre du réalisme urbain
4 Rue Ronsard
Monmartre
Paris

WHAT DID THE CARD MEAN? He probably handed them out by the dozen. Océane stuffed it in her handbag and closed her eyes again. She wanted to forget all about Jean-Jacques Riveau, his penetrating green eyes, and his strong, warm hands. It was impossible. It was as if his gaze had burned itself into her retina and her body moved uneasily on the plush chair as if his hand was still holding hers. Going to the Alps to paint with friends. What would a life like that look like?

She was on her way to her own liberty. As far as she dared to go. Giving her artistic side a free rein for a while though confined to the walls of a strict boarding school. She would never be a free spirit, to go with life where the winds took her. It was not in her.

As the train swayed and the brakes creaked and the iron wheels covered the last miles to Lausanne, her preliminary destination, Océane was wrapped in another existential crisis. And she hated herself for it.

"I had this figured out," she murmured to herself. "Why does JJ come around and muck it all up?"

JJ. Everybody in the scene called him JJ. Like she was OC to most. It didn't make her happier. They had nothing in common.

Liberté! What did the word mean anyway? She let it roll over her tongue, tasting it. Who knew? She certainly hadn't had much of a taste of it. Everything had been in the fast lane since her Radcliffe debacle. Packing, saying goodbye to friends and family, waving goodbye to her native country to make the crossing of the big pond on her own. For the very first time. It had certainly shaken her up. Especially because no one awaited her on her arrival in Le Havre.

Maxipa had wanted to be there but couldn't. He was at his Château in Picardy for the summer. It had stung her, to be honest, but he'd promised to come and pick her up once her course at the finishing school was done the next year and she would stay with him in Paris until Christmas.

"Maybe it is as well," she thought to herself. "Grandpa would have fussed over me, and I'd never learn to stand on my own two feet."

She had arranged the trip through France herself, ordering porters for her luggage and checking into the Ritz in Paris for the night. She had hardly slept in the luxurious bed, afraid she'd arrive too late at Gare de Lyon for the train to Lyon-Part Dieu, where she changed for the international train to Geneva, and then into Switzerland. But all had gone smoothly and here she was. Over 7,000 miles away from home, in an unknown country, all by herself.

Taking heart at her own courage, she decided she would breathe in all that Le Manoir had to offer with fresh energy. She would take her time to find out what she wanted her future to look like. At some point all would become clear to her, as crystal as Lake Geneva itself. She felt in the pocket of her travel jacket again, fingering her mother's last gift to her there. Her stethoscope. Her mother's sweet face came before her as Océane's head rested against the velour cushions of the train.

"Darling, you know I want you to make up your own mind about what you want to do with your life. Dad and I only want your happiness. But I wanted to give you something to remember me, now we're going to be apart for so long. I've been racking my brain what to give to you that is really from me, you know, some token for you to take on your trip to your own future." And that was when her mother had given her the stethoscope. She had looked so lovely, almost shy, as she explained, "This stethoscope had been with me throughout the first world war. It was a present from my father. Wherever I went, it was always in my pocket. Maxipa used to say he could draw me in my white coat with that stethoscope sticking out. It helped me in my darkest hours during the war.

When my German biological father conquered the front-line hospital where I was working, and I didn't know if I would live or die. Whenever that fear gripped me, I could touch this stethoscope and it would give me strength. It reminded me who I was and what I stood for. I want you to take it with you, not to force you to become a doctor but to hopefully get the same strength out of it that I did. And to feel my energy."

Her mother had stopped talking, looking a little out of breath as if she'd run some distance. It was then that Océane understood, really understood, how much her mother loved her. Her mother who breathed being a doctor with every tender breath she took.

Deeply moved but hesitant, she had replied, "But, Mom, don't you want to keep it for yourself? Don't you need it?"

"Ah, non," her mother had said, returning to her native tongue, "I don't use this one anymore. We have more modern ones these days. It's not an instrument, it's a talisman. And I want *you* to have it." Agnès had kissed her daughter on the forehead by way of giving her blessing.

Océane's fingers gripped her mother's talisman while she wondered about Agnès as a young doctor. She'd been so brave to go with Dad to the front lines to save Allied lives. No female surgeon had ever come so close to the Hindenburg line. Dad's eyes were always full of admiration when he talked of Agnès's bravery. Especially after the German occupation, and after he'd been severely injured, and she had had to save his life. She had nurtured him from being an invalid to a healthy man with the same diligent love she now bestowed on her invalid son. Her nymphlike, ethereal mother who was actually made of steel and kept the whole family together.

"I'll find my way, Mom," Océane mumbled to herself as the stethoscope slowly grew warm between her fingers.

The view became breath-taking, the lake glittering as a large diamond-studded quilt while the pristine mountains on either side rose to a majestic blue sky. For a while the train ran along Lac Leman, as the French called Lake Geneva, before finally coming to a standstill at the Gare de Lausanne. With the final screeching halt of the wheels, Océane felt as if she had traveled for an eternity, across half the globe. The journey was in her bones, her mind, her soul. She was weary and worn-out but knew this was to be a brand-new chapter.

6

LE MANOIR

Disheveled but brimming with curiosity, Océane disembarked and, while waiting for the porter to stack all her luggage on the trolley, inhaled the crisp Swiss air and stretched her stiff body. She spied around her to see if Jean-Jacques was disembarking as well but there was no sign of him.

"Just as well," she muttered to herself. "There's no place for him in my life. I'm completely on my own, just as I longed for."

"Follow me," the Swiss porter, who had a friendly face with an exuberance of whiskers and mustache under his black cap, welcomed her. "Normally the chauffeur from Le Manoir waits at the front of the station to take the young ladies to the school. He is to return any minute. You are the second one to arrive today. There was also a girl from Austria."

"Okay, thank you," she responded, not really sure how she ought to comment on his information.

Who else would be in the school held little interest for Océane. She'd come for herself, to draw, to relax, to think things through. Following the porter to the front, she saw a black car with - in golden lettering - 'Le Manoir' on the door slowly move up and stop at her feet.

A stocky, short driver clad in a black uniform hopped out and addressed the porter in Italian, *"Perché non hai portato mademoiselle in sala d'attesa?"*

The driver appeared to be rather agitated, but the porter seemed unperturbed. Océane had no idea what they were talking about but was quickly ushered into the back seat of the shiny car. The car took off immediately.

"Has mademoiselle had an agreeable journey?" The driver looked at her in his rearview mirror; his strong Italian accent had a pleasant, melodious lilt.

"Yes, Sir, thank you. It's been a long one, so glad to arrive at my destination."

"Ten minutes, no more!" he promised.

She was relieved that after this show of politeness the chauffeur showed no sign of interest in conversation as she sank into the leather upholstery to look out the window. A soft, evening glow enveloped Lausanne. The lanterns popped on and spread a yellow light over the quiet streets. Lausanne did not seem like a very lively city. Then the car started to climb, and she gasped.

Lake Geneva lay shimmering dark and inky below them with grey-blue mountain ridges climbing to the sky at the other side of the still lake. Here and there a small vessel moved like a white snail or bobbed as it lay at anchor. The stillness, the water calming her overwrought senses, the fairy-tale beauty of the surroundings, it stirred something in Océane she'd not expected. A yearning for her paintbrushes that was almost a physical pain.

She'd always loved the out of doors but had never seen it this postcard-pretty and sublime. And how the surroundings made her feel in the backseat of that lush car. Prettier herself, more feminine, more refined. A soul that lived and breathed. Jean-Jacques Riveau's handsome, virile face and posture came before her and for the first time ever she wondered, *Am I a woman? Of course I am, but that never seemed to matter. Is this the beginning of finishing school? Does this place do this, turn girls into women? What does being a woman mean?*

In Océane's upbringing, the equality between men and women

had been evident and never really a matter of discussion. And of course, her mother was feminine, very much so, but never in the sense of being interested in clothes or magazines. Mom had one best friend, but she was also a doctor, and they went to the woods with Bally, and talked about work. Mom read a book or listened to the wireless, but she never seemed to do what the mothers of her friends did. They were all homemakers, needlework and Church groups, or volunteer work for one of the many Chicago charities. Once Mom had taken her to downtown for shopping, but they had ended up browsing through the bookshop instead. Océane looked at her simple but good-quality travel dress and suddenly felt apprehensive. What if the other girls were all fashion dolls and she would have nobody to talk with?

There was no further time for musings as the chauffeur drove up a long, gravel lane. On the border of the lake, almost hidden by the dusk, Océane saw a large, rectangular building in white-washed stone with rows of square windows loom up before them. Some of the windows were illuminated. She had a flashback to the Vanderbilt building but this Swiss school in no way resembled her intellectual, strictly Christian dorm in central Boston. Le Manoir breathed opulent money and international allure.

"Here we are, Mademoiselle!" The stocky Italian quickly jumped out of the Renault to open the door for her.

"Monsieur Maltese!" Behind them a sharp female voice rang accusingly through the evening. It had a metallic ring.

Océane didn't miss the chauffeur make his face impassive before giving her a polite bow and busying himself with her luggage. Things were becoming formal. Océane turned on her heels. A slim lady of incalculable age, dressed in toned-down colors with a beige shawl draped around her shoulders, was striding towards them. Her gait was rather overrefined, as she carefully placed one foot before the other as if tight roping. *That's not a healthy way of locomotion*, shot through Océane's mind. The woman extended a manicured hand, spreading a stiff whiff of perfume and an even stiffer smile. Ai, she hadn't calculated ending up in an acting class. Maybe this was a wrong decision after all. Her hand was gripped in a super soft paw that was immediately withdrawn again.

The affected lady was ready to embark on her speech. "Welcome to *Le Manoir*, Mademoiselle Bell. I take it you had an agreeable journey?"

"Oh, yes," Océane mumbled but was instantly corrected by one eyebrow being lifted in the carefully made-up face. The lady in question was talking and didn't expect to be interrupted.

"My name is Madame Paul Vierret and I have been the headmistress of Le Manoir since 1917. The correct way to address me is Madame Paul. And as long as you stay here you are Mademoiselle Océane. Always address each other formally. As you have arrived late ..." This was said in a slightly condescending tone, though Océane thought she had no control over the train's timetable. "... and most of the young women have retired to their rooms, I will show you to your room myself. You may refresh yourself for a minute. I've asked cook to prepare you a light supper. I take it you still have an appetite despite the late hour."

What a funny way of talking she has. Maxipa would have a fit if he heard her. Océane tried hard to look as deadpan as the chauffeur, who seemed to be waiting for further instructions from the headmistress. Despite Madame Paul's artificial behavior and speech, and this film-set-like introduction, the idea of freshening up and a hot meal was a tempting prospect. Océane opened her mouth but shut it again. The rules were confusing. Was it polite or impolite to reply to Madame Paul's evening schedule for her? She followed the slender, straight back without a word.

"Room six, Filippo."

So, staff was not to be treated formally?

Océane felt bad for him, having to carry all her heavy luggage up the stairs in one go but she didn't dare come to his aid. She held on to her beauty case and handbag. They entered a huge hallway with black and white marble tiles. At least six corridors led from the hall into different directions. One magnificent mahogany staircase wound to the first-floor landing. All carved wood and shiny polish.

Apart from the clicking of their heels on the stone floor, it was silent in the school building. But when they went up the mahogany staircase, Océane discerned the muted tones of a piano being played in one of the corridors. Madame Paul halted midway up the steps, tilting her head as if deaf in one ear, lips pressed together in a disapproving way.

"You're on the first floor, Mademoiselle Océane. Your roommate also arrived today. Mademoiselle Esther apparently thinks it is still allowed to play the piano at this late hour. Tomorrow morning I'll instruct you both in Le Manoir rules. And they apply at all hours." The voice was menacing but the smile never left the painted lips.

Heavens, what a sourpuss! Doubt crept in again about choosing this school. She hadn't anticipated having to share a room, either. As long as the rule-breaking Austrian roommate was nice.

"Well, here we are!" the headmistress announced, pushing open a brown door and going in first.

Océane was glad to see it was a spacious room with two beds on either side against the wall, a big window with the shutters closed, enough space for two, a huge closet on either side, a writing table, chairs.

Madame Paul swung open another door with a theatrical wave of her arm. "And this is the bathroom that you, of course, have to share. You can leave most of the unpacking until tomorrow. Only take out the essentials. In half an hour the maid will take you down to the dining room. I'll leave you to it now."

There was one pressing matter on Océane's mind that could not wait. "Madame," she began, made immediately aware that omitting the 'Paul' was probably the wrong start when the eyebrow went up again. In the light of the room, she could see the hard glint in the celestite blue eye. "Madame Paul, is it possible for me to make a phone call to my grandfather in France, you know, to tell him I've arrived safely? He will then phone my parents in the States. You know, I've been traveling on my own for the first time and my parents will want to know I've arrived in one piece."

For a moment she thought her French was inadequate because the headmistress just stared at her with those hard eyes and pressed lips. Océane looked away, her gaze falling on a photograph of a young couple on the bedside table of her roommate. So, the Austrian was probably engaged. Two things happened in rapid succession. Madame Paul, instead of answering her, followed her gaze and went over to pick up the framed photo. She opened the top drawer of the bedside table and put it in.

"No pictures of men in the bedrooms," she said sternly, directing the probing gaze to Océane again. "Mademoiselle Océane, it is praiseworthy for an American to speak such good French but please refrain from using stop words like 'you know' in your speech. They are unnecessary and pollute your conversation. Furthermore, don't use colloquial expressions such as 'have arrived in one piece'. Correct speech is not inbred, it is learned, and I will personally take it upon myself to polish your conversational style." She took an unnecessary pause before saying, "The mademoiselles are not given free access to the telephone, but I will telephone your grandfather myself and give him your regards."

"But …" Océane started, then seeing it would be useless, closed her mouth again. No chat with Maxipa.

"Two letters per week are allowed, two out, two in. Those are the rules, Mademoiselle Océane. Well, I'll leave you to it now. I will see you tomorrow morning at breakfast. It is served in the breakfast room at 8:00 a.m. As this is the first time for both you and Mademoiselle Esther, you'll be escorted downstairs by one of the girls. Make sure you're ready at a quarter to eight. Good night, Mademoiselle Océane."

"Goodnight, Madame Paul."

OCÉANE FELT her mood drop below freezing point. She was bone-tired and homesick. She just needed a little friendliness. Following the orders, she dragged herself to the bathroom to wash her hands and face, before sitting down on her bed to wait. There was a soft tap on the door. It was immediately opened. A tall blonde girl, her light-green eyes glittering with tears, stepped hesitantly across the threshold. Océane understood this was her roommate but seeing her cry sent her on high alert. The girl seemed lovely and easygoing enough, not a troublemaker. She began to think they'd arrived in some kind of prison camp. What a cold, nasty place. If these were manners, she had a set of her own!

"What's going on? Sorry, I'm Océane Bell. Why are you crying?"

The girl retrieved an embroidered handkerchief from her sleeve and dabbed her sage eyes. "I'm sorry," she sniffed, "I didn't want to upset you, but I had nowhere else to go. I'm Esther by the way." She shook Océane's hand, still sniffling.

Océane's protectiveness surfaced and still holding the soft hand, she guided the girl to the bed she'd been sitting on. "Tell me what happened. I've got a minute before I'll have to go down to supper."

Esther sat on the bed next to her. She was still crying but slowly calming down. The doctor in Océane let the distraught girl take her time to recover. Her own mind was racing in the meantime. She did not like Le Manoir one bit and already regretted her foolishness of traveling half the world to a country that didn't seem as hospitable as she'd imagined, nor was it likely she would be able to dabble freely in her art.

She was thinking aloud, as she muttered, "Well, I can always leave, can't I? It's not like they can keep me here against my will. I'll just get hold of a telephone somewhere and tell Maxipa to come and fetch me. No one in my family would want me to suffer here."

Esther stopped crying. In her German-laced French, she said, "I arrived in Switzerland this afternoon. I'm also not sure whether I should have come. After the Anschluss in March, and the Nazis all over Austria, my country has not been the same anymore. Life for us Jews is getting more and more complicated. I was worried about leaving Mutti and Papi and ... of course ... my fiancé Carl." At this she looked at her nightstand. A strange squeaky sound came out of her throat.

Océane jumped up and opened the drawer for her. "Don't worry, Esther, it is here. Madame Paul says we cannot have pictures of men standing around but she's not going to take it away from you. Just keep it hidden in your drawer."

Esther sat with the picture in her hands, stroking the glass, looking as lonely and forlorn as Océane felt.

"What happened just then? What made you cry?"

Esther looked up from the photo, her clear eyes full of love. She emanated a wonderful kindness that made Océane think she looked more like an angel than a human being. The blondness and fairness of this creature puzzled her; Esther looked more like her own German-blooded mother than like the dark-haired, dark-eyed Jewish women with whom she'd studied at Radcliffe. But all that was of no importance. She wanted to comfort the rattled girl and simultaneously comfort her own misgivings about this finishing school.

Esther brought her lips to the glass before putting the picture back in the drawer. Folding her hands in her lap, she said, "Madame Paul was not very friendly when I arrived. How was that for you?"

"Same here," Océane grumbled, "but she's not going to see me in tears. I swear so much."

"It wasn't Madame Paul who sent me over the edge. It was the other girls."

"What did they do to you?"

"I ... I don't know if they do it to all the newcomers, you know, make them do things that are forbidden just to make Madame Paul lash out at you. Well, at least you've been warned by what they did to me." Esther sighed, fighting the brimming tears once again. "I so much wanted to come here. Both my mother and my grandmother did their year at Le Manoir before they married. It is like a tradition in my family. My mother was here before Madame Paul took over; it was during the first world war. Strange to think schools like this just continued but Switzerland likes to stay neutral in any war. That was why my parents wanted me to go now. They know I want to learn everything I can here so I can be a good wife and great host when I marry Carl. Viennese and international relations are important to us. So, I came here hoping to make no mistakes, to be always top of the class as my mother had been, to be proud of myself, have the same impeccable reputation as my mother and grandmother who are very revered hostesses back home." Esther stopped, looking at Océane with a strange longing in her eyes.

"Go on," she urged.

"I never talk that much about myself. It's not appropriate. I'm sure I'm boring you and am sounding biased. Well, that's why I'm here, I guess."

"Oh, fiddlesticks," Océane exclaimed, "I like you already, but just quickly tell me what the girls did before I go down and they start grilling me, too."

"Well, after dinner one of the French girls asked me if I played an instrument, so I said yes, the piano, and then they asked me to play something for them. I thought it was an innocent request and I wanted to be liked so I started playing a modern jazz piece they wanted to hear, though I usually play classical music. And then they kept asking me to play more songs but ... but suddenly Madame Paul stormed in and looked at me with those queer eyes. She didn't say anything at first, just stood there as if she had asked a question and I was supposed to answer it. I didn't know what to do. My hands were still in mid-air over the keys when I heard a muffled laughter behind me and Madame Paul saying in very slow, deliberate syllables, *there-is-no-playing-on-the-piano-after-dinner.* I felt mortified, not so much by her reprimand but because the girls were clearly enjoying that I was put on the spot. It was mean. They knew the rules and should never have encouraged me. Now my first impression on Madame Paul is not a positive one, when I thought I was doing something nice, you know, to entertain them."

Without a second thought Océane sided with her new friend. "That's mean indeed. Well, I'm glad Madame Paul put us newbies together so we can have each other's back. Shall we make a pact? I used to do that in college with my best friend Eliza and it always worked. Two are stronger than one."

Esther's eyes opened wide. "You went to college? You mean like university? Heavens, you must be smart."

Océane shrugged. "It's not important right now, I'll tell you all about it later. So do you want us to be friends and stick up for each other?"

But Esther was still mesmerized by her new roommate's academic achievements. It quite took her out of her own misery. "University," and she let the word roll on her tongue. "What did you study? Now I look at you closer I can see it clearly; you look very learned."

"Horsefeathers!" Still, Océane was glad her presumably superior brain seemed to take Esther's anguish away. She would gladly use her gray cells if it could help her new friend gain Madame Paul's praise.

"Mademoiselle Océane!" There was another rap on the door and a female voice calling her.

As she made for the door, Esther whispered, "Thank you, OC. Is it okay to call you that? We'll be best friends. I know it."

"I much prefer OC to *Mademoiselle Océane*." She spoke in Madame Paul's haughty voice.

Esther giggled.

She winked back at her.

AFTER OCÉANE HAD WOLFED down a plate of *charcuterie,* pickles and brown bread, she felt much better. Not just because of the first-class food in her stomach but over the idea that she'd once again been blessed with a female friend in life. Physically Esther looked very different from the slight, dark-blond Eliza, but character-wise they were quite alike. Both were kind-hearted, soft-hearted women who wanted to do nothing but good in this world.

It will rub off on me hopefully, Océane thought as she wiped her mouth and took a large gulp of fresh apple juice.

But then her father's voice rang in her ear. "My beautiful daughter, you have such a fierce, loyal heart and bright mind. You could singlehandedly lead this world like the second Jeanne D'Arc if called upon in the moment of truth."

As she finished her meal, she pondered what he had meant by that, why she always shoved compliments aside; what her stance in the world was or could be; how people saw her and what she was to learn here at Le Manoir that would be useful in her future life.

Though she was sleepy, her mind was wide awake. For the first time in her young life, Océane felt she was closer to her calling, though she had no idea what it entailed or why she suddenly felt it so strongly here in untroubled Switzerland.

She fell asleep that night feeling she was about to find her Northern star.

7

THE FUTURE

It was a good thing that Océane and Esther forged a deep friendship from the first day at Le Manoir because as novices they were tried and tested by the other girls. Madame Paul's reign over the finishing school resulted in a rigid, ruthless regime sprinkled lavishly with such mottos as 'for your own good', 'what is expected of you in the real world', 'no mistake is made when you thoroughly prepare'.

Her suppression of the girls, who by and large were used to more freedom in their upper-class upbringings, led to underground revolt and much bullying when Madame Paul was not looking. Neither the American nor the Austrian girl had been subject to such vile attacks before. Standing shoulder to shoulder and looking out for each other, they endured the first weeks.

One day there was a dead mouse at their door when they wanted to go down to breakfast. Esther was the first to leave the room and screamed out in fright. Océane just looked puzzled, but because Esther raised her voice in an unladylike manner, Madame Paul acted with disdain towards them for two days. Then there was the deliberate mixing up of their table setting, which resulted in Madame Paul puffing with extravagant sighs.

"Monsieur Petrov has explained the routine in straightforward French. Can you please both pay better attention?"

Esther had bit her lip and Océane clenched her fists. She was near to crying out, "If you think Monsieur Petrov speaks straight-forward French, you should have your ears cleaned. The man speaks Russian all the time and his teaching is in his gestures."

Océane and Esther struggled on, side by side, and revived themselves when together in their room, chatting about life before Le Manoir and after.

On a cold, dark night in January 1939, while the wind howled and a snowstorm blasted against the shutters, they were lying in bed with down quilts tucked up to their noses. Their bed lamps were still switched on.

"You're awake, Es?"

"Hmmm ... half. We should be sleeping." Esther turned on her side, the beautiful sea-green eyes, those of a sleepy mermaid, always lit up at the sight of her friend.

"I've been thinking ..." Océane started, which evoked a chuckle from Esther.

"Now, have you?"

"Seriously, Es, it's only because of you that I can bear the place. Though Christmas was terribly hard, wasn't it? I'd never imagined Switzerland such a cold place, not just temperature wise but also the people here at the school. But you've made all the difference. That's just what I wanted you to know."

Always beat-up, always sweet-mouthed Esther, still hanging onto her dream to become the mistress of a grand house, replied, "I think we're actually making good progress, OC. Yesterday Madame Paul gave me my first ever compliment on my flower arrangement, And she keeps telling you that your paintings are superb."

"That's true. I love how you are always so optimistic. Oh, and I'm dying to go skiing in St Moritz next week. Closest I've come to a ski slope was watching the ski-jumping tournament at Soldier Field in Chicago last year. That was quite spectacular, but I can't wait to try it out myself. What about you?"

"Thank God, at least I'll be able to excel at one thing here! We've been alpine skiing since I was a little girl. We have so many great slopes in Austria. My family has been going to Obertauern every winter for twenty years now. One of the fun things is that my father always brings his Leica to take pictures of us. My mother pastes them in albums and we love sitting around the fireplace, going through these albums. We see ourselves grow year by year, my big sister Rebecca and my little brother Adam and me, wearing the ski jackets and trousers that the eldest have outgrown. It's the only time the women in my family wear trousers. Can you imagine flying down the track in a skirt?"

Esther laughed her tingling laugh. The thought of her family under happy circumstances cheered her up. Sweet as her character was, she added, "I guess Madame Paul has ski instructors in St Moritz for us, but I can teach you if you want. Outside the lessons. My Papi always says, 'it looks like you were born on skis, dear'. I could outski the Nazis, if necessary."

A dark shadow slid over her smooth, lovely face and a sudden chill went through Océane. "Let's hope that's never necessary," she said in her most upbeat voice. "Now let us sleep or we'll never hear the alarm. I couldn't stand one more session walking with books on top of my head. Argggh. They'll all land on the floor again, that vile Sable and her cronies laughing their heads off."

"I don't understand why some of the girls find it necessary to be so disagreeable," Esther said in a sleepy voice.

"Oh, I do," Océane replied, still wide awake and full of energy. "Don't you see? They actually fit this whole concept of finishing school perfectly. All they want from life is a strong man who reigns them in and keeps them in check. Until then, they'll try out their nasty behavior with other women, but as soon as they're married, they'll become all docile and pliable. Still, they'll never be nice to other women. My two cents."

"I don't know ..." Esther's voice trailed off.

As Océane listened to her friend's even breathing, she wondered if girls like Sable Montgomery would ever truly change and why Madame Paul condoned such undermining behavior when she was so corrective with her and Esther.

On the whole, they were maneuvering through the course as best as they could. The one thing that made up for all the anguish and belittling were the painting lessons by the queer, gray-bearded Monsieur Georges. Though not the best of teachers, being much more interested in his own art than that of his pupils, Océane had ample opportunity to indulge in hours of oil painting, sketching and lithography.

Where Esther had chosen music as a special subject, she had chosen painting. Even in her free time she had access to Monsieur Georges' large, light studio at the back of the school, where it was quiet, as none of the other girls seemed to enjoy painting. Most of the time she had the studio to herself and her daydreams. Still, two minds, science or art, art or science.

That day she had finished her first modern painting, letting her imagination run wild. It had resulted in a carnival of colors, in which she'd etched the contours of the Arc de Triomphe in fine black lines, the tomb of the unknown soldier underneath. A birthday gift for her grandfather. Yes, she was really coming into her own, developing her own style. Even self-centered Monsieur Georges had nodded his broad head approvingly.

"*Vous avez du talent!*" he had exclaimed in his affected voice, drawing Madame Paul's attention to his gifted pupil while lapping up all the credit for it himself.

"Maybe an exhibition at Easter, Mademoiselle Océane?" the headmistress had suggested.

She'd been so proud at that moment. If only Mom and Dad could come and see her work. As she was dozing off, Océane was almost certain she would enroll at *L'École des Beaux-Arts* and say goodbye to medicine for good. There was nothing that would make her happier. Art over science.

WEEKS TURNED INTO MONTHS. Despite Switzerland's neutrality from the ripples of fear and devastation that Hitler's regime was creating in central Europe, the Spring of 1939 did bring a change to Esther's family in Vienna. Océane found her one day, tears in her beautiful eyes, the sheets of a letter in her lap. She was instantly on high alert; both had been going strong for a month now, looking towards the future with more confidence. Esther to a successful marriage with her Carl, Océane going to Paris to study art.

"What is it? Is it Carl?"

Esther shook her blonde head. "No, it's my family. Apparently, Vienna has become a terribly hostile place to Jews. Mutti has finally persuaded Papi to move to Norway. They already talked about leaving Austria when I was still at home, but they've left now. Just like that. To Oslo. I had no idea." Tears spilled over Esther's cheeks, her shoulders shaking in the gray merino cardigan with its alpine flower embroidery.

Océane was at her side in two steps and put a firm arm around the trembling shoulders. "Tell me!" she urged, but Esther was too upset to talk. She was working herself in a frenzy, the pale cheeks flushed while she was having difficulty breathing. Océane routinely took her pulse. "Not good," she mumbled. "Lie down, sweetie, you'll become very dizzy in a moment. I'll just pop to the bathroom to get a cool flannel but I'll be back in a sec. Try to breathe a little deeper, so you won't get a hyperventilation attack."

When she returned, she saw Esther was about to faint, so she quickly stuffed a cushion under her head. A steely calm settled on Océane. This she could handle. Here she was in control. Mentally she recalled Kerr's diagnosis, knowing that now Esther had lost consciousness, her automatic nervous system would take over and her breathing would stabilize by itself. There was nothing of importance to do right now.

Putting a hand on Esther's flat tummy, she helped her breathe deeper by guiding her breath deeper into her body, a technique her mother had taught her. The stillness in the room, the stillness in Océane's soul. This was nothing like Arthur's wild, uncontrolled epileptic attacks. This was a soft fall from consciousness, the body's normal reaction. She listened to Esther breathing evenly, the ticking of the Swiss clock on the wall, the high-pitched voices of the other girls on the terrace. Somewhere a dog barked and a gull screamed. Slowly, Esther came by, opening her sealike eyes, bewilderment on her face.

"It's okay, Es, you passed out because your system couldn't handle the stress. Breathe as calmly as you can, stretch your limbs, waggle your fingers, whatever. Don't worry, I'm here. You're safe."

It hadn't occurred to Océane to call on the nurse on standby day and night at Le Manoir, as one girl had female troubles, another a headache or a cut finger. She could handle this simple medical situation. Though she might be punished for it if Esther let slip a word. But she would never do that.

Lost in her thoughts, she shot up as Esther addressed her in her normal singsong voice. "Going to art school would be an absolute waste of your talent as a healer, OC. You're a natural doctor. You are radiating so much assurance and confidence right now."

The soft eyes were steadfast and clear. The words Esther spoke aloud hit Océane as a Eureka. The calm, the concentration, the conviction. Esther brought it home to her. Art was passion. Medicine was knowing. She'd have to choose between passion and simple, steadfast knowing. Healing people was her mission. As soon as the physical body was hurting, she knew what to do, where to be, how to act.

Now it was Océane's eyes turn to fill with tears. "You're right," she sniffled, "I can't fight what I'm supposed to do here on earth. And you of all people letting me see that. Thank you so much."

The hand in her pocket closed around the stethoscope her mother had given her. She instantly felt the presence of both her parents with her in the room. It was true, every time she was needed in an emergency, she was right where she needed to be. It was providence, for sure. She was a born doctor.

Esther hugged her. "You're welcome, Doctor Océane Bell. I wish you could be my doctor all my life. I'm so glad to see how you can use your superior brain to help humanity. Not many people are carved out to be a doctor, but you're one of them."

Knowing she would have to digest this new insight at some point on her own, Océane steered the conversation away from herself. "Are you feeling a little better now?" One hand on Esther's clammy forehead, she checked her pulse with her other. "Can you tell me what upset you so? You're still marrying Carl when you're done here?"

Esther shook her head, her lip quivering. "No. My parents are going to live with my father's sister, Aunt Isabel, and her husband. They've got a shop in Oslo. They want me to come to Oslo as soon as I finish the course here. Carl is supposed to come up north later ... only ..." She hesitated, breathing as Océane had instructed to calm herself, her eyes big and scared like a frightened deer.

"Only what?"

"Carl's parents also own a jeweler's shop in Vienna, near the Naschmarkt, quite a beautiful one. Our families have been friends and competitors for years." Her face temporarily relaxed in a wan smile, as she remembered her Vienna life. "Both his parents are frail and old. They are suffering so much from Hitler's vilification of the Jewish community. The Bernsteins live over the shop. When they came down one morning, *Jude* and the Star of David was painted all over the shop window. Old Mr. Bernstein had a heart attack and since then he's bedridden. Carl is the only son in the family, so he's running the shop. That is, for as long as they may still be open. It's all so awful.

"My parents try to cheer me up by telling me Carl will come to Oslo as soon as he can. We'll get married there. But, you see, I don't think he can leave his elderly, ailing parents behind. So, so ..." She sighed, twisting her engagement ring around her finger. "Can't say I didn't see something of the sort coming. Just tried hard not to believe the worst. Mutti and Papi forbid me to go back to Vienna on my own. I can't go against their wishes, but I'm torn. I want to be with Carl. More than anything in the world."

"What does Carl say?" Océane stroked her friend's back, trying to soothe some of her anguish.

"Carl's last letters were cautiously optimistic, but I can read between the lines. Vienna is clearly insufferable for us at the moment. God knows how long it will last. There's no sign of Hitler slowing his occupational frenzy. He's recently occupied Czechoslovakia."

Océane, who'd paid little attention to belligerent Germany and the geopolitical shifts taking place in the Old World, began to see the situation through her Jewish friend's eyes. So far, she'd believed it would all die like an old fire and the Nazi dictator would be handcuffed and put behind bars. But Esther's tale made it slowly dawn on Océane that Europe might indeed be on the brink of war.

"What will you do?"

Esther shook her shoulders. "I'll wait for Carl's letter to decide, though I already know what he will say. Go to Oslo and wait for me. Do I have a choice?"

"I guess not. At least you'll be safe there. Hitler seems more interested in the middle of Europe than in the northern countries."

"Let's hope so."

That evening as Esther slept, Océane pondered her future, for the first time from a moral standpoint and not her own desires. What if war broke out when she was still in Switzerland and she could not return to Chicago? Or should she go back home now and enroll in the Boston University School of Medicine after all?

In the dark she shook her head. Whatever happened while she was in Europe, she'd stay and finish her course. If she went to medical school, it would be at the Sorbonne in Paris. She'd ask permission from her parents to stay with her grandfather and study at her mother's university. Composing the letter in her mind, Océane fell asleep.

8

THE NEW GIRL

July 1939

Politics were strictly forbidden at Le Manoir, so it was hard to know what was going on in the world. Madame Paul considered politics crude and unrefined, menfolk talk in back rooms over cigars and whiskey. Something her students steered clear from at all times. As mistress of the house, they should only know how to smooth a debate that became too heated. That was all. Le Manoir's policy was a reflection of the country at large. It had worked so far, so it would work always.

Through all that refinery and etiquette and social manners, anti-Semitism still managed to trickle down the corridors of the posh finishing school on Lake Geneva. It was never openly instigated by Madame Paul, but the teachers had started to isolate the two Jewish girls still boarding there, Esther Weiss from Vienna and Anna Levi from London. It came in sneaky remarks and hidden reprimands but escalated towards the end of June with the two girls being separated from their roommates and put together at the end of a corridor on the third floor that - under normal circumstances - was reserved for the staff.

Both Océane and Esther were devastated by this cruel separation, hanging on to each other during the day as much as they were still allowed. The number of girls at Le Manoir was slimming down with the rumors of war growing. Girls were called home, parents were worried. While Océane's confidence in herself and her future became stronger by the day, Esther withdrew more and more inside herself. She had no news from Oslo or Vienna and the spotlight on her gnawed at her and eroded her beautiful soul.

One day, having a rare moment of alone time together while setting the table for afternoon tea, she confided in Océane, "I wonder what good my Le Manoir diploma will do for my future. I fear I'll never be able to put everything we've learned into practice."

"Don't be silly, Essie, you will. Trust me. I wonder if I'll ever come across situations where I can implement this stuff. I guess it's always a good thing to know how to behave in posh places. Who knows, we might become spies one day and we'll be able to double-talk ourselves out of tricky corners with our fine manners."

"Don't say that, OC!" Esther raised her voice a notch, which she rarely did. "That's dangerous talk. I hope I will only use what we've learned in honest and pretty surroundings, just as we've been taught."

"I'm just joking! I have no inclination to have anything to do with whichever side in whatever conflict. I'm going to be a doctor, remember? Doctors don't take sides."

That afternoon there was a lot of hush-hush going on in Madame Paul's office. One of the bolder French girls put her ear to the door and whispered, "They're saying there's a new girl coming. Apparently not from a family Madame Paul is in favor of but it's some kind of emergency because she was involved in something. Couldn't hear what it was but for sure it must be a scandal. That's going to perk this place up. A little bit of scandal! For sure, it's a fallen girl!"

"What is all this gossiping in the corridor?" Madame Paul, perfect eyebrows high, put on her glasses that invariably hung from a pearl string on her bosom, inspecting the groups of girls standing idly together. "Isn't it time for your afternoon walk to collect Alpine plants to identify and dry?" As the girls dispersed with a stifled giggle, Madame Paul said in her nasal voice, "Mademoiselle Océane, could you please step into my office for a moment?"

"What have I done now?" Océane murmured under her breath to Esther but giving Madame Paul a short nod, went with her, feeling her friend's eyes in her back. In the past months there had hardly been any corrections on her behavior, or the way she carried out her tasks. It was Esther who had regularly and unfairly been picked on by the demanding headmistress.

Océane was bored; she knew the drill by now and the course held no new insights for her inquisitive mind. Often she pondered leaving the unpleasant atmosphere but the reminder of her Radcliffe debacle made her grit her teeth and sit it out. *Two more months, for the diploma and for Esther's sake.*

She sat herself opposite Madame Paul on the edge of the seat. The matron resided behind her massive mahogany desk.

"You'll have a roommate as of today. Her name is Mademoiselle Liliane Hamilton. Just like you she's half French but she's arriving from England." The sour look on Madame Paul's face revealed the dissatisfaction with this new arrival.

Why let her come if you don't want her? Océane thought, rather puzzled. Had not Marie-Christine said something about a fallen girl? Whatever that was. Supposing she was not to reply as Madame Paul had not asked a question, she stayed silent with an agreeable smile on her face. Just as she had been taught.

But Madame Paul asked, "Well, Mademoiselle Océane, what do you have to say about that?"

"Me? I don't think I have anything to say in the matter. I just hope she's nice, though she's not going to be able to replace Esther."

"Ahhh," Madame Paul sighed rather unduly, "I wish you would pay less attention to Mademoiselle Esther, who after all now has Mademoiselle Anna as her friend. You are to concentrate on the new girl. Good God, she will need some steering from your common sense, Mademoiselle Océane."

Océane was again unsure whether this was a question or a statement, but curiosity won. "Is there something I need to know about Mademoiselle Liliane, Madame Paul?"

She certainly fell from one amazement to another when Madame Paul with all her stateliness bowed confidentially over the desk and whispered rather excitedly, "The girls in that family are notoriously unruly. My predecessor had her difficulties with this girl's aunt, but I've encountered the worst situation of all with this girl's French mother, Mademoiselle Madeleine. My heartbeat still goes up when I think about it."

The celestite eyes swerved to the window. Océane thought the velvet-covered, sumptuous bosom of the headmistress indeed rose and fell rather fast. The conspiratorial tone was back when she returned her gaze to her visitor.

"Mademoiselle Madeleine ran away from here one evening in March 1918. Just like that. Ran away. Can you imagine? It's unheard of. The thing kitchen maids do. Mind you, it was even in the middle of the Great War. She left no note, nothing. We had a search party for her all night, but the little madam had boarded a train back to France and later played havoc somewhere at the German frontlines. For which she was - heaven knows why - decorated lavishly. At least, that's what I heard later. Utter disrespect is all I got from her. And a short letter full of misspellings after the war, telling me she was grateful for my lessons but needed to be where all the action was. Do you hear me? How irresponsible can one be? And also, don't think that the little countess's parents apologized to me. Oh no! The mother apparently is some kind of artist, French nobility, of course. You know the type."

Océane did not but was certainly fired up by the story, thinking of her own mother and father fighting to save soldiers' lives at the same time, also on the frontlines. Yet this was 1939 and she had no idea what the daughter had done wrong.

"Mademoiselle Madeleine went on to marry some commoner

she'd met during her pranks at the front. A Major Hamilton, so now she's Mrs. Hamilton. Just tells you the sort of girl she was, getting involved with army folk during the war. She called me last week to tell me they are having difficulties with their nineteen-year-old daughter and if she please - last-minute - can come to Le Manoir to prevent some ruffles in their English circles."

"But what has Mademoiselle Liliane done?" Océane couldn't help asking. She quite enjoyed the confidences Madame Paul was scattering over her. It gave her bored mind something to figure out.

"Well, what do you guess?" The eyebrows went up again and a mocking look settled in the cold blue stare.

The question was rhetorical, Océane assumed, and she was right. The Le Manoir lessons were paying off. She understood diplomacy in conversations so much better now. When to talk and when to be silent to hear more.

"She broke off her engagement to a suitable man!" Madame Paul cried out in great triumphant as if this was a crime Mademoiselle Liliane would be punished for, for the rest of her earthly existence.

"Oh." It sounded deflated. Océane was far from impressed by the severity of the mishap. What, after all, was wrong with breaking off an engagement? However, she understood this was just grist to the mill for the headmistress. It made clear as sunshine all that was wrong with this family.

Océane wanted to blurt out, *why do you let her come if she's such a hopeless case?* She knew the answer. Fewer and fewer girls arrived due to the threat of war. Madame Paul probably needed the money. But she also enjoyed working herself up about this family. There was nothing the headmistress liked more than correcting what she thought were faulty manners and here came a girl she could give her best grounding to.

"Well, Mademoiselle Océane, that will be all for now. I'm sure that *you* with your solid and sound background - two wonderful doctors as parents - will have a good influence on the unfortunate girl but do not hesitate to contact me should you discern any improper behavior from her."

Gosh, Océane thought, *now I've been promoted to police officer or governess for the good cause. What will be next?* She would never snitch on one of the others, unlike some of the girls, so she made a gesture with her head that held the middle of a nod and a shake.

OCÉANE IMMEDIATELY WENT in search of Esther to tell her what Madame Paul had just told her. Her table setting was Esther's exam piece that day, so she was making a great deal of fuss over the exact location of the plates, the cutlery and the glasses. Despite the stress to do everything right, Esther seemed chirpy. Table setting was the subject she liked best, where Océane detested it. Seeing her friend so concentrated, she halted in her tracks. It wasn't the right time to tell her the tale of a new, difficult roommate arriving any minute.

Esther looked up, a happy smile on her fair face. "What do you think? I want it to be sublime, so I get no comments."

"Looks good to me?" Océane answered disinterestedly.

"Oh, did you hear there's a new girl arriving from England today? Isn't it exciting? I hope she and Anna will get on well, you know, as Brits among each other, and that we can hang out together more often again."

"So you heard?"

"Yes, don't you like the idea?"

"Don't start about it," Océane grumbled as she sat down in one of the wicker chairs that stood around Esther's table on the terrace. Esther was measuring the distance between each plate and cup with a ruler. "I've just had an entire lecture on guarding that new girl. She's kind of wild according to Madame P. But what's worse, she's going to be my roommate. Not something I'm looking forward to. I only want you as a roommate, Essie."

Esther shot her a viridian glance and sighing deeply, came over to give her a hug. "I want that, too, but I don't think it will happen again. But you and I will always be best friends, OC. And if she's really horrible, there will be no other option but to tell her straight out. We can't have your last months here being wrecked by a spoiled brat. Don't worry, I'll help you."

At that moment they heard the Renault come up the driveway. Unable to restrain their curiosity, they sneaked up to the corner of the building from where they could watch the gravel parking place in front of the school. They were too far away to hear what Madame Paul was saying to the girl. She stood rather forlornly on the spot, clearly uncomfortable with the sermon and heat. Red curls peeped from under her fashionable hat. She looked far from dangerous or haughty.

"If that's a fallen girl, I'm the devil myself," Océane whispered.

"Yes, she looks rather nice, and the way Madame Paul is talking to her, all airs and stiffness, is surely making her feel terrible," Esther added.

As if she had heard talk of the devil, Madame Paul looked in their direction. They quickly withdrew their heads, giggling in the ivy leaves that grew along the south wall.

"Let me help you with the last part of the table setting," Océane remarked, "meanwhile we'll wait for the new girl to come down to tea. So far, I see no reason not to be nice to her. Imagine arriving here when almost everyone has finished the course."

Esther agreed. "And with a war almost certainly erupting any moment. Can't be fun being separated from your family at a moment like this."

HALF AN HOUR later when they were putting the final touches to Esther's table display, the new girl in an expensive navy-blue Elsa Schiaparelli suit came sauntering towards them. She was all shyness and freckles. Océane's quick inspection told her this was perhaps a spirited girl but certainly not a bad girl. In fact, she took an instant liking to her, the way she exuded a mix of diffidence and determined resolution.

"Hi," they all said at the same time.

Océane extended a hand to greet the newcomer, who was taking her in with intelligent aquamarine eyes. She looked lovely, with a pale, translucent skin and soft red curls. A true descendant of the Celtic race, Océane thought.

"Hi," she said again, shaking the slender white hand. "I'm Océane Bell. You must be my new roommate." She saw she'd adopted the right tone, as a smile hovered on the girl's red lips.

"Lili Hamilton, enchanté."

Océane's inbred attitude to put people at ease made her add, "Just sit at the table and watch us slave. It'll give you an idea what is in store for you."

Lili looked at her with disbelief, wrinkling her pretty nose. "Do we have to do the waitressing, too?"

"Oh yes," Esther chimed in, "if you want to be the mistress of a grand house, you have to know all the details of what that means. We cook, we clean, we polish, we set tables, and we do the waitressing."

While Océane adjusted the cushions on the wicker chairs around the long, damask-clothed table, Lili remarked, "Heavens, I've never done any of these things in my life."

The ice was broken, and the table done. Océane glanced once more at the red-haired girl as if to ascertain that she'd really like her. She decided again there was nothing that pointed to the contrary. Lili was just nervous and tired from the long journey. They would get along just fine. She sensed Esther, whose every emotion she knew so intimately by now, agreed with her. This girl was different from the other hoity-toity damsels with whom they had nothing in common.

"We've been where you are right now," she assured her. "Don't worry. We'll help you in any way we can. Just stick with us."

For a moment she hesitated. Had she not just discussed with

Esther that the two of them would be closer together and they would leave the new girl to Anna? But to her relief Esther nodded.

For an instant Lili's smile was a little less tense before another shadow glided over her face. "Madame Paul told me you'll both be leaving soon."

"Es and I will be here for another two months. We'll have time to help you settle in."

Right then Madame Paul came parading in as a mother hen with the rest of the girls as her chicks trickling behind her.

Immediately the atmosphere changed and Océane whispered to Lili, "Sit with us, we'll help you."

Despite Madame Paul's penetrating look in their direction, she maneuvered Lili by the elbow and made sure she was secure in between them. For some reason, the newcomer evoked something maternal in her, a feeling she'd never had before. Both her best friends Eliza and Esther had not seemed to need protection from her, even-tempered and down-to-earth as they both were. With Lili she sensed something radical, uncrystallized, a longing to jump too early and too far. In an odd way it made her feel older and more mature, though they were probably the same age. Now it was her turn not to feel the inexperienced one.

HOURS LATER, after Lili had unpacked and they were lying in bed on either side of the room with the fresh evening breeze streaming in through the open shutters, Océane was still filled with wonder over feeling so protective of Lili. Though still missing Esther, there was a new, fresh air around the Hamilton girl. It gave her another energy, reminding Océane she was young too, too young to marry. Something only Esther wanted. It was ages since she'd even thought of the ravishing Jean-Jacques, who would never be hers anyway.

Lili's posh British accent interrupted her daydream. "I saw a stethoscope in the bathroom. Is it yours?"

"Yes, it is. Well, it's actually my mom's."

"So, are you a doctor, or why do you have it here?"

This made Océane chuckle. "Not yet, but I will be."

"Gosh," Lili's voice was full of admiration, "that's wonderful. I want to be a journalist, but a doctor? Wow. And is your mom a doctor, too?"

"She is. She used to study at the Sorbonne, and she went with my father to the frontlines during the Great War. That's when they fell in love."

"Wait!" Lili sounded quite breathless. "What's your mother's name?"

"Agnès Bell, but her maiden name is De Saint-Aubin. Why?"

Lili clapped her hands. "Really?"

"Yes, what do you mean?"

"I think our parents know each other from the frontlines. It must be your mother. There were so very few female surgeons at the time. I heard my parents talk about a Doctor De Saint Aubin and a Doctor Bell. They worked at my grandparents' château in Picardy in 1918."

"Incredible!" Océane cried out, as excited as Lili now. "That's them indeed! That's where they were. What a coincidence! What's your mom's last name?"

"De Dragoncourt. After the castle."

For Océane these names, though not having been on her parents' tongue for a long time, now rang a bell as well.

"Do you think our parents are still in touch with each other?" Lili sat up in bed, eager and wide-awake.

"I don't know. I don't think so, but they should rekindle their acquaintance because of us. Don't you agree?"

"Yes, we will make that happen!"

9

WAR IN EUROPE

Le Manoir, 3 September 1939

Océane continued to be happy with Lili as her new roommate. During the day they spent as much time as they could with Esther. A tender friendship was forged among the three girls. Though they were all very different in temperament and their outlook in life, and views for the future had little in common, somehow it worked.

She was happy that the last months at Le Manoir drawing to a close were at least brightened by great friendships. Just like with Eliza and Martin in Boston, she was sure Esther and Lili would somehow form part of her future. But for the rest, the day-to-day monotony of the courses and their Madame Paul's antics no longer held her interest.

Maxipa had written he would be motoring down to Lausanne to pick her up. A bright new university life was waiting for her in Paris in a couple of weeks. How her brain longed for the stimulus of studying and books, as her soul yearned for Paris. Even painting had lost some of its luster as she'd now come to a conclusion regarding her future career.

Yet she could never have anticipated how her year in Lausanne would end. It was a blustery day, quite unusual for the time of year in southern Switzerland. She was alone in her room, reading a letter from her mother.

Chicago, 10 August 1939

My dearest daughter,

How happy Dad and I were to receive your letter dated 10 July. This year has been so long without you! We've never before celebrated Thanksgiving, Christmas and Easter and, of course, your birthday on 8 August without you. I don't want to make you sad but know you're sorely missed.

So you've come to the decision that you want to study medicine at La Sorbonne. Dad and I have discussed it at length. Of course, we are delighted, my darling, now we know this is your very own desire, uninfluenced by us.

To reach this conclusion on your own must have been impactful for you. Again Dad and I regret having unconsciously pressured you to go to Radcliffe. Perhaps you were still too young. We missed the signals as you were always such a bright little thing, far ahead of your age group. It might have been too much responsibility for you at too early an age. But that is all sorted now, and we're absolutely delighted you've made up your mind and will – after all – follow in our footsteps. Words are inadequate to tell you how my heart bursts with pride.

When you get this letter your last weeks at Le Manoir will have arrived. We were glad to hear you got to know Lili Hamilton, Madeleine and Gerald's daughter. What a coincidence! Or maybe not after all. Dad and I were talking about the Hamiltons on your birthday, which, of course, always brings us back to 8 August 1918 when Dad was shot down outside the Château de Dragoncourt and I had to perform that difficult operation on him in very primitive and dangerous circumstances. In the hope he could walk again someday.

Your birth a year later on that same date, is – as you know – always a double celebration. Anyway, we were talking about that time during the war and reminiscing about the people we met there and befriended. Not just Lili's parents but also her Uncle Jacques and Aunt Elle.

We really intended to stay in close contact with them because we went through so much together, but with us moving to the States it was first letters and then it became Christmas cards and ultimately communication stopped altogether.

But now that you met and befriended the next generation, I will make sure I write to Madeleine and ask for the addresses of her siblings and the other staff to whom I owe also Dad's recovery, a Scottish nurse called Bridget McGovern and a French nurse Marie-Christine Brest without whom Dad wouldn't be the dad he is today.

Anyway, my darling, we're in agreement that you may continue your studies at the Sorbonne and live with Maxipa. I've already asked my father and he has assured me he would want nothing else but fears you'll soon be bored to death living with an old man. So he's already looking into buying you a small flat near the Sorbonne. Dad insists we should do that on your behalf. That way, we'll have our own pied-à-terre whenever we visit Paris.

So, my dear daughter, here's the surprise. We've bought tickets to cross the Atlantic from New York on the SS Normandie on the 3rd of September to see you and to go flat-hunting together. And yes, of course, we'll take Arthur with us. We've run some new tests on him, especially behavioral ones, and consulted new specialists. Everything points to the assurance that we can bring him as long as we stick to his routines as much as possible and keep him away from too many and new stimuli. That's why we'll bring his favorite nurse Betty, who will give him his own food and stay with him when we go out.

Our friends, Doctor Martin and Doctor Brown, will replace us at the clinic and Dad has been able to switch his Harvard classes to the second semester so there are no impediments left. I'm so excited! I can't wait for this trip that's taken way too many years now, first and foremost to see you, of course, but also to see my beloved father and Paris once again!

So, my darling, expect us in Paris when you return there with grandpapa. We've organized special transport to Paris so Arthur will be comfortable.

Dad sends you much love and promises to write to you next week.

Big kiss, also from Arthur,

Your Maman

xxx

They were on their way right now! It was the most exciting news Océane had had for a long time. Suddenly the dreariness of the day didn't matter anymore. All that mattered was the warmth in her heart, that she would soon see her beloved family again. And Maxipa was almost here. She thought the day would never come and now everything happened in a whirlwind.

It had been a hard tug of war on her heart, returning to the States and her family, or to go to Paris. Now these blended as one. It would make her new life in the French capital so much easier. Spending time with Mom and Dad and Arthur. She almost couldn't wait any longer. Océane sprang up from the bed and rushed out of the room in search of Esther and Lili.

Downstairs she was met by a very gloomy Madame Paul who immediately ushered her into the library. To her astonishment Océane saw everyone huddled around the old wireless, the girls, the teachers, the chauffeur, the gardeners, even the stable boys and the kitchen maids, listening intently to the voice that came out of the radio set.

She sidled in next to Lili. "What's going on?"

"Great-Britain has declared war on Germany."

"What? Noooo!" Océane cowered in fear, the letter from her mother still crumpled in her hand.

The news she'd just received burst like a soap bubble. Then the next blow hit her. They were already crossing the ocean. By God, what would happen to them? Océane never panicked but she was close to it now. Not just the declaration of war but her family bobbing helplessly on the sea sailing right into the danger. Shivering she tried to understand what Neville Chamberlain was saying but her ears buzzed and the shrieks in the room didn't help to follow the thread of the announcement.

"France has also declared war on Germany," she heard the Italian driver say, which was followed by more cries of anguish. "Because Poland was invaded by Hitler." It didn't make sense to her. What did Britain and France have to do with Hitler in Poland?

Trying to ignore the thrumming of the blood in her ears, she crumbled her letter further. Despite herself she started to cry, for the first time ever not taking care of others but overwhelmed by her own fear and pain. She wasn't the only one. Soon complete panic broke out and girls were shouting to each other and to the staff that they wanted to go home. Now! The telephone started ringing in Madame Paul's office and did not stop anymore. Girls were being summoned home immediately while travel was still possible.

Bit by bit, Océane became aware of her two friends, seated on either side of her on the hard wooden library chairs. They gripped each other's hands and held on tight. As if they would come through this war together instead of likely having to go home separated. While the nurse calmed the hysterical fits that some girls had fallen into, the Swiss staff sat silent and ghostlike, possibly wondering if their home country would again be able to keep up their neutrality while war rippled over the rest of Europe. Madame Paul was not her usual self either, looking pale as a peeled turnip, putting her glasses on the pearl strings on her nose and then taking them off again, all the while sighing.

"My-oh-my, what to do now?" She didn't seem in control of herself or the school anymore. Etiquette rules were no longer operational. All the veneer chipped away in one single hour.

After her own initial shock wore off, Océane became most worried about Esther. How was she going to travel to Norway through enemy territory? Maybe she should take her with her to Paris, but she immediately tossed aside that idea. Esther would want to be with her own family, now more than ever. She probably could travel through France and take a boat from La Havre. Lili would be okay. The fighting was east of Germany, so she'd probably be able to get home to England safely.

And what would *she* do now? Stay with her grandfather for the time being, reconsider if she could get home safely? But first and foremost, find out where her family was. So many things went through her head as all around her arrangements started for most girls to leave straight away.

Through the cacophony Madame Paul called her name. "The Baron on the phone for you, Mademoiselle Océane."

Releasing her friends' hands, she went forward and gingerly took the receiver that Madame Paul offered her. "Maxipa." She wasn't able to bring out more than a wheeze.

"*Bonjour, ma petite*, how are you? Awful news, right?"

"Yes, Grandpa. I just got a letter from Mom that they ..." Tears gushed down her cheeks.

"Don't worry about them, my girl. Sad as it is they won't be coming, they decided not to take the risk when forewarned in New York. Thank God for your parents' wisdom. No matter how much we would have liked to be all together. So, it'll be just the two of us in sackcloth and ashes. When can I come to Lausanne to take you home?"

"Oh, Maxipa, that's wonderful news. That Mom and Dad and Arthur are safe in the States. Let me ask Madame Paul when you can come but honestly, I don't think it matters. It's complete chaos here. Any time that's convenient to you."

She tried to attract Madame Paul's attention, but the headmistress was walking around like a clubbed catfish. Océane knew she would have to carry her own weight. With the news of war exploding as a bomb, all rigid regime and stiff protocol had instantly been cast aside and sheer anarchy had settled on the once so orderly institute.

"Well, if you have carte-blanche, my dear, give me a day to pack up here, close the Nice house for the season and dispense with my local staff. I can be at your service the morn of Wednesday 6 September. Will that work?"

"I'll be ready, grandpa."

A hasty lunch was served at the school. After that, they all found themselves again around the wireless listening this time to *le Président du Conseil français* is Édouard Daladier explaining why France had also declared war on Germany. Océane wondered if the

United States would soon follow but nothing was said on that account.

The weather had changed as well, the rains dispelled, the wind gone, and it was in fact a pristine, clear afternoon, with the small waves of Lake Geneva lapping friendly over the sandy shoreline and the sun radiating a pleasant warmth. There were no longer any organized classes, so after dinner the three friends went down to the shore to discuss the new situation and start taking leave of each other.

Dipping their bare feet in the pleasantly cool water, something they would never have dared to do when Madame Paul's reign was supreme, while the sun sank further down the mountain ridge across the water, Océane broke the silence. "We must somehow stay in touch. It may be difficult if the mail's not working properly, but at least we must try."

Lili and Esther nodded.

"And after the war - which will hopefully only last a couple of weeks - we must meet up again. What would be a good place, you think?

"Paris!" they said in unison, which made them chuckle.

"Let's swear on it," Océane suggested.

Three pairs of slim hands, one light brown, one white, and one rosy, were put on top of each other as they swore alliance to their friendship and to their reunion.

"I'm so afraid about this war," Esther admitted, her voice catching in her throat.

"Hopefully it will be over very soon," Océane comforted her, while Lili put an arm around Esther, remarking grimly, "Stupid men. It's always men who want to fight and conquer other countries. It's never women wanting to own another piece of land and its people."

Esther, feeling strengthened by her two more feisty friends, agreed in a milder tone. "I don't get it either. All I want is peace and everything ordinary. Not these big shocks and millions of people terrified as their lives are turned upside down."

With her usual vehemence Lili said, "I believe that sometimes it's necessary to make your stand and fight back. If I were in Poland right now, I'd fight the Nazis with all my might."

"Of course," Océane agreed, "that's logical, but if Hitler invaded France - which, by God, I hope he won't - I'm not sure I'd fight. I'd do everything I could to help the wounded, but I don't think I would run up the barricades and shoot a bullet at the enemy. It's just not for me."

"Neither would I," Esther added, the golden glow of the sunset catching the silver-green in her eyes. "I would cook for the men fighting, and help them, but I would not do any fighting myself. That would just not be right for me."

"I would!" Lili declared with vigor. "I definitely would. I think we women are equal to men and we should be there, shoulder to shoulder with our men when our country is attacked. But maybe it's easy for me to say because Hitler is never going to try and conquer Britain. That would be sheer suicide. But my French roots would fight at the barricades in Paris, so if he decides to turn westwards, I might join any Resistance movement that rises up."

The other two girls looked at Lili with admiration but also a trace of doubt. All bold and invigorated, the little Celt went a step further. "I'm a Communist, you know. Now I think I can say it out loud, as Madame Paul can't harm me anymore. I've secretly been getting information from the head of the Communist party in London, Leo Oppenheim."

Both girls stared at Lili open-mouthed. Then Esther put a hand over her mouth not to cry out while Océane studied Lili with a level-minded yet surprised look.

"Well, Lili, if you believe in that, you must do what you think best, but it's my feeling that the Communists will not be successful here in Western Europe. I know they're in power in Russia, since the people have been oppressed there for centuries, but here? No way. But I understand your ideals, and if you're happy with it, by all means go for it."

"Enough talk of strife and sides," Esther chimed in, in line with her diplomacy lessons. "I'll never understand politics and I don't want to. Let us talk about where and when we shall meet up."

"How about the weekend of 28 October this year. We can all stay at my grandfather's house in Neuilly-sur-Seine if I haven't got my own flat yet," Océane put forward.

"Fine!" they agreed.

Esther added, "That is if the war is really over. I don't know if I can travel all the way south again when there are still squabbles here and there."

"Of course," Océane agreed, "Only if and when the war is over. We must remain positive. If it takes longer, we postpone."

"We need to exchange addresses," Lili proposed. They all scribbled down their new addresses and exchanged them.

"Let's choose the oldest restaurant in Paris, *À La Petit Chaise* on the Rue de Montserrat in the 7th Arrondissement," Océane continued.

"Oh, yes," Lili cheered, "I know that one! It's the place for us!"

Océane felt melancholy mixed with hope as she studied her friends' faces. So dear to her, so familiar and soon so far away.

10

FALLING HARD

Paris, End of September 1939

Despite being at war with neighboring Germany, French life continued floating numbly in status quo. The Paris spirit in particular was to sit out this phony war that wouldn't last more than two months. The Treaty of Versailles was still fresh on everyone's mind and had brought the Germans to their knees. Hitler's rise to power and his conquering of surrounding countries was nothing new on the European stage and would certainly be brought to a halt now he was facing war with the two mighty powers, Britain and France. Ally Poland had been sacrificed, as had been Austria and Czechoslovakia, but those countries were just pawns on the board. The German wouldn't dare to come westward. That was the general spirit.

Paris was still half in its post Great War period. The hopeful atmosphere expressed itself in the growing numbers of parties and jazz clubs, its surge having begun in the Roaring Twenties, temporarily torpedoed by the Great Depression and now reviving. In the wake of Duke Ellington and Louis Armstrong, black musicians from across the pond arrived to spark up the City of Light.

Young French musicians eagerly promoted the jazz music, among them the guitarist Django Reinhardt with his Jazz Manouche. Writers also returned to the French capital, leaving their stamp, The Ernest Hemingways and Scott Fitzgeralds of the epoch. American creatives, just like at the end of the 19th Century, rediscovered Paris and transformed it for good. Paris in the Fall of 1939 was like a drunk man stumbling around in the dark, desperate to get to the party lights. The growing fear drowned in alcohol and too much fun.

On the other side of the spectrum, serious and studious Océane did not follow the stir her fellow countrymen caused. She was studying hard after having been admitted to the Sorbonne Medical School. But she was as happy as the partygoers to be back in Paris and had fitted in seamlessly at her grandfather's stately house on the Seine Boulevard. After her brain cells had only occupied themselves with silverware and conversational rules at finishing school, she dove into epidemiology and clinical medicine with a passion she'd never had at Radcliffe.

Eleanora Rosenkrantz, a young female professor in the practice of medicine, was her favorite teacher. The Jewish refugee from the University of Munich taught communication skills between doctor and patient. She had developed a method with emphasis on patient-focused, compassionate and professional behavior. Océane had seen her mother adopt this method naturally, but she now greatly enjoyed the scientific research that showed patients had a greater chance of healing if they were actively involved in their therapy. It also was a complete reverse of Madame Paul's etiquette lessons that had mainly centered around getting your way as a woman in a shrewd and diplomatic way. While taking in Professor Rozenkrantz lessons like a sponge, Océane instinctively knew both teachings were supposed to blend within her. Somehow. Somewhere.

In 1933 Eleanora Rosenkrantz had already understood that Hitler's rise to power was going to impact Jewish jobs, therefore a year later she'd moved to Paris to become - at the age of twenty-seven - the youngest female professor ever at the age-old institute. As Océane listened to the slight, dark-haired woman with her white, almost shiny skin and dark-brown eyes under strong eyebrows and a strong nose, her thoughts invariably went to Esther. Would she have made it safely to Oslo? Would there be a letter soon?

The sweet, very feminine voice with the strong German accent, rounding off her words harshly at the end where the French tended to ingest word ends, was explaining how to prepare patients for physical examinations that might be unpleasant to them. The professor interrupted herself and addressed the first row of students with Océane in their midst.

"On a side note, I've been requested by staff at the Hôtel-Dieu de Paris hospital, if there are students in my class who want to gain first-hand practice in the hospital. They're getting short-staffed now with many of the male doctors being called under arms."

Océane was sure her dark eyes rested on her, and she jerked up, raising her hand as a sign she wanted to say something. "I'd love to, Professor Rosenkrantz, if they'll have me."

The young professor smiled, which made her pretty, narrow face shine in a youthful, almost girlish way. "I'll take down names of volunteers and will let you know in the next lecture how many of you can apply."

All hands rose as one. The first-year students didn't just like their professor, they all longed for the practical experience that would prepare them in this war. No one knew what was coming next.

OCÉANE HAPPENED to leave the lecture room at the same time as her professor. They left the building together, descending the marble steps into the cool fall air on Rue Cujas.

Eleanora gazed sideways at her student. "So, Océane, you seem eager to work at the hospital? From your enrolment papers I see you already did pre-med in America. You also come from a family of doctors. That will give you a head start, for sure. I happen to know the head-physician in Hôtel-Dieu de Paris' cardiac ward. Would that be of interest to you? Say, two days a week unless you have lectures?"

Océane's own heart skipped a beat at this proposal. Now she'd decided to become a doctor, her next question had been which specialization attracted her most. This might be the way to find out.

"Do you think I could? I'd love nothing better."

"Why not? You're way ahead of the French students. The sooner you start working, the better you'll understand the theory. These are exceptional times. It would of course be better to have the knowledge first and only start working when you're better equipped theoretically. You'll get a crash course on the spot."

"I'll need to ask my grandfather as I live with him and I'm still underage. But knowing him, he won't have any objections. He's used to it. My mother was just eighteen when she enrolled at the Sorbonne and five years later - in 1918 - she was the first surgeon ever on the frontlines in Picardy."

"That's amazing!" Professor Rozenkrantz's friendly eyes shot her another glance. "I have so much admiration for your mother. I glance at her plaque here at the Sorbonne every time I pass it. Agnès De Saint-Aubin was a pioneer. She paved the way for the next generation of female doctors and university professors. It was your mother who taught us there's nothing women can't do professionally."

Océane didn't know how to answer the singing of her mother's praises. Of course, she was proud of her mother's plaque in *Cour de Physique*. It was an honor but also put a lot of pressure on her young shoulders as 'the daughter of'. She just smiled, uncertain of her own fate.

They had meanwhile halted under a large chestnut tree, the leaves of which were turning deep yellow and brown. The wind swept up the fallen leaves, whirling them across the street.

Eleanora looked imploringly at her, then smiled warmly. "It's okay to see your mother just as your mother. That's what she mainly is to you."

It made Océane find her tongue. "I guess so. Of course, I was always aware that Mom was different from other moms. Most of my friends' moms were home makers but mine went out to work every day, just like my dad. I think it's mainly because of my grandfather. He was always freethinking and urged Mom to go to university."

"What about your grandmother?" The voice was kind and soft.

"I never knew her and neither did my mother. She died when Mom was three days old. Puerperal pyrexiai."

The dark, friendly eyes still rested on her and Océane felt tested but not in a bad way.

"I'll make a phone call to Doctor Ribaud tonight. I know him well." The name made Professor Rozenkrantz blush. Now it was Océane's turn to be surprised. In a rather flushed voice, her teacher added, "Maybe I can set up a meeting with him this week? After you have your grandfather's formal consent?"

"Absolutely."

"Au revoir, Océane"

"Au revoir, Professor Rozenkrantz.

OCÉANE'S first day in the cardiac ward of Hôtel-Dieu de Paris was both chaotic and exhilarating. Because it was so busy, they had no time to instruct her properly and let her do things she'd never done before. Used to emergency situations, Océane blended in well, constantly navigating around the doctors and nurses who were in a rush to look after the patients. There were patients in all stages, some on the brink of an operation, some in the recovery rooms, some brought in after a heart attack and some with serious heart conditions such as coronary artery disease, congenital heart disease, arrhythmia. She was learning the names, the medications, the procedures as fast as her quick mind allowed, thriving in the buzz and necessity of her presence.

The cardiac ward was large with at least a hundred beds but greatly understaffed. By midday she was already taking care of the distribution of pills to relieve the nurses. She listened in on talks between doctors and patients, felt pulses and took temperatures. Anything to make herself as helpful as possible.

Towards the end of her first day, she was dispensing pills to the last patient in the corridor when she heard a deep male voice call from a bed behind a closed curtain.

"Nurse... can you come over here, please. I'm short of breath."

Looking around her to see if she could call a nurse, she saw there were none. The voice came from one of the private rooms.

"I am no nurse," she said through the curtain. "I'll go and get you one, sir?"

"No, just come over here and help me up."

Hesitantly she did as she was asked, peeking around the curtain, ready to run for help. In the bed lay a middle-aged man with short, stubbly hair that was graying at his temples. He didn't give the impression of being very ill, given his ruddy complexion and healthy build, but despite being in the ward for just one day, Océane had already understood that exterior appearances in these patients were deceptive. They could have serious conditions and look as healthy as a May morning. A tricky disease indeed.

"Help me up," he ordered. "I'll be okay when I can sit more upright. You're new here, aren't you?"

As Océane stuffed more cushions behind his back while he tried extremely hard to raise himself, she answered, "Yes, it's my first day here. Also my first year at the Sorbonne. I'm not a nurse, sir, I'm training to be a doctor."

He ignored that, observing, "You're not from here, are you?"

"No, I mean, half of me is Parisian, but I was born and raised in the States."

"Aha, I thought so, a Yank. Can always spot an accent."

"Are you more comfortable like this, sir?" Océane took a step back and looked at him.

After he had rearranged his pajama top, he patted the bed. "Do you have a minute for a chat, little doctor? I get so bored being here on my own all day. How long till visiting hours?"

Océane declined his invitation to sit on the bed, perching instead on a chair nearby. Just one minute, she thought, remembering Professor Rozenkrantz's lessons on building trust with patients. He asked, she should give. The Frenchman seemed friendly enough and perhaps she could ask him why he was here. Her preliminary diagnosis was that he was recovering from a coronary artery operation as he was still on a drip and had that after-operation aureole.

"I think visiting hour will start soon, sir, but I'm not yet acquainted with the times."

"Six till eight. Then we get dinner."

"I hope you'll have a nice time with your family, sir. I really should be going now."

"Wait. Can't you stay a little longer. I've been alone all day." He lifted his blue-green eyes to her, his mouth in a half-smile. "Please?"

"Alright, two minutes, sir, but I don't want the regular staff to think I'm just standing here chatting to patients on my first day."

"What's your first name? It only says O. Bell, Medical Student, on your tag. *Belle* you are certainly but I'm curious what the O stands for."

"Océane, sir. My dad is American, and my mom is French. They called me the space between them."

"What a funny thing to do, but I love it, anything that has to do with water. I love water, lakes and ponds, the sea, rivers. I have a little boat here in the Seine, at the Pont Neuf. What about you, do you like water?"

Not knowing where this conversation with the strange middle-aged man was going, she just nodded, shifting on the edge of her chair.

"My name is Gilbert R–" At that moment the curtain was ripped aside rather wildly, and a boisterous young woman stepped inside in a whiff of perfume, all blond curls and tailored dress.

"Papi!" she exclaimed, rushing towards him, and embracing

him despite the tubes in his body, kissing him heartily on the cheeks and caressing his stubbly hair. She was unaware there was another person in the room. "How are you today? Have they told you when you can come home?"

Océane rose to her feet, ready to sneak out of the curtain unseen, but stood for a moment, mesmerized by the glamorous girl, somewhere in her mid-twenties, obviously the patient's daughter.

"Hello, Margot, but where's Remix? I thought you would both come?" the father answered her enthusiastic greeting.

"Sure, Papi, he's parking the car. He'll be up in a minute." The young woman turned to look around the small cubicle inside the curtains, perceiving Océane standing in the corner. "Oh, hello," she said in a tingling soprano voice, "sorry, I didn't see you. Was I inter-rupting a medical examination? Sorry." Her lively eyes, the same blue green as her father's took her in with interest.

She looked vaguely familiar, but Océane could not recall where she'd seen her before. Maybe an actress or performer, posing on some poster. She certainly had the poise and confidence of a star.

"No, no. I was just keeping your father company until you arrived. I'll be going …"

At that moment the curtain was once again swept aside and to Océane's absolute consternation she found herself eye to eye with Jean-Jacques Riveau. *Remix?* shot through her mind. *Why did the man call him Remix and what's he doing here? Is the patient his father?* She tried to make her way out, rather wildly pulling the curtains aside, all the while feeling these moss-green eyes and the snarky smile take her in.

"What in the world!" he cried, his handsome face breaking into a wild smile now, showing beautiful white teeth and the most endearing grin. "Third time lucky! This time you're not going to escape me, Diana!"

"Her name is Océane," his father chuckled from the bed. "I had no idea you two knew each other."

"No, sir, I don't know him. If you will excuse me now."

And she dashed outside and almost ran to the nurse's quarter where she had left her bag and was to sign off for the day. She felt her heart race in her chest, all the while scolding herself for her clumsy reaction. But how was she to know that Gilbert was his father? Her mind raced as her cheeks reddened.

I would never have stayed to talk with him if I'd known. And Margot, now it makes sense, she looks just like him, that's why I thought I knew her.

Once she was safely inside the nurse's quarters, she waited until her heartbeat calmed down. Then she finalized her first day by filling out a list. After saying goodbye to the secretary, she made for the door. Stay away from Gilbert until he was released from Hôtel-Dieu de Paris. That would be her advice. Not run into Jean-Jacques one more time. Ever!

Why are you so afraid to meet him again? He seemed quite friendly on the train. She was asking herself this as she descended the marble steps from the hospital, grateful to fill her lungs with the fresh evening air.

But soon she froze in her tracks. There he was, smoking a cigarette and gazing up at her, the dark-blonde hair lit up by the streetlamp. He had been waiting for her. So much was sure. She thought about retracing her steps, going back inside but the child-ishness of it was too apparent. Slowly, in seconds that seemed like sluggish minutes, she closed the distance between them and stopped in front of him.

"Hi," she said softly, "how are you?" She thought it sounded rather lame but knew nothing else to say.

"O-cé-an-e." He did it again. Spreading out the letters of her name, as if tasting its texture on his tongue. "Océane Bell, *enchanté.* So glad to see you again."

He did not shake her hand, just studied her with those green artist eyes as if inspecting a work in progress on the canvas. As he flicked away the butt of his cigarette, she saw his fingers were still smeared with paint. His face broke into that awry half-smile she'd seen before, which made him irresistible, unattainable. Certainly a thread of glamor ran through the Riveau family like a vein of gold in a robust rock.

"I'm just curious, no, that's not the right word. I'm spellbound to know who you are. First you call out my name in the Museum of Fine Arts in Boston and subsequently vanish like a phantom. Then I see you on the train heading for Switzerland, we share a few words, then part. I hoped you'd contact me when back in Paris, but you never did." He sounded offended.

Océane didn't know if he was serious or not. She still said nothing, twisting and untwisting the leather handle of her medical bag as they stood under the light of the street lantern, people rushing in and out of the hospital, the arrival of an ambulance cutting through the air with its shrill siren.

"And now our paths cross again. I meanwhile found out that your grandfather is Baron Max. He's a dear family friend, so before you dash off again like a wild horse on the prairie, give me a sec to explain, okay? I know it was my fault on the train, but I really couldn't stay any longer. I've waited for a message from you ever since."

He stopped talking, probably waiting for her to ask after the relationship with her grandfather, but she was still tongue-tied, catching herself wanting to bolt off like that prairie horse. Everything about this man made her uncomfortable. He was so present, so self-assured ... so captivating.

He lit another cigarette and took a step in her direction. "Please listen for a moment. I know you want to get away from me at your first opportunity because I'm not in your league. But don't you see that being at my father's hospital bed in the capacity of his assistant doctor is a sign for us? Third time lucky, they call it. You, Doctor Bell, intrigue me and the word doesn't even do you justice. By God, I'm not good at this. Forgive my rambling." He hit his forehead with a flat hand. "Forgive me. You're free to go. I sound like an impostor."

It was as if some of the light in his amazing eyes died. At that, Océane couldn't help opening her mouth to reassure him. "No, it's not that. I'm ... it's ... the opposite. And I didn't know you knew my grandfather. It's a big surprise." She bit her tongue having kind of admitted her infatuation with him, but the words were spoken and could not be swallowed again.

It was agony but there was a sweetness to it that kept her nailed right there to the pavement, a soft, brown, curly lock waving in front of her face in the evening breeze, her silk shawl slipping from her shoulder, which he caught in a swift duck before it reached the ground. Instead of giving it back to her, he spread the square fabric with the colorful paisley pattern and held it to the light.

"Hermès. Good taste."

"It was my mom's," she said apologetically, as if he would consider such an expensive shawl an extravagancy. "I found it at Grandpa's."

He folded the shawl into a drape and handed it back to her. The green eyes focused on her again. "So the Baron being your grandfather; it was a surprise for me as well. You're not just a doctor but also come from one of the grandest families in the history of France. Indeed, way out of my league." He gave her a mock sad face, which made her smile. He could be more disarming than she'd given him credit for.

"Don't say that," she protested meekly. "I've long admired your work, at least five years. I think I've read every article about you, every time you were featured in a magazine. I love art myself, you know, but I'm not good enough. That's why I've decided to return to medicine. I never think I'm that important and nor do I think my heritage is."

Why am I rambling this way? she thought, distraught Scanning his face, she saw his expression was sincere. It held a strange longing mixed with a tinge of what looked like disbelief.

"Océane." Again, he said her name in a way that caused funny ripples in her belly. "I didn't know. I'd love to see your work. I'm sure you downplay your art as you seem to do everything concerning yourself. Will you show it to me?"

"No, I can't," she whispered. "It would make me very uncomfortable. I really ought to go now. It's late. My grandfather will be worried about me."

"I understand. I'm sorry to have kept you. Do you want me to drive you home? My sister will be with my father for another hour. And he … he already understood I needed to talk to you."

Though the offer was enticing, she shook her head. "I'll take a taxi. It's no problem."

"Please?" His face was one big begging badge.

It made her smile. "Alright, if you insist. It would be very convenient, I must say."

"Come, give me your bag. I've never before in my life carried a medical bag, so let me feel how that feels." The lighter tone suited them both better. As Jean-Jacques guided her to the hospital parking lot, he seemed to hesitate for a moment. "I'm afraid you're used to much more luxurious cars. Mine's rather old and run down."

Océane thought it endearing he seemed to care what she thought of his car. It was the last topic in the world she was concerned about, as she cared nothing for any kind of transport.

He continued, "It rumbles long right through Paris. My friends keep laughing at my stinginess regarding transport, but I paid my price. Paris doesn't deserve nice cars. I used to have this lovely Cadillac La Salle, had it specially shipped from the States, but one night the mirrors were stolen and then a couple of days later some individual banged into the side door, leaving La Salle damaged for life. No note, nothing. I still have her, but she's parked at my grandfather's estate at the Loire. Anyway, I bought myself this hideous mouse-gray Peugeot 4023, but no one bangs into it or steals from it, so it works for me. Question is, will it work for you?"

The moss green eyes took her in, and she saw he wasn't mocking her. He really thought she was rather spoiled because her grandfather was exceedingly rich and loved to spend money on cars.

"Heavens, I don't care in the slightest what means of transport I'm in. Let's go and try out your hideous car."

As he was driving from Hôtel-Dieu de Paris in the direction of Neuilly, they were silent for a while. Océane thought he'd indeed not warned her for nothing. The Peugeot creaked and protested but it rumbled along and soon they were going west along the Seine.

"This makes me happy," Jean-Jacques said in the dark of the car, steering with one hand and fishing a Camel from a crumpled package with his other. "You want one?"

"No thanks, I don't smoke."

"You mind if I do?"

"No, of course not."

He inhaled the smoke eagerly and shot her a quick glance. Océane kept looking straight ahead, forcing herself not to return his gaze. Somehow sitting in the car with him was very intimate but also awkward. He was suddenly so near, so human. Nothing like the great artist she'd idolized for years. Why was he doing this to her? There must be a string of girls ...

"I'm not with someone if that's what you think." His words were arrows in the night. Swift and accurate. Could he read her mind? "What about you?"

"No, no!" she stuttered, glad that the night covered her crimson cheeks.

He deftly parked the Renault outside her grandfather's house but there was no way she could open the door and leave right now. Not yet. There was so much between them in the cramped confinement of the car. She was glad he kept her there, continuing to talk.

"I may seem all world wise and famous, but I spend most of my waking hours in my atelier, I mean I did, until my father fell ill. I'm not what you may think I am. I live for my art."

His words were like sweet syrup on her pancake. He was free. She had to believe him. But why did he tell her? Could he be interested in her as well? Or did he just admire her, or her blue-blooded family?

Through the mist of her misgivings, she heard him say, "Listen, I don't like beating about the bush. I don't know how to do this thing. Believe it or not, I'm no Don Juan. I think it's all my father's fault." He chuckled, drawing on his cigarette. The orange flash lighting up in the dark, illuminating his face.

"What do you mean?" She now turned towards him, taking in the strong profile, inhaling the stingy smoke in her lungs. She knew she was falling, falling fast, and tried to fight but her weapons were weak.

"Dad's been asking about you ever since I came back from the States. I told him about an amazing girl calling out my name and then before I could do anything, she'd left the museum as Cinderella at midnight. Only I had no clue, as you left me no shoe. Then I screwed up on the train. I didn't want to hit on you, you seemed ... unhappy, withdrawn, and I didn't think it was up to me to draw it out of you. I was also hard hit at the time. No inspiration, flat mood, you know that kind of thing. Though the remembrance of your sweet face helped me through the next rough weeks, it took a while before the Muse returned to me. Then just when I was in the groove again, my father fell ill, and I was preoccupied with his health. It was one thing after the other. Then tonight of all nights!" Again, the chuckle.

She felt her blood beginning to sing. It couldn't be true. Or could it?

"I'd almost think Dad knew it was you and that that was the reason he kept you talking at his bedside but that's pure superstition on my part, of course."

He extinguished the cigarette in the ashtray and put a strong hand on her sleeve. The electrical charged field between them was made palpable. He gave her arm a little squeeze.

"You know what?" He was gazing straight at her now.

In the wordless moment that followed, she could see how he saw lines and shapes and colors in her face in the light of the street-lamp, just as she did in his, beauty always intermingled with art, the form and the content of it.

"Can we make an appointment to grab a coffee this week? Would you want that? Have time for that?"

Some of the tension left her. Her own voice, though still somewhat constricted, answered. "I'd love that."

"Can I pick you up here? At your grandfather's place? That way I'll know you won't set me up and not show up." He grinned, showing wonderful teeth. "Oh, and I'll promise I'll wash my hands." He turned his paint-smeared hands in front of her. "I'd completely lost the time when Margot rang my bell to go to the hospital. I just left my easel like this, but I promise I'll smarten up. To the extent that I can." He added the latter rather mischievously.

"Just a coffee then?" Océane inquired, giggling now. "If you decide to smarten up, I need to know the dress code myself."

"You wear whatever you want to wear, Hèrmes-shawl girl. You look like royalty no matter what you drape yourself in. Would Tuesday at four do? I'll show you my favorite café."

Océane blushed, but this time didn't care whether he saw it or not. No man had ever given her such a compliment. She locked the words in her heart as she hopped out of the car before he had time to open her door for her.

"Tuesday it is!"

A last wave, a promise.

11

NO ESCAPE

"A h non, chérie, pas ça! Too sophisticated for an artist date." Her grandfather sat in his usual armchair, his legs in the gray flannel trousers crossed at the knee, sipping a Courvoisier and shaking his silver head. He had been as excited to hear that Océane had met the grandson of one of his best friends and now insisted on helping her with choosing a dress for the occasion.

"Your mother was always so particular in choosing all her outfits herself. I had no say in it. And she cared so little for clothes. She often threatened to only wear her white doctor's coat if I told her to make an effort to impress your dad with her feminine charms. But you, my dear, are much more pliable. Like me, you actually enjoy a good piece of clothing."

Océane agreed. This was fun and also necessary, as her grandfather was a Parisian in heart and soul. Although he'd been a widower for forty years, he had a keen eye for fashion for both sexes. She admired his excellent judgment on what was appropriate and what would be a faux pas. Paris was a complicated society to Océane's American eyes but unlike her mother, she didn't want to be traipsing around only in her white coat. She was still discovering Paris's secrets and charms. And now it was paramount she make the right impression on Jean-Jacques.

Whirling around in a red cocktail dress she'd once worn to a party at Harvard she attended with Martin, Grandpa shook his silver head while puffing on his LeRoy cigar. "I'd say not avant-garde enough. Dare to be a little bolder, my dear. Maybe trousers or do you insist on a dress?"

"Jean-Jacques is taking me to his favorite café, but I don't know which one."

"Aha, that helps a lot!" the Baron exclaimed. "I know it's ..."

"... no, Maxipa, don't tell me! I want it to be a surprise."

"*De jure*! But now I know that you can definitely wear your black trousers with a floral blouse. Something wild and exotic." He jumped up from his chair as if he was twenty instead of over seventy and started rummaging in her closet.

"Granddad, you may be greatly in love with color, but I love toned-down garments. I don't want to stand out on my first date."

Her grandfather stopped his search for her most extravagant top and turned on his heels, smiling wildly under his luxurious mustache, while he teased her. "So, you're telling me it's not just coffee between two acquaintances but a proper first date? Well, I must say, my dear, you certainly stepped up your game from not wanting to have anything to do with the young man, shunning him as if he was a dangerous criminal, to dating him. My old head is spinning."

"Stop it, Maxipa." But she was giggling as well. "You knew right away that I liked him, didn't you? Well, what do you make of Jean-Jacques Riveau now that he's taking me out for a coffee?"

Her grandfather gaily brought the tips of his fingers to his mouth and kissed them. "Excellent choice, ma chérie! But I had not expected otherwise. Instantly liked your father as well, first moment he bumped his head against my chandelier and had the funniest, boyish apology on his handsome face. That's a man you can love."

"Oh, Maxipa, you're so funny. Is that really true? Did Dad hit his head when you first met him?"

"Sure as eggs in April. I still hear him say 'damn length' in that funny accent and I was sold. Took your mother a little longer to acknowledge she was smitten with him, but I kept them both in my sights." His face darkened for a moment. "Except for the time they were at the front, and I was in the house in Nice, you know, during the last year of the Great War. I had consented to letting Agnès follow her dream to save as many lives as she could at the front. We were all devastated after our dear housekeeper Petipat was killed by that damn German cannon. The Bochs called it the Paris Gun, but never mind. I'm digressing, as usual. You should be getting ready for your grand entrée."

"Do tell me, Maxipa! I have another hour and will only be twiddling my thumps waiting for Jean-Jacques to arrive. I've only heard fragments of Mom and Dad's early romance during the war. They didn't like talking about that time, which I get, with Dad getting wounded and Mom in real danger because of her German blood."

"Alright then. Only the basics. Not the juicy parts." Her grandfather smirked, settling himself once again in the Louis Quinze chair in her boudoir, the room that had also been her mother's bedroom when - apart from the servants - Maxipa and her mother had been the sole family members living under this roof.

Her grandfather loved deeply and fiercely, first her grandmother, then his daughter. His love had not been bestowed on another female since. Océane knew she could do her grandfather no greater favor than talking about the time he was still with his beloved, adopted daughter. Agnès had been the apple of his eye, always and forever. Now, she, Océane, was quickly becoming a worthy successor to that love. How she bathed in it.

After refilling his glass and lighting another cigar, he said in his musical, baritone voice that filled every room, "It was the Spring of 1918. We'd already suffered four long years of siege here in Paris, when my housekeeper, who'd run the Saint-Aubin household since I was in diapers, died from her wounds under Agnès's and Alan's hands in the Lycée Pasteur. It was our breaking point. We could take it no more or we'd drown in our grief. I buried myself in my music in the south of France while Agnès went north with Alan, right to the German front. Knowing my daughter was at least with the man she adored eased some of my pain over our separation. Though there was nothing romantic going on between them at the time. Of course, I knew your father was still married to that French Cubist painter - what was her name again? Ah yes, Suzanne Blanchard - but that's beside the point."

"I knew Dad had been married before, but I didn't know to whom. An artist, you said. What a coincidence. I have to read about her work."

Her grandfather winked at her. "I'd dare say it is a coincidence. But it's no use spilling your time on Suzanne Blanchard, my dear. She was just a short-time highflyer. Didn't go into the annals as a famous painter. It was her extravagant lifestyle that caught the headlines. Understood your father had fallen for her but not his marrying her. She was a great beauty in her prime. Nothing like the sweet allure of your mother, though. But you're as bad as I am. Sidetracking me all the time. What's the time?"

"I'm good, Maxipa. Just tell me the story."

"Throughout the war I prayed the fairies would sprinkle some magic on those two, but it took forever. Your father is every inch the gentleman and although the divorce proceedings against his estranged wife had been set in motion, he waited with proposing to *ma fille* until it was all settled. That was on Armistice Day. A day I'll never forget for so many reasons. They were engaged shortly after and married in early spring."

Océane's eyes grew wide as she sank into the armchairs across from her grandfather, a question mark on her face. That was why her parents had always been so vague. The cat was out of the bag now as she did her calculations. They'd never celebrated their wedding anniversary, never giving the exact date, talking around it. Now she understood.

Her grandfather saw her counting on her fingers, bursting out in a merry laugh, "Aha, you've finally figured it out, haven't you? The scandal! I certainly didn't encourage such free behavior in my daughter, but I couldn't scold her either. Your mother is a fiercely loving creature, my dear, and when they were finally certain they were made for each other, there was no holding her back. It wasn't your father. It was that little nymph of a daughter of mine." He chuckled again. "They would've married immediately but your father couldn't walk from his back injury until February of 1919. He insisted he wanted to walk down the aisle unaided, so that's why they postponed the marriage. But, believe me, dear child, your mom and dad were married the day they openly declared their love for each other and that was on 11 November 1918. Apart from my own wedding and the birth of your mother, that was the third happiest day of my life. It had taken these two fools five years to find out they were in love with each other, while it was as clear as the notes of a cavalry bugle to everyone else." He ended, stubbing his cigar rather enthusiastically in the ashtray.

Océane could see how sincere he was, how the memory moved him. "You must miss them so much," she said softly.

"I do, my dear. But I'm very grateful I have their love child under my roof now. That evens the odds out, so to say."

Feeling they were really on confidential terms now, she ventured on. "Why did you never remarry, Maxipa?"

He crossed one flannelled leg over the other, then rested his slim, tanned, musician hands on his knees. He pondered her question for a while, not offended, deep in thought. "I have no real answer to that, my dear girl. Sometimes I think of myself as a swan. I loved once, I loved deeply, but I know it's not the answer. It just did not happen again, but it doesn't mean that I've always been alone. There have been ... you know ... a couple of flings, but they never resulted in anything. Now I'm too old and women don't look at me anymore." He raised in hands in an 'alas' gesture.

"Nonsense, Grandpa, you're not old at all and I'm sure women are still mad about you. You're so sophisticated and humorous and a real gentleman."

"Thank you, dear girl, that makes my old heart gladsome but these days I'm quite content with my life, my music, my beautiful, talented granddaughter, my friends. I lack very little, you know, except seeing my little Agnès more often. But enough talk of me; let's get you in a fine outfit now." He checked his chain watch. "That young Valentine is going to be here shortly, and I've planned a performance at Le Trianon with my friend Bertrand Riveau, you know, JJ's grandfather. We two get to enjoy ourselves for as long as this awful war is not on our doorstep."

Océane had meanwhile selected her clothes. The suggested black trousers but with a modest white blouse, a brown jacket and flat shoes.

"Are you going to tell your friend about me, about us?" she implored, as he got up to let her get dressed.

"Of course, that's the whole reason for meeting him. We old men can gossip as well as womenfolk. Well, my dear, don't make it too late, no curfew yet, thank God, but the times are changing."

"Maxipa," she retorted indignantly, "it's only a coffee appointment. I've got lectures at nine tomorrow. I'll be home for dinner."

"Okay, no need to parent you. You're as faultless as your dear mother, aren't you?" He winked at her with a mischievous glint in his brown eyes.

"Grandpa!" she exclaimed. "You are quite something."

He kissed her forehead and bid her adieu.

WAITING FOR JEAN-JACQUES TO ARRIVE, while the Baron had withdrawn to his music room, Océane became fidgety, doubting whether she'd made the right decision to go out with an artist. Her father's story clung to her like a bad dream. Multiple times she was at the brink of asking her grandfather for his friend's telephone number, so she could cancel the date, but her grandfather would never give it to her, so she felt cornered. Hadn't Jean-Jacques said he expressly wanted to pick her up here where she wouldn't escape him? Just coffee and a chat, she kept repeating to herself, going to the mirror a dozen times to redo her long, dark curls, wondering if she should opt for a dress after all, lipstick or no lipstick. In a moment of extreme self-doubt, she grabbed her mom's stethoscope and jabbed it into the pocket of her jacket.

"I'm totally insane," she told her mirror image, "but it gives me comfort and Mom always had it when she was around Dad."

No longer able to back out of the inevitable, she descended the stairs and waited in the front parlor. At last, the front doorbell rang. She had to hold herself back until she heard the maid Gaël answer the door, pacing the room like a caged lion.

"Mademoiselle Océane, a visitor for you."

Before she knew it, he stood before her, handsome, strong and whole as if he had just come from the countryside, his hair wind-blown, his eyes shining. In his hands, without a trace of paint, he held a bouquet of red roses. Océane was sure the color that shot to her cheeks were the same shade of red.

"For you," he said with that endearing half-smile. "Hardly any roses to be begotten in Paris these days but I was lucky!"

She uttered a "thank you", glad to be putting her nose among the sweet-smelling petals to give herself a pose.

Gaël, who had been observing the young couple with interest, interrupted. "Shall I take them for you, Mademoiselle. I can put the vase in your room, if you want. Will you be out for dinner?"

"Yes, thank you, Gaël. No, I'll eat at home." She looked questioningly at Jean-Jacques.

He nodded. "I'll make sure she's back by that time, Madame."

Gaël, who had taken Petipat's position as housekeeper after the latter's death, had been in the Baron's household since before the Great War. Although she had no official authority over his grand-daughter, she felt protective of her anyway, nicknaming her little Miss America. The middle-aged woman gave Jean-Jacques a friendly nod, satisfied with the arrangement.

"So, shall we go," He raised a dark-blond eyebrow, "or are you having second thoughts?"

"Always," she giggled, "but I'll get over it. Gaël here can testify that I'm not usually so shy."

"That I can, little Miss America," the housekeeper, her arm full of roses, admitted.

"Are you telling me I'm the cause of your change in character? What on earth have I done to you?"

"I'm not going to tell you," she teased. Seeing him in the flesh, real and solid and full of radiance, made her instantly more at ease.

"The place I'm taking you will help you let your hair down. I promise."

"I can't wait to see it. My grandfather knew but I told him not to spoil it for me."

"He knows? Ah, I guess I'm predictable after all, despite posing as an avant-garde artist. There you go, my entire reputation in ruin even before our first date."

"Don't worry," Océane assured him. It felt as if she'd known him a long time. Nothing was difficult about Jean-Jacques.

"I've got the old car waiting and hope she'll obey today. Yesterday I got stranded on the Place Pigalle. Thought that was rather funny. Hookers all around me asking if I needed help."

Now it was Océane's turn to raise an eyebrow, while Gaël looked shocked.

"No, no, no!" Jean-Jacques roared with laughter. "My friend Thierry Chevalier has an atelier there. He wanted to show me some new work. It was all very modest and proper."

The door opened and her grandfather glided into the room like a silver fox. Océane saw Jean-Jacques' eyes light up.

"Baron Max," he exclaimed, as the two men shook hands, Jean-Jacques towering a good head above her slender, finely built grandfather.

"*Mon garçon*," he replied warmly, "I hope you haven't told Grandpa Bertrand? I want to surprise him tonight."

"No, of course not," the young artist laughed. "I wouldn't want to be the damper on your piece of gossip." Turning to Océane, he added, "We really must go, or I'm afraid they'll give our table to someone else. Au revoir, Baron Max. Madame." Bowing to them both, he grabbed her by the hand and pulled her towards the door.

"Have fun," her grandfather shouted after them.

"Mademoiselle, your overcoat, it's going to be chilly tonight, and your umbrella." Gaël rushed after them with the accessories, as much in a longing to fuss over the young mistress as to have a good look at the gentleman's automobile that did not sound a reliable mode of transport.

Used as Gaël was to the quirkiness of the old Baron and many of his friends, she was well acquainted with what she called 'those bohemian troupes' but she would have preferred a man like Océane's father, a doctor or a professor with a steady job and a straightforward outlook on life. The look on her face spoke volumes as Jean-Jacques, in an attempt to open the car door for Océane, held the handle in his hand.

With a rather prim look on her round face, Gaël shouted from the front door, "Do let me know if you decide to dine out after all, Mademoiselle. And have fun."

"The car has taken a turn for the worse this week," Jean-Jacques observed as it started with a lot of grumbling and noise. "One of the windscreen wipers has come off but at least we have a radio."

He took his place behind the steering wheel but before taking off turned to look deep into her eyes. Océane felt the blood rush to her cheeks, it was such an intimate stare that she thought he was going to kiss her on the spot. It made her body tingle all over. Then he extended the thumb of his right hand and caressed the rounding of her chin as if moving a paintbrush over his canvas, a tender but firm stroke. He sighed, then smiled and drove off.

"You could easily be what Adele Bloch-Bauer was for Gustav Klimt," he said as the Paris traffic raced by and a soft drizzle made the light of the streetlamps dance. "Your face is an inspiration for every artist."

Océane didn't know what to reply to another compliment. Nobody had ever in such frank and sensual terms called her beautiful. It was far from unpleasant.

Jean-Jacques had meanwhile turned his attention to the mundane again. "Off to the 8th Arondissement then. I promised you relaxation, not work."

He was a good driver, a confident one. More than once he muttered an accusation under his breath when the car before him did not accelerate fast enough at the traffic lights or hesitated taking right of way. Patience was not his strongest asset, so much was clear. He steered the car deftly around the Arc De Triomphe and along the Champs-Elysées until he turned into Avenue Georges V and after some more turns shot the gray car into a narrow parking slot.

"*Et voilà!* Have you been to *Le Boeuf sur le Toit* before?"

Océane gazed at the crème-stoned façade, a building identical to most of Paris old architecture, and wondered. She'd certainly heard of the place. "Is that where the German diplomat Ernst von Rahm was killed by that young Jewish man, which led to the Kristallnacht all through Germany last November?"

"Yes, in fact it is. Hadn't thought about that when I brought you here. Horrible repercussions by those despicable Nazis. Way out of proportion but shows you what they're capable of. Well, the German wasn't actually killed in Le Boeuf but apparently, he and Herschel Grynszpan met there for the first time. Do you still want to go in? I mean it's not as fun as it used to be in the twenties but it's still one of the freest bars I know. I quite like it and thought you might take a peek, but we can go somewhere else."

"No, I'm intrigued! Of course, I want to see it. I want to see Paris through your eyes."

"Okay then, my Adele, let's go!"

He put an arm around her shoulders in a protective gesture. It felt pleasant, almost normal, and she let herself be led to the café entrance. Releasing her to push open the front door for her, they stepped inside. It was as if walking into a wall of sound; everyone present seemed to be talking at the top of their voice. Somewhere the tones of a piano jingle jangled over the noise that fell and rose like a roaring ocean. Oceáne wondered how on earth anyone could have a conversation of any kind. Jean-Jacques steered her into the crowd. They were instantly surrounded by waiters swishing by with trays filled to the brim with coffee cups and cocktail glasses, shouting, "Attention, attention!". Cautiously she stepped forward.

It was extremely hot, a steamy and upbeat energy that enveloped her as a warm, wet blanket. Staying close to Jean-Jacques, she looked around her with interest. Though she'd been to bars in Chicago and Boston, this cacophonic phenomenon was unknown to her. When in a bar in the States, people sat at tables and conversed quietly. Here most of the guest were standing, some were even dancing, and there was no order in the jolly chaos. It was an eruption of sound, scent and smiles.

"You want to stay?" Jean-Jacques yelled in her ear.

She nodded.

He grabbed her hand and zigzagged with her through the crowds, but they moved very slowly as he was recognized everywhere. Though it was almost impossible to strike up a conversation, he was patted on the back, or kissed on the cheek, or his hand shaken. It was clear he was a regular. When one of the waiters caught sight of him, suddenly the crowds stepped aside and let them pass. Oceáne, still holding onto his hand, moved closely along. His grip on her hand tightened, which felt safe and secure.

They went underneath a portico and entered a backroom of the café that was far quieter. It was where the pianist was positioned, a black man with striking white teeth, who played an acoustic version of 'Over the Rainbow' on an old piano in the corner, swaying on his stool. Here people sat at tables, some in pairs, some in groups. The waiter who had accompanied them went to a secluded corner that was obviously Jean-Jacques' regular place. Someone closed the door to the busy part of the bar and the noise levels went down further. It now seemed like a normal bar.

"What are you having?"

They sat down next to each other on the velvet-covered bench with a dark-brown, stained table in front of them.

"Coffee, please, black."

"Anything to go with it, cognac, brandy?"

"Thanks, just coffee."

"Alright, I'll have the same but with Rémy Martin."

Heads turned at the other tables to look at them, some waved or nodded in Jean-Jacques's direction, some shot a curious glance at Océane, but no one came over to interrupt them.

"I'm lucky," he explained. "This is my table. We'll get privacy here. If I'm at this table, it means I'm with someone I want to talk with. It's always colleagues so that's why you're getting the odd glance. They're trying to figure out what kind of artist you are, and they can't place you."

He gave her his dashing smile, which made her think everyone understood she was here for a different reason, but she couldn't care less. However, as she stirred her coffee, some of the apprehension returned. Now they were in public, it became obvious how famous an artist Jean-Jacques Riveau was here in Paris. She was not used to people staring at her while he seemed to shrug off the whole celebrity thing as a frog shrugs off water from his back.

"Why did your father call you Remix?" she asked, thinking that if he'd not used this nickname, they wouldn't be sitting here now.

"He did? Gosh, the old man must have felt sentimental. It's from the time I started painting. I was about twelve at the time, but I was constantly making a mess of my palette and apparently claimed I needed to remix my colors. That's when Margot, my sister, whom you met at the hospital, started to call me Remix. Dad thought all that sloshing of paint on the canvas rather a waste of time and money. He at first refused to have anything to do with it but when I sold my first painting at fifteen for the handsome price of twenty-five Francs, he decided I was a Remix after all." Jean-Jacques smiled at the memory, the snarky smile she'd come to like so much. "But enough about me, tell me about yourself."

Taking a sip from her black coffee, she pondered what she

should tell him about her life; it seemed so unadventurous compared to his. "Just ask me a question," she eventually said, "then I'll know where to start."

"Oh, that's easy," he grinned. "What's that thing sticking out of your pocket?" He fished the stethoscope into the air and inspected it. "I have a feeling your whole life is connected to this, and it will follow you around for a long time. So tell me."

And she told him about her upbringing in Chicago, Arthur's accident, Radcliffe and the final debacle, which made her decide to go to Switzerland. The more she told him, the easier it became. She laid her life before him as a map and he seemed to read it effortlessly, following her down every road she'd so far taken until she was home with him. She had no idea how long she had been unburdening herself to him - another coffee arrived. Then she accepted a brandy while he smoked another cigarette as she talked on, and he listened. And then she knew as certain as her shadow would follow her that he was the first person who understood her, really understood her, even her wavering choice between art and medicine.

"You're a miracle, O-cé-an-e Bell." He brought her fingers to his lips and kissed them.

His eyes full of light searched hers, and she saw her own reflection in them. She knew, he knew. All was good as long as he was here with her, for her. No one had ever been there for her like he was, a connection deep and wordless, despite all the words, a flowing river of color and captivation and comprehension. She thought her heart would burst any minute now.

Taking her hand in his, he studied her fingers. Counting them from thumb to little finger, he summed up, "Doctor-painter-doctor-painter-doctor. Yes, *ma belle*, your destination has always been in the stars, but my atelier is yours any time you want to relax and paint." Then he shook his head. "Life isn't fair. You have such a head start over me. All *I* can do is paint. But look at you, both sides of your brain equally developed. *Pauvre moi!*"

"Now you know everything, and I know little about you except why you're called Remix." Checking her watch, she saw it was almost six 'o clock.

"You may know all my secrets. If I had them. So why not phone Madame Gaël and tell her you'll have dinner with me after all? I know a quiet little restaurant just around the corner."

"I don't know. I have an anatomy class at nine in the morning and I still have to prepare for it. You now know I can't take a chance at failing an exam again. That would ruin everything."

"Fair enough! But can we see each other again? Then you can ask any question you want."

JEAN-JACQUES PARKED the car in front of her grandfather's house. They sat together in the car without moving, unable to leave each other without some form of a seal. A kiss seemed too intimate, but what then? He took the lead, taking her hand again and kissing her fingers.

"May I call you JJ? Everyone calls me OC," she asked.

Without looking at her, he said, in a low voice hoarse with emotion, "I'd love nothing better, OC."

"JJ, it is."

He was still playing with her fingers, unable to let her go. "Can I pick you up at the Sorbonne tomorrow after your lectures?"

Surprised and excited, she replied, "Of course, but do you not have to work?"

"I can't paint right now. My heart is too full, but it doesn't matter. Everything for the exhibition next week is ready, so I can take some time off. Five o'clock then? I'll take you to my restaurant."

"But I'll have to change first."

"Then I'll take you home. And I'll wait for you in the car."

"Nonsense, my grandfather will love to entertain you while I change."

"Deal then?" He kissed her fingers a last time and said softly,

"You're the noblest, most beautiful creature I've ever seen. I'll need all of tonight to come to terms with that."

"I already knew all this when I saw you in Boston, maybe even before," she whispered, "but it frightens me terribly. What will happen to us, JJ?"

"You knew, too?" He shot her that all-seeing gaze, eyes that opened her soul wide. "Heavens, and I thought I'd lost you for good. Especially after messing everything up on the train. Now go before I can't stop myself from kissing you all over. We'll be fine as gossamer, my darling OC. Don't you worry!"

At that Jean-Jacques jumped out of the car and raced around to open her door. They hesitated on the pavement but then she turned and with a quick wave of her arm, tripped up the stone steps to the red door with the golden lettering, and let herself in. Panting for breath as she closed the heavy door behind her.

This was it. This was all.

12

A WHIRLWIND ROMANCE

Over the next weeks as Fall fell over France and the phony war rumbled on, Océane's life turned into a whirlwind of love and exhilarating expeditions.

She saw Jean-Jacques almost every day because one could hardly breathe without the other. Invariably the gray Peugeot stood parked at the Sorbonne or the Hôtel-Dieu de Paris, depending on where Océane was. Together they discovered new and old restaurants and bars, the interior of which had little interest for them; all they had eyes for was each other.

But other things in Océane's life were also shifting at breakneck speed. Professor Rosenkrantz, who understood Océane's advance over the other students, had asked her to become her assistant, helping the other first-year students with their coursework. She'd hesitated to accept the position, feeling she would be in the same shoes as Martin had been with Professor Lock at Radcliffe. What if she would be compromised by one of her fellow-students, too?

When she'd laid her doubts before Eleanora, the professor who was quickly becoming her friend, had answered, "You've learnt your lesson, OC. And I assume Martin has learned his. You're too smart to make the same mistake twice. By the way, did he ever mention if he was allowed back into Harvard?"

"A year ago, yes. It eased my conscience somehow. Took some work on my father's part to smooth the ruffled feathers. I miss Martin and I miss my friend Eliza. She's a second-year student at Boston School of Medicine now, top of her class, fast on her way to become the first genealogist in her Congregationalist family." Océane's eyes had a misty, faraway look.

"You'll see them soon, once this crazy war is over," Eleanora comforted her. "I've never even been to the States, but Boston has always been my shining dream on the hill. Hopefully we can travel there together."

Océane's eyes lit up. "I'd love that. Yes! But let's first finish my Sorbonne education."

The third great change in Océane's life was that her parents bought her a flat on the Rue Saint-Jacques, a two-room apartment where she could set up her own life if she wanted. She had been doubtful about this as she loved living with her grandfather and his house on the Boulevard Seine was large enough for both of them, but the idea of having something of her own and being able to see Jean-Jacques whenever she wanted was enticing. It seemed an extravagant luxury but after her grandfather assured her he wanted her to have her independence, she said yes. Soon she and Jean-Jacques were redecorating and furbishing the cute little flat on the second floor of an old apartment block.

They had just hauled a secondhand, dark blue sofa up two flights of stairs and dumped it on the floor.

Panting Océane sat on it. "Gosh, you almost carried that single-handedly. I was just steering, nothing else. How come you are so strong?"

"Next to painting, I've been sculpting for a couple of years. Believe me, hacking in marble for a day makes you strong as an ox. I'd love to get back into sculpting one day but the demand for my paintings keeps me busy. Luxury problem, of course, but I do miss it. Good thing you've some heavy stuff for me to haul around so I can stay in shape. Because hauling you around won't do the trick. You're as light as a feather, my American elf." He lifted her from the sofa and threw her in the air, catching her again.

Océane cried out but laughed at the same time. "Put me down, JJ. I'm not a feather. I have weighty brains."

"I agree," he laughed, tightening his arms around her and burying his nose in her lush curls, "your weightiest part is for sure your brains. The rest is just a wisp without any substance."

She let her body relax against his but could not stop laughing. "You make me feel light as a feather because I'm so incredibly happy, but I'm not a wisp. I protest!"

He slipped his hands around her slender waist and squeezed them together. "You see, nothing there, the fingers of both hands touch. You're a wisp, just admit it!"

The bantering went on for a while but as always ended in a sensuous embrace that meant abandoning the decorating to lie in bed together for hours. As the light over Paris turned from pale gray to midnight blue, the city lit up with millions of streetlamps and shop lights. Jean-Jacques was smoking his Camel cigarette, a scent she'd come to adore, while her head rested on his broad chest, listening to his heartbeat. In the contentment of lying in his arms, secure and protected, while love spilled from all their senses, she began to believe that nothing would ever tear them apart.

Raising herself on her elbow, she studied his half-closed eyes with the thick, dark-blond lashes, the stubble of his beard, the blonde hair a scoop on her pillow. "Do you think I should tell my parents about you, I mean, about us?"

He squinted, one green eye focusing on her, a smile curling his lips. "What do you think their reaction would be? I mean, are they liberal thinking or would they be totally shocked by how I ravished their precious daughter?"

"You didn't ravish me, you brute. You only abducted my heart. The rest is still as intact as it can be."

"That can be changed instantly!" He threw his cigarette in the ashtray next to the bed and made a move to embrace her again.

"No, stop," she giggled, "seriously, JJ. I mean how much did you tell your parents about us?"

"My dad and Margot know, of course, and they are delighted. They keep badgering me to bring you over. My mother doesn't know." He stopped for a moment, hesitating.

Océane realized he had hardly mentioned his mother before and for some reason she had not asked. It seemed a sensitive part of him. Madame Riveau had also not been at the hospital to see her sick husband.

"What's with your mom?"

"Nothing serious, she's just been in the countryside since the declaration of war. My grandparents, you know, Senator Riveau - who's your grandfather's friend - own a house near Vichy. Mother has been there since, running the family's lace factory."

"Is she afraid of the war?"

"Well, she *is* Jewish, if that's what you mean, and no Jew is safe anywhere in Europe although they want to believe so with all their might. Dad wanted her to get to the States, to be really safe, but she refuses. Says, she'll stay anonymously in the countryside.'

"Is it hard to miss her?" Océane kissed his bare arm in a gesture of comfort but also because that muscled bicep looked so enticing.

"Not harder than it must be for you not to see your family. I can at least see her when I go down there. And we phone each other regularly."

"So that makes you half Jewish as well. Are you afraid?"

He laughed a scornful laugh. "Me, afraid? No way. If they call me up to fight those Nazi bastards - and I suppose it's only a matter of weeks before I have to enlist - I'll do it with my whole heart. My father and my uncles fought in the Great War, and I'll fight in this one."

Her heart sank low in her body. Her hand went limp, stopped caressing him. It had never even crossed her mind that her new love could be disrupted by anything. But here it was, war crushing down on them, Jean-Jacques saying he was to go under arms.

Seeing her face drop, he kissed her lips tenderly. "Don't worry about it, my darling. Sorry I even mentioned it. Let's go back to your original question. When to tell your parents about us." He went on to kiss her eyelids and then her earlobes, trying everything to make her forget his upcoming soldier's life and the split between them.

It took a while, but she let him seduce her in the end.

"Mom will instantly insist on planning my wedding if she hears about you and me," she said pensively. "Dad will take a more nuanced approach, asking me all sorts of questions about you, how I feel about you, how I see you fitting into my busy schedule of studying and working to become a doctor. But I really want to write to them soon. I'm afraid if I don't, my grandfather will not be able to keep his mouth shut for much longer. He's over the moon with you, as you know."

"I know what we will do. I will ask my friend Henri Cartier-Bresson, you know the photographer for the Communist Paper *Ce Soir*, to take our picture."

"You know him, too? Gosh, you know *tout le monde*. Did he not cover the coronation of King George VI? I think Grandpa knows him."

"Sure, he did that. And he played in Jean Renoir's films. He'll do it if I ask him. Then we send your parents the photograph with your letter so they can see we're serious."

"Are we serious?" She said it in banter but was not prepared for the fierce look that landed on her next.

There was raw emotion and a strange pain that almost contorted his attractive features as he said, "Darling, it's that damn war that's making our tomorrow so unsure, but I'd marry you today if we could. I've never been surer of anything in my life than I am of you and me. I can't stop painting, I'm so inspired, and it's all because of you. I feel my best, my richest period, is just around the corner because ... because I'm totally in love. Like you, I knew

Cupid had shot his arrow that moment in the Boston Museum of Fine Arts. I just knew that you were the girl I'd been waiting for all these years."

The fire in his eyes. His love, his declaration of love, made her eyes misty. Feeling overwhelmed by the immensity of his words, she nestled back in his arms, his naked torso warm and close by. If only they could always stay like this.

Dear God, don't take him, she prayed silently.

But Jean-Jacques wasn't done. "Océane Bell, my dear OC, you're my everything. If I wasn't a left-wing rascal with the odd mix of artistry and politics slung in, I'd say you are my alpha and my omega because I think I finally understand what the sweet Jesus meant by that. You're my religion. So, are we serious? Deadly serious. As soon as we can have our families together, we'll get married. That is, if you will have me."

He fell silent, gazing at her through his thick eyelashes. Océane had to smile at the shadow of uncertainty he expressed. Jean-Jacques was always so confident in everything he did; even in his work he was almost cocksure of his talent and place among the 1930s painters. She often thought he was the most unfazed person she'd ever met. But now he was in doubt.

Taking his left hand, the hand that created these masterpieces, she said soberly, "Of course, I want you, you're my other half. I don't exist without you, so we'll get married as soon as the war is over. I think it's a lovely idea to have that photograph made by Cartier-Bresson and send it to Chicago. I'm sure my grandfather will insist on having one as well. And your parents, of course."

"Talking about your grandfather. I think it would be a good idea to ask for his blessing in the absence of your parents," Jean-Jacques observed, winding a lock of her dark hair around his finger. "I mean, he has condoned our spending intimate time together, but it is a different matter to ask it formally. What do you think?"

At that, Océane jumped out of bed and slid her slim figure into a silk bathrobe, the sash of which she firmly knotted around her slender waist. "Let me ring him and see if he has time tonight."

"You're the boss, Madame!"

~

ON AN EARLY EVENING in late October, Océane had just returned from her shift in the hospital when the doorbell rang. Still in her overcoat with the white apron underneath, she opened the door. A delivery boy handed her a gold rimmed envelope of handmade paper.

"With the compliments of Monsieur Cartier-Bresson. Monsieur says that if you want more photo prints, just let him know." The young boy straightened his thin shoulders at the importance of the message he had delivered.

"Wait, let me give you something for your trouble," she said, searching in her purse.

"It was no trouble at all." But he gratefully accepted the francs she dropped in his palm.

Océane's heart started to beat faster as she returned to her sitting room. Should she wait for Jean-Jacques to look at the photos? He'd said he might be working late, and it was impossible to constrain her curiosity.

Kicking off her shoes and coat, she settled on her blue sofa and impatiently broke the seal on the envelope. Seconds later she was staring at the large black and white portrait. Her whole being was sucked into the image, as if she was someone else looking into another world. In that world she sat in a lush Art deco Sofa Riot chair wearing a white mousseline dress with a black leather belt that accentuated her slim waist. She sat in a posture of a glamorous actress, self-confident, blazing with love. The white stood out beautifully against her long, dark curls framing her slender face with the dark, doe like eyes.

Very unlike her, she was wearing shiny stockings and high-heeled black shoes with a thin strap. Her face with the radiant smile was turned upwards towards Jean-Jacques, who sat on the arm looking down on her with that intense look of love in his eyes.

He was dressed in a black suit with a white carnation pinned to the lapel, black and white, just as they had chosen. They complimented each other beautifully. Though in formal dress, Jean-Jacques still breathed the artist with his half-long hair falling over his cheek, the wry smile and the keen eye that were his hallmark.

"Oh-my-oh-my," Océane kept repeating, "Mom and Dad will love it. But I also want this photo in pocketsize format. Have it in my handbag, never part with it, with us, ever again."

A strange shudder went through her nervous system. No! Nothing would happen to them.

Océane was still writing the letter to her parents when Jean-Jacques planted a kiss in her neck. He picked up the photo that lay on her writing table, staring down at it. For a long time, he remained silent. Then he did something she had never seen him do before. He went to the sideboard and poured himself a large whiskey and gulped it down in one swig. The deep ocean eyes were on her as he returned to the table and sat down.

"We look like royalty," he said but his voice was flat.

"What's wrong, JJ?" She put down her pen to go over to him. She sat in his lap, stroking the dark blonde mane from his face.

"I've been called under arms, OC. I leave for training in Reims next week."

Océane gasped. Opened her mouth and then shut it again. The strange shudder she had felt earlier shook her whole body. *Nooooo! You can't go. Don't leave me!* everything in her screamed but she knew he would, she knew she had to let him go. No horsepower or love in the world would keep her hero from fighting for his fatherland.

"I'll be okay, my darling. Don't worry about me. I only have one favor to ask you, together with my father. I'm supposed to have an exhibition at the Galérie Sud in November. The paintings are almost done, I only need to finish the last one, a portrait of you. Would you be able to bring the paintings to the gallery? Dad will drive the van."

"Of course I will, but your dad? Is he strong enough? Maybe I can ask someone at the hospital or what about my Granddad?"

"No, Dad will be fine. Also, I want you to keep an eye on him. Margot will give a hand as well. If anything is sold, you collect the money. I've put the account in your name."

She didn't even hear the trust he had in her. Money was the last of her worries.

"When will you be back?"

"I don't know, darling, but I hope before Christmas. We get six-week training and then we're supposed to be sent to the Maginot line. The training ends right before Christmas. I hope they'll give us a break. Unless those blasted Germans get it in their stupid heads to attack France. I don't think it will come to that."

He kept caressing her arm in an absent manner. Océane saw he was fighting hard to stay calm himself. Despite all his bravado, he was afraid as well, afraid to part from her, afraid to lose her. She knew him so well; she knew she had to be the strong one now.

His voice was still toneless when he continued, "I just have to do my bit. Can't idle away my days as a painter. It might come in handy someday if I know how to use a weapon. But I worry about you, OC. Will you stay here? The rationing and the angsty atmosphere doesn't bode well for Paris."

"When push comes to shove, I can always move back in with Grandpa. He has so many friends in the government, Mom told me they didn't really lack anything in the Great War. I'm sure he'll be able to get extra portions again."

Jean-Jacques took her head between firm hands and kissed her lips tenderly. "It would put my soul at ease, knowing you're with him. Please consider it, darling. Leaving you is already so difficult, but leaving you here to fend for yourself, it grates at my heart."

"I'll be okay, JJ. I've got my studies and my work, increasingly more work now the men are all leaving. Professor Rosenkrantz asked me only today if I could work an extra day. We're getting way more responsibilities than first-year students should but it's an emergency situation. In my own way I'm also preparing for the war."

"Wouldn't you want to go back to the States now while it's still possible? Be safe and be with your family?"

She shook her head decidedly. "You are my main family now, JJ. You and me. I'm not leaving the country without you. Ever."

13

PARIS HAS FALLEN

14 June 1940

Awakening in her bedroom in her grandfather's house, Océane wished the day had never broken but it had, despite her will, despite France's will. No human hands could stop the arms of the clock, no matter that the day was bitter, black and frankly bizarre.

After nine months of phony war, Nazi boots were stomping all through the Paris streets. Their despicable swastika flags hanging from all official buildings and Hitler on his way to make his triumphant tour along the Champs Elysées.

All of Paris pulled out their hair in bewilderment. How could this have happened, with the scars of the Great War not yet healed? A Blitzkrieg by the German army through Holland and Belgium, the Maginot line pushed aside like a row of tin soldiers, and Paris fallen within a couple of days. How? There was no answer. Only reality. Harsh, cruel, unbending reality of a foreign hateful regime taking over their lives. Hitler made all of Europe puppets on his string and no one seemed able to stop the dictator.

Océane hid her head under the bedclothes. She wasn't so much frightened - she was furious. There wasn't anything she really feared for herself. Her US citizenship made her no threat to the Germans. Her worries lay with the two men in her life, her elderly grandfather and her beloved. Maxipa seemed to have grown frailer overnight, blaming himself for not sending her overseas earlier, and then there was Jean-Jacques still at the front that no longer existed. Had he been taken captive? Where was he now?

Messages trickled down to Paris that the Nazis had crashed through the French resistance like snapping pieces of matchsticks, but it had been over a week, and nothing had been heard, nothing specific. Tales of brutal murder and whole garrisons been taken prisoner and sent to work camps in Germany couldn't be confirmed.

As in all crises in her life, Océane mainly stayed level-headed and practical, yet a growing unrest permanently settled in her stomach area. This was so vast, so unpredictable. She wasn't sure she'd be able to handle it properly and keep her men safe.

University lectures had stopped overnight. Just in time, she'd managed to pass her first Sorbonne year with flying colors. Professor Rozenkrantz was very proud of her. Doctor Ferron and the young professor had taken Océane under their wing at the cardiac ward of Hôtel-Dieu de Paris. The two women worked side by side, almost as equals. For Océane it was a steep learning curve, but she was up to the challenge, able to diagnose most heart diseases and perform all the necessary actions apart from the operations.

"War is always a time of great advance for medicine, Océane, so make use of it," Eleanora told her more than once.

She had no idea if they would be given access to the hospital today under the new circumstances, but she was adamant to treat the day as business as usual. Jean-Jacques' old Peugeot would take her. He'd given her the car before he'd left for his military training in the fall and the car had not failed her once. She treated its good behavior as providence. All would be well. One day. Maybe not today. But soon. For sure this idiocy couldn't last very long. Just like in the Great War, the Allies would soon stand ready to liberate France.

Only it had taken them four years the last time. Four years. Océane shuddered as she hoisted herself in her hospital outfit and put on her sturdy walking shoes.

"Be well, my love, and come back to me today."

Kissing their portrait that stood on her armoire, she said a short prayer for Jean-Jacques. Though not religious in any way, she'd taken to praying since he'd left. Only two reunions since, at Christmas and a surprise visit in February. He'd appeared chirpy enough, clearly enjoying the hard physical labor that his strong body always craved. His intense hate of the Nazis and what they stood for had been the wood that kindled his fire. He had returned much more like a soldier, his eyes hard with hate. It had been difficult to see his soft side. He couldn't dig deep enough to get to his love, not even for her. But Océane had patience. And she understood. This wasn't a time to lament or be clingy.

Removing the blackout from the windows, she stared down at the scars of Paris. It was a beautiful early spring day with fresh young leaves on the trees in front of her grandfather's house. The Boulevard was eerily silent in comparison to a normal, bustling Friday. Only German jeeps and motorcycles filled with khaki soldiers or SS officers in menacing black uniforms raced along the Seine. To Océane it felt as all of Paris was holding its breath. Even the bells of the nearby church seemed subdued and out of tune.

Not waiting for Gaël to come up and inform her about breakfast, she made her way downstairs. The small household staff was at their wit's end, all vividly remembering the first war that had ripped Madame Petit from them.

The frightened, pinched face of Gaël peeked around the living room door, and Océane straightened her slender back. She would have to lead these frightened ones, comfort them, staff or patients, and be strong, stronger than anything in the world. There was no other option. Her task was cut out for her. Starting here.

"Is the Baron up yet?"

Her grandfather usually always slept in, but Gaël nodded.

"He's been up since before dawn, Mademoiselle. I'm so worried about him. At his age to have to live through the occupation of his city all over, it's too much."

"I know, Gaël, but that is also the case for you and for Marie. That's why I want my grandfather to go to the house in Nice, take you with him. I can look after the house while I wait for Monsieur Riveau to return. Can you ask my grandfather to join me for breakfast?"

Océane saw hesitant admiration in the housekeeper's eyes as she replied, "You're just like your dear mother, so resolute and courageous. I'll ask the Baron straight away."

And at that Océane knew the tables had turned. Until now Gaël had wanted to mother her, but she'd grown up fast and now took her position as mistress of the house.

"Maybe Madame Paul's lessons weren't wasted after all," she mumbled to herself, while waiting for her grandfather to join her.

The Baron walked in with his newspaper and cigar, looking as if he was slightly unsteady on his feet.

Océane's heart broke for him. "Gramps," she said, swallowing her tears, "we need to talk."

He shuffled to the table and sat down in his chair with a sad sigh. She went over to him, kissing the silver-haired crown of his head before sitting down opposite him. He'd still not spoken a word, which was very unlike the talkative, energetic Baron.

Océane got up again to fill his cup before pouring herself a coffee. The silence in the room was palpable. He had bags under his eyes, his always slightly tanned skin, almost ashen. Her upbeat, ever bright and breezy grandfather had turned old overnight. The shock it gave her to see him like this was immense. She decided that whatever would come her way, she'd remain at his side, even choosing him over Jean-Jacques, if necessary. In the absence of her mother, she would protect and support her Maxipa. He *was* an old man, having recently turned seventy-eight, and the renewed rationing of the past months had eaten up his already slim posture even further.

"Maxipa," she almost choked on her own voice, "I can't describe how sorry I am that you have to live through this all over again."

She hoped against hope that he would brush the whole situation aside as a joke with his usual conviviality but the somber look in his always sparkly brown eyes spoke volumes.

"A bad business indeed. Even the Imperial Army didn't manage what this despicable rapscallion has brought upon us. Disgrace *my* Arc de Triomphe with their hideous Nazi flag. How dare he! If I were a young chap, I'd join the army now, something I didn't do in the first war. So I'm glad your beau is doing his bit."

"What will you do, Gramps? It will only get worse here in Paris with all the restrictions in place and food so scarce. I want you to go to Nice. Take Gaël and Marie with you."

That did the trick. His eyes, instead of jolly and humorous, turned to a thundercloud of hailstones and storm. "Damn Hitler! Damn, damn him and his Nazi party. Never will I buckle down to that regime. I'll stay put here until these impostors in their ludicrous SS uniforms are gone from my city. I won't let myself be exiled like *I* am the criminal! Not me."

His tirade shocked her but the return of some vibrancy in him also made her hopeful. Maybe rage was better than submission. Though it was also dangerous. Knowing how passionate a man Maximilian De Saint-Aubin was, she didn't know where his new revolutionary argy-bargy would lead.

She tried again, also for her mother's sake. "I'd rather you go to Nice, Gramps, or to the countryside. You're not one for the battlefield, not just because of your age but also because making music is most important to you."

"Making music?" He looked at her as if she were a Jack-in-the-box suddenly popping up before his eyes. "There's no music in this, my dear, no music at all. All I can hear is marching music and that horrible Wagner. It hurts my ears. No, I promise I won't start killing Nazis with my bare hands. I'll keep a low profile for now, but who knows. Don't rule out a tribe of old men. If we can't outrun them, we can outsmart them."

Océane had to admit her grandfather looked rather bellicose and she had to smile at his gusto despite herself.

Seeing her smile, he softened his rhetoric. "What about you, my dear? I phoned the Port in Le Havre to see if there are still ships sailing to America. Not passenger ships, of course, but sometimes you can go aboard a cargo ship."

"My home is here!" It came out in a harsher tone than she'd intended. In a softer voice she added, "My home is with you and JJ and Paris."

"Right." He relit his cigar and sipped his coffee with more comfort. Though they'd come to an agreement, nothing was solved.

After a silence, her grandfather continued in what was more like his musical voice. "Can't say I haven't considered going to Nice, my dear. Also for Marie and Gaël. It was my first instinctive reaction just as during the first war but then I thought how cowardly I'd been then. I mean, your mother and Alan went to the front and did their bit. And what did I do? Now these Bochs are back, they'll have to step over this old body before I'll flee again."

He was winding himself up once more.

"A person can change, right? Plus, you are here. You're my responsibility, too. I knew you wouldn't go back home, even if you could. We'll sit this war out, you and me, won't we?"

"Yes, Grandad. We will. I'm also worried about Professor Rosenkrantz, who is so clearly Jewish, and Jean-Jacques's father, whose heart is still fragile. I'm responsible for them as well."

"Though they're not family, looking after them does you credit, dear girl. Concerning Professor Rozenkrantz. Wouldn't she be wiser to take to her heels to the States? The Nazis will soon make life very difficult for French Jews. Mark my words."

"Oh no, Eleonora told me in no uncertain terms she's not fleeing the country again. She's French now as she and Doctor Ribaud are married and expecting their first child."

"Eleonora?" The Baron lifted his silver eyebrows in mock

surprise, his mind temporarily taken away from the grimness of war. "Aha, so you're on first name status with her. Well, I do understand the dear doctor's reasoning. It was the same with your mother and father; you doctors are so dang loyal when it comes to sticking to your guns. I personally think the military could sometimes take an example from your heroism."

At that moment, the front doorbell could be heard clanging it's deep, coppery ring. Gaël was soon talking with a visitor.

The Baron took his golden chain watch from his pocket, furrowing his brow. "Not even eleven! Who on earth can be inclined to visit unannounced at such a malapropos time? Have all manners gone by the wayside now the Germans marched in?"

Océane couldn't help smiling at the old vigor her grandfather showed. The door to the living room swung open and, on the threshold, stood Jean-Jacques dressed from head to toe in a khaki uniform and a navy-blue beret on his dark-blonde locks. His smile was as wide as the River Seine. Océane didn't even feel her feet touch the ground as she flew to him and into his arms, ignoring the rough fabric of his uniform and his two-day beard. Even unaware her grandfather was watching, she kissed him and kissed him again. Not even giving him any time to say her name or greet her grandfather. He held her tightly against himself and she felt those strong arms, the arms of a wrestler around her, and she was safe, crying and laughing as she kept kissing him until he lifted her up and, carrying her against his chest, brought her back to the table, to her grandfather's room and to a capitulated Paris and a lost war.

The Baron had risen from his chair. Eyes moist with sadness but also with pride, he cried out, "*Vive la France!*"

Jean-Jacques, with his arm tightly around Océane, saluted and replied, "*Vive la France.*"

Revived and in command, the Baron began frantically ringing the house bell. Gaël had needed no instructions, though, and hurried in with a tray laden with fresh coffee and homemade bread.

Eyeing Jean-Jacques with shy reverence, she apologized. "We

only have surrogate coffee, Monsieur, and I had hardly any yeast left for the bread so it's not as well-risen as I usually make it."

"I've come to adore surrogate coffee these past months," he joked. "If they gave me a real cup right now, I'd kindly turn the offer down. As for the bread. I haven't eaten in two days so I assure it will taste just like brioche to me."

"Sit, rest, eat and drink," the Baron invited heartily, "then you must tell us how you got back to Paris. Tell us all. But first, do your father and grandfather know you're back?"

"No, Sir, I came straight here. Well, I first went to the Rue Saint-Jacques but when OC wasn't there I came here at a gallop."

"Do you want me to telephone your father?"

"Not yet, please; the less people know I'm back the better. I'm going to join the Resistance straightaway."

"What?" It came as a strange squeak from Océane's mouth. "No, JJ, no! You can't, you simply can't. I won't have it. You're finally back in one piece. No!" Tears sprang in her eyes.

But he didn't seem to see her anguish. "Safe!" He spat out the word. "Safe! Fiddle-faddle! No Frenchman is safe as long as these Fritzes degrade our nation!"

"Now, now, my boy," the Baron soothed him, one eye on his distressed granddaughter, "drink your coffee and eat. Then have a bath and some proper sleep. You look exhausted."

"Thank you, Sir, I'd appreciate your help. I'll need civilian clothes but I'm afraid they're already watching my house and studio, so I don't know if it's wise to go there right now."

"Who's *they*?", Océane inquired, a thousand needles piercing her heart.

"Some mates and I blew up a German airport on the way." He said it almost casually. "It was an interesting homebound trip, I can say that much."

Océane didn't like his tone at all, how cynical and hard he'd become. She needed time alone with him, to talk that idiotic plan of joining the Resistance out of his head. Jean-Jacques was a painter, an artist, he created things, didn't demolish them.

"Tut, tut," the Baron coaxed the young couple, "we'll sort out the clothing part later. Now, let's rejoice in your safe return."

Océane bit her lip, not wanting to argue, swallowing her fear and uncertainty. This changed man, bitter and brittle, was in no way the warm and tender lover she'd known and cherished. Jean-Jacques the artist was color and shade and nuance. This man was black, unbending, proud. He didn't even seem to have an eye for her. But she wanted him and needed him. Pulling her chair close, she slipped her hand in the pocket of his rough uniform and watched him ravish the bread and gulp down three cups of Gaël's instant coffee.

After he'd satisfied his worst hunger, he took her hand from his pocket and kissed her fingers. Instantly their connection was alive again and she sighed with relief, forcing down the tears that bubbled up as from an underground well. A gesture, a look, his presence, she was one soppy mess. It was as if the ring of ice around his heart broke as well. Tracing his finger over her lips, he smiled, sorrow showing on his face.

"I didn't want to scare you, my darling. I shouldn't have started about the fight ahead of me right now. How are you, how have you been?"

The eyes that took her in were Jean-Jacques's eyes again. The tightness in her chest relaxed, her blood could flow through her veins again. *He is home*, was all she could think, *home, home, home. Don't think of tomorrow. Think only of today.*

"I'm fine. I always will be fine when you're with me." It was impossible. Her eyes filled with tears of their own accord, but it was sorrow mixed with happiness.

To her shock she saw Jean-Jacques was crying as well. "Oh, my dear, oh, my dear girl," he kept repeating, hugging her tightly. There was so much agony, so much passion in his embrace.

Don't leave me!

It was a cry to the heavens.

14

A CHANGED WORLD

Three months later

Océane woke panting, stretching out her arm in a panic to feel if Jean-Jacques was there. She touched his naked back and listened. He was breathing evenly, fast asleep. In an attempt to calm herself, she turned on her back and checked her wristwatch. It was four in the morning. Blackout robbed her of any sense of time.

A heavy truck rumbled by on the Rue Saint-Jacques, clattering the windows. For the rest Paris was still, bound and gagged by the German oppressors.

What was the nightmare that had awakened her? She fought to undo herself from the frightening web.

Walking barefoot through a desert, ripples and ripples of yellow sand. In the distance a sandstorm huge as a wall came her way. She wanted to flee but knew it was useless. She would have to protect her face but as she had no shawl, she took off her blouse and tied it around her head and face. Feeling terribly exposed in her thin vest and bra, she was not just a plaything of the wind and sand but also of prying eyes that were watching her everywhere, creatures hiding in the sand.

No map, no location, no destination. Yet she knew she had to go straight through the sandstorm. Where she'd come from was too dangerous to return to. Here it came. She braced herself. The sand wall hit her body, the bare parts of her flesh, went through the cloth and nestled in her mouth, her ears, her nostrils. It stung every part of her skin, sandpapered her all over, bringing her off balance.

The heat was unbearable. The soles of her feet burned as she tried to run forward, hope against hope to get through it alive. Then the thirst set in, what she feared most, faint of thirst as she was buried under a heap of sand and die. No one would ever know where she was buried.

Suddenly she remembered why she was there. She had a message for Jean-Jacques. It was urgent. He was on the other side of the sandstorm, waiting for her at an oasis. Just as she thought she'd suffered the worst, a black boot stepped on her naked toe. She shrieked in pain. Through the slit in her blouse, she saw an SS officer looking down on her. He was clearly not going to let her pass.

"Please let me go," she begged. "I have an important message to deliver."

"Save yourself the effort. The traitor's dead. And so are you."

The SS officer took a pistol from his belt and aimed at her.

That was the moment she had woken up. She shuddered in the remembrance.

"Just a nightmare," she told herself. "Nothing to worry about."

Listening to Jean-Jacques's breathing, she fought the urge to fling her body against his. He'd loved her already and needed his sleep. It had been way after midnight when he'd barged into her bedroom, returning from a three-day secret mission, having not slept in the meantime.

Within twenty-four hours he'd be gone again, disappearing like a thief in the night, abandoning her to her sickening worries until he'd be back ... or not. Until now he'd come and gone, always hungry, tired, restless. A caged wildness around him until he rested briefly in her arms. For a few sweet hours they'd be lovers again, the war forgotten, his perilous Resistance work pushed outside the walls of her bedroom.

The fear for his safety eroded Océane's strength but she hid it from him as best as she could. Her own life was full and arduous as well. Fulltime work at the Hôtel-Dieu de Paris kept her on her feet all day, forced by the Nazis to treat German soldiers alongside the French patients. She often thought of her parents, having had to do the same in the earlier war.

The staff at the Hôtel-Dieu de Paris had shrunk to a minimum so she worked all hours. She didn't mind. It kept her from brooding over Jean-Jacques and her grandfather. No thinking, just doing, was the best strategy. Her family was a dead spot as well. All mail from the States was disrupted. No news, nothing. A prolonged silence in which her whole life hung in limbo.

The nightmare came back.

"Please give up fighting, JJ, and go back to painting," she begged the black night and his still back. "Don't take the little I have from me. I'm not strong enough for this."

But her plea always fell on deaf ears. Jean-Jacques had made clear he'd given up painting for the duration of the war. He swore he could not hold a paintbrush until he could lay down his rifle. When France was French once more. When.

It made Océane think of Lili and her fervent communist bravado. Lili also had that inbred need to fight injustice. Did she, Océane, lack something? She didn't hate the Germans she treated at the hospital. Most were young men, who needed care just like any other human being. Just as grateful when they had relief from pain and the treatment cured them, just as frightened, just as homesick.

Jean-Jacques stirred in his sleep, then turned around and sleep-drunk pulled her into his embrace. She plied her body against his in the darkness and they found each other as they always did, as magically and as natural as sunlight on the sea, light, playful but also deep and mysterious. They were one forever in a love without end.

"I love you till the end of time," he breathed into her hair.

The words so simple, so powerful and she knew it was the truth. There was no other truth.

MORNING CAME, and a quick, meagre breakfast with Jean-Jacques still asleep kept Océane fighting with the nightmare and her nauseous fear for him. To protect her, Jean-Jacques shared nothing about his Resistance work, but she wasn't stupid. The Gestapo was coming down hard on the French opposition, tracking down the leaders of the Resistance like a pack of hunting dogs.

The newly appointed SS Obergruppenführer Dieter Von Stein had even ordered posters pasted on all French official buildings with code names of the men and women they were looking for. Océane had been chilled to the bone when she saw Remix among them. There was no doubt who that was and that they had him in their vision.

Jean-Jacques, sleepy, gorgeous and dressed only in a bathrobe, stood in the door to the kitchen. A cigarette dangled from the corner of his mouth. His dark-blonde hair stood up in peaks.

"Hello, darling. Did I wake you?" She hoped her voice was even, no emotion.

"No, you didn't. But I wanted to make sure I'd catch you before you leave. Come here."

She went into his arms, smelled his musky, strong body, tobacco and leather, felt the heat of his skin.

This! She screamed inwardly. *This! This! Don't rob me of it. Please, dear God*!

As she clung to his body as if shipwrecked, she heard him say through her tears, "Darling, I want you to move back in with your grandfather again. This flat has become too obvious a target. The SS is upping their game. It will be difficult to come and see you at your grandfather's house but at least it's got a back entrance. I can slip in unseen sometimes."

"Okay," she sniffled, "I'll do that. It makes sense to go back to Gramps, like when you were at the front."

He lifted her chin and kissed the tears from her eyes.

"I know how difficult this is for you, OC. I do know and it eats at my heart. But I feel I have no choice. I want our children to grow up in a Free France. Don't fret, my darling. I'm strong and fast and much smarter than these Fritzes. Nothing will happen to me."

"Do you promise?" She said it without needing an answer. It would be an empty promise either way.

His answer was a tightening of his embrace and another kiss. "If I don't show up for a while, it will mean it's too dangerous for me to be in Paris. I'll be laying low somewhere in the countryside. But I'll make sure you'll get a message through the network. That coward Pétain and his puppet Vichy state has made it much more difficult for us to fight back. There are so many traitors among the French now."

She kissed him back, not wanting to hear the words, but he was very serious now, the moss green eyes forcing her to listen.

"If it becomes too dangerous for you here, if you feel you're being followed, please persuade your grandfather to move to Nice with you. There's more food available in the south and I'll be able to travel around with a little more ease. And one more thing. Don't be surprised if I'm disguised next time. It's security measures."

Océane gazed at him with terror in her eyes. Her worst nightmare was coming true. She could no longer hold back. "I told you so from the beginning. Why couldn't you stick to painting, JJ, if only for my sake? Life is unbearable as it is without me being constantly on edge that the Gestapo will arrest you and kill you. Can't you take a break, give us a breather and then go back when we have a better idea what the Germans want? We could go to the south together, just for a short break. I'll take time off from the hospital."

She was aware she was losing it, begging and fighting, and that it was useless. She wanted his love for her above all and was exhausted from having to fight for first place. Her words hit him.

He hung his head, acknowledging the pain his underground work caused her.

"I can't stop anymore, OC. Even if I wanted to. I lead a Resistance cell here in Paris. I know too much already. Even if I resigned, they'd still send the Gestapo after me. But I do promise you one thing. I'll discuss it with my cell, tell them I need some days with my girl. Because I see you're falling apart under the stress. That's why I want you to leave Paris, to get a different perspective. I also know how hard your life at the hospital is, having to tend to enemy soldiers. It's a right rigmarole we're in and I wish with all my heart that I could change it but it's too late."

She nodded, slowly, very slowly. He did think of her. She did come first. That was all she needed to know. She also knew the die was cast. Neither of them had a choice anymore.

"I love you, my fearless warrior." Her throat clogged up with emotion despite her will. "And I understand. Really I do."

Here was a soldier who had been forced to lay down his arms at the Maginot line, had escaped a German prison camp by smartly disguising his identity, and created havoc on his way back to the French capital, thwarting the Germans with every step he took. Remix was a formidable Resistance fighter, fluid, smart, creative and, above all, fearless.

"You're the best France has to offer right now, and I know that if anyone can stop Hitler, it's you."

"Not on my own," he said with modesty, "but I'd like to think I'm the sharp-teethed terrier at his heel."

She smiled, a wan gesture. "Well, I guess I'm as stubborn as you are. I won't leave Paris. I'll stay at the hospital. That way you'll always know where to find me."

They stood, embraced, solidified.

"I admire you so much," he said, unable to stop kissing her, "so incredibly much. I hope you understand this isn't some violent side of me or coquetting with left-wing politics; it's a cry of my soul to liberate us from a future of slavery. We have to rise to the occasion."

"I know," she replied, kissing him back. "I know you feel that way about your country, our country. I may not share your way of standing up against oppression, but I know you see it as having no choice. Neither have I. Because I love you, I'm bound to your choices."

"I'm sorry." He said again, then let her go.

She had to leave for the hospital, slipping into her white coat and sturdy flat shoes with rubber soles, then tucking her mother's stethoscope in the pocket of her doctor's coat. Ready to go, she faced Jean-Jacques one more time. He was sitting at the kitchen table, smoking a cigarette. His face glum, deep lines showing next to his mouth. It was a wordless goodbye to their flat. For how long they didn't know. Her heart broke for them both. Their love nest, their sanctuary, so much fun, so much passion. Here it had been just the two of them, the war a faraway phony war. Now it marched all over them, crushing all beauty in its wake.

"I'll go to my grandfather's house tonight. I'll use his car. Might be better not to be seen using the Peugeot." He nodded, unable to answer her. She went over to kiss the dark-blonde head one last time. "Au revoir, JJ, please be safe. Let me know."

"Au revoir, my darling."

Where was the promise now?

STEPPING INTO THE AUGUST MORNING, Océane felt as dejected as a wet hen. Head down, tears stinging in her eyes, she made her way to the Hôtel-Dieu de Paris. Everything seemed wrong. The nightmare, the final goodbye, her rumbling stomach, her aching heart. She felt alone and defenseless, a useless Don Quixote.

But she knew she wasn't alone. All Parisians scurried by with eyes cast down, as if it would make them invisible. These days only the Nazis held their heads and their rifles high. Paris had recoiled inside itself, a mere shadow of its former lively persona, a melancholy city where life had become no more than existence.

Queues at the baker's and the butcher's, graffiti slogans against

Jews, children playing soundlessly in the Bois de Boulogne. Silence before the storm, a sandstorm, a rainstorm, or a storm of bullets.

I'll phone Maxipa when I'm at the hospital, she reasoned, giving herself a goal. He'd look forward to having her home with him again. He was holding himself well so far.

"It's a disgrace," he'd complained to her the other day. "Despite their immoral political views, I'd have given the Germans credit for reverence for art and beauty, but these hordes are pure philistines with their parades and German-über-alles songs. It's a good thing the French foresaw this barbarism and brought our art treasures to safety. They'd destroy everything if they get a chance to lay their paws on it. I bet they couldn't distinguish an impressionist from a rococo."

Her grandfather's indignation now made her smile. The things he got worked up about seemed irrelevant compared to the huge challenges France as a nation was facing. But then again, let her grandfather stand up as the Maecenas and Patron of the Arts, if he wanted to. In place of Jean-Jacques who had no time for that position right now.

There was a great deal of commotion outside the Hôtel-Dieu de Paris, a string of khaki German jeeps, next to a stately looking black Mercedes with the swastika flags up front.

A high visitor, Océane thought with disdain. Just not what she needed today. German officers stood on guard next to the Mercedes, while others walked around the army vehicles. She hastened up the marble steps, uncomfortable with this display of power.

There was a waiting crowd of staff and walking patients near the entrance of the cardiac ward. The entrance was blocked by two SS officers, dressed from head to toe in black leather, their rifles demonstratively in front of their chests.

"Please let me through, let me through." Waving her apprentice-doctor's license, she managed to make it to the front of the crowd. "*Ich bin* Doctor Bell. *Ich arbeite hier.*" She showed the license, hoping that addressing them in German would be enough to let her pass.

"*Bitte! Personalausweis!*" one of the armed guards ordered.

Océane looked him in the eye, not knowing from where she got the courage but was surprised at what she saw. His rough demeanor was just a thin veneer. The SS officer was young, too young for his huge cap and oversized coat, with a skittish look in eyes like brown marbles. He had the fleshiness of most of his countrymen, a farm boy look, possibly recruited for a job he'd never aspired to, Paris his first taste of big city-life.

Poor sod, she thought, handing him her ID , which he studied with those innocent eyes, clearly never having seen an American passport.

"*Was machts du hier*?" Again, the gruffness but also the uncertain look.

"I'm a doctor and I work here. Can you tell me what is going on?" He deserved no further explanation why an American was working in a French hospital.

He shook his head but handed her back her passport. Then he gestured to the other SS-officer to open the door for her.

There was a strange calm on the other side, the corridor empty, only the faint hissing of equipment and here and there the beeping of a machine. She was glad to see a nurse come her way.

"What's going on?" she asked again.

The nurse was in a hurry to get to one of the patients whose drip needed a refill but as she sped by, she replied, "Some high-ranking German has been brought in. Possible heart attack."

"Is that what all the fuss is about," Océane muttered under her breath, irritated at the exceptional situation that was created for this man when they were already so busy. "Where did they bring him?"

She decided she'd take a look at him before Professor Rozenkrantz came in. They kept Eleanora away from the German patients as much as they could. An unspoken code.

"Room 8."

She opened the door. Her hand slid automatically to the stethoscope in her pocket, giving it a tight squeeze. The room was deserted but for the patient and his impressive black coat hanging on the coat rack. His tall, black boots, shiny and oversized, stood next to the bed, as if on roll call by themselves. The high-flapped cap with the silver eagle gleamed menacingly at her from the bedside table.

How strange, she thought. *No guards here when the whole hospital is swarming with them.*

She looked away from his attire to the man in the bed. He lay flat on his back, still and sedated, left to fend for himself. Probably in his early forties, he was still dressed in his own white shirt, the black tie loose around his neck. He looked neither formidable nor intimidating.

The first thing that struck Océane was that he was too thin, his Adam's apple protruding like a chicken wing, with the skin hanging in loose flaps on either side. His pallor was obvious, his skin sunken, while the area around his eyes looked puffed. Not the face of a healthy man. Either stress was eating him away or he was drinking too much. She guessed the first. Though he was still almost wrinkle free, there were sharp lines between nose and mouth, which gave him a beaklike appearance. With his eyes closed she could only guess the color. Due to the strawberry blond hair and bluish white skin, it had to be pale blue. The hair was tousled and thinning at the crown. His bony hands, ringless, folded over his stomach as if in prayer.

She stood watching him for a while, uncertain what to do, void of emotion. It flitted through her mind that she could just pull out the drip and that would be it. He was at her mercy. But it was only a passing thought; the doctor in her knew otherwise. As was customary, she grabbed his pulse, but her touch made him jerk. He pulled his arm away from her, and his eyes snapped open. A haunted, fearful look. Only for a second.

"It's okay, Sir," she said calmly, "I'm Doctor Bell and I'm just checking on you. Who has been with you earlier?"

He blinked, taking her in, weighing her authority while she met his gaze. Pale-blue, cold fisheyes. She'd been right. Despite his infirmity he was now clearly struggling to regain control. The haunted look was replaced by a wall of obscurity. There was no longer an entrance into his soul.

"Is *zere* no male doctor?" he asked in clipped French.

"I'm afraid not, Sir. I'm the doctor in charge here."

"*Ich bin* General von Stein, so don't 'sir' me!"

"Sorry Si– uh … General. Before we run some tests, can you tell me why you were admitted to Hôtel-Dieu de Paris?" Océane meanwhile checked what the nurse who'd applied the drip had scribbled on his patient file.

No answer came from the bed, so she lifted her eyes from the clipped board only to meet the light-blue stare. Accustomed to read her patients' expression as well as the symptoms they suffered from, she felt she was not getting very far with this impassive German. She decided to prod him,

"Any congenital defects, swelling of the legs, irregular heartbeat, dizziness?"

"Of course!" he snapped in a cloud of self-righteous indignation. "Do you *zink*, Madame Doctor, that I would be here lying in a French hospital bed because I wanted to take a vacation? Damn it, I only arrived in Paris last week. I lead the *Sicherheitsdienst* on the Avenue Foch. Z*is* is most inconvenient. I order you to give me something so I can resume my duties today."

Seeing his agitation, which was only aggravating his heart condition, Océane calmly sat down on the chair next to his bed. She adopted as much doctorial authority as she could muster to get this man twice her age and in whose power she was, to obey her for the sake of his own health.

"General von Stein, can you please give me a brief overview of your medical record?"

"How dare you!" he cried out, his eyes rolling in their sockets. He struggled wildly to sit upright but as he tugged on the drip in his arm, the hurt pulled him back down. "I am perfectly healthy, or

Herr Hitler would not have promoted me to head of the *Sicherheits-dienst*. Get me out! Now."

It was at the tip of Océane's tongue to reply that Herr Hitler had not consulted her on the matter, but humor didn't seem General von Stein's greatest asset. Somehow, he'd managed not only to worm his way into the SS but had risen to a very high rank disguising his heart disease.

"So you were never diagnosed with heart problems before?"

"Never!"

You're a sore liar, Océane thought. The cursory chest examination she was performing clearly detected the extra sounds that were evidence of heart disease. Remembering Professor Rozenkrantz teaching, she inwardly recited, *Heart murmurs are of two types, systolic murmurs, which are synchronous with the heart beat itself, and diastolic murmurs, occurring between two beats. Systolic murmurs are the most common of the two, are usually loud, and are most easily heard. Diastolic murmurs are usually soft and difficult to hear. This simple screening is efficient in identifying patients with systolic murmurs of mitral valve insufficiency and aortic stenosis, most often the result of previous rheumatic fever in childhood. It also identifies patients with congenital heart lesions such as patent ductus arteriosus, ventricular septal defect, and coarctation of the aorta.*

Of course, it was still possible that General von Stein had harmless systolic murmurs related to the vicissitudes of blood flow and not disease, but his complaints pointed in another direction. She checked his face again; it was impassive but for the slight nervous twitch in the left corner of his mouth. He knew, she was sure, but why had he hidden his condition? Any physician carrying out a military service medical would have noticed the diastolic murmurs. Or did Von Stein join the SS without a medical examination? Had he been that dead-set on joining the SS? Whatever the reason, she had to be firm with him.

But then she hesitated, aware he was seeing her dilemma. Here was a patient who didn't want to hear he was ill, and he was the enemy. What did she care if he dropped dead that very moment?

These were the men that her Jean-Jacques fought against night and day. Also, his coldness and hostility towards her didn't warm her to this patient. It seemed an easy solution but the doctor in her won. As always.

"Um, Herr General, as your *current* physician," she expressly emphasized the word 'current', "I want to X-ray your heart to inspect the chambers. I hear some systolic murmurs that could point to a heart disease." It was as diplomatic as she could make it.

"Nonsense, I feel quite alright again. There is no need for further examinations. Get my sergeant and tell him we're out of here. If I need pills, have them delivered to 84 Avenue Foch. Now out with you!"

"I don't think I can allow that, Herr General. As long as you are here in this hospital, you are a patient and in my care. You run an enormous risk leaving without a proper diagnosis and a treatment. I cannot do that from a distance. I'm not a bogey healer of some sort."

She didn't know from where she drew the courage to contradict a man who could have her shot on the spot should he decide so. The pride in her profession made her bargain with him. She'd already diagnosed the type of man he was. He denied his condition because it made him feel lacking in manliness and strength. He wanted what he didn't have. Well, he'd have something coming if he kept harking to that path.

The General had already raised himself in his bed, careful this time not to tug on the drip. "Get that thing out of me and quit your rubbish," he roared. "You, Madame Doctor, have no authority at all over me. When I declare myself healthy, I *am* healthy."

The solution in the drip had sufficiently revived him for the time being.

She shrugged. "As you wish, General, but as a doctor it is my duty to warn you. I'll ask the nurse to remove the drip and get your sergeant for you. It's indeed unfortunate that you've had a slight ailment in your first week in office. I wish you no further drawbacks but because we have not finished the tests, I will not be able to give you the proper medication. I will, however, prescribe a tranquilizer in case you feel you need it."

If Madame Paul heard me and my diplomacy now, she would rejoice, Océane thought grimly. *Stay friendly, stay calm, don't lower yourself to his level.*

"I don't care one iota what you think or don't think, Doctor. Give whatever pills you want to my sergeant. I'll never want to see you or this hospital again."

"Good day, Herr General."

As she left his room, shaking her head, Océane thought this was by far the weirdest patient she'd ever come across but at least he had temporarily taken her mind off her own troubles.

In one aspect they were in total agreement. She also hoped never to see General von Stein again.

15

INTO THE LION'S DEN

On a gray, water-logged afternoon in mid-November 1940, Océane, dressed in black slacks and a dark-brown mackintosh, a rain hat jammed on her dark curls, found her way down Rue Ferou, looking for number 34. She approached from the other side of the street so she could get a good look at the house without coming too close, not knowing what to expect.

Also on tenterhooks regarding the movement of German officers in the neighborhood, she inched closer, but nobody seemed to be paying attention to her. Studying the house, she found it looked like an ordinary Paris building in cream limestone, three stories, a dark red front door and the shutters closed in front of all the windows.

She sought for ways to go around to the back. There was a fence at the side of the Jardin de Luxembourg. Her walking boots sloshed in the water pools in the alley while she kept her rain hat in place with her hand.

The alley was deserted. Luckily. she came to a door in the side-wall. Spying around her, she confirmed no one had entered the alley, so she knocked firmly on the door. Nothing happened. She tried again. Still no reply.

Finally, she heard a metal bolt being pushed aside and a voice calling, "*Qui est la*? Who's there?"

"I come for D'Artagnan," she called back.

At that the door was opened ajar. A young woman with very slick, shiny black hair and black painted eyebrows peered around the corner. "Who are you?" The tone wasn't nice.

"I'm Océane Bell, Jean-Jacques's girlfriend. I mean Remix."

"Blast!" The door was opened wider and Océane was ushered in hastily. The black-haired girl, who was also dressed completely in black, said in a sharp voice, "Never use names, certainly not full names. Are you out of your mind?"

Océane felt scolded like a small child as she followed the woman through a long, dimly lit corridor. They entered a stuffy room where the shutters were closed. All lights extinguished. It reeked of human sweat and stale cigarette smoke. In the dusk Océane could observe several human forms but she couldn't see whether they were men or women. The black-haired girl blended in with the dark. For a moment Océane was lost, thinking they wouldn't tell her anything, even that this might be a trap.

She almost panicked until in the dark the girl whispered in her ear, "I had to bring you in here to tell you. Not at the door. We don't know where he is. The person who came to tell you he was arrested is not here right now. Four of our cell were arrested the day before yesterday. One woman, three men. We've done what we could to trace them but nada. It stinks, as you may understand, because we don't know how much pressure they can stand before they snap. That's why we're leaving this safe house today. So don't come here anymore." She hesitated for a moment before adding, "I'm sorry. Truly sorry."

"How can I stay in touch with D'Artagnan?" Océane asked, despair tinging her voice in a squeaky manner. "I need to find him."

"He'll be in touch with you when he can." Her voice was slightly kinder now. "That's all I can say. If he has news, he'll know where to find you. The safe houses are opened for us by rich Parisians who support our cause but can't do so openly themselves. I don't know myself where we will be next."

"So I leave empty-handed? No clue?" All energy was drained from her.

"I guess so. Good luck and stay strong." The black-haired girl pushed her back through the corridor and out the door.

Not minding the rain anymore, numb and lost, Océane wandered through the 6th Arrondisement. She didn't know why but instinct kept her there. Was he somewhere here, her beloved? Had he managed to escape? He was so smart and mercurial; he might have outwitted the Nazis again. But no, that was idle thought, of course. He was captured, or he would have let her know he had to go into hiding. She had only one trump card left.

But not looking like a drowned cat, she decided.

"I'm going to dress up and do once more what I did at Radcliffe. Only this time I can't be caught. And I'd better remember Madame Paul's lessons as well."

AFTER TOSSING and turning through the night, Océane dressed in a navy-blue merino dress with white cuffs and white hem and brushed her brown curls until they shone. She even applied some light make-up and wore her best shoes. She had her doctor's coat over her arm to avoid suspicion.

"What's the fuss?"

Her grandfather was sure not to miss a different outfit.

"Nothing, grandpa. I just need to feel a bit better today, so I thought I'd put some effort in the way I look. I hope it helps. You're the one who taught me this trick."

"True," he agreed, smearing the tiniest bit of marmalade on a thin slice of bread. "The worse the situation, the more important to face it in full uniform. Best tonic for a depressed state."

She glanced at his velvet paisley jacket, the crème-colored chemise and brown flannel pants, under which he wore his favorite embroidered babouche. Her grandfather certainly lived true to his word.

"What's up at the hospital these days?" he asked, inspecting the bread on his plate as if it was an unwanted object.

Poor grandpa! So used to a lavish lifestyle.

"Oh, the usual." She made it sound casual. "I'm given too much authority because we're terribly short of staff. It's a good thing I was brought up by doctors and already know the basics, but it's irresponsible, to say the least. I do what I can, though. So far I don't think I've really blundered. I always double-check if I'm uncertain and it's really important."

"I wouldn't remotely mind if you blundered on one on these Huns." An angry look under silver eyebrows stared at her.

"Grandpa!" she cried out in a huff. "You're not implying I should deliberately make a mistake with a German patient?"

He shrugged, lighting one of his cigars, not answering.

INSTEAD OF DIRECTING her grandfather's Citroën to the Hotel-Dieu de Paris, Océane drove in the early morning towards the Avenue Foch in the 16th Arrondissement, lined with posh 19th Century mansions and rows of sky-high chestnut trees, famously known as the widest avenue in Paris. How cynical, she thought, that the Nazis had set up their headquarters in a street named after the French hero of the Great War, General Ferdinand Foch. Whether they'd done that on purpose, she didn't know.

As she parked the car in front of the ornate building now draped in a huge SS flag, a chill ran through her. No going back anymore. What had to be done, had to be done. Smoothing her best dress and taking out her handbag, she gingerly went towards the impressive front door guarded on either side by grim-looking SS officers.

Grabbing the bull by the horns, she said with as much authority as she could muster, "I'm Doctor Bell from the Hôtel-Dieu de Paris. General von Stein was my patient there. Is he in?"

"What do you need him for?" a tall, mustached Nazi with bulging eyes and rosacea cheeks asked in broken French.

"I've come to give him the results of the last tests and the medicine he needs to take."

The guard looked at her not so much with suspicion but with incredulity. "Show me your ID first, Madame. I haven't been informed of your visit."

"Aha," she said, handing him both her ID and her doctor's license, "that may be because the General was not expecting the results until next week. But his condition is ..." She hesitated, looking up at the officer with a glint of charm. "... favorable, so I think he will be happy to hear that from me."

From where the lies came, she didn't know. She accepted them gratefully. It just didn't seem right to give these guards the idea their superintendent was suffering from a serious ailment.

"So, pray tell me, is the General in?"

"No, Madame, he is not."

"Oh, that's a damn pity. He'd be delighted, I'm sure." A shadow fell over her face as if she was a skilled actress. She stood for a moment hopping from one stylish shoe to the other. Then she cocked her head. "I really have very little time; doctors are so busy at the hospital, as I'm sure you can imagine. Could I just leave it with a note on his desk and ask him to call the hospital, should he have further questions?"

She retrieved the prepared letter with the hospital stamp and the bottle of pills from her bag, holding both in the air. The guards looked at each other, rather puzzled. It was clear that such a strange request had not been put before them, certainly not so early in the morning.

Then the one who had addressed her, and apparently was higher in rank, shrugged. "Alright then, Madame Docteur. But it is absolutely forbidden to go into the building on your own and we must remain here on guard. You'll have to wait in the vestibule until another officer can take you to Herr General von Stein's office."

"No problem," she announced with a sunny smile, slipping into the marble vestibule.

The smile soon died on her lips. It was cool and pleasant in the beautifully decorated hall. That wasn't it. Something was very wrong with this building, though it was hard to say from where it came. German officers walked by her, some in haste, some leisurely. Through the open door she could peek into a large office, where female typists sat at desks rattling away on their machines. On the surface it had the appearance of an ordinary office but there was an acute smell of fear in the air that gripped her by the throat.

JJ, she thought in a panic, was he being held somewhere in this building? What were they doing to him? Were they hurting him? The idea made her sink down on one of the wooden benches that had been placed along one wall, clasping her handbag in her lap, suddenly overwhelmed by terror. Avenue Foch 84 was without doubt a place where horrible things happened, she could feel it prickling under her skin. No matter that the Germans made it appear like a business-like, ordinary day. They were good at that. At pretense. She'd have to up her game, but it was almost impossible in the face of her deadly fear.

She felt her courage slip from her like water through a sieve and bowed her head.

I'm not like you, JJ, a tiny voice whispered in her head. *I don't have the spirit to stand up to these fascists. I'm just an American girl, a doctor-trainee ... a coward.*

She heard heavy footstep approach, which stopped in front of her. Looking up, another young blond officer in black saluted her.

"Madame Docteur, follow me!"

She had no choice than to do as she was bid but her fear aggravated. What if she would never be able to leave this building as a free person again? There was so much more at stake than a failed college exam.

The officer's heavy boots sounded like dull thuds on the marble tiles as she followed him through the vestibule and into a large, oval office that overlooked a well-tended garden. Here the floor was made of parquet and sounded more muffled under the soldier's soles.

He turned to face her. "I understand from the guards that you want to leave a message for Herr General?" He spoke in that clipped French with strong German accent that Océane was now accustomed to but still struck her as peculiar.

"Yes, Herr Commandant. Here," and she opened her bag and took out the bottle of Digoxin and the letter. "This is what the General can take in case he suffers trouble with his heart again. Would you mind if I write him a note in case he has any questions? And where he can reach me?"

"No, of course not, Madam. Go ahead, here's a pen and paper. I'll wait outside the door."

This was exactly what she had hoped for. As soon as the officer had left the room she raced around the large walnut desk and shuffled through the stack of papers that were neatly piled up on one side to see if there was any mention of JJ or Remix. There was not.

While she scribbled a note, she tentatively opened the top drawer and glanced in there. Nothing on prisoners or on Resisters. She could not help herself and turned to the large filing cabinet that filled the entire wall. With German *grundlichkeit* the tabs were all in alphabetical order, so she cautiously opened the one that read PA to RU. Remix or Riveau should be in there. Her fingers slipped through the files as she held her breath. She was close now.

Behind her a gruff voice barked, "What are you doing there?"

Frozen in her tracks, her hands still in the drawer, her breath stopped. This was it. This was the end. She would *not* leave the building.

16

THE POINT OF NO RETURN

Océane was overjoyed to see Eleonora had arrived in the staff room. The soon-to-be mother was patting her growing tummy in a contented way. Though the women had become good friends over the months, working long hours side-by-side, Océane never considered her mentor an equal. They also weren't touchy-feely, always kept a friendly and respectful distance.

"Good thing you're here! I need to let off some steam." Océane poured herself a cup of coffee from the percolator and sat down at the Formica table under the bright light.

"What's up?"

"High ranking SS-er. In a bad shape but not willing to admit." She explained the whole situation with Von Stein. "I honestly don't think you'd have had a better shot with him, and he'd probably be even nastier to you."

"I'm proud of you, Océane," her mentor said. "We may not like our patients, but their race or nationality is of no concern to us. We treat anyone, notwithstanding. A lesson your parents also learned in the Great War. They would be proud of you."

"But that's the whole point," Océane protested, ignoring her reference to her parents, "I didn't treat him. He refused treatment."

"You offered it and that's what counts. You can't force a horse to drink what it doesn't want to drink. Now it's up to him to do something with the knowledge you gave him. From what you describe, we might well see him back soon."

"I hope not and frankly I don't care." Changing the subject, she asked, "So how are you? And how's the baby doing?"

Her mentor sighed. Océane saw the dark circles under her eyes.

"It's not a good time to be pregnant. And now I've lost my job."

"Oh no!" Océane cried out. "I thought you'd become a Christian being married to Doctor Ferron?"

"On paper, yes, but that's not the way the Germans see it. They're hunting down all people with Jewish blood. Even in Vichy France they've now introduced the *statut des Juifs*. All Jews in the whole of France must register with the authorities. And from October 3rd they've banned us from professions in law, university, medicine and public service."

Océane struggled hard with this news. The war suddenly became very real. There was no escape from it anymore. "What will you do? Will you go abroad?"

"No." It sounded adamant. "Yves wants me to go south. But I tell him it's no use. I'm not fleeing anymore. I worry for the sake of my child. Not so much for myself." Her mentor looked terribly dejected as she packed her last hospital belongings and stacked them in her medical bag. In a soft voice, thick of tears, she added, "I had so hoped to have escaped the hate after I left Germany in 1934. But it's right back at my doorstep."

"I'm so sorry," was all Océane could offer. She realized how meagre it was. "Maybe go south anyway. Maybe go first and Doctor Ferron can follow. Paris is a German infested city now."

"Maybe."

Eleanora looked so miserable that Océane put a hand on her shoulder, adding bitterly, "I've just had to let Jean-Jacques go. Now I'm even more afraid because he's half Jewish also. I promised to move back in with my grandfather. We said goodbye this morning and I have no idea when I'll see him again. And now I have to say goodbye to you, too. What will I do without you, Eleonora? I'm only a student, not a doctor."

"Oh, dear girl," Eleonora's voice was full of compassion, "how hard on you. Yves will support you. Don't worry and we'll stay in touch, if only via him."

They did kiss each other goodbye at that. Desperation in both of them.

WHEN OCÉANE LEFT the Hôtel-Dieu de Paris that evening, she sensed that summer was gone, and the grim Fall had begun. Perhaps the grimmest in the history of humanity. The war had come full circle for France. She shivered in her thin summer coat. Her talk with Eleonora had unnerved her more than she dared to admit.

It had been an incredibly tough day. The war was finally closing in on her, too. She'd kept it out of her periphery for as long as possible but here it was all around her. Hunger lurked for millions of Parisians while the Germans behaved more and more ornery and cocky. She passed a restaurant, one she'd been in with Jean-Jacques in the spring, but there wasn't a Parisian in sight now. The khaki and black uniforms were everywhere, loud, singing and laughing, champagne and rich food in abundance while French children went to bed with rumbling stomachs.

She suddenly saw her city through Jean-Jacques's eyes, through Eleonora's eyes. She, a privileged American, still fed at the hospital, still earning an income while all around her the craters of suppression became visible. Not actual craters, as no bomb had fallen, but the craters in the French soul.

She could see it now.

Young French women whoring to stay alive, Jews being extricated, the French spirit broken in the bowed heads and skittish looks, civil servants actively licking the German boots. More and more of those. While the enemy cared nothing about any of them and partied on.

Something snapped in Océane. The war *was* real. The net closed slowly but certainly around them all. *Accès interdit aux Juifs* was everywhere, and the French people condoned it. Closed their eyes to it. She had, too. It all felt so overwhelming, so impossible to stop the hate train set in motion by the German propaganda machine. They were all turned into tiny mechanisms, where right and wrong had become too difficult a question to answer.

The minute minority of brave men and women who secretly took up arms, sabotaging the Nazis where they could, risking being killed on the spot or tortured until they betrayed their comrades, people like her Jean-Jacques, they stood upright, looked the enemy in the eye. But the price they paid for their courage was exorbitant.

The first French Resistance fighter who'd died at the hand of the Germans was a nineteen-year-old boy, Pierre Roche. On 7 September he'd been caught cutting the phone lines between Royan and La Rochelle. The military governor of France, General Otto von Stülpnagel, had announced that no mercy would be granted to those engaging in sabotage and all saboteurs would be shot. But the brave ones hadn't listened. Louis Lallier, a farmer, shot for sabotage on 11 September in Epinal, Marcel Rossier, a mechanic, shot in Rennes on 12 September. And more and more followed.

It was a matter of time before Jean-Jacques Riveau, alias Remix, would be among them.

Océane shivered again. "Don't think that," she reprimanded herself. "He has promised to come home to me, hasn't he?"

DAYS TURNED into weeks without a sign of life from Jean-Jacques. Océane began to give up hope. Pale and thin, she dragged herself to the hospital every day with less and less enthusiasm. Everything was hard. Sleeping, getting out of bed, eating, even concentrating on her patients. Her world had become small and lusterless. Eleanora gone, Jean-Jacques gone, Marie and Gaël scared and skittish, her grandfather's violin silent.

She was downing a cup of surrogate coffee on a rainy morning in early November when Gaël called her.

"Mademoiselle, there's somebody at the backdoor."

As fast as her feet could carry her, Océane sped through the chilly hall. Could it be? No, if it was JJ, he would've come in. Her feet slowed; her shoulders slumped. She suddenly didn't want to go on anymore. It could only be a bad message. Gaël was following close on her heels, forcing her forwards. She went through the scullery to the rough wooden door that was ajar, the exit the staff used to get to the alley at the back of the house. She pushed it open to come face to face with an unknown man who had a dripping wet Trilby deep over his eyes, a long, equally wet overcoat hiding his figure.

"Bonjour, Mademoiselle, I have a message from Remix." His accent was more Spanish than French.

"Yes?" Her eyes went wide open. There was hope! But when he didn't hand her a letter and he didn't move, despair set in.

"I'm afraid Remix has been arrested by the SS."

There it was.

"Nooooo!" she howled, her knees becoming as jelly and her vision blurring. She had to steady herself with a hand against the doorpost.

Alarmed by the wounded cry, Gaël came hurrying towards them, drying her hands on her apron. She gave the stranger a foul look. "What is going on here? Who are you?"

"I'm D'Artagnan, Madame. I'm sorry for the message. Here." He fetched a note from his wet pocket, the blue ink already watermarked. "It's an address in the 6th Arrondissement. Go there incognito. Make sure nobody sees you. Go tomorrow, not today. They'll be watching closely today. Many have been arrested. I can't guarantee but by tomorrow they might know where the

Gestapo brought the prisoners. That's all I can offer right now. I'm sorry."

Océane stood rigid with anxiety. All the air was sucked out of her lungs, and she was swaying on her legs. Gaël gripped her firmly by the elbow while D'Artagnan made a slight nod and disappeared down the alley. Her last connection to Jean-Jacques.

"D'Artagnan, D'Artagnan," she kept repeating, as if the name was the string to which her beloved was attached. As a sleepwalker she let herself be led back into the house. Gaël made her sit on a chair while she kept repeating the stranger's name, his code name, no doubt.

A glass of cognac was brought to her lips, and she swallowed obediently but soon sputtered out the golden liquid in a fit of coughing. Tears streamed down her cheeks while Gaël gently tapped her back. Marie hurried in with a cold cloth to wipe Océane's clammy forehead.

All these actions seemed to take place in a parallel world; it did not sink in but wormed itself into her body. JJ was no longer fighting, he was arrested. He was gone. He would not return to her. After the initial shock that benumbed and froze her, she now began to shiver all over. Gaël tried to get hot tea into her instead of the cognac, but she couldn't swallow.

"Marie, go and fetch the Baron," Gaël ordered the spindly maid who stood wringing her hands in the corner. To Océane she said, "Let me take you to the living room. You have to lie down for a moment."

"I need to go to the hospital. My shift starts in half an hour." Her voice sounded like an automaton.

"You're not going there today. I'll phone the Hôtel-Dieu de Paris to tell them you are indisposed."

She helped Océane up and they made their way to the living room with Océane leaning on the housekeeper. When she was installed on the sofa with a blanket over her, she doubted this decision when she heard Gaël speak on the phone. Working might be best. She couldn't face a day here, her mind going crazy about JJ's fate. Here the full horror of his imprisonment would be with her all day, the minutes creeping forward until she could go to the address D'Artagnan had given her.

At that moment the Baron, ashen under his always tanned skin, stormed in. "What horrible gargoyles they are! How dare they! Oh, my darling, what a blow this is but I'm here and we're going to hotfoot this immediately! What can I do? Here, let me first assist you. Gaël, quickly make some broth, the girl needs some nourishment in her, take anything you have but be fast."

"Maxipa, please don't fuss," she pleaded but she secretly had to admit that it was exactly his fussing and his care that lifted her spirit.

His extravagant manner of taking care of her made her almost smile despite herself. He was such a character, even the arrest of her boyfriend made him want to move heaven and earth so that she would not suffer, but he did it in such a comical, over the top way that it actually worked.

"Let me nit-pick when I choose so, dear girl. As soon as you're back on your feet, we have to plot an idea how to find out Riveau's whereabouts. I'll start with phoning the Senator, of course. Jean-Jacques' grandfather has to throw his weight behind this as well. It's outrageous. The Riveaus may not be as old a family as De Saint-Aubins but they have vouchsafed *la République Française* for generations as loyal, hardworking citizens. *Scandaleux!*"

"Grandpa, please!" She was smiling now but there was no stopping him.

"It's an outrage that one of our own patriots would be held in custody by a pack of these Krauts. Both the Senator's weight and mine, my dear, must certainly be enough to bring them to their knees and free the poor boy."

As he continued to rave and rant, Gaël hastened in with the quickly prepared soup. Taking the bowl from her, he set out to spoon-feed her the hot liquid himself.

Océane slowly came to her senses and understood how upset her grandfather was. All the commotion he was making - although meant to calm her - was a demonstration of his love for her and how much he cared for Jean-Jacques as well. It was exactly what she needed to regain her strength. And perhaps there was some truth in his words? The Baron de Saint-Aubin was well acquainted with French ministers and other people in high places. It remained to be seen if these people still had any influence on the German rulers, though.

She hoisted herself up, also determined to take action instead of waiting passively.

"How are you going to do that, Grandpa? The Germans may never find out that you or your friends know JJ. And they may never find out the connection with me."

"*Biensur*! I understand that, *ma petite*. I'll ask in a circumspect way. Leave that to me. Your grandfather has been among diplomats all his life and although I've never had ambition for a political position myself, I've seen how it's done and I'm a good copycat. No trace will lead to you."

He pulled a coy face before gazing at her with an impassive yet friendly expression. It was his best attempt at toning down his expressive face to look like the diplomat.

"Now, I'll go out as fast as my two nimble feet can carry me. You, however, *ma grande-fille*, have to promise me that you stay indoors today and rest. Can you do that for me? I know it will be very hard and your head will be wondering and your heart aching but the very best you can do right now is stay calm and wait until I'm back. Hopefully with some news!"

"But I thought you were going to phone your friends, Maxipa?"

"On second thought I've decided to drive over to Senator Riveau. I've got some petrol left and it seems best that Bertrand and I speak face to face. You never know these days who's listening in on phone lines."

"Please be careful. They might already keep an eye on JJ's family, and I hope to God they don't know about me or, you know … that they've, uh … tortured him and he's given them my name."

Her grandfather looked at her in dismay. "First of all, JJ would never do that and secondly, he has no reason. You're not a Resistance fighter. They want *their* names, not of girlfriends. But enough talk. I'll be back as soon as possible."

After her grandfather had left the house, Océane stared at the blotched slip of paper D'Artagnan had given her. It was an address on the Rue Ferou, close to Le Jardin du Luxembourg. She wondered who lived there and what the connection was to Jean-Jacques. Had he stayed there, eaten meals, discussed tactics, slept in a room? Were these friends or just people he trusted?

Unable to stay put any longer, she rang the bell for Gaël. "Please, bring me my coat and bag. I'm going to the hospital. I can't sit here another minute, twiddling my thumbs."

"But, mademoiselle! You promised the Baron to rest. Please stay home, at least until he returns."

"Let him phone the hospital if he has news and I'll come back. But not until then."

The housekeeper's light-blue eyes pleaded with her, but Océane had made up her mind. From her parents she had learned to get on with things. When life was tough - just like after Arthur's accident - they had not sat on the couch and wept. They had done all that was in their might to get him the best medical care, next to continuing to run their clinic. She could still hear her father's words ring in her ears.

"Even in the sight of the greatest advisory, you go on, my daughter. That's how your mother and I got through the war. No, let me correct myself, that's how your mother got *me* through the war after I was shot down and paralyzed. Fighting is the best medicine, always and everywhere. Never give up and you'll never give up on hope."

"Well, this is *my* paralysis, Dad, JJ being arrested by the Gestapo. I don't know if I'll be as brave as you and Mom were under *your* German occupation, but I'll do my best. All I do know is that I can relieve some suffering at the hospital today, so let's start there."

SURPRISINGLY, she found out she could focus on her work and push the thought of JJ and what he was facing to the back of her mind. A young German soldier was brought in with chest pains. He looked so scared and forlorn that for a moment the war was forgotten, and she became the impartial doctor again.

"What's your name, Sergeant?"

"Hans Arenberg, *Madame Docteur.*"

"Right, Sergeant. What exactly are you feeling in your chest?"

He gazed at her with dove-gray eyes, big with fright, his jaws clenched, his hands tightened into fists. His whole body was rigid as if the uniform he was in was a cocoon that closed around him too tightly, like a shrine.

This is no Nazi, flitted through Océane's mind, *this is a boy who wants to go home to his Heimat.*

"I can't breathe, doctor. Please help me."

Her now experienced eye when it came to heart and respiratory problems told her there was nothing physically wrong with this patient. He had a panic attack. She wanted to put her hand on his stomach, but he shot away from her, trying to leave the bed. He even cried out, a deep, long-drawn moan that made Océane startle.

"Heavens, what's happened to you?"

"Nothing!" he shrieked. "Please let me go. I promise I will man up."

"What are you talking about? Pray, tell me."

But he continued to scuttle out of the bed, away from her. This puzzled Océane. German patients could be rude, uncooperative, but most were just patients glad to accept treatment. Plenty of French patients had panic attacks but not the oppressors. Something else was going on here.

"I only wanted to instruct you how to deepen your breath," she said as calm as possible. "Don't be afraid. There's nothing wrong with you. We just need to calm you before we have a little chat."

"Nothing's been going on." The wild fear in his eyes told her otherwise.

"Look," she said, "I'm going to sit on this chair here. I won't touch you. I promise."

He eyed her suspiciously but clearly decided she was not going to harm him right there and then.

"So where are you from, Sergeant?"

The answer came more promptly than she'd expected. "From near Hanover, Madame. I am the son of a Junker; we own an estate south of Hanover. I'm the middle son and my father wanted me to go into the army. He said General von Stein would ... would look after me because ... because he's from the same region."

"Von Stein?" Océane tried to hide the surprise in her voice.

"Yes, Ma'am, General von Stein."

The emphasis was on 'general'. There was reverence but also something else in the young soldier's voice. Océane tried to read his expression but could not. He looked away, as if ashamed of something. Something had happened with Von Stein who'd lain in that very bed a couple of weeks earlier. She didn't want to probe but the dots slowly connected. Von Stein was a dangerous man, not just for the French but also for his own soldiers.

"What happened?" she asked it as warmly as she could, but he kept his head turned away. His chest began heaving fast again. "Breathe," she ordered, "to your tummy! Tell me about your family."

She pushed the right button. His breath calmed and words flowed out of him as if of their own accord. "We live on a farm. We have cows, sheep, horses, ducks, you name it. Plenty of animals. I tended to them all. It was a simple life, but it was enough for me, ploughing the fields, horse riding, being out of doors all day. I'm ... I'm not good in cities."

"Then why did you leave?"

"It wasn't me. It was my father's wish. I've always been on the delicate side despite all the physical work. My father wanted me to toughen up, so that's why he sent me to the Hitler Jugend. From one came the other." His voice became shallow again.

"Homesick," Océane murmured.

"I hate the war," he said with more vehemence, revealing the farm-life tenacity that lurked under his fear. "I obeyed my father because he's a good man. He really believes that he made the right choice for me but for me it's different. I don't believe in this war. I believe people are best off in their own countries." He hesitated, flitting gray eyes in her direction. It was dangerous to say what he'd just said, and the walls had ears. There was obstinacy there as well. An interesting mix. "I think General von Stein guesses my wavering dedication and that's made him ... you know ..."

The fear was back, stifling him. Von Stein had clearly manhandled him in some way or other.

"... do what?"

"I can't tell. He'd shoot me on the spot."

"That bad, huh?"

He nodded.

"I understand you don't like being in France," she assured him, "but there is little you can do about it. Maybe listening to your father's advice is your best option. Become as strong as an ox for when you return."

He seemed to ponder this for a moment but then shook his pale head. "I don't think that will happen, Madame Docteur. The Germans are here to stay. All of Europe is now the Third Reich and going home is not in the cards. But you are right. I will have to stick it out. I just hope I'll be transferred to another place, you know, away from the General."

"Is that likely?"

He looked skeptical. "I don't know. I've only been here since last month after finishing my training at the SS Junker Schule in Braunschweig."

"I could write a note as your doctor to say you're incapacitated to work at the SS Headquarters due to heart problems. The General himself was here for heart troubles. He might condone it."

"You think so?"

The hopefulness in the young man's voice made Océane want to fight for him. If she couldn't fight for Jean-Jacques, maybe she could fight for this Hans Arenberg, who in no way resembled his compatriots terrorizing Paris and the rest of France.

"I'll write that note. You can stay the night for observation but there's nothing wrong with your heart. The dizziness and tightness in the chest are caused by your shallow breathing. It disturbs the amount of oxygen and carbon dioxide in your lungs. Remember to breathe deeper, or even into a paper bag. Good day, Sergeant Arenberg. I'll check in later."

"I can't thank you enough, Madame Docteur, you're by far the kindest person I've so far met in France."

"And you helped me forget my own troubles for a while," she mumbled as she left the room.

IT WAS A SHORT-LIVED RELIEF. As soon as she left the hospital the familiar pang of anxiety was back, and she rushed home, hoping against hope that her grandfather had been able to pry some information out of his compadres.

"And?" she cried out to the newspaper he was holding in front of his face.

Slowly the paper was lowered, and her grandfather shook his head, clearly distressed.

"Nothing, my dear. Nobody is willing to say anything, but I found out the Gestapo brings Resistance fighters to La Santé, Cherche-Midi or Fresnes Prison, so there are several locations where he could be. It's rumored that they're often transported to Germany immediately to work as prisoners-of-war. I'm so sorry, my dear. I wish I'd been able to bring you a better message. All we can do is wait."

"No!" Océane stamped her foot in red-hot anger. "I *will* find out where JJ is. I need to know, or I won't be able to sleep."

"But what can you do?"

"That man D'Artagnan gave me an address in the Rue Ferou in

the 6th Arrondissement. I go there tomorrow morning. If that doesn't yield any results, I'll visit the SS Headquarters myself."

"No, you won't! Have you gone mad?"

She'd never heard her grandfather speak so bluntly to her before. She was temporarily taken aback.

"I've treated the General who's in charge for heart problems in the hospital. I'll lie that I've come to bring him his prescribed medication. That is, if I run into him, which I hope not."

"It will quite likely prove to be a pointless exercise, but I must say, my child, you sound very much like your mother right now. So full of ardor and fearlessness. I quite admire you for your plan but it's a firm no. I forbid it."

"You can't forbid me to do what I have to do, Maxipa." It was said in a soft tone, but the meaning of her words was crystal clear.

Von Spiegler had put her with her back to the wall. Time to show her true colors. No more wavering, no more weariness, no way out. But could she pull it off?

17

A NEW CAREER

Without even having to look over her shoulder she knew General von Stein had come into the room and had caught her red-handed rummaging through his files. *Death sentence, torture, labor camp in Germany.* All the options clicked through her mind as metal bullets. She stood still as a corpse. Whatever would come down on her, she was now in the same situation as the man she'd tried to save.

His after-shave heady and too flowery for a man wafted into her nostrils. A sickening ball sank into her stomach. She couldn't gag. Not now.

"Turn around."

It was an order but not as infuriated or threatening as she'd expected. It was still an order. She did as she was told, her arms hanging limply alongside her body, head bowed, trying hard to stop the trembling of her hands. The smart dress and shoes would not help her now.

"What are you doing?" He repeated his question, but she couldn't answer.

Didn't dare to look at him, felt like her whole life was just a crumpled piece of paper in his hand. Without a warning from her body, she burst out in tears, first softly but soon all the tension and all the fear erupted from her slight frame, taking it over. Her shoulders shook and long sobs escaped her mouth. It was impossible to answer him now, though she knew she must. He was waiting for an explanation when there was none. None that would satisfy him.

To her surprise he walked around his desk and sat down. He ignored her and her crying, pulled a stack of papers towards him and started reading. Not her note. He didn't glance at the brown bottle with pills either. He just acted as if she wasn't there at all.

"I'm sorry," she finally managed to bring out, "I couldn't help myself."

"Sit!" Through her tears she saw he pointed to the chair on the other side of his desk. "Go!" Von Stein ordered to the commandant who knocked on the door and came in. "Wait. Bring us two strong coffees. No phone calls or interruptions."

Oh no, what's going to happen now, Océane thought desperately.

Von Stein picked up her scribbled note and inspected the pills. When the coffee arrived on a tray, he poured her a cup himself. It was real coffee. The smell made her both ravenous and sick.

"Cream, sugar?"

"Just black, please."

She ventured to look at him, wondering what this was all about, whether this was a set up for the torture that would for sure soon begin, but he seemed to be concentrating on stirring his coffee. With chattering teeth, she put the cup to her mouth and tried to drink without spilling the contents on her.

As if she'd not just been snooping around in the Sicherheitsdienst secret documents, he asked, "So why do you recommend these pills, Madame? I told you I was perfectly healthy."

Returning with all her might to her position as medic, she stammered, "That's what I wrote on the note, Herr General; you don't have to use Digoxin, but I brought the pills just in case you feel unwell again. They are perfectly harmless, made from the foxglove plant, Digitalis Iatana."

She knew they could be quite high risk, especially when the

dose was not accurate, but there was no way she could tell him that. It would undermine her.

"Aha, I see," he said in a strange, syrupy voice, "and why do you care to bring them to me when I told you in no uncertain words that I wouldn't take medication. It strikes me as rather strange that you would care so much for your ex-patients, Madame, that you go all the way, distributing unwanted pills around Paris."

He tapped his thin, white fingers together and stared at her with ice-cold, blue eyes. It then dawned on her that he was playing a game with her, a cruel game and that she very likely would be the one who got the short stick. Still, she clung to the thin thread of hope he'd not bring up her nosing around and would continue to enjoy provoking her with this not-being-ill game.

"Because I care about my patients, Herr General, and although you don't want to believe it, it would be better for you to carry these pills with you, just in case."

He put his cup carefully back on the saucer, seemingly contemplating this. "You know, Madame Bell, I would almost be humored into believing your true sentiment if it hadn't come to my attention that you are looking for someone." The light-blue eyes fixed on her as orbs of burning suns as she sat as transfixed in her chair.

He knew, of course, he knew!

Nothing would escape this man's attention. He was a maven when it came to finding out about French opposition to the Germans. Her cheeks reddened and she clasped the handles of her handbag tighter between her fingers. He was waiting, studying every move in her face, the cold eyes never leaving her. She swallowed hard. Straightened her back. She was not going to give it to him. Whatever the price. Everything she could say would betray her real reason for being there. She had to stick with the medical story. Find a plausible reason to be going through his files only if he asked.

Think straight, Océane, use your brains!

Von Stein knew everything, of that she was sure, but she wouldn't hand it to him on a platter. Not if she could help it. Then a strange calm settled on her. Maybe it was bluff. In no way could Von Stein connect her to JJ. Or had he talked? Her mind went in circles, but she refused to show her confusion in words.

I'm not going to give an explanation unless he asks me straight out.

In the end, the German rose to his feet and although he was not of an impressive length, towered over her. "Well, aren't you?"

"Am I what, Herr General?"

"Looking for someone?"

"No, I'm not, Herr General." The lie was easier than she'd thought.

"Aha!" His voice went down a timbre. He took to pacing the room, his leather boots creaking as he marched over the expensive woolen carpet. "I see. The love must run deep."

"I don't know what you are talking about, Herr General." She also rose from her chair, feeling suddenly that she'd suffocate in that room if she stayed another second. In a vain hope for escape, she spied towards the door, ready to run.

Von Stein had no plan of letting her go. "You know, I could jail you for snooping around in my office, don't you?" He halted in front of her, and she winced.

"What for, Sir? I mean. Herr General."

"Stop playing games with me, Miss." It was the closest he came to raising his voice. "I have a proposition to make to you." A small grin spread over his white face, showing a row of rather yellow teeth.

"What proposition?"

"Well, you and I are the only ones in Paris who know this ticker isn't as it should be." He pointed to his chest. She startled, surprised at his candid declaration. "That gives me the advantage because I don't want anyone else to know. So ..." He paused, for the first time dropping his acting and coming as close to being sincere as he could. "... what if I hired you as my personal physician? Of course, we're not going to tell people why I need a young female physician but given my rank and position I can have everything I want. In exchange, you stack your bags with the right equipment and pills from your hospital. Under the disguise of acting as my personal assistant, you keep an eye on my health. In return, you're close to the fire you so want to be close to."

He raised his light eyebrows, the sinister eyes focusing hard on her. Océane gasped. Her head spun. It was too much. She couldn't take in what he was actually proposing.

"But could I still work at the hospital, you know, and live ... um ... at home?"

"To the first question, no. To the second, for the time being, you can stay with the Baron Maximilian De Saint-Aubin."

"You know my grandfather?" She fell from one bewilderment into the other. Biting her tongue. No names. Had the black-haired girl not told her? But he knew already. Tears began to sting again.

"I know what I need to know." The answer was cryptic. "Now go and do as you're told, and report here tomorrow at nine. Good day, Madame Docteur."

He turned away from her and stiffly marched around the large desk. Sitting down, he opened the file in front of him.

Océane kept standing on the carpet, not understanding if she was free or not, should say something or not, protest or not.

"Good day, Herr General."

As if already under his complete influence, she moved with stiff steps to the door where the guard stood waiting to escort her to the exit.

As she stepped outside the iron gates of 84 Avenue Foch, Océane felt she was walking in some strange parallel universe where she no longer knew who she was. She had been offered a job by the most despicable man in Paris, well, not offered, been forced to take it. He was probably only offering it to her because he wanted to play with her and her fear for JJ. Of course, she had no choice, she had to go to the hospital and hand in her notice.

Then there was this other side, Von Stein's realization that he *had* a heart condition that needed monitoring. But she was no cardiac specialist, she was a second-year medical student, so why her? It was all terribly confusing, and her strongest instinct was to run and hide. Not to report the next morning.

But what if he would be willing to give her information on JJ, when she did her best to help him with his heart? Would he want to help *her*? It seemed unlikely. No matter how she looked at it, there were parts in his story and his strange request that didn't fit. This man was the biggest enigma she'd ever met but her gut feeling also told her he was also the evilest and most relentless one.

"One thing is certain," she told herself as she slowly made her way to the car, "he can order his own supplies from the hospital. I'm not going to take scarce supplies away from my colleagues. I don't want to have that on my conscience."

Océane's last working day at the Hôtel-Dieu de Paris was a sad one, one filled with lies and uncertainties and so much fear that it rattled the very bones in her body.

18

MADAME DOCTEUR

On opening her eyes the next morning, Océane felt a heavy load weighing on her chest. For the first time ever, she was depressed. Her eyelids felt like lead and her body was limp and lifeless. All liveliness and hope had seeped out of her in the night, and she was certain she'd done the stupidest thing in her entire life the moment she'd stepped inside 84 Avenue Foch.

It was one thing to forge an exam result, it was quite another to infiltrate the Sicherheits office and believe one could come out unscathed. How she could have been so naïve and so blind. And now it was of the greatest importance to hide this truth from her grandfather. If he knew, he'd insist she left for Nice and from there to the States directly. That way she would leave JJ for good. She couldn't do that. She had to know where he was.

The only sliver of hope she had was that she could convince Von Stein to let JJ go, that by working hard and giving him what he wanted, she would soften his defenses. It was idle hope, but it was all she had. Maybe she should return to her own flat, so she could come and go without questions from her grandfather or Gaël. But that would upset him as well.

Evading her grandfather that morning proved impossible. As she tried to sneak out the door, even foregoing a much-needed breakfast, she heard him call from the front parlor,

"Océane, my dear, is that you? Can you come in for a minute? I need to ask your advice on something."

Hoping it was a quick question she could answer without giving away her motive to leave the house so early, she peeked around the door. "What is it, Maxipa?"

"Do come in for a moment and close that door behind you. There's an awful draught this morning and Gaël finds it impossible to feed the fire with enough wood. Everything is rationed now and I can't even heat my own house anymore."

"Is that what you wanted to talk about, Maxipa, because I'm really in a hurry. An emergency at the hospital." The lie came far too easy.

"No, no!" He shook his silver head.

Only then did she see the concerned look on his face. Perching on the edge of the Louis Quinze settee, she asked, "Is something wrong with you, gramps? You look awfully pale. Do you want me to take your temperature?"

Again he shook his head. "Nothing wrong with me. It's you I'm worried about."

She shifted uneasily on her seat. For sure, he couldn't suspect anything. But if Océane had learned one thing from being around her grandfather, it was not to underestimate him. He was shrewd and had a wide network of friends and acquaintances, quite possibly he was one of Paris best informed citizens.

"We need to talk." It was all he could wedge in before Gaël knocked on the door announcing breakfast. With an irritated gesture, he added, "Yes, by all means, bring us that God-awful surrogate coffee! We haven't had quite enough of it."

This wasn't her pleasant, always polite grandfather who treated the staff as family.

She saw the shock on Gaël's face and hastened to add in, "It's okay, Gaël, I'll have mine standing as I have to leave in a minute."

"Of course, Sir, Mademoiselle." The housekeeper quickly placed the tray on the table and hastened out as fast as her legs could carry her.

"What's wrong, Maxipa?" Maybe using his favorite name would put him in a better mood. She waited, a whirl of thoughts in her head until he came clear.

"What were you thinking, going to 84 Avenue Foch, Océane? The most dangerous place in Paris. Are you out of your mind?"

She shot him a glance through her eyelashes and saw her grandfather angry for the first time in her life. Ashamed and caught out, she shrunk inside herself like a tight ball. A familiar feeling from when her father confronted her with her exam forgery. But this was much more severe, human lives were at stake.

"Who told you?" It was barely audible.

"Does that matter? Answer the question, young lady!"

"You know what I was doing there, Grandpa, trying to find out about JJ."

"Silly, silly girl! I assume you're in grave danger now, aren't you?"

She nodded, staring at her coffee that was getting cold. Her stomach couldn't take in anything anyway.

"Tell me what happened and then I will see what I can do. I could try to draw on my network."

Now it was Océane's turn to become indignant. "You're not saying you're collaborating with the Germans?"

"Under no circumstances! God forbid you even think such a thought. I'm a patriot, dear girl, a patriot!"

"Sorry, grandpa, I'm all confused."

"Then tell me what happened, and we'll see how we can fix it."

As she told him all that had passed while she was inside the German headquarters, the Baron whistled between his teeth, continuing to murmur, "*C'est pas vrai, c'est pas vrai.* It can't be true." Relief flooded through her at being able to share the horrors of what she'd gone through with someone else, and she ventured a sip of the cold coffee. But then the shivers returned. Her whole life seemed over, her job gone, JJ gone, her grandfather in mortal danger and all because of her.

"There's only one solution," the Baron concluded, exactly as Océane had foreseen, "you go to Nice. Maybe we can still get you a ticket to go back to the States or you slip into neutral Switzerland until this lunacy here in Paris is over."

"I can't, grandpa. I have to go through with this idiotic plan to become Von Stein's doctor. That's the only way we as a family can possibly stay safe. I may not be able to save JJ, but I can at least try to save us. I could even play the trump card and tell him I'm half German by birth through my mother. That might placate him?"

"I don't think anything will placate these Huns, but I see your reasoning. When you don't show up today, they will come looking for you here. They know who I am, they possibly have a file on the family already. Have no qualms that he doesn't know about you and JJ. What I don't understand is what he wants from you."

"Well, I'll have to find that out, won't I, as prudently as I can."

"I fear it is what all these German officers are doing all over Paris, turn you into his mistress."

"Grandpa!" Océane was mortified.

"Well, hadn't you considered the possibility yourself?"

"No way, he doesn't seem that kind of predator and he doesn't look at me that way. I may not have much experience with flirtatious men, but I feel it's something else he wants from me. Not my body."

Her grandfather sighed deeply. "We're in a nice pickle, my dear. Well, I suppose you will have to keep up this charade for a while until we come up with a better plan. Know, in the meantime, I'll get my contacts working on a new identity for us. We have to get out of here as soon as possible. Together!"

She kissed her grandfather on the cheeks and left the house feeling terribly guilty and depressed. Her own safety at risk was already stupid but her ageing grandfather did not deserve this.

I'm made for trouble, so much is clear, she thought sadly as she drove to her new job.

As she parked the car for the second time outside the gates of 84 Avenue Foch and stepped out, she was shaken to the core by a high-pitched, long-drawn scream that came from the top floor of the building. It pierced the cold morning air, which seemed to reverberate for a moment after the scream died.

A woman, Océane thought, *it's a woman.*

And then it occurred again, chilling to the bone until it ended in the same foggy silence. Her body revolted and the sickness in her stomach led to throwing up the earlier coffee into a nearby bush. A sharp pain cramped her stomach and wastepipe together. Could it be even worse than what she'd fathomed?

It was all too clear what that hair-raising cry meant. She sensed that the few Parisians quickly passing along the avenue, scurrying away from the tomes of torture, also knew. But they didn't want to hear, to see, to know. She, Océane Bell, had no choice but to enter this place of horrors. As a doctor. What were they expecting from her? The bells of death were ringing for her as - deathly pale and doubled over with cramps - she made her way to the guarded door.

Trying to control her shivering self, she showed her pass to the guards. The same ritual was repeated as the day before. She was directed to the bench inside and had to wait until being taken to Von Stein's office. Queasy and with trepidation, she sat trembling despite her winter coat with fur collar. It was not giving her any warmth. She already envisioned tortured victims, binding their wounds, even closing their eyelids over maimed faces for the last time. And what if... what if one of them was JJ?

Lost in her painful thoughts, Océane startled as a kind voice above her asked in reasonable French, "Madame Docteur?"

She looked up to gaze into the light-gray eyes of Sergeant Hans Arenberg. He smiled as he recognized her, and she instantly felt better.

"How are you?" she asked, trying hard to focus on another

human being, pushing away her morbid thoughts. "How's your breathing been?"

Together they walked in the direction of Von Stein's office. The tall, slender man at her side in his stiff SS uniform with the clicking boots on the marble, outwardly identical to the other Nazis, somehow felt different, closer to her, accessible even, although he was the enemy.

"I've been physically much better with your instructions, Madame." He left it at that. What he didn't say, she read between the lines.

"I hope to be able to keep an eye on you, too, now I'm here," she said, her voice as kind as possible in her own shakiness.

"Yes, I heard you'd been transferred to Headquarters. It surprised me. But then again, General von Stein must have great confidence in your skills."

"Thank you." she said and without further speech they made their way through the building towards the garden room, which was Von Stein's office. As he was about to open the door for her, she whispered, "Do you know what is expected of me, Sergeant?"

He gazed down on her, shaking his head under the enormous black cap with the eagle emblem. "No, Madame, I'm sorry but I don't. I do wish you luck, though, and hope to see you more often."

Océane was ushered into the room without further ado. It was a slight comfort there was at least one kind German in the building. She took a deep breath.

"*Kommen Sie her!*" Von Stein, pale and with a lined face, sat writing behind his desk but fixed his pale blue eyes on her when she approached. "Madame Docteur."

She was surprised by the almost reverential tone in which he addressed her, but her hackles rose at the same time. Something was off. This man was not to be trusted under any circumstances. *Don't let your guard down. Don't be tempted by false friendliness.*

"Coffee? *Pain au chocolat*?"

The idea of a *petit pain au chocolat* made her tired brain vaguely remember its taste and without warning it produced saliva in her mouth, repressing the former sickness. She had not tasted anything remotely like a *petit pain of chocolat* since the beginning of the war. Brains were funny things. That moment the unhuman cries rang in her ears, and she faltered.

In a muffled voice she answered, "Just coffee would be fine, Herr General."

He gave the order in the mouthpiece of his phone and then continued his reading. She had no idea if she was supposed to sit down or remain standing. Her sturdy brown shoes felt like blocks of lead on her feet.

"Why are you not wearing your white coat?" It was asked indignantly.

"I beg your pardon, Sir?"

"Don't 'Sir' me!" His anger was quick to flare.

"Sorry, Herr General. I thought you'd instructed me not to openly be your physician."

"I've changed my mind. Now, why aren't you? You are *my* doctor."

"I didn't know I was supposed to bring my uniform, Herr General."

"Uniforms is what we all wear. Whatever function we have. We all do our bit for the Reich."

"I could go back home and collect my coat?"

A young woman, about her own age but heavily made up and with stylish dark hair wearing an expensive women's suit, brought in a tray with the coffee and the delicious smelling *petit pains au chocolat*. Océane immediately understood she was French. Likely in the same position as herself, forced to work for the Germans. The young woman didn't make eye contact but fussed with the tray, clearly wanting to win the favor of the high-ranking officer. This taught Océane a second thing about her. She was not like her; this woman had adapted to the Nazis and was rewarded for it.

"Thank you, Amélie, that will be all." Von Stein brushed her off like an irritant beetle, which made her press her red painted lips together in a huffy way while black eyes shot a bad-tempered look in Océane's direction.

In a honeyed voice of broken German, she lisped, "Just let me know if you need anything else, Herr General."

"I won't. Now go!"

After the brunette had left, filling the room with her swirl of perfume, Von Stein set out to pour Océane her coffee as he had done the day before. She studied him, trying to figure out not only what he wanted from her but who he was. There was something about him that was different from all the people she had met so far but it didn't have to do with his Germanness. At least she didn't think so. He had mannerisms for sure, a studied way of moving and acting that hid something profound, but she couldn't put her finger on it. Not yet. Her advanced people's studies would reveal it in time. If she was given that time.

Whomever Dieter von Stein was, and what it was he wanted to conceal from the world, it didn't intrigue her, it appalled her. He was a people user, that was clear, and a relentless bully, but peeling away his secret would be her mission. She'd study him minutely, reveal his vulnerability. His undoing would be her salvation, if ever she would be able to escape.

"Do sit," he ordered. "You and I need to have a chat but first do me the pleasure of eating one of these buns. I had them especially delivered for you."

"Why?" she asked before she could check herself.

He raised his light eyebrows to the fringe of same-colored hair. "Why?" he repeated affectedly. "Because I know all French people love them and I like to treat my personnel well."

"I'll try, Herr General, but I'm not terribly hungry."

"You look like you haven't had a decent meal in ages. All of that will change. You'll now dine in the fanciest restaurants. Well, at least as long as it lasts."

She refrained from commenting on the new information. It confused her. The trap certainly lurked around the corner. These niceties were like sugar on vermin but when she took the first bite of the flaky pastry with its soft chocolate heart, she melted. There was no way to stop herself stuffing the whole bun in her mouth in one go, licking her fingers for the last crumbs. Yet, it sank like a bomb in her stomach, a betrayal, another stupid naivety.

"Good!" he nodded. "Now let's have a look at your first day in office at Gestapo Headquarters. My adjutant Sergeant Arenberg will drive you to the hospital with one of our trucks to load as many materials, medicine and equipment as you can load. The supplies will be stored in the former library here. Don't forget to bring some sets of uniforms for yourself. After your return, we will have lunch at the Ritz. You and me."

The aftertaste of the *petit pain of chocolat* and the real *café noir*, though superlative in every sense, was sour in her mouth. It was clear Von Stein was doing all he could to drive a wedge between her and JJ. Rescuing him seemed more impossible than ever.

"Yes, Herr Commandant."

Stiffly rising from her chair on her way to rob her own hospital of its much-needed supplies. *Why?* her soul cried. *Why me?* She was being punished for every stupid action on her part.

It was a small consolation that she was going to see Sergeant Arenberg again but also that made her doubt this General. He knew Arenberg had been to the cardiac ward of Hôtel-Dieu de Paris. What was his plan in putting them together now? Arenberg had hinted at the General's doubts about his loyalty. Whatever it was, they were both following orders they couldn't refuse, swimming along with the current, in her case becoming a Nazi collaborator. How much worse could it become?

It began to dawn on her that this was what JJ had been trying to convey to her all the time when she wouldn't listen to his political talk. That she needed to take a stance, to choose sides or it would be too late. Her dapper hero had chosen the right path but what had it brought him? And she, by trying to save him, had fallen in the obvious trap and become a German compliant.

"You're ready?" Sergeant Arenberg asked as they made their way to the truck.

Océane was too glum to answer, preparing how she was going to inform her colleagues that she was just showing her face to rob them for the sake of the Germans. When they were finally alone in the army truck, she could no longer hold back and burst into tears, clamping her hands before her face in utter shame and humiliation. He had the decency to let her cry, obviously understanding in what position she'd been placed.

Steering the big truck along the Place de la Concorde, he said softly, "I have an idea, Madame Docteur. It may help unburden your heavy heart. What if I go in and order them to hand the supplies over to me? There will be guards at the hospital whom I can give instructions to help me. I'll take the General's list and you stay in the truck. That way no one will blame you."

She looked at him through her tears. His sharp profile as he concentrated on the Paris streets. This man was truly kind, and he understood her. "Thank you," she said sniffing in her handkerchief. "Can you ... could you in some way tell my colleagues why I haven't shown up. They don't know what happened."

"I will, don't worry. Here." He handed her a thermos and a bar of chocolate. "I'm told every woman's heart becomes lighter when they see chocolate." He gave her a sideways grin and Océane managed the ghost of a smile herself.

"Thank you, Sergeant."

"I'll leave the engine on. That way the cabin will stay warm. I will be back soon."

After he was gone, Océane tentatively screwed the metal lid from the thermos and poured herself some of the black liquid in the top cap. She put the chocolate in her bag, keeping it as a treat for her grandfather and Gaël and Marie.

Gazing out of the small cabin window at the hospital that had been like a second home for her the past two years, she could hardly imagine she wouldn't be working there anymore. First Professor Rozenkrantz and Doctor Ferron gone, now she. She hadn't heard from her mentor in months, had no idea where she was. If she was safe. War tore every friendship apart.

Her thoughts returned to that odd and sinister Dieter von Stein. The man sent cold shivers up her spine, but she also reeled at the power he held over her. She needed to get to his plan for her fast. There was no time to waste. He didn't need a fulltime doctor. *What is it, what can it be?*

She sensed in a macabre way that it had to do with her relationship with JJ but why he didn't interrogate her if he wanted to draw information out of her, was mystifying. Not that she knew anything. Apart from the name D'Artagnan and the house on the Rue Fitou and that hadn't come up at all. Von Stein had access to a piece of information that she had not.

While her thoughts went in dark and morbid circles, she took in the almost deserted square in front of the hospital. Parisians didn't dare to visit the hospital unless it was a matter of life and death. The ambulances that did arrive transported German soldiers. The guards and patrols were all Germans as well.

A flock of gray homing pigeons were picking crumbs from between the cobbled stones, their little heads moving swiftly up and down. They flew up in a fluttering swarm as soon as a car drove by but returned to their picking when the square fell into quiet again.

Paris so deadly silent in the middle of the day was ill-omened. The City of Light had become the City of Darkness and she was right in the middle of it.

19

TRAPPED IN LUXURY

A German truck filled with confiscated hospital equipment and first aid materials rumbled away from the hospital grounds. Océane took a last glance at the familiar building with its many archways. The goodbye was almost physical, as if with her leaving the hospital the last sliver of her partisanship was stripped from her. Now she was completely in the claws of the Nazi occupiers.

At the wheel, Sergeant Arenberg was probably having his own thoughts, as he remained silent, though now and then glancing in her direction. She felt unspoken compassion from him. Here was a farmer's son from a neighboring country in the wrong uniform with his heart in the right place. Océane knew she had to snap herself out of her weariness before returning to Headquarters; this was her only opportunity to find out what Hans Arenberg knew.

Clearing her throat she said in a muffled voice, "Do you ... do you think General von Stein knows that we've met before? Does he have a plan?"

Arenberg smiled wryly. "No, Madame Docteur, but I've asked myself the same question. I'm not high enough in the ranks to have any inside information. After, um, the incident that brought me to the Hotel-Dieu de Paris, I've been downgraded. But I promise you that if I find out something, I'll try to pass on the information. You must under all circumstances remain one hundred precent alert. General von Stein is a capricious person, very capricious."

He threw her another sympathizing look and for some reason she felt sorry for both of them. He hadn't recovered from whatever Von Stein had done to him. He just kept his chin up, as she would.

"I had already noticed that. If you need any help and I can give it, let me know."

"Thank you, Madame Docteur, you've already done more than enough for me. And my breathing is fine. The rest I'll deal with myself."

He parked the lorry inside the iron gates of the SS Headquarters and accompanied her to the door.

"I hope to see you soon, Madame, and please take good care of yourself."

The idea of parting from him without any clue, made her desperate. Still out of earshot from the guards, she whispered, "Do you by any chance know anything about a French resistance fighter by the name of Remix? I need to know where he is."

The young men's gray eyes opened wide, instantly grasping why she was there. He thought for an instant, then shook his head. "No, Madame, I have no information on prisoners of war. Again, my rank doesn't permit that, you see. But I'll keep my eyes and ears open. Please, be very careful. You're on perilous grounds."

Océane's hope sank into her shoes, but she managed to give him a tiny goodbye smile. Sergeant Arenberg couldn't help his position, but hopefully he was on *her* side. She was almost certain of it. Almost.

Making her way to the entrance of the house of horrors, her shoulders sagging, she couldn't care less what happened to the content of the lorry. Nothing was of interest to her anymore.

THE LUNCH with Von Stein at the Ritz turned out to be a gruesome affair despite all the luxury and the animosity the German officers around them created. Most of the Germans were already under the influence at the beginning of the afternoon, moving through the gilded rooms as if it were a cheap taverna, staining the costly carpets with dirty boots and red wine, or knocking the century-old Chinese vases off their pedestals. Shattered fragments, bloody stains.

For Océane it was the first time being surrounded by her oppressors while they were spending their leisure time and she didn't know where to look. Everywhere she glanced, her eyes were met by chaos and deliberate destruction. French waiters hurried around serving bottles of champagne and plateaus of roasted duck, stepping over the debris in an attempt to serve their non-paying, debauched customers. Their eyes filled with fear and horror while the crescendo kept rising.

Océane sat at a table in the middle of the large dining room with General von Stein, who had a tiny, dry smile lingering in the corner of his thin lips. He was enjoying the devastation, she thought with a shock. He didn't partake but condoned it, nevertheless. It gave her another porthole glimpse into his soul.

Contrary to his fellow countrymen, Von Stein didn't drink alcohol, at least not there and then. He ordered himself a lemon squash and a bottle of champagne for her. The flute of sparkling Dom Perignon stood untouched next to her Laurent Buttazzoni fleur rose plate. She knew that at some point he would force her to drink it but until then she would refuse. She watched him eat. For the lean man he was he had a good appetite, diving into his roasted duck, fresh potatoes and green beans. She watched and watched, taking mental notes. She would find the key to this man. Maybe not today, but some day.

"Are you not hungry." It wasn't a question. It was '*der Befehl*' she'd been waiting for.

Dutifully she took three tiny bites from her deliciously baked sole, took a sip of the champagne. With every taste of luxury, her resistance rose. She was becoming someone else, someone Dieter von Stein would never know. He was not going to get a porthole look into *her* soul if she could help it.

He tried to make small talk, dabbing the corners of his mouth with the damask serviette rather dandyishly. "I take it you've been at the Ritz before, Madame Bell?"

"*Biensûr,* it is always a pleasure to be here. The best hotel Paris has to offer." She gave him a sweet smile, very Madame Paul-like. She wasn't going to disclose to him that her grandfather was good friends with the owner Charles Ritz and that the Baron had given many a violin recital in the Bar Hemingway. It was none of his business.

"Well, this table is always reserved for me. Any time of the night or day I might want to make use of it," Von Stein said rather importantly. "I'm right next to Hermann Göring's table but our commander-in-chief of the *Luftwaffe* isn't in Paris at the moment."

Heavens, you boasting peacock, Océane thought while nodding amiably.

She sat back in her velvet upholstered chair at the damask-covered table that could easily have seated eight more, feeling as if she'd suddenly fallen into a cheap B-movie.

"That's very interesting, Herr General. I had no idea Herr Göring was often in Paris as well."

What had Sergeant Arenberg said? To be vigilant. At all times. She could see the shrewdness in the pale-blue eyes across from her. Cat and mouse, mouse and cat.

The clipped voice, now slightly nasal, as if sensing something had changed in her, took control. "After lunch you and I are meeting someone here."

The blood stopped in Océane's veins, faltered and then started flowing again. She had not seen this one coming.

"Someone I know?" She tried hard to sound unruffled, but her voice betrayed the anxiety underneath.

The same mean little smile wafted her way. "I think so. Can't imagine such a famous name not being known in Paris."

Breathe, don't gape.

"I'm all ears, Herr General."

"I thought so." He took his time stirring the coffee the flustered *garçon* had put in front of him. "I think you and her will get on well with each other. Both hard-headed women."

"A she?" Océane breathed out with some relief. Unless, unless it was the black-haired Resistance fighter.

"Yes, a 'she' by the name of Coco Chanel."

Now Océane did gape. "Coco Chanel, Herr General?"

Her mind raced. What had the French fashion designer to do with a German Gestapo leader? Or was it pure coincidence? Von Stein certainly made her fall from one surprise into the other.

"You and I, Madame, are soon going on a little trip and I want Madame Chanel to fluff you up a bit. Just consider it a small token of appreciation."

Her hackles raised, as did her pulse. "Wait a minute, Herr General. I'm confused. A trip and new clothes? Could you please be more specific?"

Everything jumbled to the forefront of her thoughts, being taken to Germany, used as a German Spy against the French, being made a high-class whore. What was he aiming at and why? She saw he enjoyed her confusion. Temporarily her fighter spirit let her down. She wasn't enjoying this game, not in the least.

"Ha!" The general took a minute to savor his triumph over her in this round. "I can't tell you all the details yet, Madame, but there's nothing you should worry about. If you treat me with respect and do as you're told, I will do the same. Now do we have an understanding?"

No, we don't! she almost cried out but instead nodded her head. She took a sip of her own coffee, feeling more wretched by the minute. *Go where, do what?* She had the terrifying idea she wasn't going back to her grandfather's house that evening.

Von Stein turned his interest to two young SS officers sitting at another table and beckoned them to join theirs. They acknowledged Océane with a curt nod but immediately started conversing with their boss in German. Still struggling with her discomfort about her uncertain fate, she tried to listen in to the best of her ability. Her German wasn't perfect but enough to understand they were discussing the logistics of troops and material sent from Paris to the Atlantic Wall.

Then she pricked up her ears when they went on to talking about *Freischärlerei*, which she knew was their word for Resistance fighters. Eager to learn more, she was soon disappointed. There was nothing specific as they were only discussing how to strengthen their ties with the *Milice*, which was the feared French paramilitary, especially in Vichy-France. No individual names were mentioned, no recent raids announced.

Von Stein waved an impatient movement with his white hand and his two guests politely withdrew back to their own table. Océane found herself once again in the sole presence of this enigmatic man, who acted as if he was heading his dinner table at home.

"Are you finished?" he asked, ignoring that she'd hardly touched food or drink.

With an acute pain, she suddenly longed for home, for Chicago, for her own family, for safety. The intensity of the feeling made her slightly giddy. She wasn't sure her legs would carry her if she stood up.

I have to force down the food next time if I want to stay strong. At least, I have food, which you, my darling JJ, must possibly go without. I'll do it for you.

She looked him in the eye, as if drawing strength from her hatred of him. Somewhere, somehow, he would make a mistake and then she'd pull the rug from underneath his feet. He answered her gaze. Nothing flinched. Yet.

As she followed Von Stein to the elevator, she had to watch her every step as she felt increasingly queasy and unwell. The doctor in her took the necessary precautions to survive. Breathe, slow down, concentrate.

The lift boy asked Von Stein which floor he wanted to go to, and he pointed to the top gilded button. Océane braced herself. This was going to be the next phase in her unasked-for adventure. She'd have to undress, forego her identity, forget about JJ and follow what this pale-skinned, phlegmatic German ordered her to do. There was little choice.

She stood next to him as he pressed the buzzer and a young, very elegant woman with platinum blond hair in a black designer suit opened the door, a cigarette in a long holder deftly between her fingers.

"Yes?" Perfectly painted eyebrows wrinkled an otherwise smooth forehead.

"Is Madame Chanel in?"

Océane felt the unsteadiness in her legs increase as the blonde cried over her shoulder, "*Chérie*, are you in?"

A smoked-through female voice called back, "Who's there?"

"*Un ami de* Hans Günther?"

"Which one?"

"Dieter, of course."

"Let him come in but I'm in the bath. Give him a Courvoisier."

The blonde hesitated before she called again. "He's not alone, he's brought one of his ... uh ... secretaries." She gave Océane a haughty look.

Von Dieter clearly was becoming impatient with this calling to and fro, so he resolutely stepped across the threshold, almost pushing the blonde over. Ash scattered from her cigarette on the thick carpet. She rubbed it in with her bare feet with painted toenails.

"I've come for business," he snapped, "not on a social call. Coco, *venez ici s'il vous plaît!* Come here!"

Océane followed behind them. Curiosity battled with her misery as she peeked around the luxurious apartment. It was not only extravagantly furnished, it also had racks of Chanel ladies suits and cocktail dresses and the air was heady with Chanel No 5. Her mother's favorite scent. Pain and chagrin had no place in this little palace and for a moment she felt like Alice in Wonderland, close to France's greatest style icon. The thrill of it!

The style icon herself came into the room barefoot, draped in a cream-colored silk peignoir, a turban wrapped around her onyx hair. She was every inch the mysterious beauty from the photographs in Le Matin and Paris Monde. Impressive and regal despite her petite frame.

Sauntering over to Von Stein, she let him give her a peck on the palm and with only a quick glance at Océane lay down on the chaise longue, stretching out her elegant legs as the peignoir fell open, revealing a pair of tanned thighs.

"To what do I owe this visit, Steiny?" she said in her languid voice, accepting a glass of amber colored liquid in a large, round glass from the blonde. Her helper also lit a cigarette for her from a golden case with CC embossed on it. She handed it to Coco, who drew on it eagerly.

Océane was already busy painting the designer in her sketchbook. The chaise, the woman, her body, the glass, the slender, naked arm holding up the cigarette. So much decadent beauty and goddess-like femininity. It was a picture worth imprinting on her mind.

"Do you have anything left from your summer collection, Coco?" he asked as he sat down on a straight chair across from her, his bones and boots creaking.

"Not so uptight, Steiny! Have a drink first, then we'll talk. I'm always so sleepy when I come out of my bath. I can't talk business like that." She snapped her fingers with the pointed red nails.

Océane was meanwhile still standing near the door, unobserved by the others, not knowing whether she was supposed to come forward or stay where she was. Coco finished her glass in a few large gulps, put her cigarette in the ashtray, and sat up. Black eyes with black lines around them took her in from head to toe. Then she slowly clacked her tongue.

"Superb!" she said, winking at Von Stein.

Raising her catlike body from the chaise longue, she pattered over to Océane, all the while scanning her with those unfathomable eyes. Just when Océane thought she was going to bump right into her, Coco took a turn for one of the clothes' racks. With nimble movements she picked a number of items from their hangers and threw them towards the blonde, who caught them deftly.

"Bedroom!" she ordered. "Babette, help Mademoiselle with the garments while I chat with Steiny." And to Océane she lisped, "Show me every item but make sure *you* wear them, instead of *them* wearing you. Understood?"

Flabbergasted, Océane nodded but had no idea what she meant. Clothes had never been of much interest to her, but she had to admit it felt extraordinary to been given the opportunity to dress in Coco Chanel's high-couture. If only everything wasn't so complicated and confusing.

Blonde Babette's attitude changed completely as she closed the bedroom door behind them and the two of them found themselves in a bedroom that had only one color: gold-beige. From the carpet to the curtains to the bedclothes and the furniture, beige was the ground tone, and all accents were in gold, like the knobs of drawers, the sashes of the curtains and the roses woven into the wall-to-wall carpet.

"Are you okay?" Babette asked in a husky voice. "You look like a scared kitten. I know this stuff may sound intimidating to you but believe me, we all play our part and it's best to make the best of it and play along and have some fun as long as it lasts. Those Nazis are going to turn our lives even more sour within months, mark my words."

Océane glanced at the glamorous blonde with relief. A nice and understanding French woman. But could she be trusted? Well, latching onto friendly faces like Babette's and Arenberg's seemed the only thing she had at the moment.

"Not really," she answered honestly. "I have no idea what Von Stein wants from me but I'm sure it's no good."

"Dieter?" The blonde raised her eyebrows and let out a smirky smile. "Don't worry, he won't touch you. He's not like that. But here, let's get you into that striped summer dress. Coco's patience is ever so short."

She wanted to ask much more about Von Stein but didn't dare to. What if they were found out talking in the bedroom, so she stuck to the clothing.

"Why summer's clothes in winter?" Océane asked, taking off her belted gabardine coat and standing awkwardly in her dark-green merino dress.

"God knows," Babette shrugged, "but it's not our place to ask questions. We obey orders and meanwhile keep our eyes open for our own options."

"You're the second one to tell me that today," Océane observed listlessly, taking off her dress while Babette opened the front buttons of the calf-length, navy blue and white linen dress.

"Then you'd better listen to that advice, Miss. Here, this is a size 4. I think it's perfect. Gosh, you're so thin. Parisians are supposed to be thin, but you're way too bony. Here," and she retrieved some food coupons from the pocket of her suit jacket and stuffed them in Océane's coat. "That'll guarantee you some flesh on your bones."

"Thank you, you're awfully kind." Océane instantly felt better, not just because of the kind gesture but also because the dress felt marvelous on her skin and swirled around her legs like a dream.

"There's a mirror." Babette pointed to the life size mirror next to the bed. "I think you can adjust the belt just one more hole. Gosh, it looks like Coco designed this one just for you. Here put on this hat and you'll look like a mannequin. Just a pity about the shoes."

Though Océane's best pair of shoes, they were of the practical and sensible type, just like she was. Far from elegant or dainty. She concentrated solely on the dress and hat and for a moment felt she was dreaming, hardly able to peel her eyes away from her own reflection.

Madame Chanel called from the other room. "*Venez ici!* I want to see."

So Océane stepped rather self-consciously into the room and

approached Madame Chanel who had reclined on her chaise longue again. She was fingering the spring of pearls around her neck while holding a topped-up glass in her other hand. Languid dark eyes studied her in detail and for an exceptionally long time. Then the dark head nodded in approval.

Océane cast a quick glance in Von Stein's direction, but he was reading a French newspaper and didn't look her way. His attitude made clear this dressing-up party was orchestrated by his friend Chanel.

"Another," Madame ordered. "I want to see her in the wide black trousers with the short jacket."

The dressing party went on for a good one and a half hour until Océane became rather exasperated, changing in and out of outfits and parading in front of the famous French designer, who approved or disapproved at a whim. No one told her what this charade was all about, but her keen sense told her that neither of the other women knew what was going on. Only the silent reading General knew, and he had no intention of revealing his plans yet.

Finally, the arrangements seemed to be to Coco's satisfaction and several items were put in a large box.

"I guess they have to be sent to Headquarters, Steiny?" The designer got up, stretched as a cat and tapped her long fingernails against his newspaper. "Order champagne and oysters for Steiny, Babette, while I get dressed. We simply *must* celebrate and suddenly I'm *terribly* hungry."

"Yes, sent to Headquarters and no, Coco, I can't stay." Von Stein folded the newspaper and got up from his chair.

Océane's practiced eye saw he had difficulty breathing but he was hiding it well.

"What a pity, Steiny, I'll give you a rain check on the oysters then. When will you be back?"

"No idea, Coco, but I'll let you know, either myself or via Hans Günther."

Her face looked sulky. "Hansie has been neglecting me of late.

You men are so busy with your war games, and I can't even reopen my shop. I'm a prisoner of the Ritz. Isn't it sad?"

"You're no such thing, Coco, and you know it. Didn't Hans Günther take you to Monte Carlo last week? Well, I must be off and thank you for your help. I'll tell my chauffeur to come and collect the box in a minute."

He brushed Océane out of the door as if she was a tin soldier. She just managed to wave at Babette, who made a face at her. A little bit of warmth in all the chill.

Under any other circumstances it would have been fabulous to meet the great Coco Chanel but now everything was blurred, without luster or lure. The big dame herself played a dubious game in it all.

20

A FORCED EXILE

W hen they were seated in the back of the black Mercedes with the Nazi flags flapping up front, the box with the golden lettering CC in the boot, Océane could no longer restrain herself.

"Herr General, could you please explain what this is all about?" She looked straight ahead as she spoke, her eyes fixed on the hideous flags while her heart rammed wildly against her ribs.

"We're going to Libya for a bit." He said it as if it lay in the next street.

"Pardon? Libya, why Libya?" It was a mere whisper.

"It's none of your business, Madame, but if you insist on knowing. I have to clear a cell of Resistance Fighters there. They're obstructing our North African campaign."

Keep staring at the flags and keep breathing. It cost all she had.

"Why do you want me to go with you?" she managed to squeeze out.

He laughed his joyless laughter. "Because you are my private physician."

"Then why the posh clothes?"

"Madame, you ask too many questions. I thought you were smarter than that. This is not a business for *nosy* people."

Nosy people. He'd caught her ruffling through his papers. He was poking fun at her while her heart bled. This man was going to take her hundreds of miles away from Paris, from her family, from JJ. Wherever he was. There was no holding her back anymore.

"Where is he?"

No answer. She almost squeezed her hands to bruises expecting a torrent of angry words but after a long silence, his voice was perfectly calm. "I cannot tell you that."

"Can you tell me if he is alive?"

"No."

"Are you holding me because you think I know something about the Resistance?"

"No, I know you don't, and we'd better keep it that way, don't you agree? It's much safer for you and for those who may want to get in touch with you."

It was all rather cryptic, but it was something. A tiny, tiny bit of hope. Although Von Stein gave no answers, she took heart from the fact he hadn't said out loud that JJ was dead.

"When are we leaving?"

"You ask too many questions, Madame."

"Doctors ask questions. That's how they get to the cause and the cure."

"Alright then. We fly out tonight."

"Tonight?" She heard her voice finally break. "Can I ... can I at least say goodbye to my grandfather?"

"No. It's best nobody knows where you are."

At this, Océane's shoulders started shaking as she sobbed uncontrollably, but her eyes remained strangely dry. It was as if her whole body was taken through the wringer and all blood and body fluids dried up. Her throat just made a bizarre, dry croak and she broke.

Just for an instant she broke.

Then an icy steel entered her veins. He'd gone too far. He would pay. One way or another he would pay for this. For the first time since she'd laid eyes on him in that hospital bed three months prior, their eyes met full on. The gold flecks in her hazel eyes glimmered as she felt her anger flare up to a smoldering heat. For a moment there was a trace of uncertainty in Von Stein's ashy-blue eyes, but he instantly recollected himself and adopted his usual offhand authoritarian look. Her own brain became calm, as in every crisis, while weighing her practical options. Fleeing was one of them but the chances of survival too small. Going along, but until which point? And then it became clear to her. Libya might not be such a bad idea after all. Escaping from there was probably easier than in densely populated Paris. Her only hope was that Sergeant Arenberg would be going with them.

"Has Madame run out of questions?"

The chauffeur was taking the bend into Avenue Foch.

"Yes. For the time being I have."

She was aware of the sarcasm in her voice but was beyond care. The focus was on herself now. Her whole life had been a preparation for what was before her. Whatever way it would go. She now understood what Jean-Jacques stood for. Von Stein was not the problem, he was a mere obstacle on their path. The German occupation of France was the real problem.

While the Mercedes came to a halt in front of the Gestapo Headquarters, Océane was already inwardly saying goodbye to her beloved Paris, swearing silently that if she would see it again, if she managed to stay alive. she would fight for its liberation. An eye for an eye, tooth and nail.

It felt good to finally choose sides, know right from wrong, be honest with herself. JJ would be so proud of her. He'd forgive her sitting at the Ritz with a high-ranking Nazi, driving around in his armored car with expensive Chanel clothes in the boot. She was not going to be a traitor, a Fritz Fraulein, *une collaborateure horizontale*. No matter how it might seem to all that looked at her now.

"I'll prove you all wrong," she said between gritted teeth and, as in the old days, realized she had spoken her thoughts aloud before she could check herself.

"What was that?" The German was quick to react.

"Nothing, sorry, I was thinking to myself." She hesitated a moment and then said as clarification, "I was thinking about my family. That I'll prove I can be a good doctor."

"Did they think you wouldn't?"

There was a sudden, strange yearning in his eyes, which she couldn't place but it made her uncomfortable. He looked like a predator ready to jump on her. Did he want her after all?

Shaking off the nasty feeling, she said in a neutral voice, "No, never. I myself had doubts about my medical career."

That was as personal as she would get with him. Meanwhile she was on high alert. A crack in the veneer. He had shown passion, but she couldn't fit the pieces of the puzzle yet. Why did it matter to him if her parents thought her a good doctor or not? She made a mental note of the predator look.

The big, black car turned into the gates of 84 Avenue Foch. She braced herself for possible cries from the top floor but, as the chauffeur opened the back door and she slid out, the building was silent. Its pain hid inside the thick stone walls but crept inside her veins, nonetheless.

She straightened her back.

From this time forward she would not be a victim anymore, no matter how much Von Stein or other Germans tried to humiliate or bully her. Glancing up at the already darkening, late afternoon sky, she inhaled the Paris air deeply, as if wanting to take with her part of the air that had once been solely French, a mixture of coffee, perfume, cigarette smoke, roasted chestnuts and fresh bread from the boulangerie. That was how *she* would remember her Paris; not what the Germans had made of it, the smell of fear and pain, beer, bratwurst and black leather.

Following Von Stein and the chauffeur carrying the Chanel box, she was glad to see Sergeant Arenberg on duty, but she was not pleased with the way his face fell as soon as Von Stein addressed him. He was clearly ill at ease with his whimsical General.

"Sergeant Arenberg, come to my office after your duty. I need you for my final arrangements here."

"Yes, Herr General." He saluted and managed to give Océane a glimmer of a smile.

After they returned to Von Stein's office, the white Chanel box sitting ostentatiously on a corner of his desk, Océane lost some of her induced courage as the General sat signing the papers on his desk and she was left to her own devices.

It crossed her mind to sneak out and go home to her grandfather, ask him to take her to neutral Switzerland, but the cunning German seemed to guess her thoughts as he suddenly looked up at her.

"I've made a list of what I think you will personally need for the African trip. Please check and correct if I have forgotten anything. Sergeant Arenberg can go and buy the supplies for you. We leave in two hours. Now go to the library to check the medical supplies we will need in Africa. Take anything you think will be necessary, but you won't be working in a hospital. You're just there to look after me." The menacing look again, the grin.

She swallowed hard as he handed her the list. "Two hours?"

Sweat in her palms as she took the slip of paper on which he had listed toiletry, undergarments, even a couple of French novels. Blurry eyed, she was hardly able to read the list. She nodded, handing it back to him.

"Now move," he ordered. "I have an important meeting with General Brinkel who will take command here during my absence."

As Von Stein shouted a command for the Sergeant in his phone, Océane left the office, momentarily thinking she might be able to just walk out the building and go home but an officer stood ready to take her to the library.

The net was closing around her.

21

LIBYA

The next days passed by in a blur and Océane wasn't sure if she was awake or entangled in a dreadful dream.

From boarding the Junker Ju 90 of the German Luftwaffe at the Aeroport Charles De Gaulle, to flying in an airplane for the very first time, to arriving in a war territory where her accommodation was a large canvas tent with hardly any comfort.

For the first time since the war started, she was only surrounded by enemies. They were of a different caliber than the black leather-clad SS officers that had flooded Paris to have fun. Here they were close to the frontlines and the soldiers, both the German and the Italians, were dressed in khaki, covered in sand most of the time, with hard-lined faces and grim eyes, never without their camouflage helmets. There was nothing jolly or extravagant about them and they eyed her, the only woman in the camp, with curiosity and sometimes untamed lust.

The first days she had been tossing and turning on her camp bed, sick from the sudden climate change, sweating in her Chanel outfit that seemed horrendously out of place. It had been winter in Paris when they left, almost below zero, but here heat hit her in waves, way over 95 degrees. Blistering sun and dry winds all day.

She hadn't seen Von Stein during her first African days. He'd left immediately upon arrival to visit General Rommel stationed closer to the coast. Her guard was a young, lanky man with a pock-marked face and strangely large hands who hardly said a word and seemed to be smoking all day, an Eckstein cigarette either held between a thick thumb and forefinger or dangling from underneath his mustache. The only thing Océane knew about him was that his comrades called him Pok, which seemed rather derogative.

As soon as she became more used to the heat and could leave her bed and eat a little again, Océane started thinking about escape, but she realized Von Stein had outsmarted her. There was no way she was ever going to get away from this place alive.

It was at the end of her third day in Libya that she left her tent to inspect her surroundings. Dressed in one of Chanel's summer dresses with a large-brimmed hat on her dark curls, she stood on feeble legs looking around her. They'd arrived in the night, after which she'd been quickly ushered into her tent, so she was surprised to see how big the camp was. Rows of identical canvas tents stood in lines over a large stretch of stony area with tanks, car and lorries parked in their midst. Soldiers moved around the terrain like ants. The heat, the dust and the wind were all relentless.

Behind her she heard Pok say in a drawling voice, "Where are you going, Miss?"

"To the Headquarters tent over there," she answered resolutely. "I want to know what's expected of me."

"But I had instructions from General von Stein to show you around the camp when you were well enough."

Océane turned around on her heels to face the tall German with his eternal cigarette hanging from his bottom lip. "In this outfit?" she scowled. "I don't think so."

"Well, I can't help your outfit, Madame, but I can show you around."

"Alright, then. If you insist, but when will the General be back?"

"He's expected tonight."

"Good. Because I have some questions for your boss."

The tall, pockmarked German just shrugged, neither impressed - as it seemed - by her obstinacy nor about his boss's comings and goings.

"Life must be tough out here in the desert," she added, a little more friendly, but he shrugged again, lighting his Eckstein cigarette.

Her professional eye suddenly detected the sullenness and depression, not just in Pok, but in all the officers that moved past them like slow ants on an endless sand path. There was no joy here, no victorious, drunken song, no loud and boisterous propaganda. All there was as far as the eye could see was a huge sandpit that stripped them of their individuality and slowly, very slowly, killed all hope of ever going home again. The fear here was not so much the death of the bullet, but the death of the human soul.

"I'm not going there." She'd said it aloud before she knew to stop herself.

Her unexpected spoken thought seemed to wake up something in Pok. "I beg your pardon, Madame. You were saying?"

"Nothing. I was thinking aloud. Take me to the first aid tent, or whatever you call it."

"But, Madame ..."

"Either you bring me there or I go there on my own."

There must have been enough authority in her voice because Pok shrugged a disinterested 'alright'.

"I'm first going to oversee if the medical supplies that were flown in from Paris are all in place."

Armed with a white coat over her designer outfit, her mother's stethoscope in her pocket, a shawl around head and mouth and a pair of sunglasses, an unrecognizable Océane set out to work.

Work will keep me sane, she told herself, *and who knows what my ears may pick up.*

She was busy placing supplies in cupboards so they would be protected from the sand when she heard the zip of the tent being opened behind her. A German army doctor who looked as if the desert had dried up all the fluids in his body startled in surprise at seeing her there. Despite her situation, Océane chuckled. She'd scared the wits out of him.

The wiry, wrinkled doctor, dressed in the same khaki uniform as the rest but with a red cross band on his arm, moved towards her with swift movements and in a surprisingly young voice said, "I hadn't expected anyone here, Madame. My name is Fritz Webel. I'm the *Oberarzt* here. Who are you?" He shook her hand with one that was as withered as the rest of him, and eyes dried-out as old currants pierced into hers.

"Pleasure to meet you, Oberartz Webel. I'm Doctor Bell. Sorry for intruding into your place without warning."

"No problem." He gave her another nod without further interest before disappearing through a flap that divided the tent in two, leaving her to continue her stocking.

What a weird place, she thought.

The next section of the tent was apparently a temporary hospital. As it had been mouse quiet on that side, she hadn't expected anyone to be in there.

Océane sat down on one of the trunks with gauze and bandages, her chin cupped in her hands as her elbows rested on her knees. The heat was oppressive, and for once the vague smell of chlorine didn't perk her up but made her sick. It was the smell that had been the thread through her life, always wafting in and out of her nostrils, calming, reassuring her she was home. But not this time. She was further away from all that she loved than ever. All alone, only herself to defend, no one to depend on. It was scary, it was sinister.

Don't go there! No idly sitting down!

She forced herself to open another box with supplies stolen from the French. How much robbing could one nation do? With a sudden pang she thought of Eleonora, and another morbid thought crept into her heart. Her mentor had vanished from the earth and so had her husband and the baby that must have been born by now. Whichever way she tried, the heat, her unsettlement, the strange environment, her thoughts turned dark every time and she had to bend them with her will.

Océane managed to concentrate on organizing the confiscated goods, but she jumped high into the air when Von Stein's clayey voice sounded behind her.

"Ah, I see you're back on your feet and settling in nicely, Madame."

Without looking at him, with her heart still jolting in her chest, she answered flatly, "I'm just keeping busy."

"There was no need for that. The *Oberarzt* could have managed finely on his own. Now come and have tea with me in my tent. I want to discuss matters with you."

Oh no, Océane thought, *here we go again*. But she said in the same monotonous voice, "As you wish. I'll just finish emptying this box."

"Sergeant Arenberg is waiting outside and will bring you to my tent."

She couldn't help but turn to face him, trying to keep her face straight while she feared it would light up in a smile. She suddenly felt a whole lot better. "I didn't know he was here, Herr General."

"I like to keep my favorite people close to me."

It was said in a clipped voice, but his gaze revealed he had seen her face transform. There was nothing that escaped this man and she instantly felt pummeled again. *Favorite people.* Was she one of them? It didn't bode well.

Von Stein looked tired and worn-out; the trip through the heat and sand to see his superiors hadn't done his health any good. His breath was shallow and his pallor even grayer and more parched than normal. The doctor won, as always.

"Are you feeling alright, Herr General?"

"Why wouldn't I?" The tone was terse, but he seemed to pick up her clue. "Well, to tell you the truth, I had a couple of bad nights in Tripoli. I'll see you in fifteen minutes."

"Should I bring my medical bag, Herr General?"

"Yes, do."

After he strode out, Océane placed the bottles of morphine in the airtight cabinet. She was shaking so badly she was afraid to break the fragile glass bottles. Finally, she put the injection needles in the same container and snapped it shut. Von Stein was acting stranger. She had to be on her *qui vive*. Even more than before.

"Madame Docteur." Ruddy-faced Hans Arenberg, now clad in a khaki uniform instead of the black SS outfit, smiled widely as she stepped into the blistering Libyan afternoon sun. "I wouldn't have recognized you should I have bumped into you in Paris. But you look ravishing."

The compliment, though out of place and unnecessary, made her feel slightly better, but it was his presence that made all the difference.

"I'm so glad to see a familiar face in the desert."

"So am I, Miss Bell."

She gazed at him, blinking in surprise. He'd never called her that before. There was something different about the squire son, but she couldn't put her finger on it. Well, she supposed everyone changed in these conditions, with heat and sand and close to the firing lines. It had suddenly become a totally different war.

"Better take me to the General." She fastened the buttons of her white coat and picked up her brown leather medic's bag. "I think your boss is coming down with something."

"Oh." It sounded disinterested as he strode off in northern direction.

Océane hastened to come abreast with him. "You're okay, Sarge?"

"As okay as I can be. I had hoped to be delivered from that evil." He nodded his head in the direction of a large tent that stood slightly apart from the smaller ones next to it.

"That bad, huh?" she sympathized. "The General seems to take a liking to folks who don't reciprocate it."

"I suppose that's his whole plan."

Arenberg sounded morose but Océane was immediately on the alert. "What plan? Why do you say that? Do you think he's got something planned for you? And for me?"

"Of course that old fox knows what he's doing. Makes it all the more sinister."

"Please explain, Sergeant. You frighten me." Océane felt a shiver go down her spine.

"Not now. We're here. But soon."

Sergeant Arenberg saluted and turned on his heels, leaving her puzzled and even more ill at ease. There was no time to think about a plan or not. Not knowing how to announce her arrival as there was nowhere to knock and there were no guards at the General's tent, she called out.

"I'm here."

"Come in!"

It was snapped in the same gruff way she'd become accustomed to. The General lay stretched out on his camp bed in his full uniform with only his cap lying next to him, the wisps of sandy-yellow hair wet with perspiration. He was breathing heavily with his mouth open and sweat was pouring down the sides of his narrow face, filling up the deep lines next to his mouth. The blue eyes, never very clear, were now even paler, the whites of his eyes red-veined and bulging.

"You are not well, Herr General. Let me check on you."

Océane hastened towards him, meanwhile wondering why she thought she had to. She swiftly pushed that thought to the back of her mind.

"Don't fuss over me, Madame. I'm just slightly overwhelmed by the heat and lack of sleep. That's all."

But Océane had already retrieved a stethoscope from her bag - not her mother's, a newer one. "Could you please open your jacket and your shirt, Herr General?"

She looked at him expectantly as she had no intention of doing that for a patient capable of doing so himself. He followed her orders as if in slow motion, his movements rigid as he bared his almost hairless chest.

What Océane heard was not good. His heart was very irregular with almost inaudible beats in between.

"Have you been taking your Digoxin pills, Herr General?"

"I forgot to take them with me to Tripoli. Is that all there is to it?"

Océane removed her stethoscope, cleaned it and put it back in her bag while the General dressed himself again. "I hope so," she said. "It's really important you take the pills, if needed. I thought I made that clear. For the time being, I order a two-day bedrest. Lie flat, try to sleep as much as possible, and no stress."

The General made a movement as if wanting to sit up but thought the better of it when he was halfway risen.

"You're dizzy, Sir?"

"Don't 'sir' me."

"Sorry. But I told you not to rise. Is there anything I can get you?" She couldn't bring herself to adding the 'Herr General' bit.

"Well, I ordered tea because I wanted to have a chat with you. I didn't plan on falling ill."

"Can I get you your tea?"

Meeker than she'd ever seen him, he nodded his head. "The canteen sergeant was supposed to bring it, but I don't know what's gotten into him. Everybody is so slow here. Must be the climate and the fatigue from fighting."

"I'll have a look." Océane got up and then realized how hungry and thirsty she was herself. After having risen from her own sickbed, she'd hardly taken time to eat and drink.

"The canteen is right opposite my tent." The General pointed to the exit.

"I'll be back in a sec. Don't try to sit up."

As she found her way to the army canteen, she wondered again why she bothered and what was it in the air that seemed to alter people's dynamics. Something in the General had changed, had mellowed him, but she wasn't sure she welcomed the change. He was even more diabolical in his weak state.

Caution, caution, she told herself, returning with a tray and on it a pot of tea, tea glasses and sweet looking gum the canteen sergeant told her was something like candied fruit. Sugar would certainly revive the sick man, as would a glass of brandy, though of the cheap sort.

When she entered, she saw the General had fallen asleep, so she set the tray next to his bed, grabbed a glass of tea and felt the sugared fruit melt in her mouth. Just as she was about to leave, he opened his eyes, studying her.

Drowning a "damn" with the last bit of her tea, she said in an overly chirpy voice, "Ah, you're awake again."

"Yes." He accepted the tea but refused the sugary fruit. "I'm not hungry."

"Shall I pour you some brandy, Herr General? That might do you some good."

"I don't drink alcohol."

"Okay, then have your tea and your tablets. And do try to eat something later."

She sat down on one of the camp chairs, stirring the sugar in another cup of black tea. It was as if she was looking at herself from out of space. The extreme oddity of sitting in a Chanel dress with a doctor's coat over it, in the middle of the North-African desert with a sick German General, seemed something out of a supernatural movie.

"If you feel up to it, Herr General, you said earlier you wanted to talk with me." Better cut the chase herself.

"Yes."

It sounded distracted and he kept drinking his tea with almost girlish, small sips. He was so affected at times. Silence followed.

Just when she supposed he'd forgotten or abandoned the idea of conversation, he said, "I wanted to be a doctor myself."

A weighed silence followed.

"That's what you wanted to talk with me about?" Her brows knitted, not getting his point but on the alert for the craziness this prelude might lead to. Then she sat up straighter in the uncomfortable linen chair. She'd better pay attention. There might be a clue here. "Then why did you not pursue a career in medicine, Herr General?"

"I failed the entrance exam, der *Medizinertest*."

"Couldn't you try again?" It was like a slap in her face with a wet cloth as she was catapulted back to her own failed test at Radcliffe. She pursed her lips. No way she'd tell him, ever.

"*Nein*." He was sweating from the hot tea, falling back in his own language.

"But, um, Herr General, I have no idea why you tell me this. Excuse me, I have to finish unpacking the medical supplies before dark." Océane rose from the chair to leave, a tactic to keep him talking.

It worked.

"There's more."

Sinking back in the chair with an air of exasperation, she folded her hands in her lap and waited as a prim schoolgirl.

"My father thought I was an absolute failure when I didn't make it into Medicine School. He's the local doctor in Sarstedt, you see, and he wanted me as his only son to take over the practice when he retired."

His voice had become a bit slow and slurry, a side-effect of the high dose of Digoxin. He now needed no further encouragement to disclose personal details that were unfiltered for once. He only needed a polite, "How unfortunate for you both." The General temporarily closed his eyes and the muscles in his clean-shaven, shallow cheek twisted. With difficulty he seemed to rip himself loose from the unhappy memory.

"That's how I ended up in the army. The only other thing my father thought a dignified profession." Another silence. In which she wondered if he would harp on about this wonderful father he'd fallen short of, but then he added, "That's why I took you with me."

"I didn't know the medical profession meant so much to you, Herr General."

He snarled, "It doesn't! Not anymore. You matter."

She wanted to ask, 'how so?' but there was something so

menacing in the way he spit out these words that it chilled her, and she bit her tongue.

"You're not going anywhere, Madame Docteur, and neither is that fellow of yours. You're both in my power."

"I-I don't understand, Herr General."

It was little more than a squeaky moan. Why did he bring up JJ now? What was going on? Then his words made her blow relieved air through her teeth. Did it mean JJ was alive? Von Stein wouldn't talk about him being in his power if he wasn't. Her heart made little jolts in her chest before it rested in its own place again.

"You know what the *Third Reich* stands for, Madame?"

"No, Herr General, I don't. At least not in detail."

"Control!" He yelled the word at the top of his lungs.

It made Océane shrink against the canvas back of her chair as if she could disappear in it. He certainly had gone crazy now. She tried to recollect if she'd accidentally given him the wrong medicine.

He shrieked, "Control!" once again, before gasping for air.

Watching the spectacle with a combination of fear and anticipation, she waited for the moment it would be her task to step in, should he start foaming at the mouth. So far, he only seemed to work himself up into a frenzy, which wasn't going to help his heart condition, but nothing she'd say right now would calm him. On the contrary. It took him a good few minutes to catch his breath again, while he lay sweating and dead-pale in the cushions.

In a less voluminous and more coherent voice he continued, "Der Führer has set it as our task to eradicate everything that opposes his control, and I am here to help him with that."

Océane fell from one puzzlement to the next. What had this to do with the man's longing to be a doctor? It made no sense. She wanted to keep him on that track as it might lead to insights she needed. She racked her brain, thinking of a question to lead him back to his weakness.

"I understand that, Herr General. I would be surprised if you didn't, but I fail to see what it has to do with me. Or with ... the person I know."

If his dead-fish eyes would have been able to glare, they would have at that moment, but all they did was bulge a little further out of their sockets. It made him look like a desperate sea monster.

"Huricana's here and so are you! Oh, sweet revenge!"

His mad cry revealed everything and nothing, while Océane's overworked brain was pulled in two opposite directions. She had no idea who Huricana was but now understood the General had linked her to the wrong Resistance fighter. There was now only her own skin to save and get back to Paris to find JJ.

"Why bring me all the way from Paris if you wanted to get rid of me in the first place? You could've made it a lot easier."

He smirked. "The fellow will show up. You're just bait, my dear. It will be slow, ever so slow."

With all she had in her, she manned herself and said through gritted teeth, "I don't know a Huricana, so please let me go."

"Liar!"

Icy calm in her veins. Another crisis. Her mind pieced the fragments of his rage together until she would know how they fitted. She still needed more information. He wasn't going to kill her. At least not yet. He used her as bait to catch someone else.

"If you manage to catch the man you want, am I then allowed to go free, Herr General?

"Ha!"

It was all he said for a long time and, as his breathing became more regular, Océane thought he had dozed off but then he said, in a very low but steady voice, "I like being the cat playing with my favorite mice. I'm always the one that catches them. That will be all. You're dismissed, Madame Docteur."

22

INTO THE WILD

O céane staggered back to her own tent, bewildered, befuddled, but also hell-bent on escape. She'd hoped to run into Hans Arenberg on her way, but he was nowhere in sight. And he couldn't help her anyway, not with escape and not with the crazy General.

The late afternoon heat hung like a heavy sheet over the desert. The distant drone of airplanes sounded high above her in the hazy-blue sky. The camp was deserted. It was either nap or dinner time but for Océane it was neither. The volatile Von Stein puzzle was becoming clear, and it didn't portend well for her.

A mouse, a trapped mouse, that was indeed how she felt. He had not wanted her as his doctor but as a mouse to play with.

What an evil, evil man, was all she could think as she zipped open the tent and stepped inside the small, hot confinement that reeked of tarpaulin and rancid food. She was tempted to throw herself on the camp bed and cry her eyes out but with her last strength she pulled herself together and sat in the folded chair at the small camp table. She had to write a goodbye letter, just in case. She'd entrust it to Arenberg and ask him to post it for her if push came to shove.

Thinking for a long time before she put pen to paper, she finally wrote as quickly as she could and before she could change her mind.

FEBRUARY 1942

DEAR MOM AND DAD,

IT SEEMS I've done everything wrong in my life. I've disappointed you and then I made a total mess of my life in Paris while trying to find more information on a dear friend who had been captured by the occupying force. For matters of security, I cannot mention his name here, but grandfather can give you the details. I hope you accept that he was important to me, or I wouldn't have jeopardized my own safety.

YOU WON'T BELIEVE it but I'm now in a desert in Libya, far away from civilization in the company of a German general called Dieter von Stein. On paper I serve as his personal physician because he has a heart condition.

IF I HADN'T BEEN SO foolish, I would probably still be working at the Hôtel-Dieu de Paris and live with grandpapa. But it is what it is and I'm paying the price for it. I'm fully aware that this is not how you raised me, and my biggest punishment is that I've not only let you down but also myself.

I DO HOPE I will see you again when the war is over. I send you all my love and hope you are well.

. . .

BIG KISS FOR ARTHUR,
    Your daughter,
    Océane.

SHE COULDN'T BRING herself to tell them her life was in dire danger. It seemed too theatrical, too grotesque, too improbable. Folding the paper in four, she slipped it into an envelope, on which she scribbled their name and address.

Then she tore off a second sheet and with the same decisive haste wrote in her clear handwriting.

DEAR GRANDFATHER,

ENCLOSED *you will find a letter that I ask you to forward to my parents in Chicago as soon as that is possible. Should the war take much longer, then please keep it as long as needed. About the same content is in this letter to you.*

I APOLOGIZE *for having been a reckless and disobedient granddaughter. My love for you-know-who certainly blinded me into taking actions that have had dire consequences. I'm currently in Libya as the so-called personal physician to the German high commander Dieter von Stein and I have no idea how long I will be here or whether I will be able to return to Paris in due time. I hope you understand that for censorship reasons I cannot elaborate on any details. I'm physically well and try to keep my spirits up as best as I can.*

I LOVE YOU, *grandfather, and thank you for all that you've done for me. I hope I will one day be able to make it up to you.*

. . .

Please forgive me. I hope you and Gaël and Marie are in good health.

Your loving granddaughter,
   Océane Bell.

REREADING IT, she wondered if it would ever pass censoring. Probably not but it was the best she could do. She also folded this letter and put it in a slightly bigger envelope with the letter for her parents inside.

She slipped back into her shoes and went outside. An ink black sky with millions of tiny stars enveloped the still camp. Night had fallen just like that. The hard wind had died down, letting the sand rest. A chill in the air made her shiver.

"What now?" she asked herself. Having no torch and with the camp in blackout it was hard to see a hand in front of her eyes. No one had come her way to ask if she needed anything. For a moment she froze in her tracks. Had they all gone and left her behind? Was she all by herself in the desert?

But then she saw just the glimmer of a light from within one of the tents and cautiously headed that way, hoping against hope it would be Arenberg's tent. She stopped to listen for the sound of voices from within, but everything was quiet. Just the soft rustling of the evening breeze and the always present muffled drum from the war further up north.

"Sergeant Arenberg?" she called out softly, not sure what gave her the courage. Nothing moved. "Sergeant Arenberg, are you there?"

There was some movement inside and the tent was zipped open. To her relief it *was* him crouched in the opening, in his shirt sleeves, the suspenders undone. He looked like a ghost in the flicker of an oil lamp.

"What is it, Madame Docteur?" His voice was hasty. "Anyone ill?"

"No, but I need your help."

The look he gave her was even more worried. "I'm not sure I can ..."

"You have to, Sergeant. My life is in danger. I have a favor to ask you. Please?" Although she kept her voice to a whisper, there was an urgency in it that made it sound like she was calling out for help.

"Alright. Come in for a minute, but we have to be very vigilant."

"I know."

She slipped in and he zipped up the tent again. In the dim light she could see it had the same bare essentials as her own, but she was surprised to see a copy of Albert Camus' L'Etranger lie open on his field bed. Following her eyes, he quickly closed the book and stuffed it under his pillow.

"I didn't know you read French." He looked haunted but she held up her hand. "Don't worry. I won't tell anyone, and the Nazis didn't forbid its publication, did they?"

"Not initially, no." He sighed, relieved. "So what is it you need, Madame?"

Océane retrieved the envelope from her coat jacket. "I don't know what the General's plans are with me, but it doesn't look good. This is a letter to my grandfather in Paris. Could you please see he gets it in case anything should happen to me?"

He took the envelope from her and read the address at the front. Then his eyes, flickering in the light of the lamp, met hers. "Do you think it's that bad?"

In an attempt to downplay her own concerns, she shrugged. "Could be. So will you do it?"

"If I come out without a scratch, I will. I promise."

"For sure, the General is not against his own people?"

It was meant to give him a shot in the arm but the look in his gray eyes told her otherwise. "I'm not so sure my fate is any better than yours, Madame. Now please leave before we're both heading for the rocks."

"One more question. Who is Huricana?" The look in his eyes told her he had no idea what she was talking about, so she explained. "Apparently the General came to Libya to round up a French Resistance cell that's sabotaging the German offensive here. One of them is called Huricana."

"You know more than I do, Madame. I told you I'm not in the loop."

"But you must have heard something?" Her plea was urgent. "Von Stein is convinced I know that Resistance fighter. Please, find out what you can."

"I will, Madame, I promise, but you must go now. And please don't say anything about Camus' book. I'll burn it tonight."

"I never would! Don't you know me by now?"

Their eyes met in the flicker of the oil lamp. Hazel ones burning into grays. A bond of trust and friendship was forged.

"I believe you, Madame, and thank you."

A little later, back in her own tent, Océane sat down on her camp bed with her head in her hands. One thing was clear to her in her despair. Sergeant Arenberg had to stay alive. He was her only ally and her only possible rescue.

SOMEHOW, she must have fallen asleep despite hunger and fear because she woke to the sound of voices outside her tent. Raising herself on an arm, she listened while she became aware of the prickly army blanket scorching her naked legs.

"*Attacke*" was the only word she picked up from the passing voices before she hurled herself out of bed. Was the camp under attack? Heavens, what now? She stopped in her tracks. What if the Allies would seize the camp and she came out alive? Crisis mode. She had her American and her French passport hidden in a back pocket of her medical bag. Von Stein didn't know, didn't search her belongings. Just to make sure, she checked they were still there.

This might be her ticket out of this hell. She only prayed they wouldn't bomb the camp and erase men and material from the earth. She needed a white flag. Already hoisting the sheet from her bed and looking for a pole to attach it to, she heard the General's voice outside her tent.

"Come here!"

"Just a minute!" she shouted in what she hoped was a steady voice.

"Make it quick if you want to stay alive."

"Why should you care?" she muttered under her breath but when she stepped outside in what appeared to be a glorious warm and sunny morning, she did see concern in his face. For his own fate, or hers? It was unclear.

"We've just received news that an Allied attack is expected on Tripoli today or tomorrow. This camp is right in the firing line. We'll take you to an underground bunker a little west from the camp. You'll be safe there."

No! she screamed inwardly. *I want to stay here. I want to be rescued by my own people.*

He must have seen the horror on her face. "I understand this is a sudden change of event. It is not what I had planned, either."

There was little else to do other than to obey. Running or escaping was currently impossible.

"Let me grab my bags." Her voice was so toneless, it was as if she was writing her own death sentence.

"Hurry up. I've got the jeep ready, and I'll drive you there myself. I want to see the bunkers my men have created before I return to defend the camp. It's a short drive."

Grabbing her medical bag and her duffel bag with the fancy attributes Von Stein had obtained for her in Paris, she followed him to the jeep that stood with rumbling engine at the entrance to the camp.

Océane was overjoyed to see Sergeant Arenberg taking the passenger seat after giving her a lopsided smile. All the while the rumbling in the air became louder and Von Stein sped away, leaving a large dust cloud behind them. The jeep bumped over sand dunes and through dust tracks until they came to what looked like a recently constructed brick road.

"Here," Sergeant Arenberg handed her a brown paper bag and a thermos, "the road will be level for a few miles so you can eat something now."

Océane thankfully drank the lukewarm tea with loads of sugar and sank her teeth into the dark-brown bread that was slightly sour, smeared with cheese spread. There was even a wrinkled red apple on the bottom of the bag. She hadn't had so much luxury since the uneaten lunch at the Ritz and greedily finished everything way too fast.

"Thank you, I needed that."

"Don't worry, I packed loads more, sausages and canned vegetables and fruit. Even chocolate and beer."

"How long do you think I'll have to stay there?"

No direct answer came from the front seat and panic fought with the food in her stomach.

"We don't know how long the attack will last, so we'd better be safe than sorry," Arenberg answered instead of the General.

She hung on to the 'we'.

If only Arenberg stayed with her, she'd be less afraid. But there was no saying what the General would decide. She watched the back of his head, the wisp of sandy hair that curled over his collar from under that ridiculously high cap. The black leather coat, way too warm in this climate, was too big at his shoulders and the gloved hands that gripped the Jeep's steering wheel shivered. Not just from the vibration of the engine.

It was puzzling to say the least that the Nazis sent a General who was clearly in such bad health to such a remote area. She wondered whether it was a sign of weakness on their part, that they no longer had enough capable and strong commanders to run their ludicrous show. Or was it Dieter von Stein's wish to run his own show till his very last breath?

After a dusty drive, Von Stein jerked on the steering wheel, and they left the track. The wheels of the jeep were ploughing through loose sand. There was sand everywhere, forcing Océane to cover her mouth and nose. Not a soul in sight, no bird, no plant, no water.

Just the war sound coming closer, first rumbling, now roaring. She could see the glittering engines hanging in the cloudless sky. It was unclear from which side they were.

Was Von Stein telling the truth?

Her stomach suddenly jolted, making her almost throw up the recent breakfast. He was going to kill them both. He'd brought them to the wilderness to get them both killed, removed from his agenda under the pretense of an attack. No one would ever know.

Or ... only to kill her?

Sergeant Arenberg had betrayed her after all. The Germans had managed to catch that man they called Huricana. There was no need for her anymore. But it didn't make sense. Her gut told her she could trust the farmer's son. And Arenberg was armed as well. He would come to her rescue.

The click-click-click of her brain cells didn't go fast enough for her liking, but her left hand gripped the door handle anyway, ready to run.

"Here we are." The General stopped the jeep and took off his heavy cap to wipe the sweat from his forehead with a pristine white handkerchief.

"Where are we?" It was more a gasp than a human sound that came out of her.

There was no bunker and deadly fear tightened her throat. The morning sun was relentless. It felt like sitting in the middle of a hot stove while the dull drone overhead slowly became deafening.

"Over there!" The General adjusted his binoculars, scanning the barren landscape. "I can't take the jeep any further or the wheels might get stuck. We'll have to walk the last part."

"I don't want to go." The words rushed out.

"I promise it will be cool and sheltered in there."

"Why ... why is there a bunker here in the middle of nowhere?"

"Aha, that." Von Stein seemed to find it a perfectly normal question. "That's what we call German *gründlichkeit*. We build bunkers wherever we conquer land. Simple as that."

"How long do I have to stay there?"

"Madame Docteur, too many questions again. We have no time for that."

Arenberg was standing at the back of the jeep opening the canvas hood. "Herr General, do you want me to take all the equipment and the food?"

"Everything, Sergeant. Just in case. I'll be going back to camp soon. I just want to make sure the doctor is settled in and safe."

"I'm not going to stay here on my own."

The General, who was already trudging through the hot sand in his impossibly high boots, turned to face her with an irritated look on his face. "Of course not. Sergeant Arenberg will stay with you. After the coast is clear, we'll come and fetch you both."

He now set out with determination towards what looked like a heap of dead trees piled together, but he was making slow progress, dragging his right leg, panting in the heat and in his heavy leather coat. Arenberg and a relieved Océane followed him. The sergeant was carrying the box with food and ammunition, while she held her bags and a small crate with medical supplies.

They exchanged a look, saying to each other without words what they thought. Was this going to be their one chance?

The roar of the airplanes was suddenly very near and very loud.

The General shrieked, "Hurry up! We must seek cover! Now!"

He was scrambling as fast as he could in his heavy boots over the cracked, bone-dry surface as if negotiating a giant beehive. All three increased their pace. They could already hear the rat-tat-tat from the machine guns pelting on the camp with not one antiaircraft battery responding. How could the camp be undefended? It felt to Océane as if she had landed in a surreal landscape, where the reality of what she was experiencing had become a figment of the imagination.

This is your one option! Your one option!

Even that seemed surreal. The General couldn't have made such a huge mistake, made himself vulnerable like this. Where was the trap? Her brain fought to find it but couldn't.

As the General reached the pile of collapsed trees, he began to pull at them frantically, sweat pouring down the sides of his shallow face, his large cap askew. It struck her that he was as frightened as a chased deer. Dieter von Stein wasn't a combat commander; he was a salon commander who bullied from behind his desk. He wasn't even remotely prepared for real action; his fingernails had always remained gunpowder free. He let others do the killing for him.

"Please, Herr General, let me do that." Sergeant Arenberg dropped the box he had been carrying and hurried closer.

The General raised himself, swaying on his legs, his pale eyes turning helplessly to the sky. "They'll kill us all, those damned Tommies!" he wailed, trying to bring his binoculars to his eyes with quivering hands.

Arenberg had meanwhile cleared the trees away with his strong arms. The entrance to the bunker was revealed. With difficulty he raised the heavy wooden trapdoor and peered down the earthen steps. Océane was looking over his shoulder. Down the five steps was a small square room shored up with wooden beams. Dry dust and sand whirled up into the air but under the circumstances it looked invitingly enough.

"Quickly, go inside!"

The sergeant took the lead now and ushered both the bewildered Océane and the sick General into the cramped space. He ran up the steps again to collect their belongings and shut the lid over the underground shelter just in time. The immense rumbling in the air grew to a crescendo and the ground around them vibrated as if a herd of buffalos trampled overhead.

Océane listened but no further explosions sounded nearby.

Perhaps they're only on their way to Tripoli and it's all over, she thought wistfully.

Then something even more alarming happened. The rambling of vehicles over the terrain.

The jeep, was all she could think, *they'll see the jeep and then we're lost.*

Her own mind was playing tricks with her now. This was *not* the enemy; these were *her* people. She should push open the lid, get out and wave a white banner. Instead, she sat silent and trembling with her hands locked around her knees.

The cars and lorries seem to speed by for what seemed eternity, while her eyes adjusted to the darkness of the space around her, to the diffuse light that came through the cracks in the wooden planks overhead.

To her horror she saw that the sergeant was bent over the General on the ground. Only now did she notice his wheezing breath. She shook herself out of her stupor and, grabbing her medical bag, shuffled over to the other corner.

"Could you give me a light?" she asked Arenberg. "Let me listen to his heart rate."

As a second wave of airplanes rushed overhead, she inspected the General who lay limp and pale as a sheet on the dusty ground. With difficulty they heaved his arms out of the heavy leather coat and using his coat as a protective layer underneath, she set out, first lifting the eyelids of his closed eyes and then listening to his pulse.

"Sir, are you awake?" She hoped that by using 'sir' she would raise his anger and he would react, but nothing happened. "He's unconscious," she murmured, "heart failure. I'll need to resuscitate him."

What are you doing! her mind screamed. *Let him die! Let him die*!

She couldn't. Her professional oath forbade it.

"Do you want me to do it?" The sergeant's voice beside her was soft but strong. "I can very well understand you don't want to do this."

For a moment she hesitated. "I am torn," she admitted, "but do you have the experience?"

"We all get that in our military training." Arenberg did not hesitate for one moment, handed her the torch and was already pumping the General's chest with two hands pressed together.

"More pressure," Océane instructed, while her mind raced.

How on earth were they going to get this sick man back in the open and back to the camp with Allied forces all around? It was a very compromising situation, indeed. Likely the Allies were looking for the high-ranking Major-General von Stein who'd sown nothing but hate in his Paris days. As much as he might be looking for Huricana, Huricana and the Allies were looking for him. The tide might be turning.

The General came back to life with a jerk, taking hesitant gulps of air. Arenberg gazed at her in the semi-dark. She saw defeat in his eyes. He was facing her grim dilemma. Life and death.

"Job well done," she said, "thank you. Now let me administer his medicine."

She was already preparing a shot of morphine when her eye fell on the bottle of insulin that was also in her bag. An accidental dose? Arenberg needn't know. Nobody needed to know. She shivered, fought, wrestled with her conscience. It was so very tempting. But it wouldn't solve anything. She would still be a German prisoner of war.

In the cramped space with the General half conscious, she wanted to ask Arenberg where his loyalties lay but couldn't. She shook her head at herself. For now, they were trapped rats. When the Allied attack was over and there were survivors in the German camp, they would come in search of their General. They knew where he was. She couldn't let him die now. It would be suspicious. She jabbed the right medicine into his shriveled arm and watched him doze off.

"That will keep him sedated for the next hour," she observed as Arenberg covered him with a horse blanket he had brought in with the provisions.

"Care for a schnapps?"

The care in the kind German's eyes calmed her somewhat. "That would be great."

They sat side by side against the beamed wall of the bunker while Arenberg's metal flask went from hand to hand.

"What now?" Océane observed, wiping the back of her hand over her mouth while the hot liquid burnt her stomach.

The General was asleep, restless and taking irregular breaths but the immediate danger for his life seemed at bay.

"It seems the heat of the attack has somewhat died down," the sergeant observed. "I'll wait a little longer and then I'll go and take stock. See if the jeep is still there."

"We're in a real pickle if it isn't." Her voice was calm, but she felt far from it.

"Let's not think the worst yet." The stealthy iron in his voice made clear Hans Arenberg could take command should necessity call him to it.

Océane was dying to ask him about his loyalty in the war, about his obvious dislike of Von Stein. She even played with the idea of suggesting to him to run to freedom with her towards the open arms of the Allies. But she shrugged that outrageous thought off. He'd be killed on the spot. Nobody would believe a German wanting to turn against his own people.

While the General shifted fitfully on his makeshift leather bed, Arenberg screwed the porcelain lid back on his flask and got to his feet. He had to bend over in the low space.

"Give me a light until I open the lid, then switch it off immediately," he said as he pushed open the wooden cover a couple of inches and listened intently.

There was only the vague rumble in the distance that was always there, and he put his head outside looking in all directions. Océane held her breath, expecting his head to be blown off any second, but nothing happened.

"Seems safe," he observed, "will be back in a sec."

He jumped out of the hole with great agility. Océane also peeked over the edge. Arenberg lay flat on his stomach in the dunes that had formed due to the turbulence of the planes flying over at low altitude. The cave was meanwhile suddenly filled with bright light, and she had to blink. To keep the General asleep, she put the shawl she had used to cover her mouth over his head. He stirred, mumbled "Hansie" and was gone again. *Hansie*? She frowned in puzzlement but then shrugged. It was probably his brother or his dog.

A little later Arenberg returned and jumped back into the cave. He closed the cover door halfway, so they had light but were still relatively unseen from above.

"Jeep's still there, completely covered in sand. That's probably been our rescue. The engine started after some spluttering."

"No signs of Allies anymore?"

"Nope. So, what we'll do now is get some food inside us and then decide how we're going to make a stretcher to carry the General to the Jeep. It's going to be a challenge, but we somehow have to get him to the sickbay at camp."

Océane nodded. "He'll probably die if we don't get help soon." She kept her face deadpan but was aware of Arenberg's gray gaze on her.

"I think it would be safe to have our meal outside. We'll pile these dead trees into a kind of wigwam and sit underneath them. I need to talk with you without ... you know ..." He nodded his head in the direction of the sleeping SS-er.

Océane thought she felt her heart skip a beat. This might be the opportunity she'd been waiting for, but immediately her mood dropped again. There was no way they could pull this off. A German officer and a French American doctor driving through the desert in a German jeep. It was a sure road to their premature death.

But so was sitting here waiting for the General to revive.

23

THE CRAZY GENERAL

Océane and the German sergeant ate dried sausages and dark-brown sour bread and washed it down with cold black coffee. For the time being the desert had returned to the whizzing of the wind and a faint but constant rumble in the background.

Somehow in this alien, Mars-like terrain, she could breathe freer and easier for the first time since JJ's disappearance from occupied Paris. Though every fiber in her body was strained to the utmost and the heat parched her throat and skin, her spirit revived, yearning for the removal of a heavy burden.

"Sergeant Arenberg ..." she began.

"Please don't call me that anymore. I'd rather you call me John. That would be my name in English, right?"

She gazed at him sideways, wondering what this had brought on. "Are you ... are you considering ...?"

"Yes." Decisive, simple but final.

She waited, hoping he'd say more now they were out of earshot of the drugged, half-crazy General but Hans who wanted to be John was drawing figures in the sand with a twig and evaded her gaze.

"What happened?" she asked softly. "Please tell me, John. We seem to be thrown into this bloody war that isn't ours together, so we might as well try to scramble out of it together, although I have no idea how."

He kept drawing the figures, then stared for a while to the horizon. She followed his gaze and was momentarily mesmerized by the shimmering line of dancing light that blurred in tones of ochre, gray and lemon yellow. She had no idea the desert had a captivating side as well.

"I can't tell, Madame. Not now. We have to devise a plan, but they'll come looking for us as soon as the coast is clear, so we don't have much time."

"If I'm supposed to call you John, you must call me Rose. That way we'll both have a *nom de guerre*."

He laughed a joyless laugh, taking the schnapps flask from his pocket and taking a deep swig. His long, khaki legs with the heavy army boots lay stretched out in front of him.

"Rose it is, though I've seen your name is Océane, which is the most poetic name I've ever come across."

"Thank you. Do you think I should check on the General?"

"No!" It was sharp, no nonsense. Hans was swiftly becoming John. "I'll tell you if you promise not to laugh."

"I promise."

He drew more figures, stared a little longer, then sighed with his whole body. It ended in a shudder. "It's a long story."

"How long have we got?"

"Not long, so let me make it as short as possible. I told you in the hospital that my father knows Von Stein, that we're from the same region." His voice was flat but held a tinge of desperate rage. "Von Stein's father was our family doctor before his retirement. Their house lies on the edge of our estate. It wasn't that we were close with the family or anything, but my father had trust in the medical knowledge of Von Stein Sr. I only saw the old doctor when I had to go for the usual stuff, you know. Once I broke my wrist when I fell out of an apple tree and once I had a bad measles' outbreak."

He stopped, taking another swig from the liquor, his eyes fixed on the horizon. Océane listened intently, trying to connect the dots.

"This was all way before the war, even before Hitler came to power. Von Stein Sr. retired a couple of years ago but my father who's also the mayor of Sarstedt still sat on some committees with him. Just the usual stuff, you know. I neither liked nor disliked the family doctor. He was just someone on the fringe of my orbit, a man with a round, black hat, always in a black suit, who had a hasty way of moving and a short, round body. I also knew his son Dieter, of course, this fellow."

Hans pointed with his thumb in the direction of the bunker. "It would have been hard not to be aware of him, growing up in a tight-knit community like ours. It was also a known fact that father and son were always at loggerheads, from his youth. My father told me that Dieter always was a weak and sickly boy but with a mean inclination. He'd tease animals and boast about it in public. My father once suspected that he was behind it when all the Arenberg chickens were killed one morning and hung upside down in a row around the fence of our house."

The sergeant pulled in one leg and stamped the boot angrily in the sand. "So this is where I don't get my father, who's the kindest man in the world and wouldn't harm anyone. How could he say that the General would protect me?"

"What happened?" Océane could no longer stay quiet.

"As I said, I knew of him, but I had never met him. He was already rising in the army when I was still in school. There were rumors, of course, but people like to blab. That's nothing new."

"Rumors of what?" Océane grabbed the flask from him and drank some of the burning liquid. She was bracing herself.

"That he was swinging the other way." He said it rapidly, casting his eyes down.

Océane's mouth fell open, realizing she hadn't misunderstood when the General croaked 'Hansie'. Her hand instinctively clamped over her mouth, her heart welled up with sorrow for this kind, helpless man.

"I'm so, so sorry," she gasped. "I had no idea." Immediately the physician in her woke up, "Are you alright? Do you need anything?"

"What do you think I need?" Hans said through gritted teeth, trying to keep his voice down. "It stopped for a while in Paris, but it's begun here again. All I need is to get away from him as soon and as far away as I can."

"Yes, that's what you need. And so do I, but we have to be smart about it. We're in the middle of nowhere, surrounded by both friends and enemies. It's a complete rigmarole."

She handed him the flask, which he emptied without stopping. His Adam's apple moved frantically up and down as he drank. Océane knew he needed every drop of that.

"So that time in the hospital was after the first time?" She hardly dared to ask.

He gave the slightest of nods. With the back of his hand, he wiped away a tear.

Océane thought she'd never felt more powerless in her entire life. She had to swallow hard herself before she could add, "Still, John, I think you must forgive your father. I don't think he'd deliberately put you in such a compromising position. Don't you believe that?"

He nodded again. Another tear.

She knew she had to keep going now. "I blame myself. I should have noticed something, but I guess I was too occupied with my own horrors."

"No!" His power was returning now the worst was over for him. "You couldn't know, Rose. Nobody knew. He threatened to gun me down as a traitor in front of all the officers if I ever slipped a word. It took until this moment in the damned Libyan desert with you before I could break the seal."

"Thank you for your trust. But why do you want to break with the entire German army over this?"

"I told you before that I don't care for this war. I never did and I never will, but I'm not blind. Hitler and his Von Stein cronies have whipped up the entire nation so even good boys have turned bad. I want to free my country from the tyranny, but I think I'd better operate from outside Germany to realize that."

His voice had an almost euphoric tone. He sounded so like JJ to Océane.

"I'd be court-martialed as soon as I returned to German soil, so I better fight from outside our borders. I'm convinced that this North Africa charade, in time, will be the turning point in this idiotic war. The Germans are losing, Mussolini's forces are in decline. If you could agree to it, I'll return to France with you and disguise myself as a Frenchman, joining the Resistance. I'm learning French as fast as I can."

The sun was meanwhile already sinking towards the horizon and a soft, cooler breeze filled the air.

"We still don't have a plan." Océane observed. "Do you think they'll come for us tonight? The Germans, I mean?"

"Yes." He stopped for a moment. "I do have a plan but it's a rigorous one. I see it as the only option we have."

"What?"

"I've been wanting to escape from him for a long time, and take you with me, of course," he added quickly. "I've studied the map in great detail. There's an Allied camp at Sébha at about a two-days' drive from here. That's why I packed extra food and petrol. Just in case this would be our opportunity. We drive during the night on my compass, without our headlights, and we hide during the day. When we approach the camp, we hoist a white flag on the jeep. I've even managed to sneak some civilian clothes with me so I can get rid of this hated uniform."

Océane listened quietly, her arms wrapped around her drawn up knees. Then she said drily, "You forget one thing."

He shook his head. "I forget nothing and see everything."

"What do you mean?"

"I saw you hesitate which injection you would give him earlier." He faced her, gray eyes sad, not jubilant. "If you can't do it, I'll do it for you."

She sucked in air and let it out slowly, trying to steady herself. "I can do it. I've thought about it before. You're right. It's just I still need to know from him what he knows about my boyfriend. I can't let him slip away, without extracting that knowledge from him."

The cold-bloodedness with which she spoke chilled her own bones, but evening was falling, the Germans were on their heels and freedom was lurking. Hans was right, it was now or never.

He shifted in the sand that was quickly cooling in the dusk. "I told you before, Rose, that I know nothing about your boyfriend. I've tried several times to bring it up with Von Stein, but he refused to give any details. Believe me that I've tried in so many ways. He's as obsessed with you and your man as he is with me. That's all I know. Only God knows what's going on inside that madman."

"He's truly evil," Océane agreed. "Well, let's see what's he's like now. Perhaps we're lucky and he's done himself in."

"That one? Never. He's as tough as the black leather he wears," Hans said grimly as he rose to his feet. Stamping to get the sand out of his clothes, his face was one angry growl.

She was once again gripped by the torture he must have undergone at the hands of his own commander.

When they descended into the cave and Hans flipped on the torch, they saw to their surprise that the General was sitting upright with his black coat draped around his shoulders. He'd helped himself to some tea and there was even a half-eaten sandwich at his side. The wasted blue eyes took them in. He seemed his old self again, ready to make a biting remark.

Hans was right. The man is tougher than leather.

"Where were you?" He certainly was furious.

"Just checking the surroundings to see if it would be safe to return to the camp, Herr General."

Hans managed to speak in his usual deferential tone, but Océane shifted uneasily from one foot to the other. It was apparently going to be tougher than they had anticipated.

"Time for your medicine," she said, heading over to her medical bag and pretending to be rummaging through it. "How are you feeling, Herr General?"

"I feel good. And I want to return to the camp now."

"But," she protested, "you had a serious attack earlier. Would it not be wiser to spend the night here and go back tomorrow morning?"

Anything to win time, she thought, not daring to look in Hans's direction. At this moment she would be unable to administer the lethal dose of insulin as had been her plan; instead, she decided on the strongest tranquilizer in her arsenal.

"Take this tablet, Herr General, and let it take effect for a while. If you still feel good enough to travel in half an hour, we can discuss it then."

To her surprise he agreed without protest and took the two pink tablets with a swig of cold tea. He rested his head against the beam, and she waited with bated breath for him to nod off. She felt Hans all tense and highly alert as well. Sitting in another corner of the small space, she kept her eyes fixed on the General. When would be the best time to confront him with her final question? All the muscles in her body were so tight she thought they might snap any moment. Her father's voice, loud and clear, as if he were in that cramped space in the Libyan desert with her, rang in her ear.

"Doctors don't take sides, neither in war nor in peace. We leave taking sides to politicians and soldiers. All we do is try and save as many human lives as we possibly can. That is our oath, my girl. Only that."

Still encapsulated in her fear and torn between the ground rule of her profession and the dire situation she found herself in, she glanced through her eyelids at Hans, who was sitting still as the Buddha himself, lost in his own thoughts. The farmer's son had never decided to go out and kill people either. Had he ever killed a Frenchman, a Belgian or Dutch citizen? She had no inkling, but she did know he was against this war. Yet, he now wanted to join the French Resistance to liberate his own country from the stain it was spreading. And what about herself? She now understood JJ's choice to give up painting and fight for a free France. Had she not sworn to do so herself should she come out of this situation alive? Unable to come to a conclusion as time closed in on her, she became vaguely aware the General was talking in a slurred voice.

"I ... owe you ... an explanation of some sorts ..."

"What's that, Von Stein?" Arenberg seemed to revive himself from his own mulling, but not addressing his boss properly anymore.

"You!"

He shrieked the word and the shrillness of it resonated through the cave. Océane shot upright but it was unclear whom he was addressing. Maybe both of them. She saw him open his eyes and only the whites were visible as he rolled them upwards. He was bursting with anger. The sedation clearly had not worked.

"You!" he bellowed once more.

Arenberg tried again. "What is it, Von Stein? Tell us."

The sick man slumped back and seemed resigned for a moment before he cried out in a thin but piercing voice that seemed to cost him the last of his breath. "You both have everything! Everything!"

As if tied to a mechanism larger than herself, Océane moved towards him and took his pulse. It was racing. For a moment she wondered if she'd administered the wrong medicine after all, but she was sure she hadn't. He was close to a delirium, so she tried to calm him. Still always the doctor.

"Please don't excite yourself too much, Herr General. Think of your heart."

"My heart!" he bellowed. "My heart!"

He began laughing, an eerie, inhuman laugh that made the hairs on her arms stand up. It ended in a cough and he almost toppled sideways, becoming purple in the face. Arenberg was at her side, helping him upright again. The sergeant's touch seemed to calm the crazy General to some extent, and he grabbed his hand and brought it to his purplish lips. Océane was surprised at the tenderness it held. But also disgusted, as she saw Hans quickly pulling his hand away.

"I'm sorry. I love you." The words hung like dirty washing in the bunker, but he repeated them nevertheless, his head low on his chest. "I'm sorry I loved you, Hansie."

Océane didn't dare to look at the sergeant, she hardly dared to move. At least there was an apology, at least. Could she expect clemency as well? Did he somehow know what they had in store for him? She didn't have to wait long. The apology to Hans seemed to have taken a valve from his stopped-up emotions.

"Remix is dead."

The silence after these words seemed eternal. All the air was sucked out of the cave and Océane had to fight not to faint. "What happened?" It was barely a croaked whisper. "I have to know what happened to ... JJ."

The sound of the General's laugh was beyond sinister. "What a stupid question. What do you think happened? The man refused to talk so *my men* had no choice."

Océane buried her head in her hands. All was lost now. They had killed him. She didn't even want to know how. Brutal and careless. Her love, her life. If she could've died that moment as well, she would've accepted it. All this, this whole ridiculous quest she'd gone on, had been completely useless. JJ had probably been dead the moment she walked into 84 Avenue Foch.

She looked up through the open lid into the African night that had fallen on them as if a sudden black sheet covered the earth. Stars twinkled on the firmament and the night was still. Even the soft swishing of the desert grass had subsided. It was very still inside the bunker as well but for the wheezing breath of the General. Arenberg didn't move a muscle, as if on guard to catch her should she break and fall.

Océane bit her lip, hard, until it bled, and the iron taste filled her mouth. Over and over in her head went the sentence, *JJ is dead and I'm alive. JJ is dead.* She was keenly aware she had come to a crossroad in her life. Choices had to be made to honor what she stood for, for his loss, his premature death, and she, Océane Bell, would make sure his sacrifice would not be forgotten.

"Where is he buried?" Her voice was calm, steadfast. Her mind made up.

The hazel gaze fixed on the General, unable to hide her contempt for him any longer. All fear seeped out of her as if a plug was pulled up. She functioned on automatic.

He shrugged but didn't answer.

"Where is he buried?" She raised her voice and he blinked, surprised at her change in tone.

"For heaven's sake, woman, I don't know. I don't occupy myself with the details of these matters."

She was about to lash out at him but restrained herself at the last moment. Crazy and evil as he was, he had so far spoken the truth when he offered a piece of information. He probably really didn't know. JJ was in an unknown grave. Her heart bled further but her mind was cool. She wouldn't rest until she knew where he lay.

Silence again. *Think, think, think.* And then it came. Something didn't fit.

"Then who the hell is Huricana?"

He laughed his evil laugh again. "Don't you understand, you silly American doctor? Huricana was Remix's boss. But they've caught him, too. Hahaha!"

"*Genug!*" Arenberg's voice cut through the dusk. "*Du hast zu viel Blut an deinen Händen!*"

"What's gotten into you?" The General flinched, clearly surprised by his subordinate's tone.

"The game is over, Von Stein." The words were spoken low and slow but the thunderous force beneath the syllables was unmistakable.

Despite her grief, Océane felt a sliver of hope return. It was two against one and the one was not in a condition to fight.

"What do you mean, Sergeant Arenberg? The war is not a game. It never was." The General obviously wanted to buy time by playing the innocent but his eyes were rolling wildly, while he seemed to be sinking further into his slender carcass.

"I mean," Arenberg said in the same slow, dark voice, "I mean *your* game is over, Dieter von Stein. *Ours* has just begun."

"Don't flatter yourself, Arenberg, and neither should you, Madame. I've already phoned the camp and they're on their way to pick me up and arrest you. Don't think you can outsmart me because you can't."

"That's bluff. The field phone does not work down here."

The General held out his hands in the air as if in defense. "So what do you want, Arenberg? Is it money? Promotion?"

"Retribution."

The word sounds so clean, Oceane thought, *so correct.*

A deadly calm settled on her. Arenberg was right. The game was over for Von Stein. She opened her medical bag knowing what she was looking for.

"Wait," the General cried, as if he had heard her think out loud, "there must be a way we can work together. Let me explain myself."

"What's the use?" It was her turn to address him. "For Hans and me, you've crushed everything that was good and loved. It's men like you that began this awful war in the first place. Out of spite and hatred and arrogance." She rummaged more in her bag.

"We don't have time for your shallow reasoning anymore," Arenberg added. "The fact that you were able to push two people over the edge who would never even have thought of killing another human is on your conscience, not ours."

"You're wrong there, young man." The general seemed to recover some of his former authority. "I had dreams of a better life once myself, and I was thwarted in the way I wanted to live my life. I could've been a famous doctor, but a mean little professor decided to let me fail my entrance exam. And I could've loved you, if you," his voice almost died down, "if you had let me."

He cleared his throat, having become strangely emotional. "Don't you both see it? You have everything I never had. Love, being a doctor, decency." His voice picked up before it became a hoarse cry again. "I had to crush it! I had to crush you. It's my job to break the good in weak people. I can break all that providence. I have that power! Hitler gave it to me, and you can't take it from me. The power over the dark is mine. Mine alone! You'll be crushed, crushed, crushed!"

"Shut up about your Götterdämmerung!" Arenberg jumped to his feet. "Now, Océane. I'll hold him."

He jumped on top of the General, forcing his arms behind his back, while he planted his knee in the German's crotch. With trembling fingers Océane filled the syringe with insulin.

Straight into his heart, she reminded herself. *Don't think. Just do it.*

"This is for the love and the beauty and the good in the world!" she said as she jabbed the needle into his chest.

Arenberg held the struggling General who quickly became limp and the last Océane saw of him was an evil blue eye, fixing her with a deadly stare.

The world became a whooshing dark swirl and then it was gone.

A white silence reigned.

24

THE FLIGHT

She came to with her entire body jostling like a corpse in the back of the jeep. Every bone hurt and her brain was pulp.

Then it came back to her in a flash. *Nooooooo!*

She squeezed her eyes shut, tried to hold her breath.

May I die? Please?

But life went on. She was awake. She peeked from underneath the rough horse blanket through the tarpaulin roof cover and could see the familiar stars in the black African night. The big Bear loomed brilliantly overhead as if protecting her wounded soul, but another deep gulf of misery washed over her.

JJ was dead. And she'd become a murderess as a result.

No longer able to live with the inside of her own mind, she scrambled to her feet to knock on the partition that separated the back from the cabin upfront. The jeep stopped, a door opened, Hans's pinched face showed at the back. Deep lines carved his young face and his eyes looked ages old.

"How are you?"

She hardly recognized his voice. It was as if all life had been eaten out of it.

"I'm sort of okay," she lied, trying to reassure him as much as herself. "Can I sit upfront with you?"

Some part of her registered the civilian clothes. It muddied her confusion further. She had no idea who he was, who she was, and where they were going.

"I'm glad you're okay." Flat voice, flat expression. "I actually have a better idea. We've covered quite a distance already. I think we can take a short stop. I can brew us some coffee and we can have a bite. I think it's what we both need."

Practical, down-to-earth, you-do-what-you-got-to-do farmer mentality. She just had to find that knob inside of herself again, too, and turn it on. She would. She knew she could do it even with her heart ripped out. She would go on. For JJ, for revenge.

Hans gave her a hand and she jumped out of the jeep.

"And how are you, John?"

"Have had better days, Rose."

The use of their aliases was strangely comforting. As if their real selves, their real murdering selves, were left in that bunker with the dead man.

"I think we can both do with a tranquilizer."

Grabbing her medical bag, she followed him to a small patch next to the car where he was already improvising a mobile camp stop.

"Hitler Jugend camps prove their worth now," he observed wryly. "It will be a short break because they'll be on our track soon. I've camouflaged the jeep as best as I could and removed the Nazi symbols but it's still a Kubelwagen and will be recognized as such."

He offered her a steaming cup of coffee, swiftly prepared over a small gas fire that he extinguished as soon as the coffee started percolating. It came with a slice of gingerbread on a tin plate. Though she felt as if her head was still in another world, she accepted both with gratitude.

Warming her hands around the metal cup, she blurted out before she wouldn't dare to ask anymore, "What did you do with Von Stein."

Her words hung in the still desert night as she inhaled the bitter roast of the coffee. It revived her nervous system.

"I said a couple of Hail Mary's for him and then left him, carrying you to the jeep. I went back for our supplies and then closed the lid over the bunker, rearranged the trees, camouflaged the jeep and drove off."

"Thank you. John." She swallowed. He had so much courage and she had passed out.

Hans continued, clearly having taken the lead, "The General will have been found by now. The camp knew where he was going. We're fugitives, Rose. There's no way to embellish it. We've killed one of Hitlers most high-ranking officers. If they find us, we're done."

"But they can't prove we killed him, can they?"

"That's your department. Probably not, but we're at least suspects even if they're unable to establish the how of his death. We left him for dead, disappeared with the jeep."

"Yes, you're right. And it doesn't matter anyway, whether they know, or not. I did kill him. I'll have to live with that." She shivered, drawing the horse blanket tighter around her.

"*We* killed him, Rose. You didn't do it on your own and your conscience is cleaner than mine. For you he *was* the enemy, for me he was just a personal enemy."

Océane was silent. The murder was like an immense wall before her and she couldn't climb it, didn't know how to get to the other side.

In the dark, Hans said soothingly, "Let it go, Doctor Bell. That's the only option. Don't look back. Use all your senses to look forwards not backwards. How to get us to safety. How to survive. If you keep playing the bunker film in your mind over and over, it'll drive you mad. This is war. In war we kill the enemy."

He started clearing the remnants of their sober meal.

"But ... but I'm not a soldier. I'm a doctor."

"From now on you're both, Rose. You're a doctor with a soldier's heart, fighting for freedom. Accept it. One is as noble as the other."

She pondered his words, thinking of her parents. Squeezing the stethoscope between her fingers. *Protect me, please protect me, Mom and Dad*, she prayed.

"There's one more thing," Hans added, hoisting the crate back into the jeep. "I've managed to take Von Stein's briefcase. We'll have to crack the lock, but it might be interesting to see what's inside."

Océane's eyes grew big, her heart beating wildly. "Oh, my goodness, you're quite something, John Arenberg! What if it contains information on Jean-Jacques?"

"We'll have to find out but not now let's go. It's at least a five-hour stretch we have to complete before dawn."

Océane followed him and took her seat upfront, almost unable to stop herself from cracking that lock right away. But Hans was right. They were far from safe. They had to eat all the miles they could to enlarge the distance between them and their persecutors.

As the jeep rumbled on through the dark, a new, shaky equilibrium settled on Océane. War was far from over, but she was closer to liberty than she'd been for a long time. And her cause was clear, crystal clear. She might have chosen her path months ago, but Von Stein's death had sealed it.

If I am now the most sought-after woman in the French Resistance, so be it.

Her thoughts turned to her companion. If they made it to safety, his story was still rambling. How to convince the Allies Hans's loyalty lay with *them* and that he was genuine, that he chose to be a traitor to his own people? Aha, the contents of that briefcase, of course. That would prove it.

"I think we should toss the contents of that briefcase into my medical bag after we've broken the lock. And then get rid of the briefcase. Just in case we're caught but can still talk ourselves out of it. Like having lost the way back to the camp."

He gazed at her sideways. "But I camouflaged the jeep."

"Safety reasons. Not knowing what we'd hit upon in the night."

"Smart thinking. But what will you do with the contents of your medical bag?"

"Store it in one of the food crates for the time being."

"Alright. We'll do that on our next stop."

The front screen was spattered with flies and mosquitos, blurring their sight. Without headlights and without a clear road, Hans could do no more than 25 miles per hour. They crept slowly onwards, like a camouflaged beetle through endless dunes. Hans regularly checked his compass that had fluorescent arms but now and then he had to stop to scan the map with his shaded torch lamp. It was an arduous, brutal, cold journey and the night dragged on for a million years.

"If you want me to take over the wheel, let me know," Océane offered at intervals.

"I'm okay. I'm used to long days on the farm. I've also done many night shifts in the army. But it would help if you could read maps."

"I could try. Just tell me what to look for."

"An Oasis called Sébha. If we're lucky it's still in French hands. For some reason I prefer to come across French soldiers instead of Brits or Americans. I think we can plead our case more successfully with them. They must be aware of the atrocities General von Stein committed in Paris."

Océane drew a line on the map with her finger in the dim light of the torch, suddenly wondering about the dream she had about an oasis. "Got it!" she said triumphantly. "But how can we be sure it is in French hands."

"We don't. But little is certain right now, isn't it? We have to pray we'll be safe and in one piece when we arrive there. Then we'll see what's next."

The drone of the jeep's motor and the intense days behind her made Océane terribly sleepy but she fought with all her might to stay awake. If she fell asleep, Hans would have to struggle on alone. That didn't seem fair after all he'd gone through as well. To keep herself and him occupied, she began to sing softly, French songs she remembered her mother singing for her when she was a little girl. *Frère Jacques, Sur le Pont d'Avignon* and *Au Clair de la Lune.*

"Sing that last song again, please. I love the melody and the words."

In the middle of a desert night fleeing from the Nazis, hoping to be rescued by the French army, Océane sang for her German companion:

Au clair de la Lune
mon ami Pierrot
Prête-moi ta plume
Pour écrire un mot
Ma chandelle est morte
Je n'ai plus de feu
Ouvre-moi ta porte
Pour l'amour de Dieu
Au clair de la Lune
Pierrot répondit
Je n'ai pas de plume
Je suis dans mon lit
Va chez la voisine
Je crois qu'elle y est
Car dans sa cuisine
On bat le briquet
Au clair de la Lune
On n'y voit qu'un peu
On cherche la plume
On cherche le feu
En cherchant d'la sorte
Je n'sais c'qu'on trouvera
Mais je sais qu'la porte
Sur eux se ferma

"WHAT IS IT ABOUT? Seems like a weird song but I like it." Hans even chuckled.

"Yes, absolutely irrelevant," Océane agreed. "Just what we need. I think it's actually a kind of love song. A man Lubin goes to his friend in the moonlight to ask for a pen because he wants to write a letter. But Pierrot, the friend, is already in bed and suggests he goes to their neighbor, a brunette. The last verse is telling, isn't it?"

In the light of the moon, you can barely see anything
Someone looked for a pen, someone looked for a flame
In all of that looking, I don't know what was found
But I do know that those two shut the door behind them.

"SOUNDS LIKE US," Hans observed, "in another time and in another way."

"Eerie," she agreed.

"These songs from our youth are somehow soothing. I'd almost be tempted to sing you a German nursery rhyme. It's just that everything that has to do with Germany now seems tainted. As if we have to bury everything we ever stood for. But it wasn't all bad, was it?"

"Of course not, Hans. Do you know I'm actually half German?"

He shot her a sideways glance. "No way, you can't be. You're American and French. I've seen your passports."

"It's a long story but it's true. My mother was one hundred percent German."

"But you said that your grandfather is Baron Maximilian de Saint Aubin and that your mother was raised by him? You've got me confused."

"It's a complicated story. Don't know if I should bother you with it right now."

"Please tell me, it'll keep me awake."

Océane sighed. "Okay, but I don't know all the details myself as Mom wasn't particularly fond of the story herself, but this is what I know. My grandmother, Ingrid Geschke, was a maid in the Prussian noble family of Graf von Spiegler. Apparently, she was a great beauty which had not remained unnoticed by both the son of the house, Eberhard von Spiegler, and by my grandfather the Baron, who was a music teacher to Eberhard's younger siblings at Frederik's Schloss. My grandfather had ended up in Holstein because he was heart-broken and humiliated after his Paris fiancée broke off their high-profile engagement when preferring the Duke d'Orléans after all."

"Holstein, huh?" Hans chuckled more openly now. "Yes, that's certainly where the German blood rushes most passionately."

"I wouldn't know." Océane laughed as well. "I also don't know if my grandfather fell easily in love in those days, but he soon was enraptured by the fair and angelic-looking Ingrid. However, the heir apparent, Graf Eberhard, struck first and without shame or consideration left Ingrid with child before returning to his army life."

"Bastard!" Hans grumbled.

"Well, my grandfather was besotted with Ingrid, pregnant or not, and with his great heart bleeding for the poor maid's fate, suggested taking her to Paris and making her an honest woman. That's how Ingrid Geschke became Baroness de Saint-Aubin."

"You've spoken highly of your grandfather and you're right. How kind and generous."

Océane nodded. "Sad thing is, Ingrid died shortly after giving birth to my mother. My mother was raised by her non-biological father and never knew her real parents."

"Gosh, what a story." Hans sounded moved. "Do you think Ingrid loved your grandfather?"

"I don't know. I don't even think my dear grandfather knows. They hardly had time to get to know each other and my grandmother never had time to adjust to her Paris life."

"What about your biological grandfather? Did your mother ever hear from him?"

Océane could not suppress a scornful little laugh. "That's the weirdest story in my family. Are you sure you want to hear it?"

"Of course!" Hans shot her another quick glance.

Although she could only see the whites of his eyes in the dark, she felt his eagerness to hear her story, anything to take them away from the pickle they found themselves in.

"Okay, but it's not a pretty tale."

"Tell me anyway. I'm all ears."

Océane folded her hands in her lap and thought for a while. All she knew of her mother's family was hearsay and it had been fragmentary to say the least. Her parents had told her the first World War had been a time of great confusion and they had been working at the frontline hospital under terrible conditions, while her mother feared all the while that the Germans would take over and her lineage would compromise the Allied forces and the Dragoncourt family who owned the castle where the hospital was situated.

She cleared her throat before she began. "My Mom was very young, only twenty-three, and just graduated as a surgeon when she followed my father to the frontline hospital in Picardy in 1918. They weren't a couple at the time. My dad was actually my mom's professor at the Sorbonne where he had been teaching since 1910. You know he's American, right? He was married at the time to a famous French artist, but their marriage was kind of rocky. Mom told me she'd had feelings for my dad from the very first time she'd laid eyes on him but with him being married it was a no-go."

"Sounds like an impossible love story," Hans chimed in.

"Wait!"

"Okay, I'll shut up."

"They were friends and colleagues. Dad tells me he was besotted with Mom as well, but he was at least a decade older and he's not the kind of person who'd go after her as long as he was married." Océane interrupted herself. "Gosh, I'm getting off topic here, I think, but it's all a bit muddled in my head and with all we are going through right now, I suppose I'm not the best storyteller in the world."

"Makes perfect sense to me. The start of a great story," Hans observed dryly, but then suddenly steered the vehicle off the road with a sharp tug on the steering wheel. The wheels spun around, and the vehicle came to a jerky halt.

"What was that?" Océane jolted in her seat.

"Don't know. I think it was an animal, a fox perhaps. Sorry for that, saw him at the last moment."

She saw a dim creature slink away as Hans reversed the jeep back onto the track.

"You're fast," she said with admiration, "even though you must be dead tired."

"Long time practice at the farm," he said with that same dry voice. "My dad used to say I have X-ray eyes. But let's get back to your story. That'll keep me awake for a while."

As they drove on through the dark desert night, an endless journey in a landscape without trees, without water and certainly without human life, putting more and more miles between them and the German camp and their possible trackers, Océane continued.

"I don't know how much you know about the Great War but the Hindenburg Line in the part of Picardy where the Dragoncourt Castle lay hardly moved for almost four years. Both armies were dug in their respective trenches and now and then entered into large and smaller clashes. Well, that's all over the history books, isn't it? Where my parents were, was about thirty miles east from Amiens."

"I suppose there was a big difference between what we were taught in Germany and what was taught in the rest of the world. My schoolbooks were all about Kaiser Wilhelm II and the great commander Erich Ludendorff, and, of course Hindenburg himself."

"Maybe not so different. The US glorified the role of the Yanks.

We were the decisive factor in a war in Europe. We're all nationalists, after all."

"I guess there's some truth in it. Wonder whether history is repeating itself, now it's rumored America is stepping up their game. But let's return to your story."

"Well, when my parents arrived on the front in the Spring of 1918, the Germans had just launched a huge offensive, so most of the patients that were transportable were taken south to Paris. The Germans ended up capturing the castle with only a bare minimum of medical staff inside, my mother and father among them. They became hostages. But now it comes." She hesitated a moment, but Hans urged her on.

"Come on, it's getting exciting now, just like an adventure story."

"I don't think my parents thought of it that way." Despite herself, she uttered a short laugh. How easy telling a story made them forget that they were themselves in a war, fleeing twenty-five years later, in the same mortal danger. "Anyway, the commander of the German army was Major General Eberhard Graf von Spiegler."

"No way!" Hans gasped. "Holy Moses. Did they know each other?"

"My mom knew because of his name. She was terrified but wasn't sure if he had ever known Ingrid was pregnant with his child. Remember I told you he was in the army at the time and always away. Mom confided in my dad, though, and I think that for a while they pretended to be married so she wouldn't have to give him her name, De Saint Aubin, which Von Spiegler would connect to my grandfather. That didn't work. Their passports were taken, of course, and her name and who she was revealed."

"Oh!" Hans exclaimed. "What did Von Spiegler do?"

"It turned out, he didn't know he had fathered a child with the former maid, so in that respect she was safe, but Von Spiegler had hated Baron De Saint Aubin for taking his favorite plaything away from him and marrying her in Paris. He thought my mom was the Baron's biological daughter and for that reason he constantly mocked her father and was horrible to her. That, added to the fact they now had to operate on German casualties, didn't make for a very pretty time but it did bring my parents closer. Not in a romantic sense yet, but as friends and allies."

"Was the castle recaptured again?"

"Not for months. That's the other part of the story. The youngest daughter of the De Dragoncourt family, Madeleine De Dragoncourt - she's actually the mother of a friend of mine that I met just before the war in Switzerland - managed to sneak back into the castle and retrieve the spare key to a cellar door that led to an underground escape route. Due to her action, the castle was ultimately recaptured without bloodshed."

"So, in their turn they made Von Spiegler and the other Germans prisoners of war?" Hans asked.

"Not exactly. During the counterattack, both Von Spiegler and my father became severely injured. My mom had to operate on them both at the same time. She managed to prevent my father from becoming completely paraplegic, but it meant that by the time they were liberated, she was utterly exhausted and my father in a very bad mood because he was paralyzed. At the time he didn't know if he would ever be able to walk again."

"And the General?" Hans asked again.

"He was very ill but also on the mend. Then Madeleine, that feisty little devil of a girl, decided to confront Von Spiegler with the truth, that he was my mom's biological father. Well, that went down the wrong way."

"How so?"

"I don't know why, because he'd lost the war or because he couldn't face the truth, but apparently he killed himself while Madeleine was still in the room."

"Cripes," Hans whistled through his teeth, "that's really horrible. Also for your mother."

"Yes, it was a shock for her, but I think at the time she was more involved with getting my dad back in shape. They could return to Paris at the end of the summer for his recuperation and then the war was over in November, of course."

"So how did they end up getting married?"

"Dad divorced his first wife and they married in the spring of 1919."

It sounded so matter of fact before, whereas, recounting it now to this German friend, she realized it actually *was* a great love story. She'd just never thought of it that way.

"Beautiful true story," Hans said. "I'd settle for such a romance."

Silence enveloped the interior of the jeep, making Océane slightly uncomfortable. She liked Hans but had no feelings for him whatsoever. Was he giving her a hint?

He quickly burst that bubble, though. "There is this girl in Hildesheim, Anna, whose picture is in my wallet. She is so enchanting and she's waiting for me ..."

As he said it, a couple of loud bangs sounded, and the jeep started to swirl and skid off the track.

"The tires," Hans cried, "they've hit the tires!"

Everything happened in a flash. With the jeep still fuming, its engine spluttering and protesting, they found themselves surrounded by men in combat uniform. Wild cries, even cheers.

"Stop! No further. You're under arrest. Hands up!"

From Océane's breath escaped the greatest sigh of relief of her life. They might be shouting their orders in German, but the four soldiers sported the French tricolor on their combat uniforms.

She could explain.

They were safe!

"We're French/American!" she shouted back but the Frenchmen were clearly not impressed by her words. A Kubelwagen was a Kubelwagen.

"Rauss!" the French commander bellowed. "Hands up!"

Océane shot Hans a quick glance. He was white as a moonlit sail, eyes huge, fists clenched around the steering wheel.

"Come," she coaxed him, "we can do this, John."

With gun points prodding in their backs, they were ushered to the back of a SAS jeep.

Ahead lay either the road to freedom or to new imprisonment.

25

THE WAY BACK

The ride in the back of the French jeep with a heavily armed, taciturn soldier guarding them from close-up didn't take too long. Océane was relieved she'd managed to grab her medical bag just before she was ushered out of the Kubelwagen and clamped it against her breast as if it held precious diamonds. Hans sat rigid, staring straight ahead.

Neither of their captors spoke. There was a grim, icy silence in which only the roar of two engines was audible. The Kubelwagen followed the SAS jeep, driven by one the Frenchmen.

"*Descendez!*" the French commander ordered, a small wiry man with a black mustache and short o-shaped legs. "Duval, take them to my tent for interrogation."

Océane stood mesmerized, momentarily forgetting her precarious situation. Tall palm trees softly waved in the warm night's air and the clatter of water was all around them. The citric scent of lemons combined with the sweet fragrance of loam soil made her feel as if she'd suddenly arrived in paradise. So this was what a desert Oasis was like.

"Move!" The gun pricked in her back, and she automatically

put one foot before the other, with Hans walking stiffly by her side. He had withdrawn within himself, a shadow of a man.

The French camp, though set up with the same kind of tents, couldn't have been more different than the one they had left behind. Where the German camp had been silent and orderly, here the tents stood scattered among the trees and there was a great clamor of agitated French voices mixed with Arab tongues Océane didn't recognize.

The French tricolor was everywhere but also the Cross of Lorraine Divisional Badge was proudly on display. Guards carrying MAS-36 machine guns patrolled on the outer circles and raised the alarm when the Kubelwagen came into sight. When they found out it was driven by one of their own, they let their fingers slip off the trigger and went off in a trot to inspect the foreign vehicle in the midst of merry laughter and backslapping.

Still at gunpoint, Océane and Hans were ushered into one of the tents.

"Sit down!" the French commander ordered as he pointed to two folding chairs in front of his desk. Instead of starting his interrogation, he leisurely lit a Gitane while piercing black onyxes moved swiftly from their faces to their clothes. The rising smoke was a curtain around his dark head.

Océane couldn't decide if the expression on his wiry face was friendly or stern. He was a proud man, so much was clear, but she couldn't see through the brittle exterior. His words would have to reveal his intentions.

"My name is Commandant Thierry Chevalier, and my division is part of the First Free French Division. We fought both at the Battle of Bir Hakeim and at the Second Battle of El Alaheim, from which we're only just recovering. We've finally sent Rommel packing."

No smile, just a big drag on his cigarette. And a small fist landing firmly on his desk.

Tough, weathered and hardened from his years in Africa's dustbowl, was Océane's impression. While Chevalier was talking about his victories, he was gauging his visitors with his no doubt vast knowledge of the region and its fighting forces. She saw he was unable to reach a satisfactory solution from his own scrutiny but was as yet unwilling to ask them questions.

"Tea, coffee?" he asked as he snapped his fingers and the man he had addressed as Duval stepped into the light with a deferential look on his young face. "Bring us something hot to drink and some halva." All the while Chevalier was talking, he did not divert his eyes from them.

Océane was sure he would have his pistol in his hand and pointed at them the moment one of them made the wrong move. And yet something settled in her, relaxing her tired body and mind. She was among fellow countrymen, her own language, away from the Germans. Next to her she sensed Hans's tension and would've loved to ease it for him, assuring him they would be alright. But his fate was much more precarious than hers. The tables had turned in her favor now.

During the coffee and delicious sweets, Commandant Chevalier mostly ignored them, talking with Duval about a convoy that was leaving in the morning. After he'd finished his business, he apparently concluded it was time to unmask them.

"You can imagine we have few visitors in these regions," he observed drily, "so you can imagine the excitement my men had over spotting a solitary Kubelwagen heading straight for our camp."

Hans sat up a little straighter, which Chevalier didn't miss.

"Yes, we had you in view for quite some time, *mein Herr*. I'm sure your countrymen possess night scopes as well. They're probably even of better quality than ours what with your German technology." The Commandant was not devoid of some self-deprecation.

He lit another cigarette and pushed the blue packet in their direction. Océane declined but Hans accepted one, obviously thinking this politeness might put him in a better book with the commandant. Her medical bag firmly in her lap, she had no idea if it would be out of turn to speak but she decided to cut to the core without giving Hans away.

"I was a doctor at the Hôtel-Dieu de Paris at the beginning of the war, Sir ..."

He raised a fine, small hand to stop her. "All in due time, Madame. I told you we hardly have visitors here, so I like to take my time and offer you some hospitality before we talk war again. Aren't we all a bit done with that? Especially in the middle of the night when we are still celebrating our recent victory?" He chuckled now but it sounded more like a dry cough. "Here's what we will do. I take it you had a long journey ..." he hesitated a moment. "Let me put it this way - a tumultuous departure before that. Let's all have some sleep first and after breakfast we'll *talk*. Duval will escort you to your quarters. Just don't think of leaving. We don't like our visitors disappearing as ghosts in the night."

The piercing black eyes were on them, drilling the message home. They were no apparent threat to the camp but there was to be no free movement. A huge gulf of relief washed through Océane and she felt Hans finally relax a little in the chair next to her. Chevalier had made clear he knew he was a German but putting on civilian clothes had communicated that he was no longer under arms, no longer the enemy.

That night in an outwardly similar tent to the one in the German camp, Océane felt a totally different person before she dove into a deep, blissful sleep. For once, she allowed herself not to think of the past or the future. She was safe, secure. Stable.

IN THE MORNING, she was glad to wedge in some words with Hans before they were summoned to the commandant's quarters.

"What are your thoughts on them?"

"The commandant doesn't seem too worried with our arrival. That seems a good thing but there might be a snag in it. If I was him, I'd have used the hours we slept to retrace our route and see what he could find. I think he's that shrewd, wants to make up his own opinion before he reports us to his superiors. You will be fine. But me?" He gave her a wan smile.

"I'm not going anywhere without you," she blurted out with sudden generosity. "We go back to Paris together and join the Resistance, or I'll be a prisoner of war with you. After all, I committed the murder so I'm the one that should be punished here."

"I don't think the French would consider it a murder, more a heroic deed."

Océane heard an undertone of admiration in his voice, and it warmed her. "Just to let you know. I've hidden my medical bag," she whispered. "Whatever their contents, I want to study those myself. I've got an inkling there's something about JJ or that Huricana in there."

"Good reasoning, though I don't think it will be easy to hide anything from Chevalier."

At that moment Duval showed up behind them and Océane startled, not knowing how much he'd overheard.

"Follow me to headquarters."

They found Chevalier quite chirpy, happily smoking his Gitane and sipping his black coffee. "Aha, you two!" he greeted them. "I hope you slept well in the company of my Free French division."

"I did, thank you, Sir." Océane was glad to speak the truth.

"And you, Herr Arenberg?"

Hans flinched at his name being spoken. His gaze flitted to the commander's face.

Chevalier smiled broadly, baring two rows of yellowed teeth. He certainly was a different man in the morning. "Don't worry, Sergeant. I'm not going to bite." He chuckled that strange half laugh, half cough.

"How ... how did you find out my name, Herr Commandant." In

his confusion Hans departed from his careful French and fell back into his native tongue.

Chevalier shook a wiry head and scratched grizzly grey stubbles under his cap. "I do not only command French troops, Herr Arenberg; we have Berbers and all sorts of Arab folk and oasis dwellers. These natives have lived and survived in these barren lands for ages and know how to make themselves invisible and soundless. On my command one of them had a quick look into both your passports while you were sleeping."

The yellow-toothed smile became even bigger as Océane and Hans stared at the wiry commander with incredulous eyes.

"Madame Docteur Bell." He bowed in her direction, and she saw appreciation in the beady, black eyes.

"Nice work," Hans muttered.

"Aha, there is more!" Great mirth seemed to take possession of the Frenchman now. "What did you two do with the former Head of the Paris SS? That part I haven't been able to figure out."

They looked at each other in bewilderment. One of them had to answer but it could be a trick question. How did Chevalier know?

Hans was the first to speak. "What made you think that we had anything to do with General von Stein, Sir?"

The gleefulness now seemed etched onto the commandant's face. "Could that be a phone call to the headquarters of General Montgomery?"

"But how did the British know?" Hans was clearly puzzled.

The peculiar chuckle cough followed. "Montgomery and General de Gaulle may not be the closest of pals but in times of emergency a phone call to London can do wonders. Added to that the mentioning of Hospital Hôtel-Dieu de Paris by Madame Docteur herself, it doesn't need a Sherlock Holmes to solve that a General Dieter von Stein is a missing person in North Africa. Greatly missed by some," he grinned, "and I wouldn't be surprised if Herr Hitler is throwing a big tantrum at Berchtesgaden, pulling out black whiskers from that hideous mustache."

There was some muffled sniggering from the French officers who stood on guard, but the Commandant fixed his black gaze on Hans, scrutinizing his face. All the glee evaporated from the weather-beaten face as he added, "Right! You're safe, Sergeant. No flinching when I mock your leader. Respect for your superiors but no sign of taking sides. What is your stand, my man?"

Hans hesitated, carefully choosing his words. "I am German-born, of course, Sir, and my family is of noble birth. The lineage goes back many hundreds of years. We've always been Junkers south of Hanover. The Arenberg family may well be one of the oldest in Germany."

Hans stopped talking, unsure if he should digress further but Chevalier made an impatient movement with his short arm.

"Go on!"

"I joined the SS at the request of my father, but I'd rather have stayed on the farm and taken charge of it. I don't think I have much warrior blood in me, but it was the thing to do as a German in 1938. We didn't really have a choice by then."

He swallowed with difficulty, his Adam's apple going up as if stuck in his throat. The commandant remained silent, pushing the packet of Gitanes in Hans's direction, after lighting another one himself.

Outside a group of soldiers was performing some sort of drill involving short commands in French. "*En ligne! Garde à vous! Rompez!*" Inside the stuffy tent full of the heady scent of Gitanes and coffee, a rusty fan whirled at the top making a screeching sound on every twirl. Yet the atmosphere in the camp was strangely relaxed. Whether it was the presence of the lush oasis, the lack of battle or the good-spirited Commandant Chevalier, Oceáne couldn't tell, but she felt Hans was also letting down his guard for the first time since their arrival. His fate no longer hung in the air.

"My country has undergone many changes since Imperial Germany came about in 1871. I'm by no means a historian, but I do believe the basis for the first War had its seeds in the unification.

On the one hand Germany had become a powerful nation, on the other it nurtured the feeling of being surrounded by enemies. Strength and fear can be a volatile cocktail."

"Interesting observation." Chevalier stubbed out his cigarette, which then remained smoldering in the overfull ashtray. "I fought at Verdun as a young, cocky sergeant myself."

Sidetracked from his own discourse, Hans asked in a polite voice, "Isn't that a terrible lot, Commandant, having to fight the same enemy twice within a couple of decades?"

"*Ah non, non, non!*" The French army officer jumped from his chair, waving his short arms in the air. "The Great War was a different war. An old-fashioned war, horrible as it was. It was the Germans testing the waters, so to say. An army trying to push another army back within its own borders. The age-old dilemma of expansion thrift. But this one ..."

He swooped his arm around as if encompassing the whole of Africa. "This, dear man, is a different affair. I tell you, if we don't get that beastly Nazi gang headed by Herr Hitler ten feet underground, the world as a whole is doomed. I've known soldiers all my life, I know what the soldier's heart feels, pride in the defense of country and sometimes king, each country to its own, but look where we find ourselves now. Amidst camel shit and coconut trees and nomads in dresses, a country that serves no other purpose that being Mussolini and Rommel's sandpit. No oil, no precious ore, no economy. So what is this all about? You tell me, my son."

Aghast and speechless, Hans stared at Chevalier for a while but then slowly nodded. "I agree with you, Sir. The evilness of the current German regime is a danger to humanity. I came to see that when we occupied Paris and saw what the SS did, not only to the city itself, but to its inhabitants, especially forcing young women to collaborate and, of course, the treatment of ... uh ... citizens that resisted the occupation of their city. I don't recognize myself in this Germany."

"I'm glad to hear it."

Hans cast Océane a quick look.

The French commander was quick to pick up on the emotional undercurrent. "The torture and fusillade of brave Parisians is indeed one of the biggest atrocities this foreign regime has exercised on the Free French. They spare no cruelty for what they consider their opponents whether they are resistance fighters or innocent Jews. And yet, would you two be up for that?"

"For what, Sir?" Océane shivered despite herself.

"For the job, of course!" the jovial Commander exclaimed. "Go back to Paris. Undermine the clique that's currently poisoning everything French." His quick black eyes went from her face to Hans's.

"Do you know who Huricana is?" Her voice almost choked as she asked it.

This clearly took the Frenchman off guard. He hesitated, his eyes going to Duval, who raised his shoulders almost imperceptibly.

It didn't escape Océane. "Are you?"

He didn't answer directly, then slowly shook his head. "I wish I was, but I can't even stand in the shadow of that man." Chevalier sounded humbled for the first time.

"Then who is Huricana and why did Von Stein say he was in North Africa?"

"I think, Madame Docteur, if you want answers to your questions, you'd better make a personal phone call to General de Gaulle. I know a lot, but I don't know everything. I do know that we wouldn't have won the battles in this sandpit without him and his cell. That will be my final word on it."

"So, Von Stein lied. He said Huricana was caught by the Germans."

He had lied. Von Stein had *lied*. What else had he lied about?

The way Thierry Chevalier shrugged his shoulders, Océane could see he would keep any cards he had close to his chest.

Hans, meanwhile, had his own cards to deal with. "If Docteur Bell and I were to go back to Paris, how do you suggest a German could be helpful in the Resistance?"

The Frenchman let his hands with the short fingers fall on his desk with a bang. "Don't you see it, Arenberg? You're perfect for the job. I'm not into the business of spying myself, being more the bang-bang-bang type but you could do counterespionage without even having to lift your little finger. As we speak, new identities are created for both of you." He bared his yellow teeth at their surprise. "Oh yeah! And don't worry, Sergeant, we'll create some new German position and new look for you, not at the SS Headquarters, of course, where you might run into some old pals. Someplace else, enough to choose from; for the time being the Germans still swarm the place." Grinning even wider, Chevalier added, "And you, Madame, you can return to your work in the hospital, but Hans will be your informer and link to the Maquis."

Both Océane and Hans now gaped at him. This petite Frenchman had certainly pulled some fast strings.

He raised his hands in defense, making his cough-like chuckle. "Don't shoot me! It's not my plan. Instructions from General de Gaulle himself. Tonight, one of the French pilots will take you to Cairo with a Dewoitine D.520s. From there the RAF will take you to Vichy France. I haven't got the details. They will be given to you personally. With instructions. Is that understood?"

Silence. Then both at the same time, they uttered a hesitant, "Yes."

The chess pieces on the table were moving at rapid speed. It would be back to combat soon. Only at a higher level.

"Well, then," Chevalier said, rising from his chair while extinguishing one of his eternal cigarettes, "I'll let you enjoy the day at the Oasis as pleases you. Make sure you're ready by 4 p.m. sharp."

They also rose to their feet. Océane felt more like a Radcliffe student after a tough medical exam than a secret agent with a mission. Her head spun, but through all the confusion one thing exhilarated her. She would be going back to Paris, maybe see her grandfather ... then the real hole in her heart broke open once again.

JJ was gone.

Paris would not be Paris for her ever again. And she herself would be in so much danger this time. All she'd lived through so far had only been a preparation for this next episode. A Resistance fighter.

Would she be up to the task?

26

BECOMING THE ROSE

Nice, March 1942

Océane drifted between sleep and wakefulness when a scent both familiar and foreign entered her nose. She was lying in a summer field of cornflowers and daisies and the sky above her was blue and cloudless. Somehow the smell of cigars and whiskey clashed with the natural scent of the flowers. Her eyelids fluttered, she wanted to stay in the field with all her might.

Someone was coming for her. She had to stay put. It was someone she longed to see with all her heart but who was he? The vision escaped her memory every time she tried to focus.

Him.

"Océane, *ma chérie.*"

A voice was whispering above her. The smell of cigars came closer.

"Not yet, he will come," she murmured but someone shook her shoulder and the sky evaporated, the field disappeared. She opened her eyes, blinking, blinking, blinking.

"Maxipa!" She grabbed his outstretched hands, crushed his

frailness with her all her might. "Maxipa! Is it really you? Or am I dreaming?"

Warm brown, gold-flaked eyes took in her whole being. His grave face nodded; the silver hairs danced. "*Je suis pas un mirage*, I am real," he smiled under his white mustache, bent over her and kissed her forehead.

She struggled to sit up and his hand on her shoulder pressed her down again.

"Rest a little more, my dear. Your last voyage has enfeebled you greatly."

"Where am I?" She turned her head but didn't recognize the furniture.

"We are in a safe house in Nice, dearest. I have been for a while. We decided it would be the best base station for the time being."

"We, base station? What are you talking about, grandfather?"

"Nothing of importance right now. We'll discuss all that later. For now, I'm going to ask the new maid to make you some bouillon while I go and see how our other guest is faring."

"Where are Gaël and Marie?"

"They're in Paris, dearest. It's safer that way."

"What other guest are you talking about?"

Océane's mind was befuddled, so she didn't understand what was going on. Raising herself on her elbow, she looked around a pristine bedroom, with the window overlooking the azure calm of the Mediterranean. A huge gray battleship lay at anchor just a mile away, bobbing on the brilliant sea surface.

"Don't you remember a certain gentleman by the name of Hans that you traveled with."

Slowly, as slowly as two black-headed gulls swam towards the battleship, the long trip from Sébha via Egypt to France drifted back into her mind. It had been too much. She'd self-sedated. The dull headache explained it.

"Grandpa," she called after him as he made his way to the door, "have you heard anything about Eleonora and Yves Ferron?"

Her throat tightened as she saw his shoulders droop.

"The last I heard was that Madame Ferron was arrested during a razzia in Lyon and deported to Germany. Her husband fought to keep her by his side, and he was shot dead by the SS on the spot."

"What about the baby?"

Her grandfather looked at the carpet. "She was deported with her mother."

"She, a girl," Océane murmured, before burying her hands in her face. Her lovely, kind and intelligent mentor. And her protective French husband.

She heard her grandfather say resolutely, "That's why we have to fight these Huns, tooth and nail."

His vehemence made her look up through her tears. "Grandpa, you're almost eighty. You mustn't put yourself in danger."

"It's too late for that now, my dear. Nothing can change my mind. Not after that execrable creature abducted you and almost had you killed. I've been a coward in the Great War. This is my time to set that right."

"Please, please, be careful, Maxipa!" Océane begged, forgetting her sorrow at the recklessness of her elderly grandfather.

"We will be, *ma grand-fille*, after all, we're a lot foxier and agile than those German brick heads. Now let me go and be a proper host to our double-spy."

He seemed to have regained some of his former posture, as she watched him flip-flopping out of the room on his embroidered babouches, his silver mane disappearing around the corner.

The real work starts now, Océane thought as her gaze fixed on the sea again. And there would be so much to be done. Her eye fell on her old medical bag, the dark brown leather creased and the silver buckle now a tarnished dull gray.

Curious to see if anyone had opened her bag and inspected its unusual contents, she slipped from the bed and retrieved it from the chair. Holding her breath as she unclasped the buckle, she pulled the sides apart with anticipation. It was still filled to the brim with documents, handwritten and typed.

She tossed them all on top of her bedspread and gazed at them.

SS stamps, the Swastika, the double headed eagle, *der Reichadler* and then Von Stein's signature on most of them. Although she had no idea what they were, she was sure this was tremendous loot for the French Resistance. But for Océane there was only one thing she was looking for: the name Remix or even Jean-Jacques Rousseau.

Folding the pieces of paper neatly, she started to stack them, one by one, scanning them, hoping against hope. She was almost three-quarters through the pile when her eye fell on D'Artagnan and she gasped. JJ's comrade, the man in the Trilby whose eyes she never saw, who'd come to her grandfather's house in Paris to tell her of his arrest.

Her eyes flew over the document, but it revealed nothing. Only that he had escaped but the SS in all occupied France were alerted to be on the look-out for him. The document was dated 1 October 1940. More than two-and-a-half years ago.

Her interest was piqued. Why would Von Stein keep an announcement for an arrest of a French Resistance fighter among his most important documents for two years? She searched further and soon realized all the documents were about the French Resistance, so she combed through them more vigilantly.

In more recent documents the name Huricana showed up. With a question mark after it. And, gasp, Oasis Sébha ... Thierry Chevalier. This name was circled. It was clear that the man had been obsessed with rounding them all up. That's why Von Stein had gone to the outback of Africa himself. The German camp lay closest to the Sébha oasis.

Océane sat wondering for a while amid the German documents. She had so many questions. Had Chevalier deliberately deceived them? Was he Huricana after all? His connections with Montgomery and De Gaulle? She was almost certain of it now and it made sense that he hadn't wanted to reveal his true identity. Had he been JJ's boss two years earlier? If so, she'd missed the opportunity to ask Chevalier questions. If he ever would have answered them. It was all so complicated, so elusive, so secretive. She almost hated having taken the contents of Von Stein's briefcase.

Stacking them back, her eye fell on one more.

In early October 1940 one of Von Stein's senior officers, a Major Ernst Bubel, had been ambushed by a young woman pretending to be a prostitute, and had subsequently been killed by ... and there it was: Remix.

Océane gasped again. Her JJ with his beautiful strong painters' hands in cold blood killing an SS Officer. But then her stomach dropped. Had she not done exactly the same? She was temporarily perplexed by the synchronicity of their actions. JJ had no doubt killed the Nazi with a gun. She had used her needle.

Was there more on him? And yes, there was. Von Stein's endless correspondence to find and arrest Remix and all who had helped him. Océane shuddered as she recalled the inhuman, agonized cries from the top floor of 84 Avenue Foch. Had that been the so-called prostitute, one of JJ's close allies? Had he been there as well? A triumphant document from Von Stein announced Remix's arrest on 15 October 1940 together with the Maid, clearly a reference to Jeanne d'Arc.

There was little more, which was strange, as the General clearly had been obsessed with this cell of the French Resistance. Disheartened, her eye fell on a yellow envelope. It was sealed with Von Stein's seal, but she had no scruples and broke it.

Two black-and-white photos fell out and all the blood drained from her body. It was JJ. Front and back. He hung between two SS officers, who held him by his armpits and looked down upon him with a disdainful look. JJ's head was slumped forwards, his torso naked and full of stretch marks and bruises. Blood streamed down his chest. The photo from his back was even worse, his broad, once beautiful back was one pulpy mess.

For a moment Océane closed her eyes, wishing she had not opened the envelope but, as so many other times in her life, the doctor in her won and she studied his injuries intently. They were bad, very bad, but not lethal. Unless they had done more to him, this had not killed him.

Without noticing it, still considering his injuries, she turned the photos and saw Von Stein had written something on the back. *Remix aka Jean-Jacques Rousseau, 20 October 1940, 84 Avenue Foch. Disappeared into 'Nacht und Nebel'.*

Night and fog, she wondered, *what was that*? Did that mean he was killed or transported. How sure had Von Stein been that JJ was killed after he was taken from the headquarters? For a sweet moment her hope flashed up but then it again died like a weak match. Von Stein had been so obsessed with JJ, he would've made sure he knew where they'd taken him, what had happened to him.

But what if he hadn't known? He'd lied to her about Huricana.

All the detective-like thinking hurt her foggy mind. She made a neat stack of Von Stein's paperwork and went in search of a box to put them in. Her mind was made up. She needed her medical bag for her own purposes again.

To her surprise, not just Hans, now with black hair and a black mustache, sat at the dining table but also an unknown man in his fifties with bristly gray hair and a nervous tick that made the whole left side of his face twitch. He had intense, dark eyes. Both were in civilian clothes and spoke French with each other. Her grandfather was not in the room.

"Hi," she said shyly, "I'm Océane Bell. Where's my grandfather?"

"He had an errand to run," the man with the intense eyes said. "I'm D'Artagnan. I think we've met before."

Her mouth fell open. "You?!" It was both a question and an exclamation. "Do you by any chance know anything more about Remix?"

The man shook his head and his cheek twitched.

Another dead end.

On closer inspection, she saw a scar had deformed his face and damaged the tissue. Although it had healed it was still giving him anguish. After shaking his hand, she took a seat at the table. Hans looked nervous but smiled at her.

"I was instructing Jakob on his first mission," D'Artagnan explained as Océane poured herself a coffee. "I'll come to yours next."

She nodded, fighting her tears.

"So," he faced Hans again, "your new name is Jakob Hess and here's your new passport. The former Jakob Hess was an SS Officer stationed at Bordeaux. We ... uh ... helped him to the other side. So, you've freshly arrived from Bremen and all your paperwork is in order. You go straight to Headquarters on 84 Avenue Foch and report to the current chief of staff General Walter Schmidt."

"But," Hans protested, "what if anyone recognizes me?"

"That won't happen if you play your part well. Sergeant Hans Arenberg has been extinguished as well. We know this is hard on your family, but we have no other option. And neither have you."

D'Artagnan spoke with great emphasis and Océane saw Hans cringe. His family had been told he was dead. How awful was that?

"We have no choice in the matter," D'Artagnan continued. "You know the building like the back of your hand, so that's too convenient not to use. Keep a low profile for the time being but your task is to collect information about members of the resistance movement. Where they were arrested, what they did to them, where they are sent, whether they're dead or alive. We'll give you this Minox subminiature camera."

The gray-haired resistance fighter retrieved a small, stainless steel attribute from his breast pocket. Océane thought it looked more like a cigarette lighter than a camera and was intrigued.

"Can I have a look?" she asked.

"Wait a moment. Let me first explain how it works and don't worry, Miss, you'll get one as well."

He opened the flat, rectangular device, and Océane peered over his shoulder while Hans also studied it with intent. D'Artagnan showed how to adjust the size and the precision with the two knobs on top and how to direct the tiny square lens on the side.

"A measuring chain is provided with this mini camera, which enables easy copying of letter-sized documents," he lectured, tapping the brass chassis. "This is the original Minox. It telescopes to reveal or cover the lens and viewfinder windows and is equipped with a parallax correcting viewfinder. The lens can focus as close as 20 cm, and, due to its small image size, provides such depth of field at full aperture that a diaphragm is unnecessary. The maximum focus zone is about one meter to infinity." He looked at them both. "I know this is a lot to take in and you'll get time to practice but please keep all this knowledge stored in your mind."

Hans was listening intently. "How does the camera project the image onto the negative?"

"The film is in strips 9.2 mm wide. Unlike 35 mm film, it has no sprocket holes. This film strip is rolled up in the supply side chamber of a small twin chamber cartridge, with the film leader taped to a take-up spool in the take up chamber. The film strips can be up to 50 frames in length."

Hans nodded. He understood.

Océane was not so sure she'd grasped it. "I think I've got just the right assignment for this Minox." She weighed the light gadget in her hand.

Her eyes met Hans's. They hadn't discussed sharing the contents of Von Stein's briefcase, but this seemed the moment.

WHEN SHE PUT the box on the dining table, it was D'Artagnan's turn to be flabbergasted.

The next hour kept them busy practicing with the Minox while D'Artagnan read through Von Stein's papers and made notes. The man was fluent in German, apparently. They were so deeply occupied with their affairs that they hardly noticed that the Baron had returned.

"Aha," her grandfather greeted them as he took off his Burgundy velvet coat revealing an ochre waistcoat and white chemise and a pantaloon of fine navy wool, "I see you've set out to win the war with a new device."

It might be war and her grandfather might have joined the resistance but there seemed no reason for him to give up his love of clothes. Something in Océane's heart started to bloom again while letting her eyes linger on her dear, special grandfather. Somehow, they'd make it through this war together, one way or the other.

As the dinner table was transformed into a masterplan to overthrow the fascist government in her adopted country, the new maid served *tourtière* and other savory pastries and they drank deep-red Beaujolais brought from the Baron's Paris wine cellar. Océane was happy and sad at the same time.

She would revenge Jean-Jacques's death by taking his place; he hadn't died in vain.

27

THE LAST YEAR OF THE WAR

Paris, January 1944

Océane, with a platinum-blond, pixie *la coupe*, dyed eyebrows and a passport that read Rosalie Juval, was scraping a tiny clod of white margarine on a thin slice of toast in her grandfather's breakfast room, when she heard the front doorbell chime. Seconds later Gaël's dull footsteps sounded over the tiled hall floor.

"Damn!"

Rising from her chair to flee, she already regretted having stayed at her grandfather's house for one night and putting the family in danger. But her Maxipa had come down with a nasty flu and she feared for pneumonia. She'd just had to see him and take care of him.

One night, and they were already tracking her down.

She hid in an empty cupboard that stood ready for the occasion, closing the ornate door behind her and locking it from the inside. The oak buffet was in no way an adequate hiding place for an SS axe or the butt of a revolver, but she had no time to run upstairs without being seen in the corridor. It also gave her the opportunity to listen in on conversations.

These days Océane knew little fear. The only fear she had was for her grandfather and his loyal staff. Her own life was worth so much less to her. Listening intently through the thin wooden panel, she heard Gaël chatting with the next-door neighbor who'd apparently been able to obtain real eggs from a farm outside Paris. Madame Riche had come to share the catch with the housekeeper in the hopes it would perk up the old Baron and make him leave his sickbed soon.

Océane almost cried at the kindness as she opened the cupboard door to finish her breakfast.

When oh when will it end? she thought with every dry munch.

It was these little kindnesses that jockeyed her forward to a finishing line that slowly, in snippets and snatches, was coming into sight. On all fronts the Germans were losing but their terror regime had not relented. Danger lurked around every corner she took. She survived on high doses of adrenaline and coffee and would do so for as long as it took.

"I have to go again, Gramps. I've put you and the girls in danger already."

She stroked the damp, silver threads from his wrinkled forehead, gazing into the feverish brown eyes. They hadn't lost their twinkle yet, so she was optimistic. Just this damned impossibility to get him properly fed.

"Stay hydrated and take the aspirins I've brought you. Do you promise?"

"Don't fuss, *ma chérie*," the Baron replied in a weak voice, "I have no desideratum to leave these earthly realms before the Bochs are gone. Rest assured I have every intention to dance in the streets with you once Paris is housecleaned from the Nazis. Just like I did with your mother on 11 November 1918. Every intention." He raised a bony index finger with his former vivacity.

"Deal!" she smiled. "Now let me go and bring that day one step closer. I don't know when I'll be able to visit you again, but Gaël

will send word to me if there's anything you need. I'll miss you."
Her eyes misted up.

"Come here."

They hugged each other tightly and she was so aware of his
fragility, his love for her, his longing for this endless war to be over
and see his daughter and son-in-law again. His powers were slowly
slipping away but his will was as strong as a Flander's mare.

"Hang in there, dear Maxipa!"

"You too, my feisty Rosalie Juval!"

The last she saw of him was a playful wink.

WITH HASTY STEPS Océane made her way along the Seine on her
way to the Hôtel-Dieu De Paris. Under all circumstances a walk
that was way too far and too cold in mid-winter, but she had a
strong need to clear her mind. The physical exercise would do just
that.

Leading a double life might have become second nature and
she quite liked Rosalie Juval. Rosalie was much flirtier and bubblier
than the studious, serious Océane Bell, but the constant alert, the
knowledge that if she was caught it would have a domino effect on
so many other people - that responsibility - weighed her down like
a hod of mortar.

And she had no friends, only allies. Wrong, she had one friend,
Hans Arenberg alias Jakob Hess, but they couldn't meet. Not properly anyway. They merely had the briefest exchanges in which their
eyes said more than words ever could. They'd gone through hell
together in that North African desert; now they lived mere miles
away from each other in the French capital, but never could there
be more than a wordless, "Be well. I've got your back!"

They were pawns in a large network that was spreading like
wildfire every day. Underground Paris was rumbling with revolt like
the stamping of millions of obstinate boots. It felt good to be part of
the rumble, but at the same time it was wading through loose sand.

Only the people at the top of *La Résistance* knew what was going on; the rest of the agents were mere carrier pigeons flying hither and thither. She was one of them. And it was lonely.

Next to her a car honked and Océane had to force herself not to jump at the same time as her heart, which shot to the top of her throat. Outwardly calm, a sweet smile on her scarlet-red lips, she glanced sideways at the car slowing next to her, her hand going to her coat pocket. The lethal pill.

She breathed out.

Hell, Doctor Frantz!

"Want a lift?"

I don't think so.

That lanky, unattractive Bavarian doctor was always seeking her out. Squinting eyes from behind horn-rimmed spectacles. She'd seen more than enough of him. She was about to walk on, nose in the wind, when she remembered the precarious assignment later in the day. *Perhaps play along for today.* Fritzl Frantz was as harmless as he was irritating but could well be her perfect cover-up.

Mustering her brightest smile, she chirped, "Of course, Doctor Frantz, I'd be delighted."

The cynicism in her voice made her shudder. What a bad actress she was. The beanpole physician was already hastening around his automobile to open the passenger door for her, most probably inwardly cheering at his conquest. He moved like an automated robot, the clumsiest doctor she'd ever seen in this line of work.

"I'm sorry to interrupt you on your walk, Madame Juval, but it is … um … I know of fuel shortages for the French, so that's why I thought you'd probably like the ride. Only work-related, I promise." He quickly added the latter but the look in his doggish eyes communicated something different.

She lifted one dyed eyebrow. Shockingly Océane-like, she thought.

Fritzl Frantz was waiting patiently for her to get into the Daimler, a rare German in civilian clothes, turning the rim of his felt hat in his hands. She hated the almost slavish way in which he closed the car door as if she was of porcelain.

Huddled in her tattered mink coat, Océane stared at the choppy waters of the Seine, dark-green and muddy brown, without tugging boats or other vessels. The streets were deserted as well, except for one bent housewife on her way to the baker's or butchers in hope of collecting some scraps of food for her family. Drab, that was what it was, a drab, desolate life.

German jeeps and lorries still patrolled the Paris streets and avenues, but they looked glummer and moved slower as well as the war grew old. The Reich's losses on the East front and the Allied landing in Italy had shrunk the earlier bravado and supremacy, each side holding their breath. Hitler had gone crazy, it was rumored, but no one really knew the truth.

Most of the young Germans she treated at the hospital these days just wanted to go home. Their bosses hadn't giving up yet, though; they became grimmer and uglier by the day.

Every Paris Jew had been rounded up. Those who went underground were persecuted with extreme barbarity. Resistance fighters suffered the same fate. Paris' heart was an immense crater of murdered citizens. No numbers, no names, no graves.

Océane shuddered again in her coat.

Don't think. Act!

Her cover-up in this German car in a German-led hospital was just a thin veneer for her real life that the sluggish man next to her knew nothing about.

"You're mighty quiet this morning, Madame Juval." Frantz suddenly cut through her thoughts.

"Uh, what is that?" she snapped herself back to the here and now. "Sorry, I was thinking of my family back home."

She always knew which button to press with silly Fritzl Frantz.

"Ah, me too! I was just thinking of my old Mutti, whose letter arrived yesterday. She told me there's rationing in Germany now. Can you imagine? I wish I could go home to help her."

"Don't you have a father, Herr Frantz?"

"He passed before the war and my sister lives with her husband east of Berlin and can't visit Mutti. I'm glad a neighbor is looking after her and it's a small village. I'm sure they'll have plenty of vegetables and livestock. It's just petrol and toilet paper and that sort of stuff now being rationed."

I couldn't care less about your Mutti and her unwiped bottom, Océane thought, but she gave him an understanding smile and no longer listened to his monologue on his dear Mutti, mentally preparing all the steps she had to take later that night.

~

SOMEHOW OCÉANE MANAGED to fake-smile and work through another day at the hospital and left with a "Thank you so much, dear doctor Frantz, it was a pleasure working with you," when her shift ended, and exited the hospital to become The Rose.

A black Fiat 1500 stood ready for her in the shade of a tree next to the Palais de Justice with the key in the ignition. Over time she'd grown used to driving all kinds of vehicles of unknown owners and with unknown destinations after she had used them. This was a sweet little thing, almost feminine in shape and size, with a vague scent of leather and citric perfume.

"Better than most," she grumbled as she turned the key.

Her destination tonight was a known one, so there was no need for a map.

The message this time had come straight from D'Artagnan. The gray-haired man with the twitch and probing eyes who somehow reminded her of Pablo Picasso had been the main hub in the wheel of the Paris Resistance since she joined. Huricana was also still a name on people's lips, but Océane had never received a message via him.

She hadn't seen D'Artagnan in person for at least a year, as the SS net around him was tightened by the day. He now only occasionally visited Paris, mostly operating from an unknown location in Morocco. But he always made sure through his informants they knew how to reach him.

Océane wasn't one of those. It was too dangerous for her to know too much. The Gestapo prize on her head was extravagant. That was Von Stein's legacy for her. Doctor Bell and Sergeant Hans Arenberg were the two names that still, after two years, buzzed around. High-profile anti-Nazis that needed to be caught at any price. Working in the eye of the storm, for both of them, was a matter of vigilant survival. At least the Germans believed Sergeant Arenberg was dead.

Night had fallen but it was still before curfew. The streets were already deserted, only here and there a Parisian, bent and with head down, hurried home through the lamp-less streets. German soldiers in pairs, black coats and caps, marched down the pavement, the ends of their cigarettes glowing against the dusky night.

She passed a restaurant where the lights were on and people were sitting at tables, eating and drinking. All in uniform, their female companions brightly dressed and heavily made-up, *les collaborateures horizontals*. It had more the appearance of the scene from a bizarre French comedy than the gruesome reality it represented. A modern version of Balzac's *La Comédie humaine*, indeed.

Steering the Fiat around the corner of the Boulevard Saint-Germain, Océane looked for a parking place and found one to her liking. Easy to pull out, shaded by another tree.

Never lock the car. Leave in the key.

With the mink coat pulled more closely around her and the fur collar adjusted so most of her face was hidden, she got out of the car. A felt hat hid her eyes. She walked fast in the direction of the address where the Resistance fighter by the name of Fleur de Lys had told her to come.

She was to bring a child to a safe house, probably Jewish, moving from one shelter to the next. It was only the second time in her two-year work for the French underground movement that a child was involved, so she braced herself for stepping into a heartbreaking scene.

As agreed, she saw the silhouette of the agent in the shadows of a porch. He or she - the creature was wearing a long, wide coat and hat, and was gender neutral - walked ahead, entering the much narrower Rue de Saint-Simon. She followed at a safe distance, keeping an eye on patrolling Germans. But the hour before curfew had always turned out to be their best bet. Again, this night the street was too cold and unfriendly to lure people outside.

They went at a firm pace until the agent cut a corner and disappeared in what seemed merely a crevasse between two houses. Océane increased her pace. Three taps on an almost invisible door under an archway. It was opened within seconds and Océane entered while the agent disappeared through the crevasse and was gone. No word was exchanged, just strangers passing in the night. All with one mission. Free France.

A woman carrying a lantern with a tiny light led her through a long alleyway until they came to a backdoor with two steps up. It looked quite similar to the back entrance of her grandfather's house on the Seine. She knew this door would lead to the servants' quarters and the kitchen.

No word was spoken as the woman opened the backdoor and let her into a large square space that obviously had been the larder before the war but most of the shelves were now empty. A single lightbulb hung from the ceiling and illuminated the barren space with a cold and hard light as if it were an interrogation chamber at a police station.

The woman dressed entirely in black turned to Océane and she saw she was an elderly woman, probably the housekeeper or someone left in charge to look after the family's Paris mansion.

"We have little time," she said in a low and hoarse whisper. "My employers were arrested by the SS this morning. Just in time I managed to hide their son Daniel in a cupboard. They were not Jews," she added, "but with the Resistance. Those awful men turned the whole house upside down. It was so terrifying. But Monsieur and Madame had given me instructions in case this would happen. I must stay in the house as messages pass through here, but Daniel is to be taken to his aunt in Orléans, his father's sister. You have to take him there. This is the address. But please be careful. The aunt is also part of the network."

She handed Océane a piece of paper and pressed her hand for a moment. Her touch was warm, comforting.

"I've packed Daniel a small valise, but understand the boy is dreadfully frightened. He's supposed to stay with you tonight. A *Safe Conduite* and two train tickets for Orléans as mother and son have been put in the glove compartment of your car. I'll go and fetch the boy now and then you must be gone."

Before Océane had time to ask questions, the woman left the larder and instantly returned with a shy-looking boy of about ten years old who kept his eyes pinned to his shoes. His cheeks were streaked with tears, his hair tousled.

An involuntarily tremor shook her entire system. It wasn't just the boy's agony. He was the spitting image of her brother Arthur, the tawny-blond hair, the slight, but strong built. When he raised his tearful eyes to hers, the quivering of her limbs became even more intense. How was it possible? The same blue eyes, Mom's eyes exactly. She fought for breath, had difficulty staying grounded, to be near him. The uncanny likeness to her brother before the accident almost made her run to him and press him to her.

"You have to go now, Madame," the housekeeper urged her. "Curfew starts in thirty minutes." She turned to the boy and said in a kind but stern voice, "Now be good, Daniel. Maman et Papa will soon come to fetch you from Tante Elizabeth."

She handed Océane an old, white valise with its embossed corners and pushed them out through the back door. Océane stretched out her hand to take the boy's, but he held his arms stiff by his sides. Everything seemed stiff in him; his legs moved rigidly, and he held his little head erect as if it would topple off his neck any moment.

The housekeeper lighted them through the backyard with hasty steps and listened at the porch. "Go!" she ordered. "Now!"

As a mirage, the figure in the long, dark coat and hat reappeared. Océane thought she discerned Hans but immediately pushed that idea aside. The anonymous agent made sure they arrived safely back to the Fiat.

Big-eyed and silent, the little boy sat upright in the passenger seat, his valise at his feet. Océane was equally in shock. Nobody had forewarned her she would have to take care of a child for two days. There were other things she had to do, like getting rid of the Fiat.

"What now?" Unaware, she had said it out loud.

"I want to go back home?" Daniel's first spoken words in upper-class French was a thin, high voice cracking at the edges.

"Soon, Daniel, soon."

Océane had to think hard. She wasn't prepared for a child. There was no way she could take him with her to the safe house, a place where grim fighters crashed in full battle dress on thin mattresses, their guns as cherished trophies next to their pillows. Not a place for a child.

What now?

This was the thing about being in the Resistance. Everything was urgent and the consequences of their actions couldn't be overseen.

Thinking out loud again she reasoned with herself. "It's a risk and a blessing. Let's go to grandpapa."

"Grandpapa is dead." The thin voice held a tinge of anger.

"Not your grandpapa. Mine."

"I don't want to go to your grandpapa. I want my Maman and Papa."

"I know. So do I. But this is war, Daniel, we have no choices."

Her grown-up approach to his anguish was wrong, she was aware, but she had no time for pedagogics or fluff right now. Cold reasoning was the only weapon in her arsenal. She would keep the Fiat for tonight. *Tanpis!* Tough luck.

When they arrived at the Baron's house, minutes before curfew, Océane almost collapsed. She was so thankful to let her guard down if just for a couple of hours. Being with her family, especially for two nights in a row, was extremely dangerous but there was no time to get back to her shelter. She would have to stay. Tomorrow was another day.

That night Océane sat for a long time next to Daniel, who was propped up in the big bed in the guest room, watching him sleep the innocent slumber of children. She wasn't looking forward to the trip the next day, which would be death-defying.

There was more.

Every part of the way to Orleans she would be reminded of what she and her family had lost in Chicago. This unknown boy broke the seal around her heart and Océane wept for home, for a life in freedom she could hardly remember.

28

DANIEL

Drying her tears, Océane could not break the spell of taking in the sleeping boy's features, the beautiful, soft face of a clear conscience. A sudden, intense craving for her crayons gripped her. To capture his delicate features in her sketchbook; the long dark-blonde lashes on the pink cheeks, the little stubbed nose, charmingly dotted with small freckles, the lips pressed firmly together as if an already grown man, the limp arm in the blue pajama top resting limply on the satin pillow; but most of all that shock of blond hair.

Her brother's hair that she had ruffled so many times and even cut off a lock to take with her to Europe.

This sudden longing to give creative form to her vision struck her as strange and out of place, yet before she knew it, the sketch block was in her lap and the crayons flew over the paper as if she had never stopped drawing in the first place.

Another pang hit her as her hands worked, reminding her of JJ. What they had shared, all the qualities she'd so admired in him but had never had time to tell him. The war had prematurely torn them apart when he'd chosen to abolish his paint brushes to fight for his fatherland. She had put all her effort into trying to change his mind and now look at her. In the same boat as her beloved, even taking his place in the ranks while he was no longer. Extinguished without a trace by the Nazis.

Daniel stirred in the bed, then let out an agonized cry in his sleep.

"*Maman, non, laissez-elle!* Let her go!"

Océane's crayon froze in mid-air.

Daniel turned on his side with his face to the wall and slept on. Unable to see his features anymore, she shut her sketchbook. She sat as before, now watching the small back and anticipating their arduous and dangerous journey in the morning.

Madame Juliet Renard, a widow, and her son Jean-Claude Renard, on their way to a relative's funeral in Orléans. Another new identity. She had lost count.

At that moment she felt as if she'd never be able to pull it off. The war kept crashing down on her, leaving her more and more exhausted. She was beyond afraid, beyond care for herself. But now there was this new burden, an innocent boy who'd lost his parents, their only crime being that they'd fought the same fight as hers, as JJ's.

Océane's double life, working as a doctor under a false name in a German-run hospital during the day and being an underground worker at night, was slowly draining her of her last resources. And now there was her grandfather struggling with his health. There never was a lull in the mental weight.

But this little boy, her brother's look-alike, could well be the straw that broke the camel's back. Not knowing what she was doing, Océane wrapped a quilt around her and gently eased herself onto the double bed alongside Daniel. Listening to his soft, even breathing, feeling the small body, warm and relaxed under the bedclothes next to her, Océane fell into the abyss of sleep, stealing a few hours away from her unceasing fight. A bliss rare and nebulous these days.

A soft tapping on her shoulder woke her up.

"Arthur?" The boy shook his head, and she was awake, ashamed. Upright with a jolt, she muttered a bewildered, "I'm sorry. I know it's Daniel. You look so much like my younger brother. Forgive me."

Speaking the truth, honest words that she couldn't take back, she saw she'd caught him off guard as well. In his blue flannel pajamas, clutching his teddy bear, Daniel gazed at her, his straw-colored hair pointing in all directions.

"Where are my Maman and Papa?" He was speaking in his perfect, grown-up voice, slightly highbrow.

"They're ... they're on a journey and I'm to take you to your Tante Elizabeth."

"No, they're not. They were taken by the Germans, and I might never see them again." The child's eyes filled with tears, but he clearly wanted to act in an adult way, for he wiped the tears from his eyes with the sleeve of his pajama jacket. "Besides, I don't want to go to Tante Elizabeth. I want to stay in Paris in case Papa and Maman return and look for me."

"Oh, you courageous, little man." Océane feared her own voice would break. "But your parents wanted you to go to Orléans. They will certainly come and fetch you as soon as they're back."

"I don't know Tante Elizabeth, and I don't want to go to Orléans. Besides, I have Kiki to look after."

"Who's Kiki?"

"She's my cat and she will certainly die if I don't feed her. Madame Trude knows nothing of cats and she's afraid of Kiki. Please, Madame?"

A chubby little paw landed on her lower arm. His eyes filled up again despite his desperate attempt not to cry. As he seemed mature for his age, Océane thought it best to be honest with him.

"Daniel, do you know why your parents were taken by the Germans?"

He nodded sagely. "Because they help Jews. One of them was my friend Ben. He's been rescued."

He said the word 'rescued' with great pride and Océane only thought was that this war made children grow up before their time.

"So you must be proud of your parents? They are very good people."

"Of course." His voice was full of confidence. "If the war is still going on when I'm sixteen, I'm going to rescue Jews as well. Now, can we go and collect Kiki, Madame?"

The more Daniel talked, the more he became his own person. Though outwardly resembling Arthur, character wise the two boys couldn't be more different. Where Arthur had been wild and playful and loud, here was a studious little professor with a very precise will, hardened by the imprint of war.

Océane's mind went in different directions, trying to decide what would be best under the circumstances. An almost impossible trip to Orléans lay before them, more risks for her and the boy. Travelling with false identity papers was not as easy as it had been two years prior, the Nazis having become smarter and way crueler.

Then there was the Baron sinking into despair. Daniel's little voice in the solemn household might lift everyone's spirits. But that was a great risk as well. The Saint-Aubin house was being watched, of that she was sure. And wouldn't it be selfish wanting to keep this wise little fellow under their roof? They would become attached to him and he to them. What if his parents never returned?

Needing to buy time, to make up her mind, she said, "You know what, Daniel? We'll go and have breakfast first. See what my grandfather thinks about Kiki, then you can go and feed the ducks with the pigeon food we found in the cellar."

His little brows crumpled in a frown. "Pidgeon food for ducks? Is that good for them? What if they choke on it?"

Océane had to hide a smile while her heart swelled. What a sweet ache. These moments would help them forget the war for just the briefest of times.

HER HEART LEAPED up again when she and Daniel entered the breakfast room and she saw her grandfather reading the paper in his usual chair.

"Maxipa! You're up? How are you feeling?"

"Right as rain!" he beamed, his sunken cheeks still glowing with a slight fever, but curiously taking in the new guest. "Now who's this excellent fellow?"

"My name is Daniel Montserrat and who are you?"

"Oh-la-la!" the Baron chuckled with some of his former glee. "Enchanté, Master Daniel. I'm Max de Saint-Aubin."

"Then why does Madame call you Maxipa? She told me you are the grandfather."

"Excellent question, Master Daniel. Now come and sit down. Then we're going to ask my granddaughter how she came up with such a ridiculous name for an old man like me."

"Oh, but I can tell you," Daniel said with great importance, sitting down at the table and folding the napkin neatly over his little knees. "You see, Sir, Max is your first name, but maxi also stands for big or grand, so it is just like a contra ... contraction of two words."

"Bravo!" the Baron clapped his hands. "What an intelligent solution. Why, not in a million years could I have come up with that myself."

Daniel seemed unperturbed. "Aren't you going to ask me what I'm doing here, Monsieur Maxipa?"

The Baron wagged his finger with enthusiasm. "That sort of question, my dear fellow, I never ask before breakfast." He rang the bell cord, winking at Océane who was watching the scene with fascination.

Memories came flooding back of her summer holidays with this fun-loving, quirky grandfather. There had not been a moment she and Arthur hadn't been tricked or treated. The smile on her grandfather's face was the final push for Océane. She would phone the aunt and explain.

As coffee and breakfast was served by a puzzled-looking Gaël, the Baron continued his game. "So, Master Daniel, I have another rule in my house before I investigate where my visitors come from."

"Alright." He seemed to be enjoying both his breakfast and the banter.

"Did you sleep well?"

"I did, Sir, but I was woken up by pigeons cooing on the roof. For a moment I thought we were in our holiday house in the Champagne. We don't have pigeons in Rue Saint-Simon, you see." The boy's face fell as he mentioned his home, but he straightened his back. "And then I heard the most beautiful violin music. I don't know where that came from."

Océane cried out. "Grandpa, have you been playing? Are you feeling that well? Thank god!"

The Baron's smile made his mustache veer up. "Ahh, I suddenly felt so inspired to play Vivaldi."

"I don't know Vivaldi," Daniel remarked studiously, "but it was mighty beautiful and very jolly."

"Thank you, dear boy! How wonderful to have some animus in the house again. We needed that."

"What animal is that?" Daniel's face had a serious expression. "I have Kiki and she's completely white."

Both the Baron and Océane burst out laughing and exchanged a look. *I need to talk to you*, she mouthed. When Gaël entered to clear the breakfast table, Océane asked her to take Daniel with her to the kitchen.

She immediately laid her cards on the table. "What shall we do? I won't be here, Maxipa; I can't risk visiting you again for a while. It's also tricky to keep an unknown boy in the house with you."

"Don't break your heart over it, *ma chérie*, we'll manage for as long as it's needed. The girls and I will keep an eye on the little fellow."

"But what about the aunt in Orléans?"

"When we collect the cat, we can ask the housekeeper to telephone her."

Océane looked doubtful. "You seriously want to bring the cat here as well?

"*Biensûr*! I'll do it!" her grandfather decided. "I'm feeling so much better today, and I can drive the car. I can't imagine a day without that little chap with his funny remarks, and I believe he's much better off here than being hauled through half of France at gunpoint."

"But you still have a slight fever, Grandpa. You shouldn't be out. It's mid-winter."

"Tattle! I'll dress warmly and I'll be right back. You go to the hospital and take good care of yourself, my dear."

Océane sighed. "If we're lucky we might see an end to this war soon, Maxipa. The Allies are pressing on through Italy and the Red Army is almost in Poland."

"I'm afraid the grimmest part is yet to come." He shook his white head in sadness.

"Heaven forbid."

IT WAS impossible to stop herself. She had to steal these precious moments with her family. Daniel now sat on the floor in Gaël's kitchen stroking Kiki's white fur as she gobbled up her cat food. For a golden moment he forgot the loss of his parents, the strange environment, his professor-like little mind. He was just a ten-year-old, united with his pet, safe in the small circle of love around him.

Océane drank in that image, storing it in her heart for the last, long battle that awaited her.

29

A SOLDIER'S HEART

Spring 1944

The stolen hours at her grandfather's house were shiny pearls on Océane's string. She knew she shouldn't come but a force stronger than herself pulled her back to her grandfather and little Daniel.

After a hard mission, another comrade lost, a day full of bullying from the Germans at the hospital, she sneaked back along the path at the back at the house the hour before curfew just to be with them. She knew the risk; they all did, but it was the only thing that kept her going.

She was playing a game of dominoes with Daniel when Marie stormed into the room with a distraught look on her round face. "Mademoiselle, quickly! Come with me!"

Afraid something was the matter with her grandfather, she shot up. "You stay here, Daniel. Marie will finish the game with you."

"But I was winning!" he wailed.

"I'll be back." She gestured Marie to follow her out of hearing range. "What is it?"

"It's a man. Bleeding. At the back door."

She was already running over the tiled floor of the long corridor, shouting over her shoulder, "Distract Daniel, Marie! Keep him in the parlor."

On the threshold, bent double with his legs folded under him and heavily bleeding, Océane was aghast to see it was D'Artagnan. Gaël was leaning over him, tugging helplessly on the collar of his coat.

"I don't know who this man is but he's unconscious. What shall we do with him?"

Océane stepped in. "I know who it is. We'll have to carry him indoors. Let's put him on the sofa in the back room. Then you fetch my medical bag. It's on the side table next to the front door."

"But ... but ..." the housekeeper protested.

"You take his legs; I'll take him in the armpits. No reason to upset the Baron with this."

With a lot of shoving and pulling, the two women managed to drag the heavy, unconscious man to the nearby room and lay him on the sofa. Océane's medical eye scanned his injuries, and she could see he had been hit on both sides of his head with a heavy object, possibly with a muzzle. There were deep wounds on his wrists that suggested he had been tied up. Opening his coat and then his shirt, she was horrified to see he had wounds all over his body. His breathing was shallow, raspy and irregular. The thought that nagged her as she examined him further was how he managed to escape; how did he arrive on their doorstep? He had to have left a trail. They were all in grave danger already when she was in the house and now D'Artagnan had chosen to collapse on their doorstep. Did he have a message for her that couldn't wait?

So many questions and no answers. She would have to tend to him first.

As she dressed his wounds as best as she could and diagnosed that miraculously he had broken no bones, she weighed their options. Sedation. Clean herself up. Read the emergency note. Make a plan.

"This will keep him asleep for a while," she finally said, getting up from her knees and putting the empty morphine syringe in the tray that Gaël held ready for her. "Now I need you and Marie to take turns watching over him, while I talk to my grandfather. He and I have to make an escape plan now."

Gaël simply nodded, her face grave but composed. She knew exactly the danger they all were in. Even more so now.

Before she went in search of her grandfather, Océane broke the seal of the envelope D'Artagnan had given her the last time they met in January 1944.

"Only in emergency situations, read this note," he'd instructed, and she had kept it hidden in the false bottom of her medical bag.

The note only had two lines: *"Go to a safehouse in Blois. Ask the station master for Madame Lumière."*

She hesitated. Was it time? Should she take her grandfather and little Daniel there and leave Gaël and Marie to look after the house? D'Artagnan's arrival complicated the situation. She could hardly expect the maids to nurse the severely injured Resistance fighter. No, she would urge her grandfather and Daniel to leave, and she would stay in Paris. Come what may. But convincing her stubborn grandfather to agree to the plan would not be an easy feat.

To travel to Blois, they would need a *Safe Conduite*. For this she had to go to an intermediary by the name of Noir who lived close by in Neuilly-sur-Seine.

"Gaël, I'm running a quick errand and I'll take Daniel with me. I'll be back in half an hour. Make sure you look after our patient and my grandfather may not leave the house under any circumstance. Understood?"

"I thought you were going to talk with the Baron?"

"I will. Don't worry. This comes first."

The wide-eyed housekeeper nodded, wringing her hands. "Okay, I'll keep the Baron occupied and look after the wounded man. What else?"

Océane had no time for her wry humor. Grabbing Daniel by the hand, she announced as chirpily as she could, "We're going for a little walk, but you must promise not to let go of my hand."

~

THEY RAN along the Seine until the little boy, tugging on her hand, yawped, "Don't go so fast, OC, my feet will wear out if we keep going at this pace."

"No, they won't." But she slowed down a little.

When they arrived at the house in Boulevard Victor Hugo, a stately house with a Burgundy red front door and windowpanes in the same color, Océane rang the bell as if hell had broken loose. A maid, dressed in black with a white apron as if war had never happened, opened the grilled little window in the middle of the door,

"Yes?"

"I'm looking for Noir." Océane sounded out of breath.

"And who are you?"

"La Rose."

The door opened and she and Daniel were admitted to a posh entrance hall with a marble floor, decorated with Greek vases and various rather erotic looking sculptures on pedestals. A small woman in a long, amber-colored silk dress, with a wrinkled face and very red-painted lips, her hair a wavy white storm, and a cigarette burning at the end of a long cigarette holder, glided into the hallway. She raised her eyebrows as she approached them.

"*Ah non, La Rose,*" she said in a smoky voice, "I'm afraid you bring bad tidings?"

"Yes, Madame, D'Artagnan is at my house but he's severely wounded and I'm afraid the ... um ... you know, will be at our doorstep anytime."

She looked down at Daniel, afraid to upset him. He was taking in Madame Noir with his round blue eyes, missing her hint.

"Come in for a moment," the tiny woman said in her husky voice. "You understood I'm Noir?" She giggled, which ended in a fit of coughing. "Black is the color of the inside of my lungs." She winked and took another deep draw on her cigarette holder, blowing out a huge cloud of blue smoke. "Come in, come in. Let me see what I can do. You are the Baron's granddaughter, are you not, the doctor?"

"Yes."

The woman in her swishing dress preceded them to a large sitting room with big sofas and chairs all with red-floral designs. The walls were white-washed and adorned with huge modern paintings.

Océane froze in her tracks and unconsciously squeezed Daniel's hand so hard that he yelped. Noir followed her eyes and saw her look at a large painting of Le Pont Neuf at night with the water of the Seine reflecting the light of the old lanterns and couples strolling over the bridge. She would have recognized the style, the color, the composition anywhere and it hit her harder than she was prepared for.

"Ah, I see," Noir said quickly, "I had quite forgotten. Yes, it's a Riveau alright. I knew him well, of course, like I know your grandfather. We're actually related, but only like distant second-cousins, or so. Come and sit down for a moment while I see what I can do for you."

Océane pulled herself together and sat on one of the floral sofas. The cushions were too soft, she almost disappeared in them. Daniel tumbled on her lap as he sat down, giggled and then quickly sat upright, adopting his solemn little face.

"I need a *Safe Conduite* for Blois for three persons," she began, "and someone has to come and collect D'Artagnan as soon as he's able to be transported. Can you help us?"

Noir pulled on her cigarette, clearly thinking fast, her wrinkled face still as a statue. "Yes, of course. I'll take care of it. I'll make sure someone brings the documents this afternoon. And remember, if anything happens in the meantime, come to me. Like your grandfather, I've got friends in high places." She winked but her eyes did not smile.

With difficulty Océane clambered out of the deep sofa. "Thank you, Madame Noir, we'll be going again. I don't want to leave my grandfather for too long. I guess I won't be of much help anymore when we arrive in Blois, but I'll be eternally thankful to you and hope to see you when all of this is over again."

"Sure, sure, honey," the white-haired woman said as she remained seated, waving a weary hand. "You never know, we might see each other earlier than you and I think." The old, white hand with glittering diamonds raised the bell on the table next to her. "Nancy will let you out. Good luck, my dear. You know where to find me, don't you?"

"Yes, Madame Noir. Thank you again."

On grabbing Daniel's hand once again, Océane heard her call after them, "My name is Mireille," followed by a chuckle and a cough.

"What a strange woman," Daniel said as they hastened back to the house on the Seine.

"She rather was," Océane agreed, "but quite likeable."

"Her hair was the color of Kiki's fur," Daniel giggled.

Océane sighed a breath of relief. Not only did Daniel not seem really upset about the sudden upheaval, but she also soon would have tickets to get them to safety.

THE DARK-GREEN front door with the Baron's name in golden lettering stood open. Instinctively she pushed Daniel behind her as they crept through the hallway.

"Gaël, Marie," she shouted, "why is the door open?"

No one replied.

She ran to the kitchen with Daniel on her heels. No one there. A pot of water was simmering on a low fire, indicating someone had been there not so long ago, and Gaël and Marie's aprons were gone, indicating they had to be at work somewhere.

Leaving the deserted kitchen, she ran up to her grandfather's quarters, but he wasn't in either. Lastly, she checked on their patient in the back room. Also gone! Océane came to a screeching halt. With all her might she tried not to panic in front of the little boy, but she couldn't help clamping her hand over her mouth.

"Where are they?" Daniel's small voice piped next to her as he pulled her sleeve.

"I don't ... I don't know," she stammered. "Come!" She ran up the stairs to her own room and found what she expected.

Her room was a mess. Garments strewn out of drawers and papers all over the floor. Her medical bag had been tossed upside down so that a display of scissors, gauges, her mother's stethoscope and medical bottles and tablets lay splattered over the floor.

"Oh no, thieves!" Daniel cried. "There have been thieves in the house."

For a moment Océane was at a loss but then an icy cold settled in her veins, and she became calm and determined. This was a crisis. Quickly stuffing everything back in her medical bag, she packed a small valise for both herself and Daniel.

Then, in an almost cheerful voice, she announced, "We're going on a little trip back to that white lady and then we're going to find grandpa and Gaël and Marie."

"What about Kiki?" Daniel asked, almost crying.

"Of course, we'll take Kiki. Go and fetch her basket."

As he went to collect both the cat from his bed and her little basket, Océane made a plan.

"Whatever happens next, you can do this!" she told herself. "You've already killed one Nazi. Now adopt a soldier's heart and go rescue your family."

As they pulled the front door closed behind them and she turned the key in the lock for the last time, her mind was made up. She left the key under the flowerpot with geraniums, a place her grandfather or Gaël would look for it should they come back.

For the second time within an hour, they retraced their steps to Madame Noir.

30

THE POWER OF MADAME NOIR

Madame Noir seemed not at all surprised at seeing Océane arrive for the second time at her house with Daniel, a cat and two valises in tow.

"Come on in, my dears! Get them some hot tea and lunch, Nancy. *Vite! Vite!*"

The old lady herself apparently lived on cigarettes and Aquavit.

As she nestled herself in her armchair, she pointed to the sofa where they'd sat earlier and asked in an offhand way, "So what happened?"

Océane was still arranging their belongings on the floor, while Daniel with the cat basket on his lap sank into the sofa. Kiki was meowing as if she was being flayed.

"Do let the cat out of the bag!" Madame Noir insisted. "That meowing hurts my old ears. He won't pee on the carpet, will he?"

"Kiki is a she and she relieves herself in the garden, Madame. Do you have a garden?"

Madame Noir giggled like a young girl. "I do, son, and, boy, are you a heartbreaker."

Daniel shot her a puzzled look but was already scrambling out of the sofa to open the wicker basket. He lifted Kiki on his lap, stroking her and talking softly to her to decrease her stress.

"That's a mighty nice cat," Madame Noir observed. "She reminds me of Bella, a cat I had many eons ago."

"What is eons, Madame?" While he continued stroking the cat's fur, his lovely blue eyes rested on their host.

"Never mind that, young man," she answered. "I'd better hear what's the matter with you two bringing your entire household here."

Océane hadn't even finished explaining their situation before Madame Noir started ringing the bell next to her with a vehemence surprising for her thin old arms.

Nancy came running in as if the house was on fire. "What is it, Madame?"

"Bring me the telephone!"

The housekeeper in her black dress and white apron hastened to the other side of the room where a white marble telephone set stood on a side table. Table and telephone with its long cord was brought to Madame Noir's side in a trot. Nancy then handed her employer a black leather-bound address book.

Daniel was following the bustle with great interest and Océane also let herself sink into the sofa a little more at ease. The presence of this resolute old lady had a calming effect on her. Someone was in charge and for once it wasn't her.

"Thank you, Nancy, now bring in the lunch." Gnarled white fingers flipped through the leather-bound book until they stopped at a page. "This one will do."

She picked up the receiver and dialed the number. Even for Madame Noir her face looked very serious. "Aha, Dorothea, Mireille here; put me through to your husband, will you?"

A short wait followed in which her face relaxed. The old lady gave Daniel a wink, who in perfect imitation, set out winking, first with one and then with the other eye.

"Hugo! Thank you for answering *de suite*. It's our mutual friend Max de Saint. Please look into it *now!* ... You will? Great, I think it's the usual affair ... Right. I'll be waiting here with his granddaughter ... yes, the doctor. Thank you, again, Hugo. Au revoir."

She put the receiver down with a bang. The phone protested with a high-pitched ping.

"Now we just have to wait, my dears, while you have a proper lunch. That was ... uh ... a friend of mine, the Marquis de Rochefort. He's well informed on both sides, so to say."

"The Marquis de Rochefort?" Océane couldn't help exclaiming. "Well, I never. I thought he was thick with the Vichy Government and the Germans?"

"Oh, he is if he wants to, *chérie*," Madame Noir chuckled. "Hugo is an excellent actor but also a staunch patriot. And he adores your grandpapa. They've been chums since they were both in plus fours. He'll bend over backwards to trace the Baron's whereabouts and get him freed. So, please, relax a little and have some good food."

Hard as she tried also for Daniel's sake, Océane was on tenterhooks. It was clear Madame Noir had no doubts they were arrested. Until then she'd hoped they might have gone into hiding. But then, why would the front door be left open? It didn't rhyme.

The food Nancy served them was exquisite, things she hadn't seen or tasted in a long time. Crêpes with real flour and myrtle jam, fresh bread laden with ham and real black tea. It smelled delicious and she was happy to see Daniel dive into the food without scruples, but her own throat tightened every time she attempted to force food through. In the end she decided to just enjoy the tea with a generous scoop of fine white sugar, counting the seconds until the Marquis's reply.

"You do understand the two of you are staying with me tonight," Madame Noir stated. It was no question.

"But ..." Océane ventured.

"No buts. Do you have other options?" The old woman lifted one white brow, sipping her Aquavit and stuffing another cigarette in her holder.

Océane slowly shook her head. Daniel's temporary place was

with her grandfather, she had her safe houses; traveling to Blois right now was out of the question.

"But what about Kiki?" Daniel asked. "She was just used to a new house and now she's moving again."

"Where did you live before, boy?"

"Number 10 Rue de Saint-Simon."

Now it was Madame Noir's turn to look surprised. "Are you Montserrat's son?"

"Yes, I'm Daniel Montserrat and my parents are Marc and Antoinette Montserrat, but the Germans have taken them, so now Kiki and I belong to Océane and Maxipa because I didn't want to go to Tante Elizabeth in Orléans."

Clacking her tongue, Madame Noir looked the little boy up and down, then smiled. "You would be a bad one for the Cause, my dear. You carry your heart on your sleeve."

With an indignant look on his little face, he replied, "No, I do not. My heart is inside my body, Madame!"

Despite the tense atmosphere, Madame Noir and Océane had to laugh, while Daniel frowned angrily. At that moment the telephone rang. Madame Noir put a finger over her mouth as she picked up the receiver. Océane was dying to hear what was being said on the other side, but all Madame Noir ejaculated was, "Ah oui ... ah non ... I see ... right ... well, thank you, Hugo. That's a big help. Yes, I'll let her know." The dark eyes rested on Océane as she ended the call.

"What is it? What did the Marquis say?" Breathless, she waited.

"Your grandfather and the two maids have been taken to 84 Avenue Foch."

Océane shuddered as she heard that address and squeaked a terrified, "Oh no!"

Madame Noir raised a hand to stop her. "The Marquis has a direct line to Major-General Richter, the current head of the SS in Paris. He phoned him and told Richter in no uncertain terms that taking the Baron and his staff prisoner was a grave mistake that would not land well with high-ranking French officials. The

Germans depend more and more on them these days now they're losing the war. Hugo took a personal vow that there could be no way your grandfather was involved in the Resistance."

"But D'Artagnan? He was at our house. And what happened to him?" Océane intervened, confused.

Madame Noir's face fell. "I'll tell you in a minute," she said, her voice hoarse with emotion. "It's not a pretty story for little ears."

"You want me to go to the kitchen?" Daniel once again broke the tension, and Madame Noir nodded.

In an attempt to remain lighthearted, she said, "I take my earlier words back, Daniel - you're a super-agent!"

The smile he gave her as he and Kiki followed Nancy out of the room was priceless. As soon as the door closed, Madame Noir's eyes filled with tears. It was the first time Océane saw her as vulnerable and intensely old.

"Our brave man, our anchor from the first hour, was fusilladed immediately upon arrival at the SS Headquarters. He could hardly stand on his own two feet and had to be tied to the executioner's wall."

Oh no! D'Artagnan as well. My last tie to JJ.

Through a fog she heard, Madame Noir continue, "Cynically enough, it was fortunate that at that point your grandfather's interrogation hadn't yet begun. As your grandfather had no knowledge of the resistance fighter being in his house, no relation between the two men could be proved. D'Artagnan was dead and couldn't speak, your grandfather couldn't answer how he'd ended up in his backroom. The brave maids kept their mouths shut, just saying they helped a wounded fellow countryman not knowing who he was. He'd banged on their backdoor and they had dressed his wounds and given him a painkiller. No mention of you or Daniel."

"Will it be enough?" Océane managed to bring out, cleaving herself a way through the fog in her head.

"We'll have to see. The Marquis is dining with General Richter at the Ritz tonight and the General will be accompanied by an old friend of yours."

"Hans?" Océane's face lit up as she thought of him. "You mean Hans Arenberg?"

"The very same, only his name is now Jakob Hess, as you should remember?"

One flickering light of hope in a very dark tunnel. She grabbed hold of it with all her might.

WHEN DANIEL WAS TUCKED into bed in his new guestroom, snuggling up with Kiki close to him, his eyes already closed, he said in a sleepy voice, "OC, I have it all figured out. Maxipa should marry Madame Noir and then they can be my new grandparents forever and ever."

She smiled through her distress. "Maybe we have to let them decide that for themselves, don't you think?" She tucked the bedclothes more firmly around his little body. "But I agree they would be a great match. I don't think it will happen, though. They've known each other for years and never fell in love, so I don't think it will happen."

"We'll just have to help them a bit," the little matchmaker muttered half asleep. "I'll think of something. I'm a super-agent."

When she returned to Madame Noir's sitting room to bid her goodnight, the old lady with her invariable cigarette, motioned her. "Do you have a moment, dear?"

Océane perched on the sofa, afraid to sink too deep into it and not be able to keep open her own eyes. The events of the day had exhausted her.

"One of our agents was at the back door," the white-haired hostess said. "He brought this note for you." She retrieved a slip of paper from her lace cuff and put it on the side table. "Came straight from our Jakob Hess."

Océane lurched for the paper. *Mission accomplished. No interrogation. Apologies offered. Will return home tomorrow morning.*

"It's done! Thank you!" She rushed over and hugged the old

lady who, scattering a dust cloud of ashes around her, let out a triumphant cry.

"There! There! I told you Hugo never disappoints!"

"Why not tonight?"

The idea of her frail grandfather and the stricken maids spending a night in the house of horrors made her shudder.

"It gets better than that. General Richter has given orders to tidy up your grandfather's house after the search and he and the maids have been offered a free stay at the Ritz tonight. All expenses paid and fitted with everything they need."

"How do you know that?"

"The agent was no other than Jakob himself."

"Hans was here? Oh, how I would've loved to see him."

"You'll see enough of him soon, my dear."

Océane's eyes popped wide-open again. "What on earth do you mean?"

"Could you say the two of you work well together?" Another cigarette was lit.

"How do you know?"

"Don't ask. You don't need to know everything. Information can be deadly in this game."

"True."

"Richter seems to be having some health problems, something about backpain and a leg that's not working properly, so our mutual friend has made the suggestion to the General that he knows this excellent young Parisian doctor who could relieve his pain." Madame Noir looked straight at her, and the dark eyes bored into hers. "I've ordered my hairdresser to get rid of those dark roots of yours early in the morning. Care for some Aquavit?"

Océane gasped, opened and closed her mouth. "I might as well." She was too stunned for other words.

Madame Noir poured her a generous glass from a crystal carafe and brought it over herself. "Here, dear girl. You'll need it. *Ad fundum!*"

It burnt a hole in her stomach but cleared her head.

"Another?" The white-haired lady put a beringed hand on her shoulder and gave it a little squeeze.

She just nodded.

"You've been looking for a way to up your game, haven't you?" Madame Noir had returned to her own chair.

Océane nodded again. This war was dragging on way too long and it needed to end fast, if only for her grandfather's health. But would she have to kill again? Would the horror start all over?

"Here's what we will do." Madame Noir's voice was calm and collected. "Your grandfather has to stay out of the limelight from now on. Daniel can return to the house while the Baron and the maids keep a low profile. You, my dear girl, will come and stay with me. I'm close to the fire, but I'm also protected. Like Hans, I play the role of double agent, but that's only what the Germans think."

Océane fell from one surprise in the other. A lady, almost in her eighties, daring to take on as mighty a power as the Nazis.

The lady herself explained further. "I'm firmly on the Free France side, don't you worry. The piecemeal information I hand to the Germans never involves humans. I might give up a silo of grain or a secret route to the coast. That sort of thing." The thin smile on her face revealed even giving up these snippets hurt her proud French soul. "I've made peace with my traitor side long ago. I can handle it as long as it leads to our ultimate goal. Get rid of them!" The dark eyes flashed with burning passion.

"Does no one suspect you? Aren't you afraid?" Océane couldn't help asking.

The thin shoulders made a what-do-I-have-to-lose-at-my-age shrug. "Just so you know, I'll be a good cover-up for you. With D'Artagnan gone, we need a new Paris leader and one that is in close contact with our main source from within. It will, let me say, speed things up. They're losing, my doll, and they know it. We just have to give them that extra push."

"How much do you know, Madame, about the progress the Allies are making?"

"It won't be long now before the combined Allied forces land somewhere on the north coast of France, Calais or Normandy. British and French secret agents are ramping up their attacks. The moment the Allies are on French territory, it will be hands on deck for every secret agent and spy in Paris and all over France. It's now or never, my dear. You with your medical background will be of indispensable value in the operation. Are you ready for it?"

"I am. And I'm grateful for your protection. But there's no way I can replace D'Artagnan. I have no inside information whatsoever."

Madame Noir's lips curled in a thin smile. "No need, my dear. He didn't know everything either. I keep my agents informed as best as I can, but this is a tricky business for everyone. One slip and .... pouf." She made the gesture of pulling a trigger.

"Do you mean to say that you...?"

"Shhhh ... don't say it!" She wagged a wrinkled finger with a pointed ivory nail.

"But then you must know about Huricana, too?"

"The Moroccan guy? Heard of him but that's all. He operates from the south and I'm sure he's well informed. My terrain is Paris, only Paris." There was that nonchalant shrug again. "Now enough questions, before you start asking me about Jean-Jacques Riveau. Not even I know what happened to him. It's a mystery but chances of survival are non-existent." She eyed Océane with her beady eyes.

The mention of his name shot through Océane as a bolt of lightning. "You said you knew Jean-Jacques personally?"

"Of course, and he had the making of a giant in this line of business." Noir chuckled at the memory, then sighed and stared at the tip of her cigarette with a disgruntled look on her face. "But I don't want to upset you further. You've got your own work to focus on now, young lady, so forget the romance and do the work. Let the pain be your motivator."

It was said with the sternness of an employer and Océane understood Madame Noir was just that. This white-haired, geriatric lady governed the network of secret agents in Paris with both an empathic and an iron hand.

"Can I at least say goodbye to my grandfather before I leave?"

"Of course, my dear. We'll invite dear Max to neutral territory. I don't want you to go near the house on the Seine until after the liberation. Let the rumors around your grandfather die so he can play his own role independently from you. I'll organize a meeting. Don't worry. Now, my girl, try and get some sleep before your day breaks and the big work starts."

31

BACK AT 84 AVENUE FOCH

Itt required all Océane's strength to force herself to walk up the steps to 84 Avenue Foch. She was sick to her stomach; her legs were jelly and her vision blurred. It didn't bode well. Somehow, she felt terribly exposed with her freshly dyed and short *la coupe* and a pair of round glasses on her nose. She was sure she would be singled out as an impostor the moment she opened her mouth.

Two items gave her strength - her white coat and her mother's stethoscope.

Grandfather is safe, Daniel is safe, you can do this, she kept reminding herself. Hadn't Madame Noir said they were almost ready to overthrow the Nazi occupation? The scales were tipping. But still.

With the Minox camera hidden in the double lining of her medical bag and the knowledge she had Hans Arenberg as an ally and a friend in that hated building, she lifted her chin and addressed the guards.

"I'm to report to Major-General Richter. I'm Marianne Briand, I'm a doctor, a nerve specialist."

Don't forget the new name, remember the basics you know on neurology.

After showing her false documents, she was let in with no further ado and led to the bench where she had to wait before being taken to the office she knew so well.

Océane could hardly breathe as she sat down. It seemed as if the imposing building had imploded in the years of war. The Germans hadn't ruined it with neglect; the walls still stood and were relatively clean, the marble floors had recently been mopped. It smelled vaguely of cleaning polish, but the smell of fear and death could not be killed. There was something else, something invisible that had ripped out the building's soul. She'd never thought a building could live and could actually die.

84 Avenue Foch was dead and yet it stood and functioned. The marble hall had seen so many of her compatriots been brought in to be transported to a prison, to Germany, or to be tortured and killed on the spot. It was as if their ghosts pushed her into that desecrated building, that inferno created by a deranged leader in Germany who had put a spell over his fellow men and now reigned over almost all of Europe.

"Madame Briand?"

She shook herself from her somber thoughts to follow yet another underage German soldier to yet another cruel leader.

Madame Noir had warned her about General Richter. He wasn't the wicked, volatile and crazy General von Stein. Richter was cold, calculating, would never become emotional. He probably didn't even have emotions, at least not human ones. What she hadn't been warned about was that he would consider her first and foremost a woman and treat her as such. Océane was totally unprepared for the trespassing on her femininity.

As she walked into the very office where Von Stein had found her snooping through the files, the first thing she noticed was the tall figure of Hans Arenberg standing slightly behind the General's chair.

It was difficult to keep a straight face, she was so glad to see him, so she fixed her eyes on the thick-set man in black in the office chair. His name the Butcher of Paris befitted him, she thought sourly.

From beefy shoulders rose a thick, short neck with a red-blotched, broad head, adorned with a thick, black mustache. Pepper-and-salt whiskers showed under his high black cap, but it was in particular the icy-cold blue eyes fixing on her that made her halt in her tracks. Nailed to the carpet, she could not suppress a shudder.

Richter's eyes were hard and greedy in equal measures. He looked her up and down as if she was naked. No one had ever looked at her this way. Instinctively she pressed her medical bag to her chest to protect herself from his lust-filled gaze. She longed to turn her eyes to Hans for support but didn't dare to. There was no other way than through the fire, so she withstood the humiliating inspection with as much dignity as was in her.

"What are *you* doing here?" The 'you' was pronounced as if she was a fly ready to be squashed, had no value and no merit. Remembering Madame Noir's instructions, she prepared herself to live up to her task.

"I'm Doctor Briand and I was asked to come here to examine your backpain."

Richter turned this thick head in Arenberg's direction. "Is this your doing? My back and my leg have been perfectly fine. Are German doctors no longer supposed to be good enough?"

"Of course, Herr General, but I spoke about this with you yesterday, suggesting a second opinion. Do you not recall?"

Richter returned his cold stare to Océane, not replying to his adjutant but eyeing her with even more interest. "Aha," he finally drawled, "now I remember but only because I like her. Let's see if she can do her job. Bring her to my private chamber."

She felt Hans's concern without looking at him as she shrunk further into herself. On wooden legs that somehow still carried her, she followed the stout man trying to hide the dragging of his right leg but failing at it.

Overweight, she thought, *but probably not the cause. Maybe an old injury that has been neglected. And why do I care? I have to save my own skin here.*

Arenberg caught up, whispering, "He'll want to grab you, but you have to persuade him to do the examination first before he can get his hands on you. Tell him whatever you need. Then quickly sedate him. Don't kill him. As soon as he's asleep, I need you to follow me. Understood?"

She nodded, an adrenaline surge sweeping through her body.

Again! Here we go again! The girl and the needle.

While Richter opened a door to what apparently held something between a consultation room and an interrogation chamber, Arenberg turned on his heels and disappeared into another corridor.

Océane mind worked swifter than a lightning flash. She had to get the General to agree to lie on his stomach, she had to prepare the syringe with the right dose, she had to remember how to get back to Richter's office without leaving a trace. She could do this. Hans would be there to support her, but when she entered the room and felt Richter's icy-cold stare on her, she was not so sure she would be able to remain level-headed, to follow the steps, even to get him to obey her. This was not the swaying mind of Von Stein, this was next-level terror, and she felt her body stiffen and her mind go blank.

"Herr General," she began, "I have an idea what it might be that is both …"

"Shut up!" he barked, never letting her out of his vision.

Océane backed away from the sheer volume of his voice and the undisguised stare. She didn't know from where it came but the dignity of her profession and the awareness that time was ticking by gave her the power she needed.

"Herr General," she began again, "I guarantee you I can relieve you from your current pain. For good. I promise you'll be able to walk without impediment and the pain will be gone. It's a simple method but very effective." She saw a flicker of doubt in his eyes and continued lying her way through it. "It's a method I learnt in Boston when I was training there as a doctor. It's an innovative medicine called an epidural steroid injection and it's very, very effective. Would you not want to try it, Herr General?"

"What guarantee do I have that you're not a trickster?"

"Wasn't my service offered to you by the Marquis de Rochefort?"

The German grumbled something with less aggression while the greed in his eyes intensified. Temporarily not for her, though. Océane was winning.

Even bolder, she added, "Has my dear friend Hugo not told you that I gave him the same injection a year ago? He's never had trouble since. But I suppose he forgot to tell you. That's how it works for us humans. When the pain is gone, we forget it. Thank god."

My dear friend Hugo. What nerve!

She had no idea from where came the courage to utter such blatant lies but if everything worked out, she'd never have to see the Butcher of Paris again, so why should she care?

"I can tell you, Herr General, that Hugo's situation was much worse than yours. Have you ever, on any occasion, seen the Marquis limp?"

"Alright," the General agreed, "but how are you so sure of your diagnosis without even examining me?"

"I am not one hundred percent sure it is sciatica, Herr General, but is has all the symptoms of it. Before I take a look, please answer these questions. Do you have a constant burning sensation or a shooting pain starting in the lower back or buttock and radiating down the front or back of your thigh, sometimes through the entire leg and even your feet?

"Yes!" he barked angrily.

"Is the pain sometimes accompanied by numbness in the back of the leg, or a tingling sensation?"

"Yes!"

He was already putting his fate in her hands. She fired off the last question.

"Do you suffer from posture induced symptoms, meaning the symptoms increase while sitting, trying to stand up, bending the spine forward, twisting the spine, lying down, and while coughing? Only walking relieves the pain?"

"Yes, woman!" he snapped, working the black mustache fervently. "Well, what do you suggest?"

He was putty now. Wanting to get rid of his pain more than he wanted her.

"I need to take a quick look, Herr General. Knowing the symptoms is one thing. I need to certify my hypothesis. Could you please remove your coat and lie down on your stomach on this bed? I will quickly put pressure on certain parts of your lower back and the back of your leg to see if such an injection would be helpful for you. I certainly hope so, but it is not always the case."

He scowled at her, exactly as she had hoped. Keep it from him and he'll want it.

"If it will work in your case, I'll let you know immediately and administer it. I know you are a very busy man, so I'll prepare the injection in case."

He gave her one more suspicious look and she answered it by adopting an innocent yet decisive look in her bespectacled eyes. With trembling fingers, she prepared the strong sedative, while he grunted and puffed, getting out of his heavy coat. Her mind wanted to slip back to a bunker in Libya, but she gritted her teeth and forced herself to stay in the here and now.

No! No flashbacks! This is not a kill.

The General lay on his round belly, almost wobbling on the narrow table. She took a deep breath and quickly pressed on the spots she knew would hurt most. He groaned like a pig.

"Yes, Herr General, it is definitely sciatica. I will administer the injection in your buttock as that is the best place. Could you please let your pants drop down a little?"

Seconds later she was eye to eye with a repugnant mass of white flesh. Without second thought she jammed the needle in the blubbering fat and released the sedative. He moaned like a dying hound. Holding her breath, she was almost gagging from her act and his ugliness.

In her most cheerful voice, she announced, "Well, that was all, Herr General. No more pain for you. Now please remain lying for the medicine to do its work."

He scrambled half up to put his pants back into place but then did as she said. With eagle eyes she watched him slip into unconsciousness, quickly packed her bag and tiptoed to the door. Looking back at the passed-out, massive lump before she closed the door behind her, she scrambled back to the General's office.

"Are you okay?" Hans's voice was full of concern. "Sorry you had to do that on your own."

"He'll be in Cuckooland for the next couple of hours, but I'd better get the hell out of here. What is it you want me to do?"

Hans put his ear to the door before retrieving an envelope from a stack on Richter's desk.

"Here," he handed her the sealed envelope, "we saw no other option. Richter has been watching these documents like a hawk. I just had time to copy them. We couldn't come up with a less messy solution."

"I'm just glad I don't have to become his permanent physician. He won't want to see me again." She took the thick brown envelope and stuffed it in her medical bag.

"You never know. But as far as I know, there's no need. This will be the last blow to the system."

"So where do I take this?" The small chat with Hans was already lifting Océane's spirit.

"An agent will wait for you at Molière's tomb at Père Lachaise. Can you go there now and deliver the envelope?"

"Sure, and then?"

"You'll be contacted before the end of the afternoon. Quick, go now," he urged her. "I don't know how long I can stay here myself after this. Richter will definitely have some tough questions for me when he regains consciousness. I've played the dumb, innocent part for a long time, but it won't work for much longer."

"Will you be safe, Jakob?"

"As safe as you, Rose. Hope to see you soon."

"It's been too long," she answered, taking another long look at the friend who'd been with her in her darkest hour.

Hans saluted her formally as the door was opened and two SS officers marched in looking at her with surprise."

"Good day, Sergeant Hess."

She quickly made her way out of the oppressing building, deeply inhaling the fragrance of chestnut blossoms as she marched down the steps, not looking at the guards and out of the gate. Hoping with all that was in her that she'd never see the inside of 84 Avenue Foch ever again.

TEMPTED TO STAY OUTSIDE, take in large gulps of fresh air, but knowing it would be an almost two-hour walk and somebody was waiting for her, Océane made her way to Étoile to take Line 2 all the way round to Cimétiere Père Lachaise. The envelope burned in the bag that sat firmly in her lap. She would probably never know its contents, but it might hold the fate of millions of French citizens.

Resisting the yearning to break the seal, she gazed out of the window as the metro moved through Paris' belly. Her own face, shallow and worn, dark rings under dull-looking, bespectacled eyes and a ridiculous platinum crown on top, reflected in the glass. She didn't recognize this woman. At some point in the war, she'd stopped looking like Océane Bell.

During that long, dark ride below the surface, swaying on the metal chair, the metro shrieking and grinding in its tracks, it dawned on her. Océane was gone. She *was* La Rose, a nobody, a cog in the wheel, a desperate entity fighting for the light. Not just a new name, a new identity, but a new type of human. Made inhuman by the opposing force. Free France! How much they needed it before the last remnants of humane life were murdered.

To stop herself having these morbid thoughts - and God forbid saying them out loud - she broke her fixation on her own mirrored image and glanced around the carriage.

An elderly couple sat close together squeezing each other's hands, heads down, silent strips for mouths. Three Germans stood together talking and laughing in loud, whipped-up voices. No merriness there. Fear. Their voices mixed with the screeching wheels of the hasty metro. This was Paris at the end of May 1944. Deserted, a gloom land, Germans dancing where there was no dancing left.

Her thoughts went back to Hans. He, too, had looked as if he was at the very end of his last rope. The stress of being discovered weighed on him. He was the one mole from within. Everything stood or fell by his actions. How long before he snapped?

Just La Rose, she told herself, *just be La Rose. Not long now.*

AFTERNOON WAS ALREADY PROGRESSING as she passed through the gates of the Pere Lachaise graveyard, remembering how she had visited Chopin's grave with weeping Euterpe on top of his tomb on a sunny day in August 1934 with her grandfather. How different the world and her future had looked then.

She and Jean-Jacques had visited the famous graveyard again in the fall of 1940 when they'd just fallen in love. He'd insisted on showing her the tomb of one of his early influencers, Paul-Jacques-Aimé Baudry. She remembered every moment of standing there with him, like tiny film fragments playing in slow motion. Watching the momentous monument of grey stone, green with wear, dramatic angels around his bust and a bent pallet with a brush sticking out as if it were real. Dots of paint on the pallet. JJ talking, explaining, gesturing, smiling, vibrating.

Alive! So alive!

They'd kicked up orange and brown leaves like kids and kissed until the gray afternoon spun before her eyes.

La Rose. No more Océane!

This was the spring of 1944. This was the third time she was here. La Rose was a haunted, underweight agent without identity on her way to deliver an envelope with unknown content to another link in the cycle.

She stopped to check the map, found Molière's tomb, number 44, in the middle of the cemetery and set out at a brisk pace. When she neared the location, she spied around to see if anyone could be clearly identified as an agent. There were several visitors to the graveyard, some tending to graves, others just passing through it as if taking a shortcut.

Océane decided to sit down on a wooden bench quite close to Molière's tomb so she would be visible to the person looking for her. When she heard footsteps behind her, she didn't turn her head but waited, still as the tombs.

A young woman, no more than a girl, wearing a green felt hat and a dark trench coat, with a belt tied tightly around her slim waist, perched on the bench next to her. The strain in their bodies was like an electric current.

"La Rose?" The whisper hardly reached her ear.

"Yes."

Within seconds the envelope had changed hands and disappeared in the girl's handbag.

"You go first," she whispered. "Take the exit you came in from at Porte des Amandiers. I'll take the other one."

That was all. Done. Anonymous to anonymous.

Océane dragged her feet back to the exit and took the metro to Madame Noir's house.

Everyone knew this was the hardest spring Paris had ever seen.

32

THE STRANGEST FRIEND

Paris, 7 June 1944

May pushed itself into early June and though nature exploded in color and scent, the Boulevards and parks springing alive with leafy trees and courting birds, Paris was staggering on its last legs.

Broken by four long years of German exploitation, all Jewish citizens deported, hundreds of thousands of citizens killed. Life was reduced to finding food and waiting.

Océane was unwell, underfed, used-up. Blisters formed in her mouth and other mucous membranes due to vitamin shortage and undernutrition. There was a constant tremor in her hands she couldn't stop. She'd taken to allowing herself small doses of morphine, a precious resource from her hospital days and not meant for her personal use. She saw no way out but knew with some part of her that addiction was luring her in. Old at twenty-four, it felt as if her life was almost over. The age her mom was at the end of *her* war. Océane would squeeze the stethoscope and tell herself to take courage from her mother's fight, but it didn't help.

The lies, the uncertainties, the secret needles in the dark. Often it was her task to attack with a needle not a gun, but she had no idea what she was doing. Madame Noir, whom she met at intervals, was never clear about the goal of her missions, only about where and when La Rose was sent. Twice she'd been outside Paris with instructions to perform her deadly injections. German officials. What did it matter? Nothing mattered anymore. Nothing could leave a stain upon her soul. Not even killing instead of saving lives. She was fast falling into deep depression.

It was a warm afternoon. She sat on a bench at the Seine's quay, her mind empty, her soul vaguely remembering family, love, future. Clad in a faded cotton dress, shoes with holes in the soles, shivering, her eyes were absently following a pair of white swans gliding by in majestical unity.

Suddenly her eyes opened wide, and she was fully awake. The fog lifted. Catapulted back to a day in Boston in May 1938, where she'd been sitting on a similar bench with Martin in Fenway Park. He'd just told her she'd failed one of her finals for Radcliffe. Martin! She hadn't thought about him for years, pudgy, honest Martin who'd been her friend through thick and thin.

Would he have become the psychiatrist he wanted to be? And what about Eliza? Was she a gynecologist now? Had life continued as normal for them in the States? Should she have stayed? Her mind expanded with her thoughts. There was more in the world than just this death and destruction, hate and harassment.

She tried to imagine what her life would've been if she'd stayed home. No Switzerland, no Paris, no JJ. She couldn't erase it, start over, be just a one-time, innocent forger. She was this, too - a killer, a survivor, a fighter.

It was the moment Océane and La Rose melded together and some sort of life returned to them both. Even if it meant a life without JJ. Nature and life were stronger, pulling at her despite herself to a future that was fickle and frail.

No more morphine! she vowed.

Océane was so engrossed in her thoughts that she veered up

when a German soldier sat next to her on the bench, as if afraid he could read her mind.

As she got up, a familiar voice said, "How are you, Rose?"

"John!"

Her eyes lit up. For some reason it felt good to say the name he'd chosen for himself. This *was* a good day after all. But he looked very troubled, so her heart sank.

"What is it?"

"Time has come to take off this hated uniform."

"I thought you'd consider that good news?" She raised her dyed eyebrows.

"I'm not sure I'll make it. This isn't a tiny oasis in Africa. This is a Nazi wasp nest with very angry wasps in the middle of a metropolitan. I'm a suspect, Rose. I'm done."

"No, you're not, John. I'll help you."

"No need for that, Rose. I've come to say goodbye."

She didn't want to hear it, probed further. "What happened?"

"The Allied forces landed on the beaches of Normandy yesterday. It's been a bloody fight, but they managed to come on land. The French Resistance, you included, have done a brilliant job, giving them all the information they needed. The Maquis are now stepping up their game, as most of the German forces move in the direction of Normandy to help the troops there. We're delaying the convoy through sabotage. I'm disappearing tonight, Rose; I'm going to help them. My job here is done. I hope to see you after the liberation."

She stared at him wordless, tears filling her eyes, misting up the silly glasses that she wanted to take off and hurl into the Seine. She didn't move a muscle as her heart rate went wild.

"Is it really, finally going to happen, John?" She was sure her heart was going to burst any second now.

"Yes, Océane."

As he said her real name, the last part clicked into place. Océane still existed. This was a glorious day indeed. The end was in sight.

But then Hans's voice warned her, "It will still be a long, hard road ahead and we may still die. Can be months before Paris is liberated. I wanted to let you know you won't be getting your instructions from me anymore. Do you remember the girl in Père Lachaise?"

"Of course."

"Her code name is Luno. You will work together with her."

"Sure, but Hans ..." She hesitated a moment. "Madame Noir may well say I play an important role but I'm quite fed up not knowing what I'm doing. No matter that you and others say it's important, I'd ... I'd like to do more."

She searched his face, wanting understanding, recognition.

"I know, OC, and I think the time has come to explain a little about what's been at stake here. We've all been protecting you and using you as bait at the same time. All eyes are on you, from both sides."

Océane shivered, longing for her morphine shot, and sat on her hands to hide the tremor. "I don't get what you're saying." Her voice was thin, childlike.

"Von Stein's death made you and me the most wanted people in the whole Third Reich. The bastard for sure left that legacy. I was officially pronounced dead so the trail to me stopped. It left only you. They want your skin at all costs, and it makes them mad that they can't find you."

"Go on." Her voice was flat, depression once again replacing her brighter mood.

"It's a two-edged sword. They think that by catching you they can round up the headpieces of the Resistance. Through you they want to find Huricana."

"Huricana? I haven't even met the guy!"

"They don't know that. But to make a long story short, without knowing it, Océane, you are the leader of the French Resistance. At least in the eyes of the Gestapo. As a result, we do two things. Every agent protects you, but you cannot have too much information because they want you so badly."

"Thank you," she said, "I get it now and will play my part. Why wasn't I told all this before?"

"Even that seemed dangerous knowledge." Hans's voice dropped. "It is dangerous what we're doing here but it's essential as well."

"I wish it could last. You're my only friend, Hans."

"And you mine." He was silent for a while, staring at the waters of the Seine moving west, obviously weighing his words. As the sun set behind the Hôtel de Ville with the Nazi flag still swinging from its pole, he said in a low voice thick with emotion, "I never managed to tell you the story of Anna, did I? My fiancé from Hildesheim?"

"Do tell, if you think we can sit here a little longer and not be arrested."

Hans took a flask from his pocket and unscrewed the lid. "This seems the only thing to keep me going these days."

She thought of her morphine as he took a deep swig from his flask. Welcoming the burning liquid, she took her turn.

Hans continued. "Anna refused to become a member of the NSDAP as early as 1937. Her father had fought in the first war but contrary to many he took his experiences in the French trenches as a lesson for life. No more war for him or his children. Thank God, Frederik Holstein only had three daughters because he would certainly have run into trouble with sons."

Another swig, dark brows knitted together. "Anna took after her father, a liberal and a pacifist. She was a beautiful, freethinking spirit who believed Germany was so much more and so much better than the narrow-minded, anti-Semitic and fascist propaganda machine that had been poisoning our lives even before it ended in this xenophobic war."

Silence. Océane didn't know what to say. She held her breath.

"Anna and I met when she went to Hanover University in 1938 to study philosophy. I was there for a course in mechanical engineering, farm equipment like threshers and tractors. Not knowing better, I was an NSDAP member just like everybody else. But then

Anna opened my eyes, talking about her disappointment that the lectures were only Nazi approved philosophers such as Heidegger, Nietzsche and, of course, Alfred Rosenberg, the creator of the Nazi creeds such as antisemitism and 'Lebensraum'. Anna secretly read her own philosophers, Kierkegaard, Hegel and Kafka."

The expression on Hans's face was a mix of admiration and gloom. "Anna didn't hold back, just like her father. She refused to be silenced. I feared for her safety already then, speaking her mind with a youthful candor and directness that made me love her all the more. She just didn't realize in how much danger she was. I tried to warn her but there was no stopping Miss Anna Holstein."

He sighed deeply, seeing the fate of his beloved before him. "We got engaged just before I left for military training in April 1939. Anna was, of course, totally against me going into the army and told me we should flee together to America and start a new, free life there. I wish I had listened to her."

Again, that deep sigh and another swig from his bottle.

"What happened?" Océane could no longer hold back.

The silence that followed was laden with the grief of war. "I don't know," Hans finally managed to utter. "I told her in every letter to be careful, to sit it out, that we would go to the States eventually, that in a way I was fortunate. I've never had to engage in real battle once. I've only been here in Paris and that short trip to North Africa. So I'm sort of sticking to our promise to sit it out."

He hesitated and Océane knew why. Hans was far from speaking the truth. Actively obstructing his own army was far more dangerous than what any of his fellow countrymen did in the French capital.

"Go on ... about Anna, I mean."

"I don't know. Her letters just stopped coming. I've written to everyone I know who also knows her, even to her father, but nobody knows where she is. Whether she's still alive. She joined the White Rose, a German resistance movement, and moved to Berlin. That's the last we heard. She's either hiding or arrested or ... dead."

The water he stared at was slowly turning to an inky blue; his hands were clamped around his flask. No lampposts lit up and dusk settled around them like a thin veil.

"Can I see her picture?"

"Sure."

Hans seemed to revive for a moment as he got out his wallet and retrieved a small envelope from which he took a rectangular black and white picture. He handed it to Océane. She looked into the lightest, merriest eyes she'd ever laid eyes on and a mass of light curls around an oval face. The young woman was pretty, but it was her liveliness and the clear, open gaze that instantly drew in all attention. There was no doubt that this girl would speak her mind and speak it loudly. She was confident and intelligent, not a woman to be taken for granted, from the roots of her curly hair to the decisive, pointed chin.

"No kidding," Océane exclaimed, "what a strong picture! I can see what you mean that she will not be silenced. By God, I hope she's alright."

Hans laughed bitterly, taking the picture back, staring at it for a moment before hiding it in his wallet again.

"I'm afraid I've missed the mark. My intention for telling you about Anna's straightforwardness was to prevent you from doing the same thing but I fear my account has had the opposite effect."

"What do you mean?"

"We all want to take action now we feel the wind is in our back. It can make us reckless."

"I've listened, Hans. I'll lay low, I promise."

"The limelight is filled with boobytraps right now, OC. So many more resistance fighters are going to be killed in the last hours of this war. It's the only revenge they can take. Please take heart from your precise, physician-like approach that has helped you navigate these treacherous waters so far. Staying safe now is the most important mission we can fulfil for our loved ones." His brows knitted together while he continued to stare at the water. "Don't take an example from my dear Anna, OC. I beg you."

"I won't." She cleared her throat. "What hurts me most is that we're in the same boat. You lost contact with your Anna and I with Jean-Jacques. We both hope against hope they're alive somewhere."

"Someone has to survive this bloody war," Hans grumbled, "some of the decent ones."

"And you say the wise and secretive ones will?" she asked.

"Yes."

He looked at her directly, gray eyes bloodshot but piercing. She couldn't help but think how much he'd changed and aged since, as a young officer, he'd been brought into her examining room at Hôtel-Dieu de Paris with chest pains after being assaulted by Dieter von Stein. He had grown, matured, hardened. Life had turned them into stunted trees, still trying to grow shoots.

"OC," his voice was soft but held a kind of warm threat, "I'm the type of man who only loves once. I love Anna, she's my swan, my life companion, whether alive or dead, but you come a close second. I love you as my dearest friend. We've forged a life out of madness together. Let's vow that we'll stay alive through this wretched war so we can still be friends when we're eighty or ninety years old. How about that?"

She saw the love he held for her, admiration, deep, deep emotion of another kind, another love, worlds merging that were never supposed to merge. All offered to her with an open heart.

It was hard to find the right words.

"You've been my friend from the first time we met, Hans. You've saved my life in Libya; we've fought most of this damned war together. Of course you are my friend and I want to stay alive for you and for your promise of an *entente cordiale* until the end of our lives, but one of us can be betrayed, or we can be found out. As much as I'd like to swear with my hand on my heart that I'll stay alive, it's not entirely up to me."

"I know, but promise you'll not do anything foolish?" He took her trembling hand and pressed it with warmth.

"I promise when you promise."

"I do. And when I'm back in Paris for the liberation of your capital, I'll try to pass by your grandfather's house. Without this wretched uniform."

"I'd like that." Her smile was warm and sad at the same time. "I'll miss you, Hans-John-Jakob. The fight will be lonely without you."

"I'll miss you too, La Rose. Remember we'll be fighting on the same side."

And Hans was gone, eaten up by the shadows. Océane realized it was almost past curfew as she sped to yet another safehouse, thinking about the strangest friend she'd made in this war. The words that had been spoken between them made her strong again. Their fight was worth living for.

33

A MARK'S WOMAN

In the weeks after Hans had left Paris and spring turned into summer, Océane often pondered their conversation by the Seine. There was a constant fight in her mind between staying low key and doing important but invisible work for the Resistance, and going all in, fight side-by-side with the Maquis to overthrow German occupation.

Neither side seemed to win but she did manage to kick her addiction to morphine and tried to eat whenever food was available. The promise to Hans to stay alive pressed her on.

Working mostly with Luna now, she didn't know the young girl well enough to discuss anything with her. They kept their masks up with each other, not talking, delivering coded messages from one address in Paris to the next, idly waiting in run-down, moldy basements for the next invisible and indefinite courier action.

At the end of July Océane's patience had run out. They received no clear insights into the Allied movements over French terrain, but the wind brought rumor that they were approaching the capital. It showed in the way the Germans became increasingly more anxious and erratic in their behavior. People were shot without reason, beaten or locked up. Blood stained the Paris streets even more than before.

Stay safe, one side screamed, *go where the action is,* another side demanded.

Océane was staying at an apartment she'd been in before at the Avenue de Saxe in the 7th Arrondissement. She and Luna were eating a meagre meal of beans, a tiny potato and a piece of dry bread, listening to the motorcycles speeding by and coarse German voices shouting hurried orders. They ate in silence, a silence they were accustomed to, a silence that kept them safe.

"Luna?" Océane started, watching her black-haired companion with her inevitable green felt hat clean the runny tomato sauce from her plate with the last crumbles of her bread and popping them in her mouth. The young woman looked up, startled by a voice cutting through the still room, her big blue eyes on alert, as if attack would come any minute. Océane met her gaze with a tranquil one in her own eyes, as if by nature adopting a calming professional look.

"What's up?" Luna pushed her plate aside and lit a cigarette. She let it dangle from her painted lips.

"Have you heard any information on the progress the Allies are making?" Luna squinted her eyes as if assessing the question, so Océane quickly added, "Just wondered."

"From what I've pieced together, they captured the French port of Cherbourg at the end of June, but after that it's been a bloody fight. The Brits and the Americans are making slow progress. Why?" Luna lit her last cigarette, crumpled the package and threw it across the room.

Océane sighed. "I'm kind of tired of not knowing where they are. How long still. As a doctor I could do more. Some of our comrades must get injured. I'd like to go where the fighting is. Help out there."

Luna stared at her with big, round eyes. She looked positively puzzled, then said while exhaling a long plume of smoke, "Heavens, you're a doctor? Why didn't you tell me?"

Now it was Océane's turn to be surprised. "I thought everybody knew. But that's the point. I'm getting mad following silly instructions, never knowing where I'm sent next and for what reason. I've been doing this for the better part of the war but now we're hopefully close to the end, I want to feel like I know what I'm doing, make my own choices again, be part of a real team. Just simply be a doctor."

Luna slowly shook her head in disbelief. "Well, I'll never! I agree, Rose, what a waste of talent. I'll introduce you to Roger."

"Who's Roger?"

"You must've met him plenty of times. The tall, dark guy, quite aristocratic looking. Wouldn't be surprised he's got a generous shot of blue blood running through his veins, especially his posh French, *language soutenu*. But that's beside the point. You know who I'm talking about? He often wears a baclava but when he opens his mouth there's no mistake."

Océane pictured him and nodded. "Yes, I just didn't know his name was Roger. We meet so many of them."

"I've had a crush on Roger as long as forever, though he's probably twice my age. Always hope I'll run into him." Luna giggled, quite suddenly talkative and enjoying her own girlish voice.

It broke the ice between the agents, lessened the anxiety. Luna wasn't such a hard nut to crack, after all, Océane decided.

"So, Roger is the guy I have to talk to?"

"For sure. I'll pass on the word to Madame Noir. But so could you. Mind you, she'll be curious, as we don't exchange information unless asked to. You could also wait and hope he'll be on our agenda soon."

"I don't want to wait much longer."

Luna extinguished her cigarette and stretched her slim body like a cat. "I need to get some sleep now," she yawned. "Got an early delivery. But I'll see what I can do."

They stretched out fully dressed in their sleeping bags on the two sofas in the sparsely furnished room, trying to block out the war and get some much-needed rest. But, trained as they were, they remained on alert.

~

OCÉANE GOT WHAT SHE WANTED. One week later she was travelling in the back of a farmer's cart somewhere near Dreux on her way to receive her first instruction in shooting with firearms. It was strange after all these years of walls and stones around her, the coarse staccato shouts of the Nazis and the frightened, silent Parisians, to see greenery.

The farmer on the box was whistling 'Le Chant des Partisans', a popular French Resistance song, and everyone was generally better fed. There were women and children waving, there was sunshine in abundance. Some of the fields even had crops on them that looked promising. Life was almost normal here, an untainted summer.

The more cheerful atmosphere had its effect on her mood. It was just so good to see some color, smell flowers and hear song. If these people could bounce back, so could she.

Roger had immediately consented to Océane being sent to the country for a week's shooting lessons.

"We'll need everyone who wants and is able to shoot a gun, so I'm all for it."

First Océane had considered retracing her steps, thinking it was her doctor's skills she wanted to employ, not to cold-bloodedly shoot people to get rid of them. Her father's reminder of her oath was still nagging at her, but she pushed her doubts aside.

Revenge JJ. Revenge D'Artagnan. Revenge all the ones that have fallen.

And hadn't she shown she was able to kill if push came to shove?

"We're here!"

Deep in her own thoughts, she had not even noticed the driver had stopped both whistling and the cart. Looking around her she saw they were at a deserted farm, amidst sloping hills of corn and the fresh green of sugar beets. Chicken cackled loudly and a dog barked. For the rest, the air was peaceful and still, a great contrast to the eternal bustle of Paris and the loud chatter of her own mind.

Océane hopped off the cart, stretching. "Where are we?"

The driver, his stocky body clad in blue overalls and doffing a frayed black beret on his head, sauntered over. She was struck by the amused look in his metal-black eyes.

"You don't know?"

He chuckled and spat out a big, red phlegm of chewing tobacco. It almost landed on her worn shoes, so she jumped aside, which made the man only chuckle louder. His unfriendly demeanor made her momentarily suspect it was a trap. She looked around her furtively, ready to dash away in case she needed to escape.

"Don't worry, Mademoiselle. I won't hurt you. I just have bad manners, always had and always will. We're near Dreux. The center of the world." He laughed again, baring irregular rotten teeth. "My name's *Le Mâcheur*, the chewer, and now you understand why."

"So what do we do now?" She eyed him with a little more confidence.

"I'm taking you to the wife. She'll fatten you up a bit. You city brats are way too thin. This afternoon *Le Rat*, my son, will give you your first shooting lesson. You're here for a week, so you'd better make my son like you."

Le Mâcheur grinned rather unpleasantly at her, showing the disheveled teeth. Océane stood awkward and unsure, clasping her medical bag in one hand and her backpack in another. The ways of the French countryside were unknown to her - different rules, different dynamics.

Having no choice, she followed the farmer to a large, dirty, white farmhouse where a big dog on a leash was barking as if wanting to cough up his lungs. The scraggy dog whimpered as the farmer kicked him with his boot. Edgy and uncomfortable, she entered the reeking farmhouse.

It was somewhat of a comfort that the farmer's wife, round and dressed in a flowery apron, turned out to be a kind and maternal person. She immediately shooed her acerbic husband out of the house.

"Don't mind that buffoon. He's all talk and no teeth!" she said light-heartedly. "Now come in, you poor wench, and let me fix you a proper meal. And don't you worry about my son either. He's never come close to a Nazi yet, though they'd better watch out for my Ives as he's the best sharpshooter in the whole of the Dreux Department."

The fleshy, red-faced farmer's wife had meanwhile taken Océane by the elbow and directed her into a huge kitchen that smelled of fried onions and stewed beef. Despite her apprehension, Océane's mouth watered. Putting down her bags, she gratefully sat down at the huge kitchen table. A young girl, of about five, with dark, curly hair and very black eyes sat at the corner of the table scribbling in a coloring book. She looked up at Océane and smiled shyly.

"That's my Amélie," the farmer's wife said proudly, "the youngest of the lot and the most sensible of them all."

The girl just smiled some more and continued with her coloring. Océane wolfed down the best stew she'd tasted in years while the farmer's wife stood by, watching her and nodding in approval, red workhands resting on her round, flowery hips.

"That's more like it!" she said with contentedness. "You stay here one week, mademoiselle, and you'll be ready to crush all them Germans with a little fat on your own bones. Now Amélie, show La Rose her room while I get a meal ready for them menfolk."

"So you've never held a gun in your life?" *Le Rat*, the spitting image of his stocky father, even dressed in the same blue overalls but with lighter eyes and not chewing tobacco, didn't seem to grasp it. "I thought you were an American by birth. Your Second Amendment means every American has at least one gun. Aren't you all descendants from Billy the Kid?"

He broke out in a salvo of laughter that made Océane laugh as well.

"I may be a Mid-Western girl, but no," she admitted, "only my grandfather has a collection of guns. I don't think even my father ever touched one of them."

"Pity," Le Rat observed, "it would have made my lessons a bit easier."

"Well, I am a doctor, so I know what precision is," she retorted, which resulted in another crescendo of laughter from her companion.

"Much help that will be, but come on, lesson one is how to start. This here is a Glock ... confiscated from a dead Nazi. We like to shoot them with their own weapons, you see. More fun."

Océane wondered if Le Rat's mother knew everything about her son. It seemed he'd been close to Germans after all. Not that it was any of her business.

The gleaming, black weapon rested in Le Rat's palm. Real and dangerous and a thrill. He showed her how to hold the weapon, how to aim, how to hold her hands steady. That was the first lesson. No shooting yet. But she couldn't wait for lesson two. Adrenaline and addiction made her blood flow.

A FULL STOMACH, the peaceful, open countryside, a break in the threat of arrest, all contributed to a deep sleep. Océane, refreshed and eager, couldn't wait to get up at the crack of dawn to indulge in her new hobby. Shooting lessons. A weapon was a new form of safety. She wondered why it had taken her so long to understand that.

Le Rat had positioned an aiming board against a stack of straw bales and let Océane take position. As she concentrated, a deadly calm settled on her. Standing firmly on her feet, her legs slightly apart, she fixed her gaze and fired. The bullet hit the ring closest to the middle point.

"Not bad." There was a tinge of admiration in Le Rat's voice. "I think we can go straight to lesson three."

"You agree that a medical training actually also trains the eyes and the nerves?"

"If you say so, Doc." The farmer's son was as laid-back as he was dangerous.

Océane couldn't wait for him to prop up a life-size, stuffed-up doll marked with many bullet holes. Though it had the semblance of a person, she didn't hesitate and hit it straight in the heart.

"I'm almost tempted to take you to the place of real action tonight," Le Rat grinned, "but I don't think my mother would agree to that."

"Your mother?" Océane looked puzzled. "She said you'd not even come close to a German in your life. What are you babbling?"

Again, that laughter that would wake up the gods in heaven. "Oh, Maman has tricked you into believing we're German-abiding citizens here, has she? That's because you're an innocent city Madame!" Océane probably looked just like that because he was slapping his knees laughing now. "My mother is *L'Étoile,* the leader of the paramilitary pack here."

Océane gaped at him, speechless. "*L'Étoile*? Your mother?"

"The one and only."

Pride shone from Le Rat's face. Océane couldn't wrap her mind around it. Rumors of a notorious Madame L'Étoile had even reached Paris in the past weeks. An agile Resistance fighter who lynched Nazis by the dozens and always seemed to get away. The stout woman with her maternal air who enjoyed beefing her guest up and seeing her little daughter color her books in the corner?

War changed everyone. Dramatically.

"Maman is going to give you your F.F.I. armband tonight. Then you'll be part of General de Gaulle's French Forces of the Interior. How about that?"

"Really? Already?" Her heart did summersaults. "I suppose I'm really part of the team now?"

"I suppose you are, La Rose," he joked. "This family is not all that it seems but from the outside we look quite normal and decent, wouldn't you say?"

"I'm flabbergasted ... and honored," she hastened to add.

"Well, you're good. You proved yourself. Let's get to lesson four, shall we?"

34

THE ROAD TO PARIS

Within days Océane became an excellent sniper to the great satisfaction of both Le Rat and L'Étoile. She had, without so much as flinching once, eliminated two German officers in a jeep passing through Nonancourt.

After nightfall she patrolled along the River Eure to protect the British and International agents who were dropped behind enemy lines. Clad in black clothes and boots with a baclava that only showed her eyes, she was just one more anonymous fighter, stealthily creeping through the undergrowth, listening for the soft thud in the dark that alerted them another ally had made it to French soil. A moment's wait until the white parachute was rolled up and hidden from the German search lights, and then beckoning them with the three-flash sign. Help them safely hide in barns and cellars for the night until their own sabotage actions began.

It was soon a routine, just a few hours of sleep before dawn, up all day and half of the night. But she didn't mind. Océane became tough and strong on the farmer's wife's nutritious meals. She finally loved her life; felt she was doing real things to purge her country from the enemy and push it to liberation.

Meanwhile the rumble of the Allied forces driving the Germans further and further back became louder and an increasing number of Maquis fighters sought their refuge at Le Mâcheur's farm. They slept in the hay or just on the ground, armed to the teeth and fully prepared to create a pass way for the advancing army.

ONE DAY as Océane was sitting on the threshing floor cleaning her weapon, a young Frenchman, his face still immature and pimpled, came over to her with a deferential look in his brown eyes.

"Are you La Rose?" His voice was as young as his face and gleamed with admiration.

Océane didn't know what to make of him, so continued her cleaning with a short nod.

"Yes, I am."

"Is it true you were Remix's girlfriend?"

At his unexpected words, her shoulders stiffened, her hands stilled. She quivered. Her eyes searched his face. A hesitant "Yes" came from her lips.

"Oh, great," he said as he slid closer to her on the floor. "I met him in 1940. He taught me everything. It's so sad such a great fighter was eliminated so early in the war, but we've all heard the rumors ..."

"What rumors?" Her voice was hoarse, hurried.

"Sorry," the young man said, "I thought you'd know."

"Know what?" Océane was aware she was sounding curt and unfriendly.

"That there's a mighty fighter orchestrating things from abroad, probably Morocco or Spain that people talk about, that could be ..."

"Who told you that?" She was only able to ask monosyllable questions as her heart raced against her rib case.

"Sorry," the young man said again, "just rumors, just people talking. I thought you'd probably know more, otherwise I would never have brought it up. It might well be that people want to believe in the myth that Remix stood for, all he promised to be, but the horrible truth is that he died in October 1940 at the hands of General von Stein. That we keep hoping against hope because we don't know his grave."

Océane opened her mouth to answer when there was a loud, shrill cry she recognized as Madame l'Étoile's.

"Hey, everybody, listen up!"

The voice was both kind and authoritarian. That strange mixture kept Océane puzzled about the farmer's wife's high-ranking position in the French Resistance movement.

Quickly putting her Glöck back in its holster, she followed the pimpled, young man out of the barn, pushing thoughts of JJ to the back of her mind, though the wound remained sore, and a strange new hope suddenly clung to her like the desperate arms of a frightened child.

Not now, she ordered herself, instinctively touching the F.F.I. armband on her upper arm. The symbol steadied her, made her focus on l'Etoile's lecture while the roar of the nearing armies was all around them.

On a summer day in August, after the morning rain had left puddles in the yard, twenty Resistance fighters including Le Rat, Le Mâcheur and La Rose, listened to l'Étoile's instructions.

"We expect the 3rd United States Army to pass through Dreux any moment now. They're heading for the Seine west of Paris, whereas the 4th US Infantry Division and the 2nd Armored Division of the French Army will go straight for the heart of Paris. The F.F.I. is part of the attack force as well. I want twelve of you to continue working in this area, blowing up bridges to obstruct the Germans and continuing with our effective guerrilla tactics. The other seven under the command of La Rose return to Paris tomorrow morning. This group will join Colonel Ré who's leading the uprise in Paris at the same time as the Allied forces attack the city. You are to join him and his F.F.I. army at the Île-de-France."

Océane's eyes widened. She would be meeting the famous leader of the *Franc-Tireur et Partisans,* Alex Ré-Boffo, and actually fight side-by-side with him. She wasn't afraid, she was excited. And that she was considered capable enough to lead her own team made her glow with pride.

"Okay then, I'll hand you all the details after dinner. La Rose's team leaves with La Mâcheur at first light.

THE LAST EVENING at the farmstead with these determined fighters who had the semblance of an ordinary French family made Océane a little melancholic. She had learned so much in the past weeks. The rich food and almost cheerful and optimistic revolutionary lifestyle had helped her restore her former confidence and stamina. For the first time war had almost been fun.

She looked forward to the final battle in Paris's streets. The secret radio messages they listened to every day made clear the Germans were falling back, losing not only more and more terrain but also becoming more demoralized by the day.

The first fights on the European mainland, both on the beaches and in Normandy itself, especially the liberation of Caen, had been tougher than expected, but now Normandy was in Allied hands with the exception of some small pockets on the Atlantic coasts.

The advance to the French capital was gaining momentum and now that General de Gaulle had returned to French soil nothing could kill their optimism; they were well and truly in the final days of a horrendous world war.

Madame l'Etoile served Océane an extra portion of *tarte tatin,* a delicious cake with apples from their own orchard. Looking up, she saw the farmer's wife sending her an encouraging smile as if saying 'you can do this'. She smiled back, strengthened, her heart full of the days ahead.

As she helped clearing the table, while the menfolk went to the parlor to smoke and Amélie was sent to bed, Madame said, "The one thing you must remember, Rose, is to keep that focus of yours. That's your biggest asset. Don't start doubting and stay true to yourself. Can you do that? Your small cell is part of the bigger whole.

You're responsible for each of them but you're also an in-between. You always obey the orders of your superiors, explain to your team when there's a change of tactics."

Océane thought she'd never seem the farmer's wife so serious. She listened carefully. She could do complicated things, keep a clear head, discern main parts from sub parts. But still. She sometimes was a dreamer.

L'Étoile continued. "I have trust in you. Your seven fighters are young but well-trained and quiet. They're all from this region. I've known them all my life and I fully dare to put them under your command. They will not fail you. Don't fail them."

"I won't, but I think I'll need more instructions on what it means to lead the team. I've little, actually, *no* experience leading a unit. Only some in the hospital."

"That's something I can't teach you, Rose. I can only give you my practical experience. Everything depends on where you'll be stationed in Paris and what will be your task. I think the leading part will be mostly during the trip into Paris. After that you'll merge into larger units with Ré at the head."

"I think I can do that."

But L'Étoile's lecture was not over yet. "The F.F.I. in Paris under the command of Colonel Ré have been preparing for the uprise a long time. I'm sure the secret agents have briefed the Colonel which strategic places to occupy. In case of chaos, for example when the group is shattered or one gets killed, you're the one expected to keep a cool head and decide what to do next. That's not something you can really prepare for, but I think you've got enough ice water in your veins not to freak out. Though you're just a slip of a girl."

After these words, she hugged her tightly. For a brief instant Océane let herself be warmed and strengthened by the bear hug from the unlikely Resistance madam.

Dressed from head to toe in her black outfit with her Glöck secured to her body under her jacket and her medical bag at her feet, Océane sat swaying left and right as Le Mâcheur's cart took them back to the outskirts of Paris.

They went at a slow pace, two old horses pulling the cart with its heavy load of hay, in which eight fighters were hiding. As usual Le Mâcheur was whistling his song on the box but Océane could hear the tension in his throat as he urged the horses on.

The war was close around them on all sides. She spied the terrain through the flap of the canvas and for the first time saw American planes overhead diving deftly to evade German anti-aircraft guns. There was loud rumbling but no visible sign of ground armies yet.

The horses took a long time to reach the outskirts of Paris and it was already midday when Le Mâcheur brought them to a halt with a loud "Ho! Ho!" Then he whistled as agreed and one by one the fighters crept out of the cart and let themself fall in the tall grass of the Forest of Fausses-Reposes between Versailles and Paris, the old hunting grounds of Louis XV.

There was no waving at Le Mâcheur. No goodbye. The last she saw of him was a squat of red juice from his chewing tobacco on the dirt road. Whistling, he and his tired horses made their slow track back to Dreux.

"We're waiting here until dark," Océane instructed her fighters. "Eat lunch, then take a rest as we'll be up most of the night marching into Paris, some fourteen kilometers. We take turns keeping watch. I will start and you take over in an hour, Brique." She pointed to the young, pimpled man. "No sounds, as little move-ment as possible."

The six men and two women, some considerably older than her, all obeyed without asking anything and soon settled for a nap using their bags as cushions and pulling their horse blankets over them.

Océane sat with her back against a big oak tree, her legs stretched out in front of her. The mossy surface was pleasantly soft and the rustling of the leaves overhead a welcome, soothing sound for her attuned mind. Now and then a plane roared overhead but it was remarkably quiet and agreeable in the shadow of the age-old trees while her comrades rested around her. A red squirrel clambered up a tree trunk and with its small, red paws held on to the bark, eyeing her with round brown eyes full of curiosity. She followed the swift-moving animal with its wooly tail as it took a breather on one of the branches, never losing sight of the strange creatures in the grass below.

Somehow that little animal and this peaceful spot took the tension away. She suddenly felt herself back in Lincoln Park, racing after rabbits and climbing trees herself, while Arthur followed on her heels. She heard them laugh and shriek together, felt his little hand in hers as she pulled him up to a fork in their favorite tree. There they sat side by side eating Curtiss Butterfingers, licking their fingers afterwards.

Her hand racing through Arthur's sandy mop of hair that always fell over his eye and him poking her in her ribs, yelling "Stop touching my hair! It's mine!" Smiling wildly with his perfect white teeth.

Arthur! It seemed years since she'd thought of her little brother in his wheelchair with his head wobbling without control and his loud cries.

Arthur! There had been a time when he was perfect in every way, and they were happy and carefree. Before his body and mind had become mangled. How could she have forgotten that period? It had been perfection in every way.

Jean-Jacques! The only other period - so short, so very short - when she had been happy and carefree again. Another happiness, another perfection in every way.

Ripples of emotion flooded through Océane and she was glad to be sitting on solid ground with her sleeping comrades around her. Suddenly her life, this life of strife and constant change and uncertainty, became too momentous for her small frame. She breathed out in long expirations, calming herself, but tears were in her eyes and for a moment she let them flow. Cheeks wet, salty on her lips.

It was her birthday. 8 August 1944. She was twenty-five years old and look at her now.

No one here knew. Her false passport told otherwise. But her parents knew and Maxipa did. Where were they and what pain where they going through on her behalf?

Dear God, let me put them at ease soon, she prayed.

For the first time since she'd left the States five years earlier, Océane was comforted. Fellow Americans were on their way to liberate her adopted city. She longed to see them, to talk with them, to ask how back home was.

At that moment, the squirrel dropped a hazelnut right in her lap and she looked up at the disappearing plume of his tail. It made her smile. As if the little animal had given her a sign that she would be okay. Get this war over and done with and then return home to Chicago. To find herself again, to heal from these hard years, her broken heart.

Océane shook herself. The real work was still ahead. Why was she dreaming about the outcome? She had to stay alive. Suddenly realizing that she'd not really been paying attention to her surroundings while her mind roamed, angry at herself, she scanned the terrain and listened intently. She was in charge, had not only a duty to herself but to her people.

THEY PUSHED towards the city after nightfall, which was not ideal, as it meant that even if all went well, they'd arrive at the fringe of Paris long after midnight, with curfew in full operation.

Walking at the head of a long line, she could signal them to stop or lay low with a quick gesture of her hand. For the first miles they didn't expect much danger, as they were sheltered by the forest. Their only companions were the animals of the night, owls and night pigeons and the occasional fox or rabbit. Yet every sound, even that of a twig breaking under their feet, made her stop and listen for a counter-sound, all her senses wide open.

When they left the Forest of Fausses-Reposes behind them, their march became more perilous, moving through open field, the German searchlights swinging above them in big swoops. As general fatigue set in, they progressed much slower than she'd hoped. Océane decided not to let them rest by the side of the road, so they passed Sèvres until they finally came to the lowest loop of the River Seine, within a stone's throw of the city.

Now their largest challenge lay ahead - to get the group safely along the west side of the Seine until they came to the walk bridge of Passerelle de L'Avre. If they managed to pass over the bridge, they'd head straight into Bois de Boulogne and be under the safety of the trees. It meant a detour of an extra couple of miles but seemed safer than crossing the Seine at Sèvres and going through Boulogne-Billancourt.

She signaled with her hand and the group stopped. Turning to them, she explained her plan.

The group protested softly. "Another couple of miles. We can for sure cross at Sèvres, Rose, please."

Knowing she was probably making a mistake, she consented, being very tired as well and aware that any bridge crossing was going to be dangerous. "Alright. We'll take a brief rest here. Brique, I want you to cross the bridge, staying low so you are never above the railing. Stay as close to it as you can and drop to your belly if something moves. We will cover you. When you reach the other side, you check the premises. If it's safe, we'll follow one by one. It will take a while, but it will draw less attention to us than as a group. I'll close the ranks and cover the last person before me. Stay low at the other side, find somewhere to hide. Now go."

The plan almost fell apart when a German jeep rattled over the bridge as one of the girls was crossing, but as their headlights were darkened and she was so slight that she almost disappeared between the vertical bars of the bridge, the danger passed, and breath stopped in their throats released explosively.

An hour later they'd all reached the other side. Lying behind a low, brick wall, Océane let her team settle for a moment. All pricked their ears when they heard voices. She indicated for them to stay low, not raise their heads. Two men were talking in French, so it seemed safe, yet they remained silent as church mice listening to their conversation.

"I can get you weapons. You want weapons, don't you?" a hasty, rather high-pitched voice asked.

"What sort of weapons?" This was asked in a more sonorous tone.

"Anything you like. Rifles, pistols, hand grenades. Good price as well," squeaked number one.

"Alright. What's the price?"

"Don't you want to see them first; I've got them here."

Océane was dying to take a look but decided she needed to weigh this conversation first. At best it was two Resistance fighters making a deal but something in her gut kept her on the alert.

The first man was clearly showing his wares when the second man said, "If me and my friends pony up 100 Francs, would that be enough?"

It made the first man laughed shrilly. "You're trying to rip me. These are new German weapons I stole for you guys."

"150 francs?"

"Alright."

The buyer whistled and they heard more voices and a lot of wheeling and dealing went on for a while.

"Satisfied?" the seller asked in his high voice.

"Yup!" a dozen voices answered in chorus.

What then happened went so fast and was so unexpected that it shook the world underneath her.

"Halt!" Coarse German voices shouted from all sides and the shrill voice squeaked, "It was a trap!"

Océane's shivered as multiple shots were fired and death cries and the smell of gunpowder filled the air. Her team lay as paralyzed on the ground, almost trying to disappear in the earth. Jeeps drove off, the shrill laughter ringing above the engines. Horrified, they did not dare to look over the wall.

Silence, a deadly silence, fell over the plot and Océane knew she had to go to the other side and check on those fighters. She was a doctor, after all, and perhaps one of two were still alive. It was one of the hardest things she would ever have to do in her life, but it had to be done.

"I am a doctor," she revealed to her team, "I have to take stock. Is there anyone willing to come with me?"

"I'll come," Brique offered, standing up in the light of the moon.

She braced herself as she clambered over the wall and dropped her body and bag on the other side. Lying down, she checked the area. There were bodies everywhere, dark patches spilling from their lifeless frames. The scent of warm, human blood permeated the silent night. Ruined lives, ruined hopes.

Biting her lip, she crouched from body to body, feeling pulses, listening on chests. Brique stayed close to her, here and there shutting eyelids, and she heard him mumble Hail Marys and the Lord's Prayer for every fallen comrade. There were thirty-five in total, none alive. The massacre had been swift and relentless.

When she'd done her round, constantly listening for the Germans or the traitor returning to finish her group off as well, she motioned to Brique. "There's nothing more we can do, horrible as it is. We have to go on, to our safe house. I hope to God that in the morning the French will bury them."

"Are you sure they're all dead," he whispered, his young face taut and stricken.

"Yes, I'm sure. Let's go back to the others and try to get to the Avenue de Victor Hugo. We have to leave them for now."

Rest in peace, heroes of Boulogne-Billancourt!

35

LIBÉRATION

Paris, August 1944

Océane's first meeting with Alex Ré-Boffo the next morning was one she was sure she'd never forget. The open-faced, attractive Colonel with his thick hair combed back over his scalp was clearly not his usual cool and controlled self. He was positively foaming at the mouth, his brown eyes ablaze, as the curse words and expletives rolled from his lips.

"They'll pay for this! The cowards, the lizards! They'll pay. The damned, damned bastards. I'll round up every French traitor if needed. Every single one of them. I call for an insurrection!"

In front of him stood a group of heavily armed Resistance fighters, for once not looking victorious, but appalled and distraught, listening to their leader. Océane felt torn. She'd been so excited about meeting the formidable Colonel and to be introduced to his headquarters in the *Barrière d'Enfer*, a bunker in the 14th Arrondissement. Where she'd expected to be welcomed to the heat of triumphant revolution, she was met with dejection over the treason in Boulogne-Billancourt that had massacred thirty-five of the Colonel's best men, boys most of them, eighteen or nineteen years old.

As she shuffled her own small group into the room, Ré continued his briefing, ignoring the newcomers. "I demand a full investigation into what happened. Why, how, by whom! Axel, Briard, Savage. You're on it." The Colonel's index finger pointed to three sturdy men in the crowd, their faces hidden behind balaclavas. They disappeared immediately through a backdoor, their weapons clanking in a metallic rhythm against their thighs.

"Colonel, may I have your attention, please?" The woman with whom Océane and her group had spent the night at the Avenue de Victor Hugo spoke up. She tall with a confident demeanor and quite an impressive sight in her camouflage outfit, a rifle slung over her shoulder.

"What was that?" the Colonel roared.

"It's Féroce, Colonel. May I introduce you to La Rose. She was a witness to the massacre."

With an impatient movement of his hand, Ré ushered Océane to step forward while shouting, "Get the investigation team back here. Now!"

It felt as if she was in the line of fire herself.

"Speak up!" The Colonel took her in with impatient eyes.

Océane stumbled through her story of the ambush by the French traitor in a thin voice, feeling very self-aware. A pin-drop silence settled on the underground shelter. It was as if her voice bounced off the walls. Her final words made her wish she could disappear behind the plaster.

Ré, his anger only augmented, ignored her awkwardness at being called out. "Dogs! They're all dogs!" Then he suddenly calmed down and seemed to think of something. The brown gaze rested on her blushing face, and he added in a soft, almost warm voice, "And thank you, Madame Docteur, for your account and certainly for paying the last respects to our heroes. That won't be forgotten. Come to my office after this briefing."

Féroce nudged her. "You're in, girl! Well done."

Océane didn't know what she was in, but she was happy for her team. If it meant they could play their part in the liberation with verve, she was all the happier.

COLONEL ALEX RÉ-BOLLO was pacing his small underground office as Océane entered. He stopped, though, turned on his booted heels and faced her full-on.

"Your name is La Rose?"

"Yes, Colonel."

"Stop Colonel-ing me! The name is Ré, just Ré. So, you're one of Madame Noir's agents?

"Yes ... uh ... Ré."

"And a doctor?"

Océane wondered how far he would go ticking off her wartime curriculum vitae. She nodded. He sat down, abruptly, and pointed to the other chair across from him. She perched on the edge, in strained waiting.

"And you're Remix's girlfriend?"

The unexpectedness of his name echoing off the underground walls made her jump. Some part of her was aware she was gazing at him like a startled animal. The band around her chest tightened as she braced herself for what might come next. If there was anyone in the French Resistance who knew what had happened to JJ, it was this man. They exchanged glances and she was sure Ré knew exactly what was going on inside of her, the rip current of emotion that broke loose and washed over her.

She heard him say in French through his teeth, *"Impossible! Impossible."*

"What?" She was shouting, all restraint gone. "What do you know, Ré. Pray tell me. I can't stand it any longer."

He simply said, "Follow me."

EVEN IN HIS sleep he was everything, hallowed, hers. Her legs folded double as she kneeled at his side, trembling and thankful, like all lovers through the ages had done before her.

"Huricana arrived late last night from Spain. He crashed on arrival. I'll leave you two to it."

Some part of her registered Ré's whispered words behind her but they didn't make sense. Nothing made sense. She was numb, in shock, sure she was dreaming. La Rose took over. Not knowing from where it came, her rational mind managed to form the necessary words through the denseness in her throat.

"Ré, will you please look after my team for an hour?"

"Of course."

The door shut behind her.

They were alone.

Jean-Jacques was sleeping on his side, fully dressed for battle, his head resting with one cheek on his duffel bag, the snarky smile hovering in the corner of his mouth. She had to stretch a finger and lift the lock of dark-blonde hair that hid his closed eye just to assure herself he was real, he was alive. He stirred, mumbled something in his sleep, but didn't wake.

A desire to cry, to shout at the walls, to throw out all the pent-up emotions inside herself ravaged Océane's insides, but she remained seated, silent as a forgotten melody, biting her lips to still the tears.

Remix, Huricana. They are one and the same.

She took in all of him with intense gulps, his face, his body, his presence, longing with her whole trembling self for him to wake up and see *her*. Heaven had been benevolent. JJ was home, home with her.

Then it struck her. What if he had forgotten her? He'd been alive all this time. Why hadn't he let her know? Could he be over her? Instinctively she shrunk away from him, withdrawing to the corner of the room.

It had to be that.

Her ears rang, she wanted to get up and go to her team. Liberate Paris and then leave France. Flee to Chicago. Her other home. No more pain. No more pain. But she couldn't get up. Drawing her knees to her chest, she hid her head between them. Too drained to cry.

All was lost after all.

Think, Océane, think!

She had no thoughts. Her head was strangely empty, her heart dead. Cruel, cruel life!

Then she felt something. A hand on her platinum crown.

His voice, soft and uncertain. "OC? OC, is that you?"

Her dyed hair; of course, he was unsure. Slowly, with more fear than she'd had in the entire war, she lifted her eyes to his, waiting for the verdict. Their gaze met. She saw alarm, concern, then disbelief in the ocean green of his eyes.

"Darling!"

"JJ!"

And she was in his arms, all doubt gone, love enveloping her in the strength of his powerful arms, his warm beating heart, every, *every* last inch of him. He was crying, unrestrained, mumbling excuses and prayers at the same time but all the while repeating, "My darling, my dear, dear darling."

He drew her to him on the single bed, holding her close, kissing and hugging her, and she folded herself against him, her heart racing, her mind finally at peace. Nothing bad could happen to her anymore. Nothing could take him away from her.

LATER, as he was smoking a cigarette and she lay with her head on his naked chest, the questions came.

"What happened, JJ? Why did you make everyone believe you were dead?"

He was stroking her short, blond hair, smelling of love and warfare. "My darling, I had no choice. People helped me escape from Fresnes prison where I was taken on 14 October 1940. They were all killed on the spot. I left my false Remix ID on one of my comrades and took his. I escaped, walking and hitchhiking to Vichy France and then on to Spain. It took me a long time; I was not in good shape. My wounds wouldn't heal but I couldn't go to a doctor until I was in Spain."

Océane nestled closer to him, harrowing as it was to listen to his words. He spoke with so much control now but to her they were raw as an open wound.

"Believe me, it felt like defeat, but at the time I was mostly concerned with your fate and that of my family. I knew Von Stein wouldn't buy the story of my death. He'd tortured me himself. He knew I wasn't the dead man."

She shuddered, having felt the scars on his back.

"I knew he would hunt down everyone involved with me, but I was unable to contact anyone before I left Paris. That's been my greatest grief all these years. That I didn't know what would happen to my family or yours."

"Where are they, your mom and dad, Margot, your grandfather?"

"I don't know. I have to find out today. By God, I hope they are okay. What about you and your grandfather?" He kept stroking her arm.

"I think my grandfather is alright," she said, looking at her watch and pulling herself out of his embrace. "At least he was the last time I saw him some months ago. JJ, we can't keep them waiting any longer. Just quickly tell me about Huricana."

"You're right. One more kiss." His lips sought hers and she almost succumbed to her desire for his love again.

Struggling to free herself, she reminded him. "Huricana!"

"I'd hoped you guessed. That you'd pick up the hint it was me."

"Guessed? Hint?" She ceased getting into her fighter's outfit to look at him. "What do you mean?"

"So you never guessed. I thought it might be too far-fetched."

"Or was I stupid?" She lifted her dyed eyebrows, while lacing up her combat boots.

Jean-Jacques was slowly getting dressed as well and that was when she got a good look at his injuries. His back and legs were a crisscross of red-lined scars, old burns on his arms, the nail of one of his thumbs gone. Yet he stood upright as the mighty fighter he was, the herculean body, the proud head. Her JJ. He'd survived them all.

Taking her by the shoulders, he kissed her forehead. "A young Radcliffe student in the Boston Museum of Fine Arts. Remember where we first met?"

"The Native American Art gallery?"

His eyes were smiling at her. "One of the minor Mayan gods is called Huricana. That's why I chose the name."

She smiled back at him. "You fool. I'm a doctor. I know nothing about the Mayan culture. I could never have guessed. You're an idiot!"

It was just the banter they needed before the last battle of Paris.

36

ENOUGH OF AN ANSWER

Océane was bound at the hip to Jean-Jacques for the entire week they fought side-by-side with Colonel Ré and the F.F.I. to liberate Paris. He had his arm around her waist constantly as they stood behind the barricades of sacks filled with sand. She fired her Glock, Le Rat's gift to her, with rapid precision, reaping praise for her marksmanship, not least from her lover.

"You're born for this job," he said, kissing her neck, but she shook her blond head wearing his black beret.

"No, I'm not," she protested. "I'd still much rather save lives than take them."

"My soldier, my dapper soldier."

The third week of August was the most exhilarating of Océane's life. Making love to JJ in abandoned basements whenever they could take a break from their fighting, gaining street by street on the Germans, seeing the hated Swastika flags being replaced by the French tricolor. The message JJ received that his family was safe in their house near Vichy, his mother's Jewish identity never revealed.

It had been a long day of fighting and an impressive march from the Place Nationale to Boulogne-Billancourt where Colonel

Ré hoisted the French flag on the townhall in the afternoon. The cries, the jubilant cries, despite the bloodshed that had instigated the uprise.

~

OCÉANE STILL SAVORED the victory as she lay next to Jean-Jacques in another basement bed, listening to his even breathing, the formidable chest rising and falling under her ear.

"You're awake?" She listened but as no answer came; she closed her eyes, thinking he'd already fallen asleep.

"Yes. And you."

Her eyes opened again, staring into the dusty darkness of the blacked-out room. The relief and peace that had been with her since their reunion melted like a ring of trust around her heart. But she still wanted to ask him about Huricana, needing to fit the pieces of the puzzle together.

And she wanted to tell him how her love for him had pushed her over the edge, to do the one thing a doctor never did. She had cold-bloodedly killed a man. Shivers ran through Océane as she recalled that godforsaken bunker. Her darkest moment in the entire war. The moment she'd become a soldier, fighting for the Cause. For him, for this man who was holding her so tenderly in his strong arms.

As from the beginning of their love affair, JJ sensed her questions before she could ask them. "Do you remember I once told you about a painter friend of mine, Thierry Chevalier, who used to have an atelier off Place Pigalle?"

Océane shot up in bed, displeased that she could've forgotten. The wiry Free France fighter at Sébha Oasis. "Oh my! How stupid of me!"

"Not really. You'd never met him and there are plenty of Thierry Chevaliers in the universe."

"Were you at Sébha Oasis when I was there with Hans Arenberg?"

He drew her close to him, hiding his big head between her breasts. "Forgive me, OC. If you can. And please believe me that it was the hardest thing I've ever had to do in my life. I was drunk for three days after you left. Thierry could barely kick my ass into shape again. I honestly didn't want to live anymore. I had betrayed you in the most terrible and cowardly way possible."

"Then why? Why the secret?"

"I had no choice." He spoke through gritted teeth, his voice full of self-hatred.

"Why?" she asked again, lifting his head to look into his eyes. The whites flashed in the dark, but she couldn't see his expression. "Wait," she said, flicking on her torch, "I want to see you when you finally tell me the truth."

His voice was slow, almost slurry as if he was again under the influence. "You brought us the tiding of Von Stein's death. You'd done the impossible, you and that courageous Hans Arenberg."

Jean-Jacques was observing her through his eyelashes. She'd never seen him shy or uncertain before, but he was clearly weighing her verdict of him now. Sitting upright, outwardly calm, she inwardly relived those spine-chilling days as he continued.

"Von Stein was the last and only hunter on my trail. Then he was dead, and the Nazis would leave my dead identity in peace. Huricana had already gained a bit of a myth status as a North-African freedom fighter, but he had no known identity within the French Resistance, at least not in the lower echelons. Only Thierry knew it was me, that Huricana and Remix were one and the same, and he would've taken poison to keep my secret." He sighed, his head hanging. "I'm getting nowhere with this. You're never going to forgive me. I chose the Cause over you."

"Go on. Try me." She nudged him.

"Alright, I'll try." He lit a cigarette, drawing in the smoke to the bottom of his lungs. "At the time I was already in touch with Churchill and De Gaulle. We were about to make the last push together with the Allies to drive the Axis forces out of North-Africa and prepare the landing in the south of Italy." Another deep drag.

"My high-ranking contacts at least made sure we could get you and Hans safely back to France."

His voice dropped even lower. "Wherever I could, OC, I've tried to protect you from my choices, but it's not been enough. Not by far. My fight has been a blind madness all these years. You told me so from the beginning, but I wouldn't listen. Let it be a meagre solace to you that I'd do it different now if I could. I'd stay with you and paint. You have no idea how many days I woke up crying, hoping I could come back to you and do only that. But I chose what I chose and now it's up to you to tell me whether our journey stops here."

He extinguished his half-smoked cigarette and offered her his palms, his eyes still downcast.

"Look at me, JJ, just look at me."

His eyes were full of tears, and she saw his pain, the years he'd fought to return to her, the ambivalence that lived in the soul of a true artist. To be just that, or to fight for all that bound the soul of the artist to the *condition humaine*.

"You've chosen the right path, love of my life."

Her words were simple, both balm and burning passion.

"Look at me, JJ. Because of you I became a doctor, a freedom fighter, a lover. Is that enough of an answer for you?"

37

EPILOGUE MARTIN MILLER

Paris, 24 August 1944

Martin tipped back the khaki helmet with the red cross to wipe the sweat from his brow. It was a sultry evening indeed. Another long, hot day of progress lay behind the 4th US Infantry Division on its march to Paris. He scanned the city through his binoculars, enveloped in dusk and plumes of smoke. Temporary flashes after explosions lit up the postcard prettiness of the Eiffel Tower and the Sacre Coeur.

"Damn them all, these bloody Jerrys," he mumbled under his breath.

"What's that, Doc?" Martin's always ready medical assistant Jerry Springer skittered up to him.

"I wasn't addressing you, Jer. You're alright."

With difficulty Martin tore himself from a memory of Eliza's smiling face. She'd beamed, her sweet face incredulous but in raptures. "We're going to have our honeymoon in *Paris*?" It was four long years later and it had never happened. But they were closer to it now.

"Doc?" Jerry again cut through Martin's somber thoughts.

"What's up?" he snapped, more irritated than anything intentional. Turning to his assistant, a spindly young man who'd been assigned to him after his faithful friend and colleague Cam Mailer had been killed in the battle of Caen, he gave him a tired smile.

"Sir, I was asked to tell you that the 9th Company has broken into the city via de Porte d'Italie and that Commander Raymond Dronne is on his way to the German General Dietrich von Cholitz to demand the surrender of the German army. Our mobile Red Cross team is ordered to enter Paris right now to help with the wounded."

Martin was instantly wide awake and on his post. "Captain Dronne did that? That's phenomenal. I thought we'd have to stay put for another day or two. Now *La Nueve* is inside, I guess we may follow suit." He grinned at the prospect.

"The French were said to be singing *La Marseillaise* when the 9th entered the Town Hall square," Jerry informed him.

"Good to hear!" Martin nodded. "And they weren't rusty on the lyrics?"

Jerry thought for a moment, looking rather helpless at this request. Though loyal and hard-working, the young New Yorker had not a humorous bone in his body. "I wouldn't know, Doc. Do you want me to go and ask the scout?"

"Cut it, Jer. It's not important. Let me go over to General Barton for instructions. You prepare the truck."

Whistling *Allons enfants de la patrie, Le jour de gloire est arrivé!* Martin made his way over to the General's improvised headquarters in Gentilly.

Two hours later the US Jeep with Martin Miller at the steering wheel and Jerry reading the map by the light of a torch rattled through the Porte d'Italie without encountering even one German.

"That was easy peasy," Martin observed. "Where to now?"

"Grand Palais, Doc. We follow the entire Boulevard Raspail and then have to cross the Seine wherever we can."

Martin's dark brow knitted together. "That hound of a Hitler must have wanted to blow up all of Paris on his way out. Any indication of the number of wounded?"

"Hundreds," Springer replied as he moodily looked out of the fly-battered window.

"I was supposed to see Paris for my honeymoon, not like this." Martin's tone was as gloomy as that of his assistant. "Still, it looks like it used to be a mighty fine city."

They passed the first barricades, sandbags piled high with grim looking Free French Resistance fighters hidden behind them, only the crowns of their heads showing as shadows in the dark. When the Jeep pulled up and the fighters spotted the American flag, they came out of hiding, jumping on top of the bags, cheering and waving their heavy artillery in the air. Martin saluted. Oddly enough, one of the slender black figures waving with great gusto jolted his memory back to Océane.

He'd briefly thought of her as he landed on Omaha Beach, first time he set foot on French soil, but war and work had been in the way since. Would she still be in Paris? The last he'd heard of Océane was that she'd started her medical studies at the Sorbonne and worked at a Paris hospital. Combat training had taken Martin away from regular mail and Eliza's letters - sparse and far between - had never mentioned their old friend.

Océane Bell. An electric shock went through Martin. *She is here.* He was sure of it. What had been that story of her falling in love with a painter and then he'd disappeared?

Martin was so caught up in his thoughts that he failed to spot a huge pothole in the road ahead. He braked with all his might, jerked on the steering wheel and swerved just in time around the gaping hole, hitting the pavement with his tires. The Jeep tilted, balanced for a moment on two wheels, but bounced back on all four with a bang.

"Heck, Doc, didn't you see that?" Jerry was clinging to the door handle to prevent himself from being jolted around the cabin.

"Sorry about that. I was thinking about a girl."

"Aha!" Jerry eyed him with a puzzled look on his thin face but said no more. It was a known fact that Doctor Miller was securely engaged to his Eliza Hutchinson, taking out her portrait every evening to kiss it goodnight. All the medics knew not to invite their Captain on their brothel trips. He'd never once joined them.

It became more crowded as they got to the 6th Arrondissement. The Germans still hid in their buildings, no longer engaging in the street skirmishes, and almost every street corner was barricaded, armed with Free France fighters who kept watch. Martin had the feeling of trespassing through a minefield. They could not anticipate from where a shot would be fired at them or from which side. Though the Stars and Stripes flag was hoisted prominently at the front of the Jeep, Paris was enveloped in a moonless night, and everything was shadowy. Friend or foe was difficult to determine.

He had sweat in his palms, all his senses on extreme alert. Though a hardened soldier by now, the Harvard professor still felt awkward and ambiguous about killing humans. He had pulled the trigger on various occasions but each time it left him with a bad tang in his mouth, the taste of blood wrongly spilled.

"Lower the window, hold your rifle ready. I don't trust this hell-hole one bit."

His assistant was already following the order. Martin opened his own window and unhitched his M1911 pistol. They passed Les Invalides unharmed and came to the Pont Alexandre III. The Seine was as dark and murky as a bleeding serpent through the city's heart.

"Holy Mary," Springer gasped as they spotted the Arc de Triomphe in the distance, "we made it to Paris, Doc. I've got to pinch myself!" Relief was clearly audible in his voice.

"We sure did, Jerry, and we're almost at our destination for tonight."

Martin breathed a little freer as well. They'd managed to

maneuver the Jeep through occupied Paris with not so much as one scratch. Soon they'd be among others, their allies, and feel more protected.

"Do you think they've already surrendered?" Watchful and uncertain, Jerry scanned the dark waters of the Seine and its banks.

"Don't know, but you'd almost think so. We'll soon get more information."

Martin had seen some horrific casualties in his long trek with General Barton, but nothing had prepared him for the scene upon their arrival at the Grand Palais.

"Last spasms of the Germans' death march," Martin grumbled as he eased his heavy body out of the vehicle and looked around him.

Jerry was at his side with their medical bags.

It was as if a huge explosion had blasted human bodies apart. They were scattered all over the square, with limbs in places where they shouldn't be. The howling of the wounded fighters mixed with the eerie silence of the dead. Martin's trained eye saw he and Jerry were the first medics who'd arrived at the scene. There wasn't a minute to lose.

"What happened here?" Springer asked aloud as they set out to give first aid to those who could still make use of it.

"Massacre," Miller said through gritted teeth. He was already sinking to his knees on the cobbled stones, next to a young woman whose every breath was a gasp for air.

"I'm here to help you," he soothed her, but she just looked at him with terror in her dark eyes. "You may not understand me but I'm your friend. I'm going to help you breathe a little lighter." And to Springer he instructed, "Go check on the ones still alive and let me know when reinforcements have arrived."

Martin prepared himself for a long night full of danger and death as he went from person to person checking for signs of life. While he worked on the mutilated French casualties, his assistant kept him informed of the progress the Allies were making and that other first aid teams that had arrived in the square. He never let his attention waver, despite his tiredness and the uncomfortable position on the hard pavement. His lot was so much better than most of these poor courageous men and women.

A woman kneeled at a short distance from him, tending to one of the victims. From her swift, practiced hands he could see she was a nurse or a doctor, but she wore the combat outfit of the freedom fighters and no band with a red cross. For the first time in hours, his attention slacked. There was something familiar about her. He noticed the prong of an old stethoscope jutting from her pocket and that reminded him of ...

"Océane!"

For a moment Martin felt he was going to be unwell. So much went through his big body that it couldn't process. His brain couldn't catch up with his emotions.

The woman looked up, terrified. "Hush," she whispered. "how do you know my name? Who are you?"

Both rose to their feet, only yards apart, their hands bloody and their eyes weary.

"M-Martin," she stammered, "is that truly you?"

They embraced impulsively, both crying tears of delight, of disbelief.

"How?" Océane asked. "How is it possible, Martin? What a miracle! Thank you for coming, thank you!"

"You of all people. If only Eliza could be here as well." Martin wiped the wetness from his fleshy cheeks, for a second forgetting his work and the war, just being human, moved to the core at the sight of a dear friend.

A dark-clad man with the posture of a wrestler materialized from the shadows and moving quietly towards Océane, put a protective arm around her.

"This is JJ," she whispered, "you know, the man I wrote you

about?"

"So you made it after all, my dear fellow? That's excellent news." Martin shook Jean-Jacques' firm hand.

The two men shared a look of mutual admiration. As if a weight was lifted from Martin's shoulders, he smiled, his china-blue eyes resting on Océane with all the kindness of his big heart.

"Good! Good!" he observed, and she giggled at his unconsciously professorial remark. It snapped him back into order. "I'm afraid I'll have to get on with the job at hand, but we must meet up before I leave for the north."

"We will. Here." Océane tore a piece of paper from her notebook and scribbled an address on it. "Come to my grandfather's house when you can. We have so much to catch up on."

"I'll try," he promised.

The square had become crowded with Allied vehicles, many of them with red crosses. Martin tried to focus on his surroundings again, his team, their expectations, but his heart was so full. He longed with every fiber of his being for Eliza's presence. For her to see their college friend, the girl who'd become as skinny and wiry as a desert rat but ablaze with the fire of love.

One thing he knew for sure. Martin Miller would never have to worry about Océane again.

38

EPILOGUE 2: THE END OF THE WAR IN PARIS

The liberation of Paris began when the French Forces of the Interior - the military arm of the French Resistance - staged an uprising against the Germans when it became clear that the US Third Army, led by General George Patton, was on its way.

On the night of 24 August 1944, General Philippe Leclerc's part of 2nd French Armored Division entered the city and reached the Hôtel de Ville shortly before midnight. On the morning of 25 August, the rest of the 2nd Armored Division, the US 4th Infantry Division and other Allied units followed suit.

Despite Hitler's repeated orders that the French capital *'must not fall into the enemy's hand except lying in complete debris'*, German surrender was imminent, but it was accompanied by severe bombing of the city and blowing up of its bridges. Thousands of free fighters were killed during the liberation.

Dietrich von Choltitz, commander of the German garrison and the military governor of Paris, surrendered to the French at the Hôtel Le Meurice, the newly established French headquarters, on 25 August. General Charles de Gaulle of the French Army arrived to take control of Paris as head of the Provisional Government of the French Republic.

This was De Gaulle's speech to the nation:

"Why do you wish us to hide the emotion which seizes us all, men and women, who are here, at home, in Paris that stood up to liberate themselves and that succeeded in doing this with their own hands?

No! We will not hide this deep and sacred emotion. These are minutes which go beyond each of our poor lives. Paris! Paris outraged! Paris broken! Paris martyred! But Paris liberated! Liberated by itself, liberated by its people with the help of the French armies, with the support and the help of all France, of the France that fights, of the only France, of the real France, of the eternal France!

Since the enemy which held Paris has capitulated into our hands, France returns to Paris, to her home. She returns bloody, but quite resolute. She returns there enlightened by the immense lesson, but more certain than ever of her duties and of her rights.

I speak of her duties first, and I will sum them all up by saying that for now, it is a matter of the duties of war. The enemy is staggering, but he is not beaten yet. He remains on our soil.

It will not even be enough that we have, with the help of our dear and admirable Allies, chased him from our home for us to consider ourselves satisfied after what has happened. We want to enter his territory as is fitting, as victors.

This is why the French vanguard has entered Paris with guns blazing. This is why the great French army from Italy has landed in the south and is advancing rapidly up the Rhône valley. This is why our brave and dear Forces of the interior will arm themselves with modern weapons. It is for this revenge, this vengeance and justice, that we will keep fighting until the final day, until the day of total and complete victory.

This duty of war, all the men who are here and all those who hear us in France know that it demands national unity. We, who have lived the greatest hours of our History, we have nothing else to wish than to show ourselves, up to the end, worthy of France. Long live France!"

Between 26 and 29 August, victory parades were held in Paris comprising both the French and the Allied forces, parading 24-abreast up the *Avenue Hoche* to the Arc de Triomphe, then down the Champs Élysées. Joyous crowds greeted the victors.

Paris could start licking its wounds.

AND WHAT ABOUT **our fictive heroines and heroes?**

Professor Eleanora Rozenkrantz and her baby daughter Isabelle were arrested during the Marseille roundup on 22 January 1943. Her husband, Doctor Yves Ferron, was shot dead before her eyes when he tried to prevent her arrest. The French police was instrumental in helping the Nazis arrest all the Jews in the area.

Mother and daughter were first sent to Fréjus, then to the camp of Royallieu near Compiègne, in the Northern Zone of France, and then to Drancy internment camp, the last stop before the long train journey to Auschwitz. They were sent straight to the gas chambers on their arrival.

YOUNG DANIEL'S PARENTS, Marc and Antoinette Montserrat, were fusilladed by the Gestapo at 84 Avenue Foch on 25 January 1944. They were among the 24,000 Resistance fighters killed by the Germans during WW2.

Daniel and cat Kiki continued to live with the Baron and his staff. Daniel was eventually adopted by Océane's parents.

JUNKER HANS ARENBERG survived the war and took over his father's estate as the next squire in Hildesheim. He was never questioned about his role during WW2, not by the French and not by the Germans. He found his Anna and married her in a simple ceremony in the Fall of 1945. He and Océane remained lifelong friends. They never publicly disclosed what happened to Dieter von Stein.

· · ·

THE FICTIVE COLONEL Ré in this novel is - of course - the thinly disguised Colonel Henri Rol-Tanguy, who played such an important role in the liberation of Paris.

ON HIS RETURN TO PARIS, Thierry Chevalier, the wiry French commander of the North African regiment, apologized to Océane for having lied about his friend Jean-Jacques Riveau, whom he'd known was alive but whose identity had to be protected at all costs. Thierry and Jean-Jacques remained friends and colleagues for the rest of their days.

D'ARTAGNAN, whose real (fictive) name was Charles Prévert, was posthumously decorated with the Croix de Guerre as a war hero and given a plaque in the Avenue Foch.

AGNÈS AND ALAN BELL handed over their clinic in Chicago to colleagues and returned to Paris with Arthur in the summer of 1945. They reunited around Baron Max and remained in Paris permanently, also taking Daniel's education upon themselves.

ARTHUR'S HEALTH improved after the move to Paris and with Daniel as playmate. He was wheelchair bound for life but regained some of his faculties. From a sunny invalid boy, he grew into a man wholly at peace with his restrictions.

Alan Bell Sr and his young bride continued to thrive and bicker among Chicago's nouveau riche. The old man got his pier built in 1940, though not for amusement but for the American navy.

BARON MAX - MAXIPA - lived to the ripe old age of 96. To the great delight of Daniel, he became romantically involved with Madame

Noir, though they never lived together and didn't marry. His quirks, his violin music and his *joi de vivre* continued to inspire them all.

OCÉANE AND JEAN-JACQUES married in the Notre Dame on 15 March 1945. They never let go of each other again and were blessed by the birth of their twins Bertrand and Max a year later. Jean-Jacques took up his paint brushes once more and Océane became a renowned cardiologist who enjoyed painting in her free time.

OC AND JJ attended Martin Miller & Eliza Hutchinson's wedding in the Pilgrim Congregationalist Church on Savin Hill (Boston) in the summer of 1945. Océane became godmother to their son Martell.

IN THE SUMMER OF 1946, Lili, Océane and Esther were able to reunite at *À La Petit Chaise* on the Rue de Grenelle in the 7th Arrondissement in Paris. They remained forever friends.

THE WAR LEFT DEEP SCARS, but it also healed, bringing them great joy. More and better than they'd ever dared to dream.

I HOPE YOU ENJOYED OC and JJ's fight for the liberation of France and their ultimate happiness when they find each other back at the end of the war.

The Resistance Girl Series started with the prequel, *In Picardy's Fields* where you met Océane's parents, Agnès and Alan, while they did their bit as frontline doctors in WW1. If you haven't yet signed up for <u>my newsletter</u> please do, so you can find out what happened to Major Hamilton's sister, Rosamond Cadden. You'll get *The Black Rose* for free.

PLEASE consider leaving a REVIEW for *The Parisian Spy* if you enjoyed the book. Reviews are very important for authors, so I'd be immensely grateful if you shared your thoughts on *The Parisian Spy* with other readers. You can leave your review <u>here</u>.

BUT THERE'S MORE... *The Resistance Girl Series* continues with Lili and Océane's friend from Le Manoir, the Austrian Esther Weiss.

You can find Chapter 1 of *The Norwegian Assassin* about Esther on the next page.

So click through.

THANK YOU for having read *In Picardy's Fields*. I truly hope you enjoyed the read and look forward to welcoming you on my newsletter.

Warm greetings,
DID YOU ENJOY THE WAR STORY & GREAT LOVE OF OCÉANE AND JEAN-JACQUES?

THERE IS MORE!!

BOOK #4 *The Norwegian Assassin* tells the WW2 tale of the Jewish Esther Weiss, whose family flees to Norway, thinking they would be safe there. Now on Preorder: http://mybook.to/TheNorwegianAssassin.

READ the first Chapter of The Norwegian Assassin here or join my newsletter and/or follow the creation of Esther's journey.

39

SNEAK PEEK THE NORWEGIAN ASSASSIN

THE ENGAGEMENT

Obertauern, Austria, February 1938

A brittle sun rose over the snow-capped Radstädter Tauern Pass, scintillating the white slopes with sparkles of diamonds and splinters of ice. The sky above the rugged mountain tops was steeped in azure blue, cold, wintry, and breathtakingly beautiful. Vast and sheltered at the same time, the landscape lay as if folded by a giant hand into a crisp, white sheet of peaks, slopes and gorges. *Gottes Land.*

High up in the firmament hovered a lone black eagle, wings expanded, its watchful eye on an early solo skier zigzagging down the Pass. The air was still, the scenery was motionless, the earth was holding its breath but for the small brown figure racing down at breakneck speed.

Sheltered from the cold by a double-glass window and a roaring fire in the corner of the Himmlhof Inn's breakfast room, Esther Weiss's gaze was also fixed on the graceful movements of the skier coming towards her. A Rosenthal cup and saucer with her morning tea in one hand, she never took her sea-green eyes from the emerging figure until he forced the tips of his skis together and came to a screeching halt right outside her window. She recognized him as one of the giant blond Vikings of the Norse national skiing team staying at the inn.

Though some part of Esther's mind registered the scene, longing with every fiber in her body to race downhill herself on this glorious morning, the larger part of her thoughts was focused on the day ahead. Sipping her tea, she once again meticulously went through all the upcoming actions, checking she'd not forgotten anything.

It was going to happen today. Her day had finally come.

At that moment the door to the breakfast room opened and Esther turned to see her mother and grandmother enter together. Her mother in a flowery morning dress, already fully adorned with her most precious gold, the dark curls foamed luxuriously and the lovely chestnut eyes full of pride. She strode in as straight as a stick, and yet something was not right.

"Mutti looks tired," Esther thought, as her lips curled into a smile. "She must have been sleeping badly again."

Oma, tall, blonde and regal - a rare trait in the Austrian Jewish community, which Esther had inherited - had a demure look on her statuesque face but her eyes twinkled at seeing her beloved grand-daughter.

"Shouldn't you be getting dressed, *Bärchen*?"

"I should," Esther answered promptly, basking in the use of her pet name 'little bear'. "I just couldn't break free from the lovely scenery. It's so good to be at peace here in the mountains, isn't it?"

Seeing her mother's shoulders slump, Esther bit her tongue. Wrong move. No mentioning of the strained atmosphere at home in Vienna, where the Germans were stamping their ugly black boots at Austria's northern borders, threatening to invade any minute. The pictures in the papers of the *Kristallnacht* back in November were etched in their memory. The angry mob had created havoc against the shops of Viennese Jews as well. Thankfully neither the Weiss properties nor the Bernstein's shops had been targeted. Not yet.

· · ·

"COME and have breakfast with us, dear," her mother urged. "Carl Bernstein Sr phoned Papi an hour ago to confirm that your betrothed is on the early train and is expected to arrive in Radstadt at noon."

Her mother and grandmother had already seated themselves at the round breakfast table. Slipping the ivory rings from the damask napkins, unfolding the white squares and spreading them over their thighs, every movement the Weiss ladies made had the precise grace of good breeding and long practice. Esther followed suit.

While they waited for the maid to serve them their breakfast, her mother gave the instructions Esther already knew by heart. Repetition led to proper behavior. It could have been Naomi Weiss's life motto.

"We've still got so much to prepare. Go to your room after breakfast and Anna will come to help you dress and do your hair."

Anna was the German lady's maid they'd brought with them from Vienna. It was a great honor that she would assist Esther today as she was usually busy enough with the older generations.

"I don't know if I can get anything inside of me," Esther observed, as two maids pushed in a trolley stacked with Semmeln, fresh butter, steaming Melange coffee, cut sausages, Schinken-speck, boiled eggs, Danish buns and apricot jam. Though the smell was delicious, her stomach protested.

But her mother would hear nothing of the sort. "An empty stomach breeds weak nerves."

Another motto Naomi Weiss-Aronson lived by.

It didn't take Oma long to chime in with her daughter-in-law. "You know you're going to have a prolonged engagement, Bärchen, so you'd better grow nerves of steel. You and Carl insisted on getting engaged now when you knew you'd still have your finishing school year in Switzerland. Better grow some patience with a proper breakfast."

Esther sighed. Of course, they were right, she thought as she tentatively put her white teeth in a Danish bun. If it had to be anything, then something sweet. The scent of the sausages and Speck made her nauseous, but she suppressed her weak nerves.

She knew how the women in her family rejoiced in her engagement and her impeccable choice in Carl Bernstein. Within eighteen months she would be stepping into the shoes of her illustrious Oma and Mutti who had reigned as supreme hostesses of Viennese society for decades. Even Papi had made peace with her choice for the son of his biggest rival and now dreamed about an eventual merger of *Weiss Goldschmied* with *Bernstein & Son Juweliers*.

Carl Bernstein was to be her husband. Esther still had to pinch herself every day to believe it was true.

"At least the weather is finally behaving itself," Oma observed as if it was a living thing.

Naomi nodded, deftly cutting a slice of ham in small cubes and popping them in her mouth. "Franz was complaining this morning that he preferred a day of skiing to being packed indoors again. Men!" She shook her well-coiffed head in disbelief.

The first week that the Weiss family had taken up residence in the Himmlhof Inn for their annual skiing holidays, the weather had been cold and forbidding with incessant snowfall, even blizzards, but today was as bright and crisp as a dewy rose. At more than 6,000 feet above sea level, no open roads led to the guesthouse, and everything had to be transported by horse-drawn sledges from Radstadt village in the valley.

Trapped but snugly together, the family had passed the time playing chess and patience, going for walks when there was a lull in the snowfall. But it had been a disappointment, especially for ten-year old Adam, who grew increasingly bored and listless being cooped up inside.

Like her brother and father, Esther was itching to stand on her skis and go. They were the real skiers of the family, with her sister Rebecca and mother and grandmother more recreational skiers.

"Hopefully the weather will hold, and we can all go skiing

tomorrow." Esther spoke her longing out aloud, though it made her slightly ill at ease.

It had been *her* wish to get engaged in the exact same place where her father had gone down on one knee to ask her mother in marriage in the winter of 1920. Of course, she hadn't been there herself but Opa Weiss, then still well and alive, had recorded the event with his Ur-Leica and Oma had lovingly pasted the snapshots in one of her many snow holiday albums. The tiny, square black and whites were faded and well-thumbed by now but had never lost their romantic appeal for Esther.

This was the location she'd dreamed of since childhood. And now it was finally here.

"We'll see about doing any skiing tomorrow," her mother replied with a bleak smile. "Carl may not be in favor of such an expedition. He might prefer going for a walk. Does he ski at all? I've never known the Bernsteins to be into winter sports."

Esther's face fell. It was true. Carl didn't ski. She saw her chances of a good go at a downhill slide diminish. He would vacation with them for a week and when he left for Vienna again, they'd only have a few days left themselves.

"Don't sulk, Esther. It doesn't befit a young lady. Maybe Carl will agree to taking some lessons and you can go down the children's slope with him. Now go and get dressed."

"Yes, Mutti."

Being engaged suddenly seemed a little more complicated than she had anticipated.

TALL AS TRAINED, but inwardly quivering, Esther stood inspecting herself in the full-length mirror that Anna had propped up in the corner of the guesthouse bedroom.

"I'll let you have a minute to yourself, Fräulein Esther," the maid said, leaving on slippered feet and closing the door behind her.

Esther's breast heaved as her fingers curled into her palms and her jawbones clamped shut like the shells of an oyster. A sudden terror struck her, an almost physical attack that made her shrink backwards, away from the mirror. She had no idea where the invisible assault came from; it swished at her as the explosive lash of a whip.

Staring at her waxlike face, with her heart racing, fear washed over Esther like a dam burst. Alone and far from accomplished, she knew she wasn't ready for this new phase in her life at seventeen. It was too much, too soon. And yet. At the edge of the precipice, Esther did what she knew she could - be her mother's daughter and brace against the fear head on.

She forced her breathing to slow and deepen, in and out, as she tucked a blonde escapee under one of the many hairpins Anna had stuck into her lush, blonde curls. She adjusted the gem-stoned earrings her parents had given her for her last birthday, dabbed some powder over the tiny sweat beads on her nose bridge and finally rearranged the matching gem brooch on her chest.

"Relax!" she ordered herself, inoculating her bloodstream with her mother's potent etiquette lessons. "You know you want this, Esther Weiss, you've wanted to get married for as long as you can remember. Carl Bernstein is going to be an excellent husband and father. So stop this nonsense."

She saw the fear dissipate from her emerald eyes and proud Esther Weiss reappeared from behind the frightened mouse that had stared back at her the minute before. A Weiss woman could do this. A Weiss woman could do anything to make the men in her life happy.

"Now go!" she told her mirrored image, smoothing her ice-blue dress once more over her slender hips. One last nod. As good as perfect.

WHEN ESTHER ENTERED the Inn's dining hall she stepped into a thick wall of voices and cigarette smoke. The cacophony mingled with the blue haze triggered her already frail nerves. She blinked, looked around her in the crowded, low-ceilinged room and was glad to spot her family in their finest standing in the bay window. Another deep breath, and she purposefully strode across the room, the heels of her new shoes clicking on the red-tiled floor.

Carl was not among them.

"Hey Missie," one of the Norsemen, who were sitting in a semi-circle in front of the open fire, addressed her. They were the cause of all the cackling and thick smoke.

Esther frowned. For sure, Papi had instructed Felix the Innkeeper to make this a private family affair? She ignored them and joined her parents.

"Ah, my beautiful Essie!" Franz Weiss exclaimed, his round cheeks on display as he beamed from ear to ear. "Come and stand with your Papi. I want you close now, while I still can."

Instantly drawn into her father's jovial embrace, Esther felt the weight drop from her shoulders. She would always be Papi's little girl, no matter whether she was engaged or married.

Kissing his cologne-dabbed cheeks, she leaned into him. "Papi, the other people ...?"

"Have no worries, my dear. They're just having a hot cocoa and then they're out skiing again. Felix asked me if they could use the room just for half an hour and, as he's lending us the dining room all afternoon, I could hardly refuse the good chap, now could I?"

Safely in her father's embrace, Esther peeked in the direction of the rowdy clan near the fire and spotted the tall Norwegian who had been showing off his skiing skills an hour earlier. Their eyes met but Esther instantly cast hers down. The fierce ice blue gaze told her something she didn't want to know. Turning to her siblings, still close to her father, she complimented Adam for his deft suit. The boy looked clumsy and uncertain in his formal attire, throwing longing glances out of the window and up the Tauern Pass.

"Adam, you look like a little prince. I'm so proud of you."

The face he pulled was even more precious. "I'd rather be a rascal and fly outdoors," he sulked.

"Adam," his mother cooed over the unhappy boy, "there will be Biedermeier Torte later. That's your favorite, isn't it?"

His face lit up, revealing a coy smile. "Can I have two *Schnitte*?"

"We'll see about that."

"Do you like my dress?" Rebecca piped in, holding the hem of her soft pink skirt wide between thumb and finger and swirling around. At twelve, Rebecca, petite, slim and darkhaired, was the spitting image of their mother, but always looking up to her big sister and aping her every move.

"You're picture perfect," Esther smiled. "I'm so proud of you, Rebbie. And thank you, Papi and Mutti, for organizing this impromptu party for me."

"You're welcome, *Bärchen*." Her father gave her arm a little squeeze, turning his stout back in the pin-striped suit in such a way that he blocked his own ensemble from the rowdy Norsemen. "Now where's that fellow of yours hiding? He shouldn't be late to his own *vort*." Franz Weiss took his golden chain watch from his waistcoat pocket and frowned. "Felix sent one of the wood chopper boys down with the horse sledge over an hour ago. I hope the snow hasn't caused trouble on the track and the train is delayed."

"I'm going to be seated for a while," Oma announced, folding her rough silk morning dress neatly under her as she perched on a chair, straight as an arrow, hands folded in her lap and feet crossed at the ankles. Rebecca immediately took up the same position on the opposite couch.

All faces turned to the door, when Carl, trilby in hand and carrying a small leather valise, entered the dining room. Tall, dark and handsome, he was far from the cliché man. Bernstein exuded an imperial aura, proud and phlegmatic, the strong cheekbones set and the dark eyes in command, although not in an arrogant way. He surveyed the room, and when his eyes found Esther, he smiled, august and appeased.

Esther smiled back and her heart did a little jump. He was here. He'd come. It wasn't an elusive fantasy that she had made up in her mind. She had to stop herself from running towards him and into his arms. He crossed the distance between them with measured, decisive steps, ignoring the noise and random spectators.

As a well-bred man he shook hands in the sequence that was appropriate, his future father-in-law, Oma and then his mother-in-law. When he came to Esther, they stood for a second, both unsure what was expected of them. Carl took her ringless right hand in his firm grip and brushed it with his lips. Then he made a little bow for her with that radiant, self-assured smile.

Her lips formed the letters of his name - "Carl" - but she had no idea what to say to him. Their former life in Vienna where they had frequented the same circles since they were children, seemed located on quite another planet right now. Again it gnawed on her that choosing this simple mountain inn for their engagement, far from all that bound them and was dear, had been wrong, fanned more by romantic notions than by the level-headed, practical decisions she was supposed to make as a future wife and mistress of the house.

But Carl tried to put her at ease immediately by chatting about his adventurous trip up the mountain. "At some point I had to put on my overshoes and help push the sledge. The horses' hooves couldn't get a grip on the slippery surface anymore. We were going downhill instead of up. Never have done anything like it in my life but it was a new experience. I say, Herr Weiss, your daughter does let me travel to the end of the world for her sake. What more will be in stall for me in the future?"

As he gave her a conspiring wink, Esther felt all the ice in and around her melt. She started glowing, believing again. Carl was a great socializer and sublime breaker of ice. All would be fine.

Everyone started chatting and laughing at once as they took their seats at the nicely decked table in the middle of the room. Esther sat in between Carl and her mother, with Rebecca and

Adam opposite them. Oma and Papi resided at the respective heads of the lunch table.

"Weren't your parents frightfully disappointed not to be able to attend our engagement?" Esther whispered to Carl, who was clipping his diamond-studded tie pin to his white shirt before decking himself with his serviette.

He turned his dark eyes to her, the eyebrows knit, a studious look on his handsome face. "Somewhat," he acknowledged. "It took some explaining on my part that this place ..." He made a rather circumspect movement with his arm. "... holds a special place in your heart and that of your family. But I think they understood. Eventually."

"I'm sorry," she muttered. "We'll hold the wedding in Vienna, of course."

Felix, the giant innkeeper with hands like snow shovels, bent his grizzly head to enter under the door beam. His two adult daughters who worked at Himmlhof as waitresses followed on his heels. Felix frowned, his gray eyes glaring under bristly, white eyebrows when he saw the Norwegians still lounging around the fireplace, long stockinged legs stretched, talking loudly in their pitch-accent Viking language while smoke rose from their pipes.

"Time to leave, *meine Herren*," he roared, rather unfriendly. "This is a private room now. Your lunch will presently be served in the breakfast room."

He shooed the Norwegians away, who got up rather reluctantly and still chatting, made for the door.

The next thing happened so fast that no one understood the sequence of events. On his way to the door, the blue-eyed Norseman tripped, slid on the floor and the last contents of his cocoa landed on Esther's bodice. The brown liquid splashed onto the pale blue silk and spread as a scandalous oil spill over her breast. She jumped up and shrieked as if being flayed alive. The shock was bigger than the pain, as the cocoa was no longer hot.

Her dress was ruined. As was her day. Tears filled her eyes and spilled over her cheeks. She continued to jammer while her mother and Oma raced towards her, shouting to the waitresses for a clean cloth and some soap and water.

The culprit got to his feet, still holding the mug. He made an attempt to go towards the crying girl but was grabbed roughly at the collar by Carl and pushed out of the room. He closed the door behind the rowdy gang with a bang before hastening back to his distraught fiancé, sinking on his knees before Esther, who still sobbed uncontrollably while her mother tried to get the worst stain out of the dress.

"It's no use, Naomi," Oma observed. "You'll have to take it off, *Bärchen*, and put on your second best. There, there now. It's not the end of the world. These accidents happen and I'm sure that oaf is feeling as bad about this as you do."

The two waitresses, dressed in identical dirndl dresses, gaped open-eyed at the consternation, clearly uncertain what to do with the steaming soup terrines.

"Go and fetch Anna," Naomi instructed Rebecca, who fled as fast as her patent leather shoes would carry her.

Carl remained before Esther, his hands affectionately on her knees while she blew her nose and somewhat regained her posture. The look of love in his eyes calmed her. Carl would be good in times of calamities. It let all the tension seep out of her like the air out of a tight balloon.

"Well, at least you've seen me in the dress I had chosen," she smiled through her tears. "Now you'll have to decide if you still want me in my ordinary day dress."

"You look lovely in everything, my dear Esther."

She'd never before heard so much passion in his voice. She was slightly ashamed to admit to herself that the incident seemed to have been needed to break down the last barrier between them.

"Thank you."

Love flooded through her like a giddy, happy mess. Giving her knees a little squeeze, Carl rose to his full length. "Now I'd love to go and give that Nordic geezer a good slapping, but I suppose that's out of the question."

Playing the heroic role was certainly grist to Carl's mill and made Esther feel doubly proud of him.

THEY BROKE the white earthenware plate as was a good Jewish custom, kissed and ate Biedermeier Torte. Bliss, brilliance and benevolence settled on the happy couple as they danced to Glenn Miller's *'Doin' the Jive'* while her parents looked on and a silver sliver moon rose above the mountain tops.

Esther was sure she would never be happier than she was right now. These shining moments would sustain her should darker periods enter her life, she was sure of it.

ORDER THE NORWEGIAN ASSASSIN NOW.

AUTHOR'S NOTE

The Parisian Spy is a work of fiction that pays tribute to the brave women and men who fought in the French Resistance movement of World War 2.

This book is in no way an actual account of living persons but has sprouted in its entirety from the author's imagination. Both the military movements and the medical procedures described in *The Parisian Spy* may lack in accuracy. I'm not a historian and I only incorporate actual events when they propel my story forward. At the risk of being considered disrespectful, I use the world wars as the canvas for my heroines. But let there be no doubt! I have immense respect for the real people who stood up against the tyranny of Nazi Germany. The *Resistance Girl Series* is my way of paying tribute to the generation of my grandmothers.

What I *have* tried to portray as accurately as possible is how these women and men must have felt, what they saw, what happened to them, how it changed them. War is a beast but people are not. I've dived deep under the skin of my main characters to bring out the universal emotions of devastation, pain, courage, doubt, fear and LOVE that trying times evoke.

A few words on The French Resistance.

La Résistance was a collection of French movements that fought against the Nazi German occupation of France and the collaborationist Vichy regime. Resistance cells were small groups of armed women and men (called the Maquis in rural areas) who, in addition to their guerrilla warfare activities, were also publishers of underground newspapers, providers of first-hand intelligence information, and maintainers of escape networks that helped Allied soldiers and airmen trapped behind enemy lines. The Resistance's women and men came from all economic levels and political leanings of French society, including émigrés, academics, students, aristocrats, conservative Roman Catholics (including priests and nuns), Protestants, Jews, Muslims, liberals, anarchists, and communists.

The French Resistance played a significant role in facilitating the Allies' rapid advance through France following the invasion of Normandy on 6 June 1944. They provided military intelligence on the German defenses known as the Atlantic Wall and on Wehrmacht deployments and orders of battle for the lesser-known invasion of Provence on 15 August. The Resistance also planned, coordinated, and executed sabotage acts on the Nazi electrical power grid, transport facilities, and telecommunications networks. The Resistance's work was politically and morally important to France both during the German occupation and the decades that followed. It provided the country with an inspiring example of the patriotic fulfilment of a national imperative countering an existential threat to French nationhood. The actions of the Resistance stood in marked contrast to the collaborationism of the Vichy regime.

After the Allied landings in Normandy and Provence, the paramilitary components of the Resistance were organized more formally, into a hierarchy of operational units, collectively known as the French Forces of the Interior (F.F.I). Estimated at 100,000 fighters in June 1944, the F.F.I grew rapidly and reached approximately 400,000 by October.

Though countries like the former USSR, Yugoslavia and Poland had more female fighters, France can pride itself on having had one of the largest resistance movements on the occupied Continent.

A fifth of these Resistance fighters were WOMEN like the fictional Océane Bell. Twenty percent!

ABOUT THE AUTHOR

Hannah Byron's crib stood near the Seine in Paris, but she was raised in the south of Holland by Anglo-Dutch parents. In her best-selling WW2 historical fiction series, *The Resistance Girl Series*, Hannah's heroines also traipse from one European country to the next, very much like their creator.

Now a retired university lecturer and translator, the European traveler and avid researcher still regularly crosses borders to learn about new vistas.

What started as curiosity about her family's connection to D-Day grew into an out-of-controlish study into WW2 history. To blame, or thank, must be Uncle Tom Naylor. If he'd not landed on the beaches of Normandy and helped liberate Holland, her British mother would never have met her Dutch Dad after the war.

Strong women are at the core of Byron's clean and wholesome romance novels. Every book is a tribute to the generation that started the women's lib movement, got dirty in overalls, flew planes, and did intelligence work. Today's girl bosses can but stand on the shoulders of these amazons.

Side-by-side with their male counterparts, Byron's heroines fight for freedom, equality and... love.

As **Hannah Ivory,** she writes Historical Mysteries. *The Mrs Imogene Lynch Series* stars the kind but opinionated Victorian widow of Constable Thaddeus Lynch.

ALSO BY HANNAH BYRON

HISTORICAL FICTION

THE RESISTANCE GIRL SERIES

In Picardy's Fields

The Diamond Courier

The Parisian Spy

The Norwegian Assassin

The Highland Raven

The Crystal Butterfly (preorder)

THE AGNES DUET (Spin-off)

Miss Agnès

Doctor Agnès

HANNAH IVORY

HISTORICAL MYSTERIES

The Unsolved Case of the Secret Christmas Baby

The Peculiar Vanishing Act of Mr Ralph Herriot (preorder)